The Last Bar In NYC

3/3/17

The Last Bar In NYC

by
Brian Michels

For Diane

Setting The Bar

You are the center of the universe, someone might've told you that or you could've dreamed it up yourself. It's a wide-eyed figment so don't believe it. You might disagree. Maybe your experiences with family and friends surround your head and heart as if you're the sun. Very often strangers appear to you as movie-set extras. Dramas from life at large gravitate toward you with meaning and momentum responding to cues from your pulse. You've experienced moments when everything in the world worth knowing fills your head with galactic brilliance. The only contention is those extras. They're living a life as vivid and complex as yours and carry on invisibly around you with their own routines, friends, families and figments. Lives you'll never see save the dim twinkle in a chance passing. Lives with their own unfolding stories where you appear as the extra, that lady sitting on the subway reading her kindle, someone in line at the grocery store buying bread and ice cream, or that nervous looking guy sitting at the other end of the bar drinking a beer. Let's be honest, how many centers can the universe really have?

The number of people that act like bombastic bubbles in a Whiskey Soda thinking they outshine the mix in the glass is remarkable when you consider each of us is hardly unique. You can prove it easy. Go to a bar and sit down next to anybody order a drink and strike up a conversation. It doesn't matter what you talk about because after you've had a few drinks together you'll discover that aside from taste and the amount of money in your pocket you have more in common than not, and most common of all are your troubles. Having been disposed under chins and elbows and cocktail napkins and ashtrays and spilled drinks for decades in New York City for countless drinkers willing to confess anything to a bar top I can guarantee that. Imagine yourself at that bar, drink in one hand and an unlit cigarette craving fire in the other. You've had six martinis or six of whatever you like to drink and whatever was bothering you all day, all week or longer is chewing your ear off, keeping you from any shot at boozy comfort. The world hasn't been going your way, some prick crossed your path or you screwed up on something, maybe a cheat took your fair share of the pie or something precious disappeared. You're at your sorry best. Worse, love or the lack of it could have you cracked open. It's the same for all of us to be up against a bar with drinking and smoking convictions fully capable of recognizing all that's gone wrong in life. It sucks. But thankfully we're in a bar and because of that some sense of it all will come. It has to. We're drinking to the fact that we're not the center of the universe.

I love a good bar. It's the bottles, the wood, the rails, the smells, the mirrors, the bar tops, the floors and the stools. It's the drinks too but they needn't be stiff. The place could be a dump or it could be one of those places with fancy decor and fancier bathrooms. Alcohol is pretty good at killing germs so the glasses don't have to be perfectly clean. The simple formula for bar satisfaction: a good crowd. Mostly good, and it doesn't need to be two thirds or more, just mostly. And by good I don't mean saintly. Though they could be saints. What I mean is they need to be people who breathe warmth from an ordinary heart, have a wary connection to the instinct in their gut, and possess at least half a brain. That everyday mix that makes up the greatest hunk of the world. The ones most of us put up with, identify with, laugh with, maybe have a terrific argument with or throw a drink at, but the ones we'll take back in an hour with a nod or a pat on the back or with the meeting of the eyes out of the corner of our eyes. The ones we especially take back if they're the ones buying drinks. People you might end up standing shoulder to shoulder and singing along with at 3:30 AM on a Tuesday when everyone is in a drunken cliché' state of mind and everyone is okay with that because we all know someone will be going to work in the morning and the whole screwy enterprise that is New York City will push out another day and at the end of that day some bar will be open again with mostly good people who know better than anything that a drink with friends and strangers is part of the natural process of it all, the topsy-turvy requirement for a well-balanced life.

Drinking Age

The first time I set foot inside a bar I couldn't stand on my feet too good. I was two years old, probably still angelic. 1964. The Woodycrest up on the hill on 167th Street between Nelson Avenue and Woodycrest Avenue in Highbridge, the Bronx. A large place with a long oak top bar and a big back room with black and white photos of boats and Galway Bay hung everywhere on the walls. Behind the bar, forty or fifty bottles of booze running the full length with a cash register in the middle and a mirror above it all with some dollar bills with what could've been Gaelic hieroglyphics scribbled across them taped up behind the register. Everyday a dependable haze of smoke and an exhausted glare of sunlight would make its way only halfway into the place through a large picture frame window and the sometimes open door. Daytime boozers scattered along that bar like worn and beaten garbage cans emptied and tossed to the curb. My father had me perched at the front end of that bar top on a Saturday afternoon with a couple of cohorts standing around. He told me I was a natural, had everyone smiling and I was quick with my hands, premium traits for a barman. I was swiping maraschino cherries every time the bartender played along by turning his head pretending not to notice. I must've grabbed a dozen before my father realized it wasn't going to be cute later on when I'd be crying with a belly full of syrup soaked cherries while he'd be trying to watch the game. My father wasn't at the bar showing off his pride and joy to his noble peers. He'd been running to the supermarket while my mom was helping my grandmother hang wall paper and he'd gotten stuck with me, wanted to get a bet in with the bookie who

1

sat in the back corner of that bar and maybe grab a quick drink or two before heading out for a box of spaghetti.

Highbridge had a lot of bars and a Bronx tenement and storefront harmony of striving and struggle for survival and little more could be found in all of them. A streetwise sense of delight from experiencing the most from what little you got and sharing and making decisions basic and cooperating with them, that was the neighborhood commonality. There was gossip and trouble but genuine people and unpredictable characters in no short supply provided a better show. There were televisions but no obsessive fascination with them unlike nowadays where it's a destroyer of communities by telling lies, dividing, isolating, scaring, fueling envy and confusion, and stamping out a short list of characters that people replicate for their own personality. Today giant flat screens keep you locked inside, negate your nerve center, your point of convergence, diverts your attention to reality show trollops, murder, nonsense and all forms of negativity producing a disturbing harmony where everyone belongs to everyone with no essential root like lines of identity leaving you with your innards out and not a set of real legs to stand on rendering you to a sofa. "When you're not attentive to the reality of your own life you are merely a passive spectator to another man's show." Somebody in a bar told me that.

You could probably break up the great commonality of the old neighborhood into two camps, the Woodycrest and Kaiser's. If you were committed to drinking good beer Kaiser's was choice. Nobody in the neighborhood had money but a couple of bucks more a week more consistently than the guy down the street meant you might live in a building with an elevator and likely you'd drink at Kaiser's. My family lived on the sixth floor of a walk up and most often spread our grace at the Woodycrest. The booze and beer selection wasn't on par with Kaiser's but the atmosphere was welcoming. By five years old I could recognize the Bronx refinement of the people who drank at Kaiser's. They always looked fresh out of a shower. Whenever my father hit on a pony he'd pass on the Woodycrest and spend an extra buck or two at Kaiser's. It's the place I learned to open cans of beer. Mr. Kaiser taught me and gave me my first can opener just so long as I spent an hour walking around to the tables offering my newly trained services.

On Sunday afternoons the Woodycrest was the pliable church after a hard-boiled morning Mass and sermon. Every kid in neighborhood would be crawling all over the bar and everyone dressed their best. Men and women drinking and dancing before going home to cook dinner, and the old drunks lingering on till the weekend truly faded into the reality of a sullied bed and then work again. Many late nights my father stumbled in the door laughing his ass off coming from the Woodycrest. Of course he'd been drinking. He was always drinking but wasn't always laughing. I'd slip out of the bedroom and sit in the darkened hallway and listen to my father explain to my mother the latest riot that had happened that night as the laughs vibrated the floorboards. I'd struggle to keep quiet otherwise I'd get a drunken man sized smack on the ass that'd rattle the piss out of you. The risk was worth it. I'd imagine myself at the Woodycrest with my father and his friends and their good times, dreaming of the day I could finally get drunk and laugh like the big guys.

By the late 1960's the South Bronx was burning and we relocated. Nearly all of the white people cleared out to the suburbs of Westchester, New Jersey and Long Island. Among the ramblers it was a sign of higher stature if you left the Bronx. You still had the same job but somehow you were closer to royalty by being fifty minutes away from it all. How little did they know. How little distance my family moved. We made it out of the South Bronx, crossed the border to the north side. Sadly we left my grandparents, my mother's parents behind. It was only a fifteen-minute subway ride back to the old neighborhood so all was not lost. There were perks in the new neighborhood to help us along: Van Cortland Park filled with enough trees to make Paul Bunyon honestly earn a cold beer at the end of his day; and a Catholic school willing to reduce tuition for working stiffs, which relieved my mother's fear filled predicament of her kids being groomed in Bronx public schools for a criminal life. Helping things along most for my exiled family was the fact that there was no shortage of bars. Squeeze in an abundance of delis selling cheap beer and a bunch of liquor stores at reach and no shortage of Italians making their own wine in basements. The new neighborhood was a bar fly's breath away from kingdom come.

With a new apartment and seven kids under his belt along with stiff drinking and gambling habits my father needed at least two jobs, some years three, just to keep sale priced chicken on the table. He grabbed a night job pulling drafts and pouring whiskey at Horgan's Pub. Being the resourceful man my father was and having as many kids as he did he saw to it that a capable son could earn a couple of bucks to put toward household costs. He got me a job at the bar two afternoons a week, Mondays and Fridays. Kindergarten let out by noon so I was free to start work by 1:00 PM. Many days Pop, my grandfather, would take the subway up from the old neighborhood and meet me at the bar. He'd have a beer and then walk me home. My job was to wait for the beer and soda delivery driver in front of the bar and roll seven or eight kegs down the ramp into the basement and then help Mr. Horgan load them into the cooler. There were also cases of soda in wood crates to drag down the ramp. The job took just over an hour and I was paid a buck. That was good money, $2 a week paid half our monthly electric bill. It was dangerous work. The beer ramp was steep, the kegs were heavy and I only weighed thirty-five pounds. But like so many things in life it was all about leverage. A growing passion for beer helped my focus. I was very careful to not roll the barrels too fast because if one of them got away from me and crashed into the basement wall I'd get a serious smack in the head. It would unsettle things, fill the beer lines with foam for the first quarter of the barrel cutting deep into the profit portion, along with messing with the consistency of the beer. That's the way old man Horgan explained it to me. It made sense. "Men are planning on drinking that beer and they are counting on you," he'd tell me. He wasn't patriarchal. He was a hard ass. What mattered to him was money. What mattered to me was that I had a job, I was in a bar, and any day there was a fifty-fifty chance my grandfather Pop might show up. I thoroughly enjoyed Pop's company. I was determined to prove to him more than anyone else that I was a bona fide bar man.

Pop had come over to the United States from Ireland by himself when he was sixteen with holes in his pockets, the shirt on his back and a completely empty stomach. Before he made it to the USA he'd already "Spent a lifetime in pubs," as he always put it. On Mondays and Fridays after my kegs were in I'd head upstairs and grab a seat next to Pop. Sal, the daytime barman, would give me a small bottle of coke with a wink and a hard knock on the bar top with his knuckles that meant no charge. Sometimes Pop would tell me I did a good job and how important it is to do a good job no matter what the job is. He'd talk about the responsibility of collecting your pay and not to get cheated because the moment you fail to stand for yourself you might as well not go on living. "Never flash your money in a bar unless there's right reason to do so," Pop would say as Sal pulled a buck from the register and hand it over to me. He'd then introduce me to some of the drinkers who'd be sitting in the bar during the day, mostly pensioners and rummies. He'd break down their character for me, whether they were "authentic" or "affected." He'd say it with his Irish brogue making his "affected" sound like "affacted" which sounded a lot like the way he'd say, fuckers, which was fackers. "You need be careful with old timers. Those fackers are on tight budgets and will press nice fellers like you to buy them pints." To teach me a lesson now and then he'd take the dollar I just earned and buy a pint.

One afternoon I was sitting at the bar with Pop, the place was empty and Sal was reading the paper. I was finishing up my coke when the front door blew open nearly coming off its hinges. A skinny-necked guy with a wool cap pulled down over his ears and nearly over his eyes was standing there. It wasn't cold outside. He was wielding a gun. "Fork it over fatso!" he yelled at Sal. Pop grabbed a hold of my knee, looked me in the eye and said calmly, "Sit still, lad." Sal pulled the money from the register and put it on the bar. "Okay," Sal said to him straight, "We don't need trouble." The guy grabbed the money but then got more pissed off. "There's nine bucks here," he yelled. Sal told him, "Nobody's come in yet... Maybe come back later." Pop let out a laugh and the guy turned quickly to him, "Old man, the wallet." Pop pulled it out, handed it over. The guy ripped it open. "There's nothing in here," he yelled. "My sentiment exactly," Pop told him. After Sal handed over his wallet the guy sneered and then zeroed in on me, "Give me what you got." I couldn't believe he was talking to me. A lot of times sitting at the bar with Pop the men might not even notice me on account that I was a kid and also because I was small. But this guy was looking right at me and pointing a gun at me and demanding the money I just worked hard to earn. I told him, "I don't have anything." He said, "Empty those pockets." I didn't want to. Along with the dollar I just got paid I had my lucky quarter, 1962. I carried it around for showing off. Plus I'd shined it up earlier that morning.

He stepped up to me, pushed the gun into my belly. I could see a visible weight to it despite it being black as night. It already caused some pain by having it jammed into my gut so I started figuring fast that it might do more harm if he fired the thing. I was also thinking about the weight of the beer I rolled to earn my buck. I'd learned to handle big barrels so maybe a gun wouldn't be much different. He can't shoot a five year old, that's what I ultimately thought. I stared into his eyes because every kid on my corner knew that if you show fear you've already lost. I tried not to flinch as he pressed the gun deeper. He stared back at me for a second or two before easing up and then looked away. For that brief and gainful moment inside my small head I knew I was closer to being a man than further away. In that short stare both he and I knew that I was more true-to-life than him. It felt like the Cyclone roller coaster at Coney Island climbing to the top and ready to rip it down the steep drop and I had the front seat all to myself. It didn't last. The skinny mug started to laugh, "Empty those pockets before you piss all over the money." Pop looked at me quietly. Sal tried not to stare. I looked down at my crotch. Pop said, "Hand it over, lad." I emptied my pockets on the bar. The dollar bill lay there dead while my lucky quarter took to spinning like a top with no where to go and trying a hundred different directions to get out the place. It didn't matter. The mug slapped his hand down hard smashing the quarter flat on the bar and then swiped up my stipend and was out the door faster than a free round of whiskey shots down your gullet on Saint Patrick's Day.

"You had that two bit junkie shaking in his boots," Sal told me. "Ye earned ye honor," Pop said. Sal tried telling me that he had spilled coffee on the barstool earlier and that I simply sat on a wet stool. "Let's go rinse those pants off," Pop said. I knew the truth. We went into the john and Pop rinsed my pants in the sink and hung them over the stall. "We'll let them dry a wee bit," he said, "It's a fine time for a pint... Pray, one on the house after this ballyhoo." I sat at the bar in my wet underpants while we waited for everything to dry. Sal pulled a pint for Pop and set it on the bar. "What do you think?" Sal asked, "Does this courageous young man deserve a beer?" Without missing a beat, "Indeed," Pop said with a fast and maybe the most honest smile I'd ever seen on his face. "But you'll do fine to make it half a pint... There's no reason to explain to his mother when he sits down for dinner for smelling like beer." "Of course," Sal said as he poured my beer, "half a pint doesn't mean half a man..." "I think a toast is in order," Sal said as he put the beer in front of me. "Indeed," Pop said, "To the virility of strong and brave men." Sal quickly added, "May the world be blessed with more of them." We hoisted our glasses readying to clang them together.

I liked what they said because it made me feel better about pissing my pants. I also liked Sal a lot and I really loved Pop. But this was a bigger moment. By five years old I'd already seen plenty of partying in my house with my parents and their friends and I'd evaluated a good "cheers" and the clanging of glasses as the highlight of the drinking experience. As I do to this day. But partaking in that very first "cheers" and the clang of glasses with Pop and Sal, more than the elevating timeliness and heart-fullness of the moment, was that the glasses clanging together sounded different from all other cheers that I've ever partaken in since then. The clang took on a life, like pulling a wrinkled dollar bill out of your pocket on a windy day and it gets away from you, caught up in a gust, gone fast, out of reach thinking it's going somewhere until another gust blows it back at you making it look like that dollar bill considered the dirty places it could end up and now it's indecisively flying around your head so you can keep an eye on it, maybe help you remember the value of it. If you're quick and lucky enough you can grab a hold of it while it's airborne in front of your nose. With Sal and Pop smiling and the three of us committing to the "cheers" you could snatch up the clang of the glasses just the same. Instead of the sound from cheap beer glasses it was more like a note coming from maybe the greatest instrument ever built. It resonated off the walls and fast through my chest and skull, then off of Pop's cheek and Sal's forehead until it decided to come back to me completely without a hint of shame. It tingled and nearly shook loose a tear. Of course I summoned up a great internal effort to hold back the emotion. Pop and Sal might've mistaken the tear for fear of the mug with the gun. Right then I didn't care about a gun or about my stolen dollar or my lucky quarter or my wet trousers hanging in the john. As I sat at the bar in my underpants drinking a beer it was settled, I had arrived.

Bartender School

You wouldn't usually get a present for your birthday in my house. My mom would almost always bake a cake and you could ask for your favorite dinner with the slim chance you'd get it; steak, fish, pork, lobster and shrimp excluded. On my eighth birthday I hit the jackpot: meatloaf, mashed potatoes and cake. My father came home from his day job with a cardboard box tucked under his arm. He put it down next to the front door and told all of us kids, "Don't touch it." After the birthday song my father went to the fridge for his fifth or sixth beer and sat back down and said to me, "Go ahead." I grabbed the box and ripped it open faster than my old man opened his beer. It was amazing. "It's horrible," my mother belted out, "How dare you, Eddie." "It's a shoe shine box," my father defended himself, "What's wrong with a shoe shine box?" I loved it. She screamed, "You want the kid to make money for you." "No Mom," I tried to yell, "it's a great present." She wasn't listening to me. Neither was my father. The shoeshine box turned out to be another trigger for a fight. They didn't need much. The early days of marriage, fun and sweet babies had already grown into work, unpaid bills and ugliness. You'd probably guess they liked to fight considering how much they did. I was certain that this time was going to be no different and instead of trying to break it up I took my shoeshine box to the bedroom to flaunt it in front of my little brother.

    We were opening and closing the tins of polish. We took turns rubbing the brushes on each other's arms to determine the roughness and softness and how the brushes were top of the line. I started to explain to him how I was going to be the best shoe shiner there ever was. He was already hoping that when his birthday rolled around maybe he'd be lucky enough to get a shoeshine box. We were having a grand old time when my father pushed open the bedroom door with a bang. He was taking a break from roughing up my mother. He had two pairs of shoes tucked under his arm. "Practice," he said. He threw the shoes into the room and shut the door. One of the shoes clocked my brother on the forehead and quickly gave him a lump. We spent the next hour or so with my brother rubbing his head wearing big shoes sitting on the side of the bed while I shined. We must've shined those shoes a hundred times before my mother finally came busting in the door and yelled at us, "Quiet in here. Go to bed." Fist fighting had her stressed. I put my shoeshine box in order and carried it up to my top bunk. I put it right next to my pillow and looked at it a long time admiring the pine wood finish, the foot pedestal, the brass clasp holding it closed and secure, all while lying there half awake for an hour or so while my mother and father pummeled each other to sleep and I slowly slipped into dreams of all the shoes I'd be shining.

I woke incredibly early the next morning. My over excited and seriously naïve plan was to hit some bars on my way to school, get a head start on my shoeshine fortune. The sun was barely out before I was pulling open the door at the Mayo Inn. Surprisingly, as I pulled somebody on the other side pushed it open. A couple of drunks came stumbling out. They didn't notice me as I slipped pass them into the bar. The place was filthy. The smell of vomit infused with cigarette smoke and beer was blatant. I looked around and realized that there wasn't going to be any shoes to shine. The bartender was the only person in the place. He had his back to me sitting on the bar top with his legs hanging over the inside. He was talking on the phone to someone and smoking a cigarette. He held a bottle of Budweiser in the same hand he held his cigarette and looked amazingly cool doing it. He had longer hair. Whoever was on the other end of the phone must've been funny because he was laughing. There was a bunch of cash next to him on the bar sorted in piles. When he finally did turn his head to stretch his neck he caught a glimpse of me standing there in my Catholic School uniform and yelled, "What the fuck!" He looked tougher than I thought. He had a mustache and his black t-shirt said Slippery When Wet on the front of it. "Not you," he yelled into the phone, "There's some kid standing here in the bar..." I'm in trouble, I thought. "What the fuck are you doing in here!" he yelled. He was ready to jump off the bar. "Nothing to it, Mister," I told him, "I wanted to know if anyone needed a shoeshine." He looked down at me doing a double take noticing my shoeshine box. "Get the fuck out of here. School is down the street," he told me. "No, no, relax..," he said into the phone, "There's a screwball kid standing here asking if I want my boots shined... No kidding." He laughed more and uttered some stuff into the phone as I headed to the door in a hurry. He turned his back on me while laughing and talking. I stood at the door for a parting moment.

My dumb idea was to shine at least five pairs of shoes before school and make $1.25 maybe $1.50 with tips. Subtract the buck my dad would take, I might have a fifty cents in my pocket before I made it to school. I looked over at the bartender. He definitely was the coolest cat I'd ever seen, drinking, smoking, making a load of money, and likely talking to one of his dynamite chicks on the phone anytime he wants. I looked around the place. I mostly noticed the floor and it was giving me a clear idea about the people who drank there. Cheap black linoleum covered with spilled beer, spilled drinks, crushed cigarettes everywhere, broken bottles and glasses. The crappy jukebox was playing Come and Get It by Badfinger. I was soaking it all in at 6:15 AM, getting my first good look at what happens in a bar during the midnight hour. I saw the sliding shoe marks and imprints in the swill, spit and ash on the floor at one end of the bar. There was a woman's platform shoe not too far away lying there on its side. That's where they were dancing, I thought. I could see the remnants of dried up vomit from a lightweight near the john and another pile near the front door. I saw some lady's pink sweater left on the back of a stool; no doubt she was in a hurry to get out of there. There was an impressive Miller High Life neon beer sign behind the bar. The High Life, that's what I thought. I took a deep breath determined to remember it better than remembering my multiplication tables for a test later on at school. I then noticed the bartender looking over at

11

me eyeballing everything. "I told you to get the fuck out of here," he shouted. He put down the phone and his beer and jumped off the bar. I turned to head out and hollered, "Sorry Mister." I was five steps down along the sidewalk before the door was finished closing. It was a good thing because I heard the bartender yell, "Wait a minute! Come back." I stopped dead in my tracks. I didn't want to get my ass kicked before school, especially because I'd have to explain to the nuns what had happened. I popped my head back in the door because I was compelled to. He said, "Come in schoolboy." He didn't look so mad anymore. "What do you want?" I said in an awful attempt to channel Steve McQueen's tough guy delivery. "You gotta come in the afternoon or after work if you want to shine shoes," he said, "Nobody wants their shoes shined when they're out getting loaded... You got it?" "I got it," I told him. Of course I got it. How could I forget it? The coolest guy in the world was dishing info on how to get ahead in this world. "And lose the school uniform. You'll make the drunks feel guilty while they're trying to forget their humanity," he said it with encouragement.

In the Bronx everybody loves the Yankees and as far as Mickey Mantle goes he was more respected and loved than the Pope. I put two and two together and figured wearing my Yankee cap and my Mantle t-shirt that I'd gotten the year before at his retirement ceremony at the Stadium would be a guaranteed lure for business. Better still, my Yankee cap and Mantle t-shirt was my favorite thing to wear period. I spent the next couple of weeks mastering the art of shoe shining and making cash. I was learning plenty more about bars and how to talk to all sorts of drinkers. Mostly I was applying my grandfather Pop's lesson about people being "authentic" or "affected." If a person was authentic you could just be honest and most of the time enjoy yourself conversing, and "Be grateful for the encounter," as Pop would say. If a person was "affected" you still might enjoy yourself conversing but you had to remember that the "affected" person doesn't really listen, they feign being in the moment while their minds are lost.

I had ways to figure out if a person was "authentic" or "affected." With "authentic" people, deciding if you like them or not is quick, comes to you naturally without a headache. Most of the time, even if you have your differences you don't have ill feelings toward them. It's different with an "affected" person. Though how you felt about them was irrelevant because there was no connecting to them in the first place. An "affected" person was like a holding place for a life; or a life that was never launched; or it was launched and left a hollow body behind somehow still capable of yapping and drinking. You could pick out an "affected" person easily if you opened your eyes wide and gave them a good looking over because they tend to stand out like an aberration. They're clearly inclined to the materialistic world and could be bent on believing in their sex appeal no matter what shape they're in. Often an "affected" person talks differently than the way you thought they'd talk going by the look of their face, sort of like hearing a cat bark. They also could have a sensational personality but one that's hard to put your finger on despite everything out of their mouth sounding familiar like television commercials. The best way to discover if a person is "affected" is if they spend a preposterous amount of time talking about themselves. Pop had explained it's because "Affacted people are in great need of unnatural attention and must tend themselves." Pop would be serious as he told me, "You'll do your best to sort out the affected from the sad sacks. Abandoned hearts are abound and a good man remembers lonesome souls in his prayers and good wishes." The thing is you didn't want to mix up an "affected" person with some unfortunate guy who didn't have anyone in this world to share his thoughts with. Lonely hearts sometimes can set off talking for an hour in one breath because they don't know if they'll ever have the occasion again. Pop said, "It be a good deed to listen to them." The best thing to know when you come across an "Affacted" person is that when you finally get your opportunity to talk you should feel free to talk as fast as you like, especially if it helps sell a shoeshine.

I honed my craft. My spit shine was an odds maker for tips. My father was happy with the extra money. Things got better. My best pal Poe Poe convinced his father to buy him a shoeshine box. Poe Poe was called Poe Poe after his Aunt Betty took us when we were six years old to Edgar Allen Poe Park on the Grand Concourse to see Edgar Allen Poe's cottage. We had the run of

13

that tiny house that afternoon. His Aunt Betty had to peel us off the walls to get us home for dinner on time. By midnight that night Poe Poe was in the back of a police cruiser. He'd climbed out of bed and down the fire escape and taken the subway to Poe's cottage and broke into the place. The cops found him sleeping in Edgar Allen Poe's bed. His Uncle Joe gave him the nickname because visiting Poe's cottage once in one day wasn't enough. The best part of Poe Poe and me working the bars together was we could watch each other's back, hear great songs on the Juke Box for free, and hang out all at the same time. Poe Poe was a master at swiping half empty bottles of beer and cigarettes from the bar and passing them off to me to stash in the bathrooms for later consumption. Together we could hit bars all over the Bronx. Our favorite strip was Bainbridge Avenue. There were a bunch of bars piled up within three blocks of the D Train at 206th Street. By 5:45 PM Monday through Friday you couldn't find an empty stool. There were also enough bars that we didn't have to haunt the same places everyday and get on the nerves of the bartenders. If a bartender saw your face too often he'd chase you out of the joint, sometimes with a kick in the ass. A shoeshine kid could be a cost free additive to his bread and butter but if patrons didn't like being pestered it could upset the flow of cash for the man behind the stick. We learned fast to respect bartenders because they provided great opportunities for us, and they were our heroes.

Bainbridge Avenue bars was mostly where men who wore suits, organization men, Swells unloaded after getting off the subway from the day's work. A Swell's job required him to keep his shoes shined like mirrors. He also had more natural pride so reflexively he wanted a shine more regularly than regular stiffs. Drunk construction workers for the fuck of it would set you a challenge now and again to see if you could get their boots shined despite going back into the muck the next day. I always took the challenge and tried to hustle an extra nickel complaining about the effort required for cleaning work boots. If they said no, I'd do it for the quarter just the same. I started figuring out that there were positives and negatives about Swells and laborers. A Swell would most consistently toss you a tip no matter if he were drunk or not. A Swell more often didn't like chit chat or any fast talk from a kid while their shoes were being shined; unlike the laborers who would battle you over who could talk more or who could talk faster. The laborers would want to know everything: who's your father, your uncle, your sister, your cousin, your aunt, your neighbor. Most of the time they'd end up knowing someone on that list. The laborers rarely tipped and if they were repeat customers they'd often expect a free shine. The Swells were less hassle but they were visibly and mentally different which made working for them uncomfortable. I'd guessed it was because they had miserable jobs. I'd heard they worked downtown in corporate skyscrapers where thousands of Swells pile into the same building every day. It was hard to believe until one afternoon Poe Poe and me took the subway downtown to see the World Trade Center being constructed. The damaging effects on them Swells was obvious. At the time I often wondered if it was determined the moment you're born if you're going to be a Swell so maybe being disturbed wasn't their fault.

The first time I had trouble with a customer was with a Swell. I was down on my knees shining his shoes and all was fine until he rubbed my head. He was drunk. Plenty of guys would rub your head while you shine their shoes. Nothing to it, a sentimental gesture remembering the time when they were 8 years old. Most of the time I didn't care because most of the time it was more like a pat than a rub. Well this Swell rubs my head like a klutz and knocks off my Yankee cap. I pick it up and put it back on my head. Not ten seconds goes by when the Swell does it again and this time he fusses with my hair. I didn't like it. I also wasn't happy about my cap on the filthy bar floor for the second time. I looked up and told him, "Lay off the whiskey, boob." He looked at me with a peculiar smile. No spit shine for this guy, I thought, I'm done. "That's a quarter," I said. Well this Swell gave me another one of his peculiar smiles and peeled off a buck and said, "Keep the change." A record breaker! I was happy because I was tired and already going to be late for dinner. I told Poe Poe the good news and both of us decided to call it quits. On the way out the door Poe Poe got one more shine and he promised to make it quick. "TCB," I told him (Take Care of Business). I wanted use the bathroom and wash the shoe polish off my face because going home filthy always pissed off my mom and she never needed incentive. After I

15

cleaned up I stepped into to the toilet stall to take a piss. Just as I unzipped my fly the bathroom door opened and before the piss hit the toilet there was some guy pushing up against me. This guy is drunk, I thought. I struggled and twisted around as the creep was trying to squeeze his hands down my pants. It was the Swell who had given me the big tip. He hauled off and punched me hard in the face. It was a good thing he was as drunk as he was and I was as fast as I was because I managed to square off and punch him as hard as I could in the balls. Joe Frazier would have been proud. The Swell fell down fast and was moaning while sitting in a puddle of piss as I cleared out of there.

Poe Poe knew something was up. His last patron got a half a shine for free and the two of us were out the door. I gave him the low down. He was riled. I was jumping more than walking. The two of us were half scared and half pumped up to almost twice our size. "We should go back and murder him," Poe Poe was telling me. "He's lucky I didn't stay around long enough to do a number on him," I said. My left eye was already swollen and my nose was bleeding. Before we managed to plan the ultimate revenge we were walking pass Napoli's Pizzeria. They had the best Sicilian slices on Bainbridge Avenue. I decided to treat Poe Poe because I wanted to get rid of the dollar bill the Swell had given me. "Two Sicilians," I said to the dough flipper. "I'll take a corner slice," Poe Poe said, pointing over the counter to the one he wanted. Poe Poe asked for a cold beer and that had the dough flipper laughing. We were eating and strategizing for dealing with queers in the future or any wise guy thinking they can mess with us. We went over a list of weapons we might resort to using. Poe Poe already knew how to make a zip gun and he had access to the boiler room in his building that had all sorts of tools that could be used as weapons. Poe Poe was also complaining about not being able to drink a beer when we earned honest money to pay for it just like any stooge or swell. He was talking about a new business, no more living on our knees shining shoes. "We should open a bar for kids," he said, "Cold beer, grilled cheese and chocolate cake." When I finally arrived home at 9:00 PM my mother was waiting with the belt. It'd been almost a week since last she smashed me around so she was jonesing for a beating. The upside was I figured she'd unload on me and by morning my black eye and bloody nose would blend together with the coming bruises and if I looked bad enough she might not look at me. That way I wouldn't have to explain about getting punched in the face by the Swell. The belt with the buckle out was unleashed. By then I'd already figured out that crying didn't do any good. You're still going to get clobbered so what's the point. Though when I finally made it to bed and realized I left my shoeshine box in the pizzeria and I'd never get it back and my days of working bars was over for the foreseeable future, I had a serious round of whimpering.

The Second Coming

I had a natural talent. I no longer have that talent. Unlike other people with talents that could last a lifetime my talent was gone before any good could come of it. It's still something to have had a talent. Don't let anyone tell you that everyone has talent and it's just waiting to be discovered. Unless you consider talent the ability to open a bottle of beer or crack open a handful of peanuts; which would still leave the talent team a few men short for a warranted competition. Bottom line is plenty of people are without an ounce of talent. They might not stand out for much but talent less people are not without merit. Most of them consistently provide reliability. That measure alone probably makes talent less people more valuable in this world of ours. After all, talented and talent less alike, we all favor a reliable world. We depend on it. Maybe I'm mistaken in thinking I had a talent when in fact it was only youth and frenzy gushing through my veins. I couldn't honestly tell you at this point because there's no way of testing a talent that's no longer available. I know it's gone for sure because I've become more reliable.

I was able to run fast and steady for a long time. Imagine a sledgehammer note slammed out on a gigantic bronze bell. I nearly put that speed to use at Mount Saint Michael High School. But partaking in organized sports was a far off idea. Regardless, I had to breathe the anxiety filled air that every freshman had to breathe: try out for some team otherwise you're a queer. I loved the Yankees, Knicks, Rangers and Giants, and I liked playing sports, pickup games, and I clearly liked girls, clear as a bell. But as the old saying goes, "There's no 'I' in team," and at thirteen years old I was still just getting to know "I" and I thought "I" was a guy worth knowing better before a total surrender to some dopey coach and a bunch of sweaty jocks. On top of it all my after school schedule was already filled with two jobs: scraping the grill and cleaning the fryer at Mickey's Coffee Shop; and sweeping, mopping, cleaning up the toilets and serving as Beer Boy on Friday Night Poker at the American Legion. Plus my father as always was harassing me to find more work. If you consider I was the smallest kid in High School and not making a team meant a barrage of name-calling coming my way then maybe you'll sympathize with me when I tell you the pressure of being thirteen years old felt like I was being snuffed out under a bell.

I tried out for the baseball team but there were unerring players to compete with. I fooled myself into trying out for the football team but that only gave the rest of the kids a blatant reason for poking fun at me for being small. I wasn't without defenses. I could talk as fast as I could run and mouth off to some of the biggest lugs in school and escape blows. Being fast with foot and mouth also enabled me to be an entertainer for everybody worth knowing and kept me on the good side of a lot of the kids who were on the larger side who would stand on my side if I had nowhere to run. It didn't take long for one of the coaches to grab a hold of me and throw a tracksuit on me. "You got real talent kid," that's what the coach told me.

The thing about the track team that unnerved me most was that I was always out in front and it felt like someone was chasing me that made the sweat pouring out of me cold instead of hot which just isn't natural. Giving up two good jobs likely contributed to my overall uneasiness. Mount Saint Michael was serious about their sports and they had a number of ball fields scattered on a campus that sat on a big plot of land in the Wakefield section of the Bronx. I know the size well because the track team had to run around the perimeter of the campus everyday after school. I wanted to quit from day one because some of the older kids I beat in my first race had figured my weak spot and got around to shoving me around in the showers - the only place without enough traction to put my speed to good use. My father was very unhappy and getting a kick out of telling me regularly: "Why do you want to run around in circles? ...Doing the same thing over and over is insanity... Go make money... Pull your weight around here." I was decisively indecisive about quitting the track team and miserable for it. By the second week in October when we were having unseasonably warm weather I finally decided the track team wasn't for me. I have to get a job, that's what I was thinking as I laced up my sneakers for my last run. The decision was pure and reaffirming.

As the immutable notion of quitting solidified I thoughtlessly discovered an unknown and incredibly mutable sensation inside me. I was running along Mundy Lane and making the turn at West Sanford Boulevard when on the corner standing on the steps of the entrance to a bar was the most beautiful woman I'd ever laid eyes on. A black girl, probably twenty years old, wearing a snug yellow mesh halter top and tight-tight light brown bell-bottom corduroys. She had big brown eyes that were reflecting bits of sunlight from across the street and a perfect head of hair filled with brown curls and natural ringlets all harmonized atop a slender, lustrous neck. By that early part of October 1976 I had already taken up the habit of admiring pretty girls but it had mostly been with a sense of admiration and tenderfoot drippings of yearning for girls my own age. I'd messed around with an incorrigible girl exchanging minimal bodily fluids in shaky attempts to displace body parts into each other's body parts. I wasn't categorically a virgin but still far from able to testify to the galactic burgeoning of truly making love to a woman. But as I ran along Mundy Lane the solstice of salacious joy was finally crossed. I turned the corner onto West Sanford Boulevard and onto a new horizon opened by a Nubian goddess delivering an instant and decisive rage of sexual momentum roaring and leaving my entire body numb save for the extension of me tucked away tightly in my jock strap that was getting tighter by the second.

A Jamaican girl, had to be I thought. She was standing in front of the bar with the sign that said: Island Charm – Be Seen In The Jamaican Scene. She was smiling at me; you would've noticed it a mile away. Before I could smile in return she turned her back to me, almost politely. That's when I saw it. Splendor bedazzled and stupefied, her magnificent plump and alive, heart shaped ass with rosebud hips honestly and happily married to a set of long healthy legs. She turned back toward me like a dizzy dancer and I noticed her thin waist, her large breasts, a face like cake. Magma level heat pulses exploded in every direction inside of me nearly blowing my lid off explaining why I tripped and fell when she smiled the way she did. I lied there on my back selfishly wondering why I was introduced to true beauty this way. She stepped across the street to see if I was okay. I was better than okay. I was in love. Her smell, a shy and anomalous orange blossom that inexplicably grows without roots or soil and floats in the air would have been enough to lift me off the sidewalk but I needed to touch her, grab a hold of her long and slender arm as she helped me to my feet. Her skin was like a warm ocean at my fingertips. With lips that appeared to be made of butter and cocoa powder how could she be real? "You alright boy?" she asked with an island girl accent. Her eyelashes were like lashes on a baby giraffe setting you off quickly to dreaming of them pressed to your cheek. Up close her eyes were a kaleidoscope fragmentation of shadowed golden hues resting on petals of flowers, magic irises, no, the spirit of irises that were packed with sweet orange, fertile green and earthen brown and utterly blended by a solar flare. "Best I've ever been," I told her as I sprang to my feet. I was too overwhelmed to be embarrassed and she liked that. She was a lot taller than me. She rubbed her fingers through my hair fixing it back to a presentable style. "You look fine," she said, "Fine enough to live another day." There were no other days. There was only this day, the day when quitting turned out to be the answer for everything newly and abruptly cherished in life. Surrender to beauty, the words could have been written in the sky. Blood was beginning to re-circulate through the rest of my body. The balance of heat between my groin and head was stabilizing. She was walking back across the street, heading into the bar. She turned and waved goodbye. Spontaneity got the better of me and I yelled, "Ja-making-me crazy." I thought it'd be funny. She smiled again and then turned away. "I'll see you tomorrow," I yelled it as if it were true, as if I could convince her in an instant of a new reality, our reality, the reality of the two of us in love and enraptured in our naked embrace for eternity.

Puberty can be consuming.

I returned to the same spot the next day after school. I wasn't wearing my tracksuit. She wasn't there. I was in love. The Island Charm was open. I walked in. There was a black guy behind the bar wearing a red, yellow and green knitted vest and a green beret on his head. He was leaning on the bar top scribbling in a notebook. There was another black guy with long, funky and nappy hair in the back room fussing with a large speaker. There was some unknown type of music coming out of the other speaker hanging over a small dance floor. There was plenty of red, yellow and green garland taped to the walls, hanging from the ceiling and everywhere. I was thinking it must be a holiday or a New Year on a Jamaican calendar being celebrated in October. Behind the bar was a giant poster of some skinny black man wearing a military uniform that was too big for him that was pinned with an overdose of medals and regalia. I started imaging the island of Jamaica with militia members drinking in makeshift bars on lost mountaintop jungles.

The bartender lifted his head, popped his eyes wide when he saw me, smiled broadly and said, "Yah Mon." You might've thought he'd seen a ghost. "How you doing," I said. He said it again while shaking his head, "Yah Mon." His smile got bigger like for certain he saw a ghost. "Freddy," he shouted to the guy in the back, "Come see what the open door bring in." Freddy turned his head. He wasn't smiling. He wasn't mad either. It appeared Freddy was more interested in fixing the speaker. "Leave it be, Clifton," he said, "Me got work to do." Clifton smiled more and even laughed some trying to assume a new attitude. He asked, "What can I do you for, Mon?" This guy likes me I thought as I sat up on the stool. He looked nice enough but I hadn't ever met any Jamaicans before so who could know. "I'll take a screwdriver," I told him like I owned the place. "Right Mon.., me make one screwdriver... Coming right to you," he said. He started to make the drink with some confusion and thinking out loud about what goes in it. He was shaking his head and laughing to himself while finishing. He hadn't asked me for ID so I wasn't too concerned about him not knowing how to make a screwdriver off the top of his head. He put the drink down in front of me. "Two dollars, Mon." I took a big gulp of it quick because I wasn't sure if this was some sort of joke and I was about to be bounced out of the place. The drinking age in 1976 was 18 and though some younger teenagers could slide on account of their size I could barely pass for a teenager. I did have a decent attitude. If he bounced me at least I'd have a half drink down my gut and the beginnings of a tasty buzz to ease my heart's yearning. I pulled three bucks out and told him to keep the change. He smiled again but this time it was more down to earth. "Righteous, Mon. Really righteous," he said.

I tried making small talk with Clifton. "What time of day you open?" "You open everyday?" "I love the music... Who is it?" I asked. "Pablo All Stars," he told me. "Listen here, Freddy, him white boy like the good shit," he yelled to Freddy. Freddy still couldn't be bothered. I told Clifton I was looking for the girl who came in here yesterday. "Many girl come here, Mon." He was smiling again. I described her, described her outfit. Clifton told me I was in trouble. "Them white boy come looking for your girl, Freddy," he yelled to the back. Freddy finally turned to me. Once he got a good look at me his concern was suddenly more sincere. He started toward the bar and asked loudly, "Are you dangerous, Mon?" It only seemed natural that I answer him, "Why?" He said, "Last time me see some white boy come to take one of me women, he was no dangerous... So me want to know, are you dangerous?" Freddy continued to step closer and closer to me and then got as close to me as you can get. Clifton's smile was no longer bright or down to earth. Freddy spun the stool I was sitting on around so that I was facing him directly. He looked down at me. He was big as they come. It's true that I didn't know any Jamaicans but I did know when a man was in a mind to call all the shots and it's usually best to give him some space and stay clear of those shots. I could feel the hot air blowing through his nostrils down on my face. Freddy asked me again, "Are you dangerous, Mon?"

I had gotten myself into a jam. I already lost my three dollars on the screwdriver Clifton wasn't going to let me finish. The girl of my dreams wasn't there and she turned out to be Freddy's girl. I already quit the track team. I didn't have a job. High school was turning out to be the pits. I was queasy and heartbroken thinking I'd have to go back to chasing flat-chested, skinny teenage girls again. The only bright thing I could imagine was the fact that I was in a bar. I was in a Jamaican bar and I'd never been in a Jamaican bar. There was a gigantic black man with hair unlike any hair I'd ever seen before up close and getting extremely personal. The music was different and I liked it. My first impression of Clifton and Freddy were quick and good. "Me asking, are you dangerous?" Freddy demanded. I didn't know what was up or down so I told him, "Me real dangerous." I told him instinctually while trying my best attempt at a Jamaican accent. Maybe speaking in tones he could relate to could help him relate to me. Maybe I wasn't thinking straight because the big gulp of the screwdriver quickly found its way to my brain that was trying to calm my heart's attempt to jump out of my chest. I wasn't sure if it was my odd answer or my poor attempt at a Jamaican accent but after a death-threatening pause the two of them set off laughing. Freddy was patting me on the back fast enough. "You real cool, Mon... Me like this one Clifton," Freddy said. "No shaking alive in him," Clifton said.

Clifton let me finish my drink and Freddy went on telling me there was no chance he'd let me steal his girl. Her name was Cherine. "There be bullets with your name for it," he told me. I hoped he was joking. He told me I was intelligent and had the finest taste because Cherine was a queen. She was. He promised me one of her sisters. I hoped he was serious. He also told me Island Charm was a reggae club, his reggae club, and Rastafarians go to his club, and the music playing on the speakers was Reggae music. Best of all they were proud to serve minors any drink they wanted though he highly recommended rum and ginger beer. That was his daytime policy, before 6:00 PM. Come nighttime he recommended a skinny little white boy like myself didn't get anywhere near the place. "Tell them boys at school you cool with Freddy," he said, "And be sure you use the back door, Mon." Also, I should know that whenever I saw Clifton behind the bar and it was before 6:00 PM I could be sure he'd have dollar spliffs and nickel bags of Jamaica's' finest for sale.

Island Charm turned out to be a big positive for my life at school. I ended up creating a new after school club, The Haile

Selassie Study Group. It was a hat tip to my new Rastafarian friends who considered Haile Selassie their savior, the second coming of Christ. He was the skinny guy in the over-sized military uniform on the giant poster behind the bar, the emperor of Ethiopia. Go figure. A group of us would meet at the Island Charm on Fridays after school. Principal Smith didn't know where we we're going, thought we were into poetry because the club's name sounded lyrical. He thought we were good kids for that. There would be at least a dozen boys there every Friday and sometimes plenty more. Freddy and Clifton were appreciative of the new daytime business and treated me with the respect I earned. They introduced me to all of their friends; I'd always get a free shot of rum, sometimes two; and if I bought five loose spliffs I'd only have to pay three bucks. This left me two spliffs to sell to my friends and make two bucks. The Haile Selassie Study Group turned out to be more than just a party. Friday afternoons were a time of unconventional learning and mind expansion. It was unlike other kids at school who smoked pot while standing around the schoolyard zoning out to absurd heroic cartoon fantasies with Pink Floyd or Led Zeppelin on cheap radios and cassette tape players. We were sitting around drinking beer, booze and smoking cigarettes and ganja inside of a bar, learning the rules for serious minded conversations, hanging out with Rastafarian gangsters who carried machine guns under their coats, and listening to dub sound in a stereophonic overture for a fulfilling contemplated life ahead of us.

The unique thing was there was not one eager student in the bunch yet while we sat around the Island Charm with Freddy and Clifton and the Rastafarian gangsters and their ganja filled duffel bags we learned worldly matters thoroughly. Clifton informed us, "Rastafarianism is full body experience, Mon. Your mind and flesh both need to liven up." We would talk about women, religion and Christ, money and international banking, bogus politics. It was a different way to learn than sitting in a stuffed classroom. Drinking rum and smoking pot probably had a lot to do with it. But we also learned smoking pot is more for spiritualism and for quality learning more than for having fun. Though Freddy confirmed with his best smile, "It be real good for party too, Mon." Clifton could roll the biggest ganja cones in existence, as large as an ice cream cones, so long as it was ganja you paid for that was filling it up. He took the greatest pleasure in telling us the evils white men have carried out through history. It wasn't all white men he assured us. "It's them Bankers, Mon." he'd say, "Them got the Babylon system, make'em debt slave all man with no mind in his head." He'd put his finger on your forehead and tap it a few times just to help you comprehend. A moralizing concept was that marijuana is a plant capable of uniting a whole nation. "It rid the world of mindlessness Babylon teach the children, Mon. It bring your focus to Jah." Jah is the be all and end all, the Big I am, the presence of G*d. Clifton told all of us this stuff while at the same time billowing out streams of smoke thick enough to easily remind you of paintings of heaven. We learned international bankers are Babylon and Babylon runs politics in most countries around the world and a free and independent African people is what Babylon fears most because Africa is resource rich. We weren't learning any of this stuff at school. "Left or Right, them all the same Party for them Banker... Them Banker only divide, Mon." Most important was that if the Bankers didn't control the politics in one country, "You be sure bet, Mon. War coming soon." Clifton must've said that a hundred times.

Some of the kids who'd check out the Friday gig weren't pot smokers. Plenty of them were drinkers and happy drinkers now that they found a bar around the corner from school willing to serve drinks to any kid with a presentable dollar in his pocket. Sometimes a wall might form between the drinkers and the pot smokers. But the wall wasn't reliable because by 4:30 in the afternoon there'd be a cloud of smoke dense enough to get even the thickest booze head in the room higher than the mountains in Jamaica. The mix of booze, beer, tobacco and ganja was a special medley because without fail it fermented in every kid in that bar a pungent scintilla to talk about some topic or idea that more than likely he would never have thought about in his entire life. For a group of kids who were all more or less coming of age, you couldn't have dreamed of a better bar for them to sanctify the solidification of their bones and to drink up to the realization that the world was nothing like we had thought it to be.

Broadway Keg

Friday night was the night to work at Fat Jack's. Bussing tables could net you $70 or $80 bucks. The real name of the bar was Jack Murphy's Broadway Grill but that didn't matter none because everyone knew the place as Fat Jack's because Jack Murphy was a fat son of a bitch - a 450-pound son of a bitch. Most people didn't consider Fat Jack a son of a bitch. They didn't have high regard for him either. When you own a popular bar patrons tend to lean toward a favorable opinion of the owner. As far as those who worked for Fat Jack they didn't consider him a son of a bitch either, nor did they consider him a kind and generous boss. He was the lard ass that signed their measly paychecks. Considering Fat Jack an out right son of a bitch was wholly my opinion of him. But when you're 16 years old vying for the opportunity to make serious cash you try to put up with a fat son of a bitch.

Jack Murphy's Broadway Grill was going to be a major jumping point for my dreams in life. I told myself that. Sadly those dreams were as clear as a moldering beer. What I did know with clarity was that $80 bucks for one night of work at 16 years old could feasibly change my life's direction. I could buy beer, pot, and tabs of acid, and with that come more good times with friends. Of course I had to have the right attitude to go along with all that dough otherwise I might lose my mind. However I added it up the chance to earn great money and eat overcooked burger-mistakes or anything out of the bus bucket buffet and the freedom to finish off half empty drinks pulled from dirty tables and the bar, it was an opportunity of a lifetime.

$80 bucks was for working on a Friday night. A Monday

night you might make $20 bucks. Monday nights were the shift I got. Making matters worse was that I had to split that $20 bucks with the Monday night cook because Fat Jack didn't pay him a decent wage. Further downgrading Monday night was your food choice was no choice at all. It wasn't a Friday night date night when some lady would order a steak and take two bites out of it and leave it to be gleaned by a quick-handed busboy. Mondays were for hoi polloi dipsomaniacs, cheap plebes, a professional patron night. Everybody would get their money's worth, plates were licked clean and all drinks finished.

"Make sure the keg is empty. Always!" the fat son of bitch yelled at me and grabbed me by the back of the neck and pushed my nose down to where the keg meets the beer line just to make sure I knew what he was talking about. That was the introduction I received from my new boss. Fat Jack was bent on every last drop in a keg. I didn't appreciate him putting his fat paws on me one bit. But it was my first night and I was trying my best to think about the future. Fat Jack blabbed at me, "Empty kegs go upstairs immediately, out the back door, inside the gate right along with the hand truck. Lock the gate... If I see empty kegs in the basement you're fired!" It made ordering new kegs easier for him, less trips down to the basement. I told him, "That sounds best, Jack." He took about two minutes explaining the rest of my busboy duties that I already knew about from my buddy, Scratch Macallen. He got me the job. There was no hourly rate, no shift pay, just tips. I was hired to buss tables and the bar, keep the toilets clean and papered, wash dishes and glasses, sort forks and knives, clean and refill condiments, help Cuban Nip the 75 year old Monday night cook prep food and salads and help on the grill if there was a rush, and also haul cases of beer from the basement and change the dead kegs. If there was any free time Fat Jack would send me to the basement to rearrange everything for no apparent reason or to sweep up the mountain loads of crumbs in his little office and bring up a stack of dirty plates sitting on his desk. If I did all that and by chance Fat Jack was busy watching Monday Night Football or talking to a customer at the bar, then I might get a minute or two to chat up the waitress. Sadly, that was no salvation. Along with the rest of the things that made Monday night suck the waitress

28

was not one of the 20-year-old gorgeous blondes Fat Jack had hired for Friday nights. Mrs. O'Leary, Fat Jack's mother's home attendant was the waitress. He wasn't paying her enough to take care of his mother so he threw her a lousy waitress shift to stave off her complaints. Mrs. O'Leary was a nice enough lady but she wasn't a looker and she couldn't take care of tables if her life depended on it. So on top of not getting a cute waitress to flirt with or any decent food to eat or half empty cocktails to drink and about $10 bucks in tips to keep, I ended up having to take orders and run most of the drinks to tables on top of all my other duties. Worst of all Fat Jack wouldn't let me hang around the bar to maybe watch a game or what I was hoping most for, to watch and learn more about the high level skill of bartending.

"You have to pay your dues," that's what my buddy Scratch told me. Scratch was a Friday night busboy. He had worked Monday nights for three months before he finally got Tuesday and Wednesday nights. Tuesday and Wednesday nights could net you $50 or $60 bucks, and no sharing tips with the cook. Once Scratch proved himself a worthy busboy, and when Michael Flynn moved backwards but forward from Friday night busboy to Monday night bartender, Scratch was given a Friday night busboy shift. Eventually Scratch was named top busboy and he could pick and choose his nights and also line up new busboys, along with being next in line to become a bartender. That was the order of things, Fat Jack's ladder of success. Scratch worked three nights and came close to making $200 bucks a week, which was nothing compared to the waitresses or the bartenders weekly take that netted $600 or $700 bucks or more. Between my Monday night busboy shift and my other job working four nights at Mavericks, a shitty fast food joint, I brought home $50 bucks. My old man took his cut and that left me with a $25 bucks and little time for a proactive social life. Some things were clear and hopeful. "You get to take acid and make money at the same time," Scratch explained to me as if he had stumbled upon a gateway to a new universe and was pointing the way. Scratch was maybe the smartest guy I knew. He had confidence in me so I tried to be patient about the job. He finished explaining his galactic insight on bussing tables at Fat Jack's, "You're gonna meet so many girls." Fat Jack's was a new

29

universe. I kept thinking how Michael Flynn was now a bartender and he too started out as a Monday night busboy, and he was only two years older than me. A future for myself appeared real.

My first day started out rough when Fat Jack put his fat paws on me and shoved my nose into a keg, but at the end of my second shift when he changed my start time from 4:30 PM to 3:30 PM ahead of the waitress and the bartender in order for me to do the entire restaurant and bar setup by myself, my vision of the future was dimming. With me on board the bartender's only responsibility was getting his cash draw counted correctly by 5:00 PM. Mrs O'Leary was having trouble with Fat Jack's nagging mother and needed extra time off to unwind before working the night shift and she didn't have to stroll in the door until 6:30 PM. Starting at 3:30 PM meant I'd have to head to work straight from school in a hurry. By coming in early I was also responsible for unloading all the deliveries and I wasn't getting paid for it. If I was just getting the short end of the stick, paying my dues, it might've been okay. But I was getting screwed. All the work and the smallest take, practically no take. I was cheerless and Fat Jack could care less.

Things went on like that for a few months and it didn't appear there was any rung on Fat Jack's ladder of success at hand. I did get to cover other busboy shifts and that put some extra cash in my pocket but it wasn't the money it should've been. If I covered a shift on a different night I'd get a reduced busboy share on Fat Jack's orders because I was the center of gravity for all bad things in Fat Jack's world. I wondered if Fat Jack had hired me in the first place because I was small and easy to pick on. He was not only stiffing me out of fair earnings but he was treating me like his whipping boy, unloading on me every night I worked with him. The weaker side of me was hoping that he'd just fire me because I was desperate for the coveted bartending opportunity down the line and there was no telling what I'd put up with for that chance.

I nearly quit the time Fat Jack tried to tell me it was part of my job to be a magician. He barked at me, "When the bartender tells you the keg is empty I want you to go downstairs and shake the keg and then go back upstairs and tell the bartender the keg isn't empty. I want at least one more pint out of it." Of course he grabbed me by the shoulders and shook me hard to illustrate the way he wanted me to shake the kegs. I couldn't figure how I could be responsible for the set amount of beer in a keg or how shaking an empty keg could create another pint. I did figure I was now responsible for running up and down out of the basement twice to change an empty barrel of beer once. I was also going to have to take the hit for missing brew when the draft beer sales didn't match up to the draft beer inventory, which happens when bartenders slide free beers across the bar or when they carelessly pull beer.

Fat jack didn't drink alcohol, which I quickly learned is a bad sign for a bar owner; unless the guy is a recovering alcoholic that might cause you to cut some sappy slack for his inability to control himself like the rest of us have to do. Fat Jack wasn't recovering from anything other than routine indigestion. The libation void likely contributed to him being a son of a bitch. No booze but he drank plenty of soda, his own version of diet soda. I'd have to mix half a glass of coca cola with half a glass of club soda. Anytime I brought him his cockamamie drink he'd send it back complaining there was too much club soda and then smack me in the back of the head. I'd have to remake it with mostly coca cola and only a splash of club soda. Then he'd want me to confirm that it was a half and half mix and of course I'd tell him, "Half and half, Jack." If the fat son of a bitch ever came into the kitchen after looking for me at the tables where he thought I should be instead of me prepping salads or helping old Cuban Nip on the grill as Fat Jack had instructed me to do, then Fat Jack in a state of confusion and rage would throw a fat fistful of utensils at me without blinking an eye. I pulled a fork out of my cheek the one time I couldn't duck out of the way fast enough. The fat son of a bitch eventually increased his bad habit of random head smacks and clumsy 450-pound shoves to clear me out of his way. Worse than all of his fuming and was his constant sweating. Imagine the sweat a fat son of a bitch can sweat once he gets worked up. He breathed out of his mouth in huffs and puffs completely ignoring the good use of the nose on his face and it produced a slight and perpetual drool. On top of all that I discovered he was a creep. He had me clean the walls of his small office one night because he lost control of his appetite for french fries with ketchup and had to crack the top off a bottle in a panic because the cap was dried shut. While wiping down the walls I knocked over a few boxes and discovered his stash of scud magazines. There must've been a hundred of them with titles like Teeny Titties, Sassy & Sexy, Bare Beaver. The covers were sickly looking girls in their panties who were a lifetime away from being women.

I got the call to fill in for one of the busboys on a Saturday night. When I walked in the door Fat Jack told me Peggy Meenhan, the early-shift waitress, was going to be late and Matt Brown, my busboy partner, was stuck in Boston. I'd have to work alone until Peggy arrived and bus tables solo all night. He was gloating when he told me, "You're still getting a smaller percentage of the tips until you prove yourself." That started the night badly but thankfully things changed when a pack of foxes rolled in the door, Nursing Students from Mount Saint Vincent's. They sat at a back table and were giggling and yakking from the moment they walked in. I got them their Seabreezes and Vodka 7up's and put their food orders in fast enough. I had a few other tables but I was amusing the future nurses and giving them first-rate service. Fat Jack was sitting at the end of the bar by the front door and craving the attention I was dishing out to the caregivers. He yelled across the room to me, "Diet coke." I ran over to the service bar and made him his coca cola with a splash of club soda and carried it down to his end of the bar. "Did you make this right?" he asked as I put the glass in front of him. "Half and half, Jack." Another group walked in the door, good-looking ladies all wearing wedding rings but dolled up like they were single and gorgeous with stored up energy to show it off. I sat them in the back next to the nurses with the intention of creating a happy hour harem for myself. Fat Jack yelled my name again. I walked to the front, "What do you need boss?" He pushed the half emptied soda across the bar top to me. "You didn't make it right," he said. Johnny Mack, the bartender, tried jumping in, "I'll get you another one Jack." Fat Jack told him, "I want him to do it." I ran over to the service bar and made him another cockamamie diet coke and then brought it to him. An older couple walked in the door and another group of five behind them and a crowd was beginning to assemble at the bar. I sat the diners and was running around trying to get all their drinks. I was delivering the narrative on the Daily Specials to the pretty housewives when Fat Jack yelled my name again. This time he was waving his arms at me. I excused myself from the table and went to the front. "You are making my night difficult," Fat Jack blabbed at me, "too much club soda." He slid the half emptied soda across the bar. Johnny Mack shot me a sympathetic look. I told him, "Right away boss." With tables backing up what I really needed to do was get my feet moving and my mind deeper into business otherwise everyone was going to end up with shitty service. I brought Fat Jack another diet soda that was pretty much straight coca cola. I apologized to the table of young housewives. They told me I was adorable and could do no wrong. I was putting out house salads for the nurses-to-be like a seasoned poker dealer when Fat Jack yelled my name again. A red headed Florence Nightingale eased my stress, "What's the fat guy's problem?" The group of them laughed.

On my end of the bargain I'd done a great job from day one for Fat Jack. He never had to instruct me on my duties or give me the layout of the place more than once. I stepped right into busboy stride and carried the slack for old Cuban Nip and Mrs. O'Leary. I covered other busboy shifts for half the money. I was putting up with physical abuse. The customers thought I was efficient, clean, appealing and funny. Maybe the real the reason Fat Jack didn't like me was because I was too good to be true. Maybe he was hoping for someone less eager to work the deadbeat shift because he feared that once I got a little experience under my belt I'd leave for better shifts at bars with better bosses. I was thinking along those lines. But Jack Murphy's Bar & Grill consistently did great business and I had staked my claim. I was also a boy of my word so there was no way I'd let down Scratch after he vouched for me to get the job. On difficult nights I tried thinking how Herman the German, the other Friday night busboy, might be quitting soon because his parents were getting divorced and hopefully he'd be moving to New Jersey with his mom.

"I said half and half," Fat Jack told me again. He slid the glass across the bar one more time. "Taste that," he said. I looked at the glass. There were persecuted bread crumbs from the Monte Cristo sandwich Fat Jack had just swallowed in two bites hanging for life on the side of the glass, some of them slipping and sinking to their death. There was oil residue from Fat Jack's sweaty lips around the rim of the glass and floating on the surface of the soda. I looked around the place. The tables were filled, not one empty stool at the bar and more customers walking in the door. My mind was already slipping into fighter-pilot mode and the afterburners in my gut were lighting up as I neared the crossover from good busboy to a nuclear powered service machine. I could hear Cuban Nip in the kitchen dropping pots and pans. Johnny Mack was holding the phone to his chest telling Fat Jack, "Peggy is stuck babysitting her niece because her sister is in the hospital." Johnny looked at me, almost apologizing for the night's work ahead. Instead of trying to figure out how his customers were going to get good service, Fat Jack told me again, "Taste that!"

My mind suddenly split. One half was preparing and hyper-prioritizing a list of requirements and actions needed for everyone in the place to get the best service, which had the wheels in my head spinning too fast. The other half of my mind was struggling to keep me standing still. Johnny Mack was back to tending customers. There were tables trying to wave me down for more drinks and their food was late. Fat Jack was breathing heavy and waiting for me to taste his soda. I looked him straight in the face, something I tried never to do. A surge came through me like biting into a watermelon-sized lemon. It was transforming. Everything in my head squeezed together tightly until an abrupt shift altered all of it to a dimension of slowness and ease. The smells in the place from burgers burning on the grill, to the young housewives wearing too much perfume, to the smell of gin and cigarettes across the bar, all of it vanished. Normalcy faded. The lights were on but it seemed they were not enough; like when your eyes adjust to a dark room and you can see everything though you couldn't honestly testify to what you're looking at. There were tables and chairs being pushed around, the bar with drinks being picked up and put down, people talking, forks and plates clinking, but the room was muted. I could've easily been sleep walking or maybe in the midst of a drunken delusion. I caught a glimpse of myself in the mirror behind the bar and it looked like a funhouse mirror. A shadowed brilliancy appeared out of nowhere. A witchy pulse of knowing what everyone else was blind to. It was enough that I could see through walls, read minds and anticipate a room full of needs and cravings. The chef, Dutch Billups, was in the kitchen drinking mouthfuls of house brandy from his coffee mug and thinking about going fishing; Cuban Nip was burning an order of Potato Skins and had forgotten to drop three orders of pasta into the boiling water; a box of tomatoes was spilled across the kitchen floor. Some guy was in the men's room and the toilet was backed up and he was on his third flush hoping everything would just go down the hole instead of spilling out under the door. The young housewife with a new perm and freshly polished nails was secretly hoping for more salad dressing but didn't dare ask for it and she was promising herself that next week would be different and she would paint her nails red in defiance of her husband. She wouldn't do it and I knew it. The girl with curly brown hair and brown eyes at the table of nursing students who didn't look me in the eye earlier really thought I was cute and sweet and I reminded her of her cousin. The pepper mill on the elderly couple's table was empty and though the old man didn't go for it yet he was going to need pepper; and his wife didn't ever deeply love him but she felt blessed just the same knowing he was a good man, a good father. It was true. I could feel the growing pains in my legs reminding me that I was not going to be allowed to stay small forever. My hands were taking on a life of their own and I had to hold them down with a conscious effort. They were reaching for Fat Jack's neck with a bad intention and dumb to the fact that they could never wrap around such girth. I starred deeper into Fat Jack's face. His mother had spoiled him, he was fat before he was young and it wasn't supposed to be that way, it wasn't his fault, and he never had to work hard for anything - this was his father's bar first. I experienced a plump pulse of sympathy for him and then the entire bar expanded bizarrely extending longer and longer. In some way I was looking at all of the bar's history and everyone that had ever sat along Fat Jack's bar and they were all looking at me or looking beyond me. I fought the urge to run down and ask everyone if they needed more drinks or something to eat or anything. It wasn't guesswork; nearly all of them had a need to be recognized. Everything was significant; the opposite of the nonchalant look on

35

Fat Jack's face. I was nailed to the floor in the present, a touchstone for that expanding backwards timeline of Fat Jack customers so they could have a new direction, forward, a future. I looked back at that the people, thousands of drinks, clouds of cigarette smoke. There was writing carved into the bar top: "We don't see things as they are, we see them as we are." A small, thin woman with big eyes and short dark hair was sitting at the bar closest to me reached for my hand, asked me, "Are you okay?" I wasn't. My perspective unintentionally changed. I was looking at the world for what it was.

I told Fat Jack, "I need a minute." I couldn't tell you about any new look that might've been on his face because I didn't bother to turn around. I walked straight toward the kitchen pass the filled bar and through the packed dining room. I gestured to all the tables calling for me that I'd be right back. In the kitchen Cuban Nip was in disaster mode and Dutch was drunk as a skunk. I couldn't do anything for them. The dishwasher was making a bad noise and plenty of dirty water was spilling out of it. I opened the back door to the alley and took a deep breath. Before I could exhale the idea was in my head. I was bouncing the hand truck down the basement stairs. I pulled a keg of Budweiser out of the cooler and put it on the hand truck and grabbed a bottle of Dewar's from the shelf and dragged the entire load up the stairs faster than a wink. I was out the back door rolling the keg down the sidewalk with the bottle tucked under my arm. In less than a minute I was on Broadway with a preprogrammed destination in my head, #1 Train at 242nd Street one block away. I climbed the stairs to the elevated platform easily pulling that keg as if it were filled with helium. I jumped onto the waiting train with my load and within seconds the doors closed. At 231st Street my heist and escape that had played out like a dance choreographed by an avalanche ended.

I guessed about ten minutes had passed since I left Fat Jack sitting at the bar waiting for me to taste his diet coke. I was already in a new territory with the Bronx end of Broadway behind me. My head was adjusting to the train ride by the time the conductor announced, "Next stop, 215th Street." I was getting off. Very likely Fat Jack was just getting off his stool and heading to the kitchen in search of me and I was already at the top of Manhattan with a portable party. Johnny Mack and Cuban Nip were going to have to forgive me for leaving them alone with a full house. Leaving all those nice customers out on a limb when they were hoping for a legitimate night out had me feeling guilty. But there was an old guy sitting across from me on the train with an encouraging smile on his face looking at my keg and the bottle of Dewar's under my arm. I was still wearing my busboy apron and there were two unsettled checks and $90 bucks stashed away in the pocket. Fat Jack was likely going to have a heart attack. But that was Fat Jack's problem. I was in search of friends to share my booty.

At 215th Street I was anew. I made it to the street and went to a payphone and made a call to my buddy Scratch's house. His brother Kyle answered and told me Scratch was at Inwood Hill Park just like he was every Saturday night. I knew that, that's where I was heading. I was hoping to catch him before he left to make sure he brought his keg pump along. Scratch was a drinker and a smoker and a talker and a taker - meaning he'd drink, smoke, talk or take anything so long as it held the smallest promise of getting him out of bounds. He was a year older than me and served as my role model throughout my junior year of High School. Scratch was from Inwood and that may have been the greatest thing about him. Inwood was the most notorious neighborhood for bars in all of New York City and Scratch was fully networked in those bars. That meant if you were in his good grace he could sometimes get you into those bars. Up, down, between Dyckman Street and 207th, there were no less than a hundred bars. Inwood was the place kids were encouraged to drink in schoolyards and parks and occasionally bars only to earn an apprenticeship before finally becoming professionals on their 18th birthday when they'd be called on to rekindle the neighborhood bar scene full time with their nearly spotless livers. Scratch didn't have to wait until his 18th birthday to be considered professional because bars were a part of his genetic code. His four older brothers were Inwood bartenders. His oldest brother Kyle was a legend at the legendary Burnside Pub. Scratch could go to any bar he chose. But at a quarter pass eight on a Saturday as the sun set late in June Scratch wouldn't be at just any bar, at least any bar of the predictable sort.

The north end ball field inside of Inwood Hill Park at the edge of Spuyten Duyvil Creek, the northern most tip of Manhattan, was the best spot in the City to hang out with your friends on a summer night. It was the same spot where the Tulip Tree under which the 'sale' of Manhattan by Americans Indians to Peter Minuit took place in 1626. If you ever sat there with friends you might imagine the blowout bash old man Minuit and his band of well-dressed pirates had in that spot after ye old prodigious land deal was closed. Maybe that was the reason why the place was great. That old Tulip tree was gone but whenever I was there with my band of adventurers there was an openness that connected your heart to the sky and it elevated a sense of getting the most out of life or at least getting a great bargain on the bit of life you've been dealt. Even if things were going bad for you it didn't matter because something good could be coming your way and you knew it just by sitting there. Add a cool breeze which would often blow down the Hudson and the many nights when stars were strong enough to shine and the tall shadowed green cliffs of the Palisades across the way displaying a form of reliability to a fault, what more could a natural born teenager want. Saturday nights the park would be swarming with sanctified Good Shepard kids. Good Shepard was Inwood's Catholic Parish and the most disciplined prayer nights weren't complete without uncounted tabs of acid. It was the communion of our times fueling abstract recklessness in search of our stripling souls.

With the bottle of Dewar's under my arm I was rolling my barrel of Budweiser on the hand-truck along the path to the north end ball field. I could see a bunch of kids assembled near the first base bench. I saw Scratch's homemade sign hanging on the fence: The Tulip Tree Pub. Scratch was standing on the pitcher's mound with Hector Cruz and Declan Finn. They'd dragged a garbage drum out to the mound and were pulling empty bottles out of it and throwing them into the backstop. I could hear the growing sound of Shake Your Groove Thing by Peaches and Herb on a radio and there was five or six girls on the grass behind first base in a line stepping left and right shaking their groove things. Declan was the first to see me. Or better put, he was the first to see the barrel of beer. A bunch of them came running out to meet me like island natives paddling canoes to meet a sailing ship filled with trinkets and treasure.

There were about twenty kids hanging out. They already had one keg tapped and it was sitting behind the first base bench up close to the bushes in front of the Spuyten Duyvil Creek just in case it had to be hidden fast from the cops. Scratch introduced me to everyone I didn't know in one shout. Four or five variables of "Hey hey" and "Party animal!" were shouted back and I was welcomed with open arms. Mary Cahill was there. That was great. Scratch was quick to asking me why I wasn't at work and where'd I get the cash to buy the beer and just how did I buy the beer. I held up the bottle of Dewar's and told him it was compliments of Fat Jack. Scratch didn't believe it, maybe because he didn't want to believe it. He'd be the one dealing with Fat Jack's fury because of me. But Scratch wasn't going to let anything spoil the party because above all he liked beer and loved Dewar's and tabs of acid reigned supreme. He put his arm around me and said, "You've proven yourself worthy to be a one of the Irregulars." The Irregulars was the name Scratch and his Inwood buddies had taken to calling themselves. If it was up to me I would have called them the Regulars and saved the other name for the rest of the world. I was honored just the same. He pulled a tab of acid from his shirt pocket and told me to, "Open wide," and then popped it in my mouth. In a glimpse I saw that he had three tabs left in his hand before he tossed them back and grabbed the bottle of Dewar's out of my hand twisted it open and took a daredevil's chug. Then with the gladdest smile and bending over in a graceful bow he said to the bunch of us standing there, "I'll see you later."

Scratch wasn't going anywhere. It was his way of saying he wasn't going to be responsible for any of his actions over the next couple of hours. It's not that he had to set any prerequisite for any of us. It was more a grand gesture to remind everyone to have a good time. That wasn't going to be a problem. We were all high. When the first keg emptied fast enough everyone was very happy that I had my keg. I tried not missing a beat and rolled the barrel into place, took the pump from the first keg and connected it to the new. I tried my best to change it with a clown's flare because I wanted to make Mary Cahill with her suddenly peculiar blue eyes laugh. I pumped it up fast and told everyone to "Line'em up!" I stood atop the keg filling everybody's cups and free pouring shots of Dewar's down their throats. I stayed on top of the keg with a delirious notion of being a luminary bartending for a select muster. It was that or I didn't want anyone to forget that it was me that brought the extra beer. I was watching some kids lying in the grass behind first base looking up at the stars. I couldn't tell if they were sleeping or traveling across the Milky Way that suddenly had parts of it reaching down into our atmosphere close enough for you to maybe swallow a star if you breathed in too hard. My acid trip was rolling. My focus kept shifting and then centering on Mary Cahill, staring at her intensely. She was looking back at me. I was still standing on top of the keg but now I was an acrobat squatting on one leg with the other leg stretched out in front of me, straight, level and rigid. I had my arms folded across my chest like a frozen Cossack dancer. My squatted leg had a magnet lock on the top of the barrel of beer and I was able to tip it back on edge for a lowbrow-balancing act. Mary was laughing at how seriously contorted my face was. I was a mesmerized goofball looking at Mary with the grass field behind her half lit up by the moonlight. The texture of the grass was growing thicker and more visible than the shadows. Mary's face was a fractal, dividing and blending and beginning to take shape a million times over on every blade of the nighttime grass. My balanced pose and my contorted face hit perfection as I lined up purely to the countless blades of grass and the million faces of Mary and I opened up all of me with a smile for all of her. She was enjoying it, a lot. "You're crazy," she said, "You're really crazy." She said it as if she was slipping down a hole and she couldn't contain her smiling and laughing the entire way down. She wanted to grab a hold of me, climb out of that hole and be on top of the keg with me.

I'd met Mary Cahill a few times before but I never had the balls to talk much to her. She was sort of Scratch's cousin. Scratch had told me plenty about her. If they made a movie of her life few would believe it. She grew up poor in Brooklyn. Her mother didn't want her. Her father wanted her too much and molested her. After her parents disappeared she lived in a halfway house. She was an exceptional student. Scratch's Uncle and Aunt adopted her at age

13. Father Rooney from Good Shepard arranged it. She had black-black hair and blue eyes, skin as pale as spilled milk and a real sweet smile. I thought she was pretty. She loved reading books. She was mostly an impossible incursion of near misses and bad luck. She could've ended up anywhere but somehow ended up with new family and friends at the Tulip Tree Pub on the edge of the Hudson at the top of Manhattan. She had a real bad attitude sometimes. Her personality forced directions, attracting and repelling at the same time. Tonight was different, she was only in one direction and that direction was me. She grabbed a hold of my outstretched leg in my goofball stance on top of the keg. She grabbed it with both arms. She hung from it. She was swinging from it. She was laughing. I was laughing. It was all fun and games until the illusion of my perfected balancing act collapsed and I came crashing down on top of her. This had the two of us laughing more. We were set off into a fit when I wanted to kiss her and it would have continued like that for a week if I hadn't I heard a crash and splash.

I sat up and surveyed the surroundings. The scene was a calamity in pieces, both peaceful and disturbing. A few of my fellow revelers, cloud heads, were dancing between first and second base to Blondie's Heart of Glass. Some of the girls had stripped Declan down to his skivvies and used his clothes to tie him standing up on Fat Jack's hand-truck. They were rolling him around the bases in a frenzy while he feared for his life. Others were on the grass just behind third base rolling like cats and dogs do. Scratch was at home plate holding court for everybody else. He was giving a bodacious lecture on how public parks are constructed and how Inwood Hill Park was not built at all. "This is an original forest!" he yelled so that everyone on both sides of the Hudson could know the importance. The park was just as natural as the day Peter Minuit bought the island for a song from the Indians who didn't know any better. Scratch was pointing in the direction of Center field asking everyone to call out for Chief Munsee Kilbuck. Only Scratch could've known who that was. Of course the group of them chanted. The chants soon enough turned to screams when an Indian Chief was seen walking toward the gang of us from deep in the outfield. I think I saw him. I must've

41

seen him because others said they saw him. Scratch was certain he saw him and ran to the outfield to make peace with the Chief. There was drama, high-pitched fear from some of the girls. Mary Cahill wasn't part of it. She was lying on the grass at my feet with nearly a far-gone face, calm as a monastic cat with eyes closed and secure amidst a mindful and momentary doze.

I wanted another beer. I turned to the keg but it was gone. I yelled out, "The keg is gone!" This sent a shrill through the gang. "The Indian took it," Hector Cruz yelled out. Others started screaming out from different spots on the baseball diamond believing the old Indian Chief had taken the keg because we disrespected sacred ground. The Chief could've been anywhere. Most of the gang scattered in different directions. I didn't want to believe that the Indian Chief took my beer. I wished real hard that even if he did take it that he'd seriously reconsider and bring it back. My acid trip was cracking, fading and I was pacing back and forth. With a bit of moonlight shining I noticed something through bushes down the embankment by the water's edge. I pushed my way through the brush to the water and there it was, the keg of beer. It had rolled out from under Mary and me down the embankment. I was glad and yelled out, "I found the beer." A few cheered and others sounded confused. I'll just show them I thought as I was going to pull the keg back up. But I slipped and slammed into it knocking it lose from the soft mud sending it into the water. The keg was probably three quarters finished or more and filled mostly with air and because of that it was floating. I stood there on the shore wondering what to do. I turned and Mary Cahill was awake again amidst the bushes up the embankment behind me. She was smiling and pointing to the water with a pure confirmation attached to a drunken wish. "You can get it," she said. I could get it. If Mary Cahill wanted me to get it you'd be damn sure I was going to get it. But if I wanted to get it I better get it quick before it gets any further away and becomes maybe impossible to get. I dove in.

I was under the water for half a minute but it felt like an hour searching for the surface. When I came up for air I was grateful for the breath. "There.., there.., there it is" I could hear Mary's voice from the shoreline. The water felt great. It was clearing the Indian phantoms from my head. Clearing things up enough to get a sure eye on the keg's bearings. It had floated further from the shore. I swam out to grab it. Once I did I rested while holding on to it like a life preserver. I tried getting behind it and kicked toward the shore. My motor skills were working except that I was motoring in the wrong direction. It was the current, the lingering beer, booze and acid, had me twisted, heading further out into the creek. I grabbed a firmer hold on the keg for another breather. I quickly drifted to the middle of the creek and the current took over. I was close to where the creek connects to the Hudson River. Only the Metro North Rail Line Bridge separated us. At first the current pushed me toward the Hudson until a whirlpool had me turned around heading back into the creek toward the Harlem River. Then I was turned back again toward the Hudson, and then back the other way again. I wasn't panicking because my head and shoulders were out of the water. But I was getting frustrated wondering if this was going to last until daylight when someone might spot me and fish me out. If I had a stronger will about it, I wondered which way would be better to go; maybe a float ride down the Harlem River to the East River would be safer than the big old Hudson. Finally the current decided for me and shot me long in the direction of the Hudson. As I floated further out and away from the trees I could hear the music on the radio in the background fading to the complete arrhythmic sound of water moving. I was readying to pass under the Metro North Rail Bridge. My plan was to kick hard toward a piling and grab a hold of it. If I could grab a hold of the bridge I could climb up out of the drink and walk the tracks to the Bronx and then just head home. I'd be too embarrassed to ever see Mary again after failing her. I kicked like crazy until I crashed into the piling. I'd kicked too hard because I bounced away from it and a stronger current had me slipping quickly under the Bridge out to the Hudson. I tried to let go but in the maneuver the keg pump snagged my belt loop and was pulling me away. There was no choice at that point the Hudson had me.

It was as beautiful as it was scary, especially from a bobbing head water line perspective. The water was choppier than inside the creek. I figured out fast that I'd need more buoyancy so I pumped the barrel and did what any aspiring barman would do, I drank some beer. It was late. I looked to both the New Jersey and New York shorelines. I was on the New York half of the river. I was floating downstream at a pretty decent rate. I could see the lights of the George Washington Bridge up ahead speckled along the span as a micro reflection of the faint celestial dome above. The view was like looking into your pocket filled with broken glass, threatening. The acid trip had faded but left inside my head a concaved mirror pointed inward reflecting a glimmer of floating paranoia. I was tired above all of it. I didn't need to swim as long as I held on to the keg. I looked up to the quarter moon. The air was warm. I decided to remain calm. I'd had a long night. I was thinking about Fat Jack, was he going to call the cops? Johnny Mack probably got hit with a workload. Plenty of customers must have walked out. I hope it didn't spell an end for old Cuban Nip. Once I got out of this river I was going to have to get a new job.

If you've ever driven across the George Washington Bridge and weren't impressed you should bet on it that when you float underneath the thing all short sightings are gone. The full magnitude of the bridge on display will help you realize sometimes a thing can truly be a thing unto its own. The bridge has carved out of time and space its own ubiquitous sensibility. Looking up at the massive lace worked steel girders and the entire length of the double deck roadway and the goliath towers and its countless suspension cables and the thousand points of light, it demanded my attention. I couldn't say it was frightful because I figured even if the colossal contraption came down on me I'd be smashed and buried into the bottom of the river faster than I could let out a scream or time to think if anyone will ever come looking for me. As I passed directly under the bridge it seemed to suck up the load of air in the vicinity leaving me short of breath. I wondered where does all that steel come from? What makes steel so strong? I was thinking about all the hands that went into putting it together. It's common knowledge that guys die building bridges. I was thinking about the guy who wanted to build it in the first place and the guy who designed it. I was thinking of all the guys who did what they did just so I could float underneath the thing. It definitely reminded me that we are not alone in this world. It was also a great reminder that plenty of guys really do something with their lives. Some can carve out a clear presence that can serve a purpose. As I moved out from underneath the bridge I thought, "What am I going to do with my life?"

I floated further along pass the Upper Westside prewar buildings with hundreds of lights on in living rooms and bedrooms. I was hoping the lights were flickering with blithe because I was coming down from the acid hard, and drinking scotch whiskey and a load of beer had my insides sponged with glum. There were lives in those apartments and I would've bet plenty of them were living purposeful lives. Lives clearly worth celebrating on a Saturday night. Despite my dim and dank outlook I was certain that cocktail parties were going on inside some of those apartments. That gave me the notion to drink more beer to try and raise my spirit. I didn't have anything to celebrate. What purpose could I serve? Can a bartender's path be a real choice, a way of life? Is it just an excuse for a party? Do I have substance? Substance like what made the George Washington Bridge - great planning, hard work and cold steel. What am I made of? I should know by 16 years old. Is my will strong? Or am I at the whim of a river, somebody who ends up floating through life at the mercy of others. Why did I let Fat Jack routinely smack me around?

By midtown I still hadn't figured anything out. The buildings and lights had changed and the apparition of an organization above it all held sway in the dark sky. It, like the bridge, had its own presence, its own interests, for better or worse, a city with something to offer the world. What are my interests? I knew I was fast on my feet and I could talk to anyone. I really liked girls. I enjoyed being around others. What could the world want from someone like me? By the time I was downtown and nearing the Twin Towers I was scared. In another twenty minutes I was maybe going to spill out into New York Harbor. After the harbor I could slip out into the bay and then Atlantic and then from there who knows where I might end up. I was water logged and getting cold. There was still some beer left in the keg. As I entered the harbor the shadowed cityscape on shore turned into a wet squint and a black and blatant emptiness swallowed me. There was so much water in my ears everything sounded like a sad trickle. I knew it was up to me at this point if I was ever going to see land again. I was tired but I put everything I had into it and kicked harder trying to steer myself to the bottom tip of Manhattan before the chance to do so disappeared.

My will had always been tangible and provided nominal results that satisfied menial goals. But willpower must be a more discernable part; it should be what identifies a person, even more than character, personality or smarts. It's the ultimate boss of you. It is you. Anyone and everyone can prance around telling themselves and everybody else how incredible and stupendous they are, and others might even believe it. But the proof is in the pudding and your will makes that pudding meld. Yet at the same time the river and the harbor had its own intentions, its currents, its own will and at the moment we were together. A bloated sense of fidelity tossed in my head as I figured the answer has to be both. There is free will but it doesn't mean you're going to get what you want no matter how hard you try. Survival of the fittest doesn't add up. The world has to be in your favor if anything was truly going to get done. It can't be you alone. The world even helps fools and weaklings get lucky sometimes. You do your part, it's required, and the world does its part. Whether you agree with it or not, providence decides. The best you can do is try to land where you want to be or get close enough to a place where you could climb out of the drink and achieve something.

I kicked harder and harder. I was swallowing and spitting out gallons of water. I could see barges floating close by and the silhouette of the Statue of Liberty out of the corner of my eye. I kicked more than I thought I could. I gave up on a direction and gave everything into kicking. I wasn't going to look up anymore until I hit something. Kick. Kick. Kick. I petered out. Holding onto the keg was more than I could handle. The currents were too strong. I slipped and went under. Once more I kicked and came to the surface. I tried reaching for the keg but it was out of sight. I was giving up because I had no choice. I was done. A bright and harsh white light clicked on in the dank darkness shining down on me. I could feel its warmth. It was too close to me to be the moon. It might've been a guardian angel taking a last look at a failure before I slipped away. Or maybe it was a craven water spirit blinding me, shrinking my consciousness down to its hollow size of white so it finally had someone to dominate and interrogate. Repulsion shined in my eyes and any honor left inside floated off. I then heard a garbled voice, "A sturgeon with a head of hair." I felt the hook grab a hold of the back of my pants and lift me with the speed and accuracy of a saintly fish gaffer. "And he's brought us beer."

The tugboat crew had a good laugh at my expense. It made light of the situation. I was definitely in the mood for it. They threw a blanket on me and I warmed up quickly as I told them what had happened up river. I'd told them my name but they were bent on calling me the proverbial Jonah. They were getting a kick out of it and I wasn't going to spoil their good time. The Captain explained how lucky I was because the Hudson has a complexity of currents, some that go upstream as well as down and I could have floated into the abysmal dark stretches and icy water heading north. I likely rode one of the mixed up warmer flows. He also said it was a very good thing that the whirlpools in Spuyten Duyvil Creek didn't spit me out to the Harlem River because I would've ended up at Hell Gate, a torrid place of rocks and converging tide-driven currents where the Long Island Sound slams and swirls into the Harlem River and East River and it has a long history of sinking boats. Imagine what it could have done to me. The Captain said loudly for the crew's entertainment, "Jonah would have needed a bigger barrel of beer." To my surprise I wasn't the first guy they pulled out of the Harbor. "It happens more often than you think," the Captain told me, "Though, most often they're dead." He grimaced and considered another thought, "You are the first gracious enough to bring along beer." Apparently it was good luck for a crew to bring a live man out of the water and even better to get him off the boat as fast as you could lest he turned your good luck bad. It had something to do with a passenger on a working crew's boat. As we motored toward a pier in lower Manhattan and after the Captain's approval the crew drew a couple of short beers from the keg and the Captain made a toast: "To the things we find by chance in life, may they all be at least half as good as beer."

They wanted to know if I was going to be okay on my own and if I needed any money to get home. Otherwise they'd have to

47

call an ambulance and the police and fill out a Harbor Incident report and they were late already with a barge waiting aimlessly in the middle of the harbor. I was fine, invigorated by the fact that I wasn't dead. They left me on the pier with my keg and a blanket. I thanked them as much as I could, maybe a hundred times as they pulled away. The sun was not up yet. The ninety bucks from Fat Jack's was still in my pocket, wet but capable of paying for a cab ride up to the Bronx. I dragged the keg over to Broadway hoping to flag down a cab. Not much activity goes on in New York City's financial district at that time of day, especially on a weekend. I 'd have to wait a while. I sat down on the steps of the US Customs House at the base of Broadway for a deserved break, leaning on the keg. I looked up Broadway through the canyon of buildings lining the street. This is the center for commerce for the world. My night started at the other end of Broadway, what was supposed to be the center of commerce for me. All was not lost. I managed to make it down Broadway from end to end without losing the keg. I would return Scratch's pump and there was a $15 dollar keg deposit I could collect. I felt sort of cheap knowing money isn't everything but it meets the bottom line. A lot of legitimate people work hard and make a lot of money in this part of town. I was certain they all like to drink. That thought was as clear as my experience at Fat Jack's bar when I could see through walls and knew the needs of others. It was also as clear as when you have to take a piss, and I had to. I was too tired to look for an ally or even stand in a doorway so I decided to piss right there on the steps of the US Customs House. The sunlight was breaking through the canyon of buildings shedding some light on the sheer number of businesses existing in New York City. As the piss poured out my blood warmed up and my ears popped and cleared. Sure enough and quick enough I was wide awake and calculating like the dickens the fact that bars can be considered something other than just a great place for partying. How could it ever be overlooked? Bars are a part of the machine, part of the business of things. Providing drinks for hard working people is as essential as world trade itself, maybe more important. A bartender is unquestionably a legitimate contribution, a great career, nothing shameful about it. It's what I'll do. With the summer morning already hot my clothes were drying quickly. I sat back down and I tried pumping the keg, maybe squeeze one last beer out of it to consummate my resolution. But like the run of all good things it was finally the end.

I, Loser

"If you touch my whiskey I will kill you." Considering it was Killer telling me that I guessed I should believe him. Though taking his threat seriously was difficult because he didn't look too much like a killer. Aside from him telling me his name was Killer and that he had "K-I-L-L" tattooed across the four front knuckles of his right fist there was barely anything menacing about him. Regardless, it was Killer's apartment and he was the one deciding who could rent rooms so if he said don't touch anything it was the way it was going to be. I was interested in living downtown after graduating from High School when my sense of adventure and my penchant for new party territory had outgrown my friends who preferred the more anchored state of affairs of uptown. As well, my habit of jumping on #4 train to the Village whenever I could and returning home at 6:00 AM had grown tired. Routinely getting mugged on the subway at 5:30 in the morning was not the best way to end a fun night out.

My favorite spot in the East Village was Mars Bar, one of the newer bars in the neighborhood. It fit in like every cracked brick on every wall on every street and the drinks were cheap and the people were crazy and everything was glad packed into a narrow room with a bar that looked like it was purchased already damaged and stools that no doubt were pulled out of the city dump. There were crude and rude paintings hung everywhere and loads of vulgar writing on the walls. The glass-brick wall facing Second Avenue provided an abstract view on the world if you didn't care about the palpable action in the place. "Get smashed" was the room's credo. Nobody gave a rat's ass about your real name, only the name you preferred to call yourself. In 1981 Most of the East Village bars reeked with that same "I'm fucking here" attitude. The neighborhood was covered in graffiti and shock art, as well as the people living there. They were mostly outliers. I hadn't ever seriously considered differences between New York City and the rest of the world so it had me wondering about people who left their hometown to come to my hometown. Everyone arrived bent on a festal angle. If you add a heavy dose of young people on bang'em up libertine vacations that stowed extra bucks to burn and girls that packed hungrier hearts with an extra layer of willingness, the East Village was heaven paved over. Pretty much in every bar you could get a beer and a boss shot of Jack Daniels for two bucks and have as many drinks as you wanted. The jukeboxes were stocked with British punk and hardcore and New York noise bands. Like it or not, that music gets you pissed off in the best way imaginable. Rip-roaring open-ness dominated the East Village. You could sit in any bar and talk to just about everyone worth meeting, musicians, art school chicks, junkies, dealers, or even old men who have lived in the neighborhood their whole life. Just walking the streets made you part of the act because the streets were filthy and sticky and it would get all over you causing you to make contact with the entire circus.

On my 18th birthday my father told me that he'd done his due and that the best way for me to get a bartending job was to move out. "You'll sink or swim," he told me. I had $400 bucks saved up so I agreed with him. Three days later, after thumbing through the classified section of the Village Voice, I was talking with Killer in his gigantic apartment taking up the entire ground floor of an old run down building on Elizabeth Street. It was on the north corner of Houston bordering desolate SoHo, close enough to Alphabet City and the remnant bum hotels on Bowery to satisfy anyone with a hankering for heroin, piss and swill. Killer had eight rooms to rent, three of them were double bedrooms. The doubles were for people who wanted to share a bedroom for a cheaper rate. He also had a half a room for rent, the space I was checking out. It was decisively not a room at all. It was the large hall closet near the front door, next to Killer's room. There was no window in my room but it was big enough to hold a platform single bed raised about five feet off the floor and underneath it was space for hanging clothes and a chair with a light. You wouldn't dare close the door completely for fear of suffocating. A far cry from a suite at the Plaza but for $75 bucks a month the deal was irresistible. In all, including Killer in his bedroom, there were thirteen people living in that apartment. There were two bathrooms and a big kitchen and a living room. No matter what room you rented Killer had a list of rules and regulations and cleaning duties posted on the fridge for everyone to follow, which he politely enforced. Needless to say, the place was a polite mess.

Roommates would change quickly. I lasted a year and a month and I was an old timer by the time I left. Most would last two months, maybe three. At any given time there would be nine or ten girls living in the place because that's the way Killer liked it. It prevented testosterone fistfights from breaking out and smashing up his apartment. As well it meant Killer could have his heart broken and healed at a consistent pace. Killer was an odd looking dude so who could blame him. He said he was thirty-three years old but I would have guessed closer to fifty. His receding hair was a messy, asymmetrical, frizzy black bush on top of his crooked face. He was skinny and short and he wore the same pair of jeans the entire time I lived in his apartment that I'm certain were never washed once. Black boots, black t-shirt and a black leather vest with a street gang styled CENTURIONS patch on the back completed his costume. His bedroom was at the front end of the apartment next to the front door, and his bedroom window faced right on to Elizabeth Street. Across the hall from my hall-closet-room and Killer's room was the living room. With my door open all the time I had a constant view into the living room, which wasn't too exciting. Considering how many people lived there you might think it was a hot bed of action. But most room renters were either out partying and working or passed out in their rooms. Killer didn't have a job to speak of. He made a profit from all the rentals and he also sold dime bags of marijuana from his bedroom window or at the kitchen table if you happened to live there. Killer would sit in his bedroom in his crappy chair all day and all night smoking joints and cigarettes, drinking and reading Asimov's entire science fiction collection or listening to talk radio and people would come knocking on his window. He hardly ever left the apartment. He'd have me run to the store for his beer, booze and smokes. He ate Chinese delivery every night. Despite his lack of taste in food or clothes, he certainly had an eye for girls. He must have been a dance fan because every girl that moved into the place told me they were dancers. It took me a week or so before I figured out that dancers really meant strippers.

Rosario Lopez was a dancer. She was there the first night I moved in. She shared one of the double bedrooms with Cindy Colon, another dancer. They were both from Queens and were older than me, 23 or 24 years old. Rosario was standing in front of the big mirror in the living room. It was late, maybe 3:30 AM. She was naked aside from the pair of black stilettos on her feet and a strip of red satin barely doing the job of covering her asset and disappearing between two fittingly sweet, round cheeks. There was a pile of clothes on the arm of the couch next to her. She was trying on different outfits. I wasn't noticing the outfits as much as I was staring at her ass and tits. If she'd managed to stand still for a minute you might've thought she was Greek statue in living color. But that was impossible because the idea of stillness and Rosario were entirely different concepts. She was gorgeous head to toe but you'd have to figure that out in a blur. Stare long enough like I was doing and she'd come into focus and shine. If you've ever heard of Tinker Bell you know what I'm talking about. Rosario's pretty face had a flickering glow hovering, bouncing and always catching your attention. You'd have to turn and twist your head to keep up, it'd make you dizzy. She finally selected a shimmering gold lame low cut tank top with no back to it. Her honey soft, tear drop breasts were mostly exposed, her olive skin shoulders glistened and the sunken line of her spine ended like a hand in a glove laying into the two dimples at the top of her ass. She was barely contained in a shiny black leather miniskirt that was so tight she might've cut off the circulation to everything below her hips and so short it could've been a wide belt she was wearing. I wasn't used to seeing girls like her up close and personal.

I had just dumped my trash bag filled with clothes on the floor and was planning on hanging them up on the rack before going to bed. I had moved in earlier that day but I was immediately out afterwards looking for a bartender's job up and down 2nd Avenue. After that I was out bouncing. No luck with the job but I was fortunate enough to get loaded. Hanging my shirts and pants on hangers was challenging while staring out of the closet at Rosario in the living room twisting right and left, vying a hundred different angles in the mirror assuring everything was perfect. While rapidly grabbing and holding up a few different outfits in a desperate final fashion showdown she caught me in the mirror staring at her. The gesture on both of our faces froze. I wasn't sure if she was going to explode or let it pass. She took a closer look at me then turned around and walked over to my little room and stood there leaning on the door. "Do you want to fuck me?" She said it so sweetly and fast that it had me confused. But a question like that no matter how many drinks I had or how it was asked didn't take long to settle and I answered as honestly as an 18 year old could, "Yes!" She smiled and told me, "I knew it." She bit down on her lower lip and winked at me. She said, "You better get used to it if you're gonna live here, I'm a bit psychic." Her million-dollar smile gleamed in my closet nearly blinding me and then she tilted her head looking at me in disbelief. "Are you okay?" I felt like I was hit over the head with a bottle of beer. We were not going to fuck. I wondered if she was screwing with my head because girls know how to tease a guy who is sweet on them. But she wasn't taunting me. Rosario really thought she was psychic. She might've been. She knew the truth.

"I just got in from partying," I told her that hoping she didn't think I was a loser with no place to go. "Take off your shirt," she said. It was off before the question was finished. She looked me up and down noticing my self-tattooed "X" on my chest without saying anything about it. She said, "Not bad for a skinny dude. You work out." I told her, "I can do fifty pushups, loads of chin-ups and I do sit-ups without counting. I just do them for an hour." She wanted to know where I was from. I told her the Bronx and that made her smile. "You're a townie like me," she said. She looked me up and down again and told me, "I'm gonna call you Mean Street." That sounded right by me. Though I would've agreed to any name she came up with. "Do you want to go out?" she asked. I couldn't imagine where she could be going at 4:00

AM but that didn't matter none because I was going follow Tinker Bell anywhere. Of course I didn't let on like that. "Where you going?" I asked as if I might've known better. She was surprised, maybe put off, "I'm going out. If you have any money you can come with me." I wanted to impress her just like with every girl I met so I pulled out my wad of cash, nearly $400 bucks and flashed it at her. "I always got money," I told her. She noticed the money but wasn't all too impressed. "Good" she said, "I like champagne and cocaine."

We got out of the cab in West Soho on King Street and Houston. We had chugged a bottle of Asti Spumanti on the ride and she was ecstatic the moment her legs were out of the car. Rosario was the sexiest girl I ever walked down a street with. "This is it?" I asked her. We were walking into a garage. Her pace had picked up to a trot out in front of me and her stiletto heels were clicking in rhythm on the concrete ramp that cars drive up when they're in search of a parking spot on the upper level. There were no cars going up or down but there was loud music coming from above. "This is Paradise," she said. That was the name of the garage. "Were you ever here before?" she asked but wasn't expecting an answer. She just kept trotting ahead up the ramp. Before I finished mumbling some lame excuse for not knowing about the spot we were on the top floor. It was a dance club and it was packed. Go figure.

Rosario was a friend of the DJ and desperate to say hello to him so she grabbed me by the hand and yanked me through the dancing crowd. Everyone was saying hello to her, many reached out for a touch as she passed. The music was loud and the crowd was like a furnace, sweat was quickly running down my back. The DJ was playing Taana Gardner's disco classic Heartbeat but he was remixing the hell out of the song. The more he did so the more the crowd went crazy. The music wasn't pure disco; it was different, more aggressive. It didn't matter what was playing because Rosario wanted to dance and that's what we did. Or that's what she did. I was mostly in disbelief. She kept spinning and falling into my arms. Every time she did my hands felt a different piece of her as if every body part was a friend she was introducing. I could dance, especially because I was athletic. At Block Parties uptown in the Bronx I'd already discovered Grandmaster Flash and the Furious Five and Kurtis Blow and I was pretty good at spinning on my back and head on ripped up sheets of linoleum and I was a natural at body popping and locking. But the DJ was into a different style, faster music than anything I'd ever heard before. He was scratching records like he was playing a set of drums. Everything he did sounded like something new was going on. I followed my instincts and Rosario's lead and we moved.

There was no bar, no cocktails or beer and that had me incredibly confused. They did serve punch out of gigantic glass bowls if you were brave enough to drink some because who knows what was in it. Plenty of people were drinking it so I went along. Rosario asked me for fifty bucks to by some coke and I gladly gave it to her. I don't know where or when she got it but suddenly we were squeezed in a corner with two of her girlfriends and we were taking turns dipping keys into the bag pulling out small heaps and snorting. That bag emptied fast enough and as soon as it did I was passing Rosario another fifty and then another bag of coke appeared just as fast. All four of us were dancing like a warlock and banshees and there were more bags of coke and more punch and then more girls and more people dancing to the point when the entire dance floor was centered on Rosario and I was the next best closest thing. It was as if a wind channel opened directly into my chest and every mad, naughty, festal and fiendish spirit in the club was pouring into me. It went on like that for a long time. When we finally rolled out of the place it was nearly noon. The party wasn't over. We had one more bag of coke and after stopping in the bodega near our apartment for a quart of orange juice I was in Rosario's bedroom with her and her two girlfriends and the four of us were rolling, moaning, licking, sucking and fucking. When the three of them had finally collapsed on the bed in an afternoon heap of tangled flesh, bumps, hair and exhausted smiles I managed to crawl out of the room and down the hall to my closet.

I woke up a few hours later not feeling right. Something different was inside me; maybe a flu bug that wasn't making me necessarily sick but feeling disparate and defeated. I'd just experienced a quasi-mystical act and should've been feeling great. My self-esteem had been hyper primed and centered on my cock that for the past five hormonal years had been the centerpiece of me. Three beautiful females had treated me as a bearer of a holy thing, a young man with a precious scepter that they could admire and yearn for and finally praise when I gave it to them. It should've been healthy for my development because rejecting them and repressing my drive would have created neurosis. There were unnumbered orgasms amidst a common meaning of life for hours that made us god-like beings striving for ecstatic unity. I was with beautiful women who were achieving profound self-esteem and excessive self-indulgence with a power to arouse a great storm of sexuality or the power to quiet that storm in a breath. The sheets were soaked with potency. It was a peak experience glorifying man and women, a transcendence that only a religious mystic could know about. But as I lay there in my bed-closet I was only terrible. Maybe it was a disastrous hangover from something in the venomous punch bowl or I'd woken from a pornographic holographic dream. Dream or poison, there was no going back to what I might've been before. I felt guilty as I looked at my arms and chest that were covered in deep scratches and bite marks. I heard footsteps coming down the hall. I hung my heavy head over the side of my bed and peeked out of the closet and caught a glimpse of two disheveled girls leaving the apartment. I was trying to decide whether or not to get out of the bed. I was tired, unsure how I was going to face Rosario. Were we suddenly boyfriend and girlfriend? Feeling sheepish had me worried. I didn't worry too long because Rosario called my name from the kitchen. I got out of bed and walked down the hall, sat at the kitchen table. She was wearing a big t-shirt and fluffy pink slippers and cooking a couple of hamburgers. She was cheerful. We sat down and ate as if nothing had happened. She told me I looked upset. "I thought you had a good time last night." I thought I did. Maybe I wasn't used to doing that much cocaine or doing anything that much. Without getting into any details I simply told her, "I spent all my money last night." "Money?" she said, "Is that it? …Mean Street, you can always get more money. You may not be alive tomorrow, and that's the only thing you should ever worry about."

Rosario and I were not boyfriend and girlfriend. We had occasional sex when it was convenient for her. Rosario had instructed me that as long as I worked out all the time and stayed a hard body I would always find work. She helped me get a job as a Bar Back at the Ritz nightclub because one of her boyfriends was the manager of the place. His name was Larry. Larry thought he was a cool guy because he was managing a cool club. Larry was exactly not cool because he was married with two kids and he was fucking Rosario and pretty much any other girl he could get his hands on, and maybe some dudes, and everyone knew about it. I didn't know if I was cool but I figured maintaining a hard body was easy enough. Larry didn't think I was cool because cool dudes can handle many things and Larry wanted me to do only one thing: "Stay up in the balcony and make sure all glasses and bottles don't go over the edge."

In the early Eighties The Ritz was the epicenter of live music in downtown Manhattan, an expansive, high ceiling, two-tiered theatre relatively perfect in every way because it also was a space for dancing. They played recorded "dancerock" interspersed with live acts when most of the crowd would stop dancing and then stand around more or less listening, and every once in a while a riot would start. The Ritz had a monumental video screen and video was all the rage on the underground music scene back then. But I wasn't part of that. I was hired for was clearing glass, which I did miraculously. Larry noticed my glass clearing skill and loved my ability to follow his commands. He upped the ante and instructed me to start grabbing half full drinks and half empty bottles of champagne. The VIP's would spend more money that way and they'd always be too embarrassed to argue about it. In a couple of weeks I proved how fast I could learn and move in the club and Larry promoted me to Bar Back. I had to reload cases of beer into the back bar coolers and bring cases of vodka, gin, rum, whiskey and tequila out of the liquor room and pull out filled trashcans from behind the bar. I loved it. I could easily make $100 bucks a night and I was behind the bar in a real professional role.

The job came with an excellent surprise, the 11 o'clock Bump. At 11 o'clock Larry would send word that he'd want to see you in his office. Sometimes you'd go alone or sometimes with a bartender or another Bar Back. You'd walk in the office and Larry would be behind his desk pretending to look for some papers on the shelves against the wall while laid out on the desk where long fat lines of cocaine. He would never look at you; just continue futzing at the shelves and say: "Is your name on one of those?" You could do more than one line if you were up for it. At first I thought it was amazingly generous but later when working at other clubs and experiencing the same thing I figured it was simply a great way to keep the staff on their toes and sell more drinks. At that time, though, Larry's 11 o'clock Bump was simply a bonus additive for a great night of work.

Life was great. I was part of the big downtown music club crew delivering the booze for everyone's good time. We were as important as the music acts. The amount of cash pouring into the registers behind the bar was mind blowing. Frank Stokes was probably the best bartender at the Ritz. His drawer was consistently the largest take. Maybe it was because he didn't steal a whole lot. "I just take taxi fare and money for breakfast after work," Stokes told me, "That's how you keep your job." Most of the other bartenders were criminals who would steal a couple of hundred bucks a night out of the club. They'd get away with it only until Larry busted them and fire them on the spot. He did that often. One night after midnight Larry told me: "You stole. You're fired. Clear out." The breaking news had a bad effect on me. Earlier that night at the 11 o'clock Bump I'd snorted four fat lines and it was contributing to my just-got-fired edge. Larry had found a bunch of crumbled five, ten and twenty dollar bills in one of the empty beer cases behind the bar next to a trashcan. He said I was swiping cash from the bar top as I cleared empty bottles and glasses and tossed the dough in the box under the bar for a later collection. Some new dude named Travis was the bartender at that end of the bar and he must've been the thief. After Larry asked him about the beer box on the floor with the cash he said I was the one stealing. Travis was a fucking liar.

I started for the door but as Larry lost sight of me I took a turn up the stairs to the balcony. I knew I could get a few free drinks before he found me again. I was drinking a rum and coke and looking over the balcony planning my revenge. I wanted to get one last good look at Travis from above. It was the first and only night I had worked with him. Maybe I wouldn't see him around for a while and I wanted to be sure the next time I ran into him that I had the right guy. I stared across the wrap around mezzanine overlooking the main floor, the crowd and the stage below. I was off kilter, crazed. A high definition of the surroundings was unfamiliar, like experiencing someone else's dream. There was a fruitcake performance band sucking it up big time on stage; anorexic silhouettes behind the video screen playing two different songs at the same time making incredibly bad noise. That was almost impossible to do in the East Village. The crowd was pissed off. I zeroed in on the other side of the room at the bar on the far wall underneath the mezzanine where I could see Travis selling drinks or stealing or whatever he was pretending to do. Abe, the new upstairs balcony glass boy surprised me by tapping me on the shoulder. He'd found a bag of coke and wanted to know if I wanted it for $10 bucks. I gave him the money and snorted the bag in front of him. He thought I was wild. He also wanted to know why wasn't I downstairs working. I ignored him. I was locked on Travis and feeling the effects of a perfect and positive cocaine fury. Normally that sort of rage worked itself out when carrying three cases of beer at a time up from the beer cooler or shuffling and busting through a crowd with jumbo trashcans filled with empties. But normally I wouldn't have been just fired. The sudden loss of work combined with the white line energy explosion had things looking like a war simmering on the horizon. I was leaning far over the edge of the balcony ready to jump across the room. I could see Travis through a mental riflescope when a surge of confidence and someone inside of me started yelling: throw a bottle. It was a long way off and Travis was a moving target and the mezzanine projected out over the bar leaving only a small angle for attack. All the mathematical figuring and trajectory calculating didn't matter one bit because in a spontaneous eruption I grabbed the first bottle of beer off the closest table and with one roundhouse rotation I let it fly. I watched the bottle soar as if it was in slow motion, capable of counting how many times it rotated and spun. With the heat raging in my head my eyes saw the bottle's hyperbola as a sleek and strung out green neon arc carved into the air above the crowd like it was part of a laser light show. I knew exactly where it would land before it did. The most vicious smile I ever had filled my face as the bottle smashed Travis on the side of his head and a burst of blood appeared instantly. He didn't know what hit him, nor did anyone around him. He was dizzy and stumbling. It spooked a few of the guys at the bar who had been sprayed with the beer and broken glass and the next thing one guy was pushing another guy and then another guy pushed another guy and so on and so on until it spilled out to the middle of the main floor were the fruitcake band was about to be dragged off stage by the pissed off crowd and then the entire place detonated into an outright riot. The crowd was storming the stage and punching through the video screen and smashing heads were everywhere. I cleared out of there as fast as I could.

I took Rosario's advice to be a hard body and also buy t-shirts and tank tops a size too small. She had told me, "You need to get noticed on a job interview." I had thought merit was most important. With some downtown experience club jobs came easy and there was no shortage of clubs in New York. The first thing I noticed about the club worker collective from an employee's perspective was that it was hard to distinguish one club from the next. Often you'd see the same people going to different clubs depending on the day of the week and more often you'd see the same faces working at different clubs no matter what day of the week. You might imagine the whole club workforce was like good-looking pile of muck slowly floating around some big pond filled with wine, liquor and beer and a kicking sound system and occasionally some of us got lumped up together in a bog. If the bog had jibe we could create a bloom, a memorable night, before a big bad rain would come and disperse everyone. Some clubs were better than others

I really liked being a Bar Back uptown at Adam's Apple because my boss Felix was a great guy and built the bar with the bartenders' convenience incorporated into the design. That made it easier to serve drinks, less bartender backaches to hear about and more drinks were sold. It was a multi level club with two suspended dance floors. The place was packed with plants and there was a giant purple-mirrored ball hanging over the main dance floor. Drunk and high you could get lost. Adam's Apple was classy and fun and that was something new to me. Cheapskates and complainers didn't frequent the place. The Upper East Side was different than Downtown, not better or worse, just different. I got to meet one of my favorite radio DJ's from childhood a bunch of times, Wolfman Jack. "Hey Wolfman, Rock 'n' Roll yourself to death," I told him that too many times. He wouldn't lose his cool no matter how many times I said it. "Rock on, baby, rock on!" is all he ever said.

I had trouble considering work in clubs a real job and often felt like someone was going to abruptly put an end to it. The money was great and every night of the week you partied because you were part of a network of friends who wouldn't wait for weekends to let it all hang out. Weekends were for Bridge and Tunnel crowds. Working all night in a club required energy so cocaine was an integral part of the job. Lazy flakes and nerds would be thinned from the work force quickly. You had to have talent too because it wasn't just about pouring drinks and making sure the bar is supplied. The right energy is what made a club great and the staff had as much to do with that as the owners, club designers, and DJ's. You had to know how to read the crowd and sort out scenarios that would serve you, the establishment, and the club goers best. That was the order of priorities. Tips were the #1 priority. Bottom line, the owners paid you but it was nominal. Your real money came from tips on your effort, and if your effort could be enhanced with an ability to read and manipulate a crowd the difference in the total tips could mean your entire month's bills settled in one night.

Bond's International Casino on Broadway was like an Ivy League school for learning crowd-tip-enhancement. The place was enormous. Maybe three thousand people could fit on the main dance floor. Plus there were multiple VIP rooms upstairs that were the size of average clubs. There was another dance floor below ground. The sound system was like something NASA might've invented to orbit earth to share the music of the universe with the good people below. The best club bartenders in New York worked there. Hugo Rodriguez was Bond's club maestro. He was a tall and handsome Puerto Rican dude with thick jet black hair and a few curls everywhere they were supposed to be and broad shoulders and long and strong arms. His best trait was the smoothness he oozed because no matter how busy it was he never appeared to be moving fast, always managed to talk to countless women, and without fail brought in the largest drawer night after night. He never had an ounce of trouble with any of the managers or the customers and his tip load was unheard of. I asked Hugo about Bartending and he told me that a bartender should always be in charge but there's no need to show off that authority. He said you need to be like an electric magnet that can turn on or off in an instant so that anytime you dealt with a customer, the moment you were face to face they'd be compelled to follow your lead. In his words, "Be positive of your work abilities, know you're doing your best every time. No lying. No time off. Then you become it. And when you it, you get the best tip all the time." He tightened his jaw, tilted his head and peered at me to let me know he was serious and then he finished, "That's where your smile comes from... You need that smile." Of course he said that with a smile, and it was magnetic and I tried to learn it.

I learned plenty more about working the nightlife. Some patrons think they're on vacation anytime they're in a club and order nuance drinks like zombies, mai tais, scorpions, etc... stuff they'd never order in their local bars. Cheap rum with a soda gun mix and "make it red" was the quick rule and most of the time was what you'd get. But nightlife was more than drinks. It's about the boogie, shaking your can and looking good doing it because it all comes down to a giant mating ritual. Clubs are about sex and when you're the bartender and have to make sure everyone gets their fill the first thing you need to do is spot the most beautiful women at the bar with the worst attitude and then turn her around because that will generate good club energy like nuclear fusion. You do it by complimenting her on her dress or her hairstyle. She'd already heard how beautiful she is her entire life but earlier that night she put effort and thoughts into choosing that dress and fixing her hair. You get closer to her heart. You also need to pay attention to the ladies with less sex appeal and make them feel more desirable because they'll start to feel desirable and that'll make them sexier. It's like watering down the booze when you need to make the most of it. You tell them how beautiful they are because they hardly ever hear it. There are only so many honestly irresistible women and there are always more horny men.

You have to deal with the men. First you spot the dude who looks like he's ready for a fight and make him feel like he's top dog. Fights are the antithesis of a good night at a club. You can ask him, "Didn't I see you knock out some chump with one punch in the Golden Gloves last year?" It'll give him the delusional power he's starving for without breaking a sweat. Or you could just give him a cheap drink and tell him some red headed bombshell sent it over to him. Then just aimlessly point into the crowd and say, "She was standing over there." You might have to do it to a few muscle heads but it doesn't matter because usually they're dumb and they'll spend the rest of the night with one eye looking for a fight and the other eye looking for the mysterious red head; dumbbells, divided and conquered. The next guy you want to look for is the man with the money. You can usually pick him out by the clothes he's wearing or more likely by the woman he's with; most of them are skinny, too skinny. The more skinny women he's with usually means the more money he has. You have to test him out because he may give you a big tip on the first round but by the second round he cuts you off. If so, cut him down to size quickly by picking the closest lesser guy and treat him with the attention and respect that the rich dude was expecting. Give the lesser guy a free shot of anything and tell him it's your specialty. By the time the rich dude's third round comes it usually turns out a big tip because he was embarrassed in front of the skinny ladies. Finally if slouches managed to get pass the doormen and they dare complain about a weak drink or the price, just don't serve them for the rest of the night and focus on the proper club goers. Ignored slouches usually leave the club on their own accord, which is best because they don't leave their negative vibe behind. Throwing people out of the club should always be the last resort. A commotion simply messes with the good time club goers are looking for. It was a great experience learning club rules and a greater opportunity to make a load of money. The downside to all of it was it was also an amazing opportunity to blow a load of money.

I was living in Hell's Kitchen, a two-bedroom railroad apartment with only one roommate, a shared bathroom with our neighbors in the hallway, and the noise and exhaust of 10th Avenue traffic always making itself at home. I was sitting at the kitchen table the night my November rent was overdue. It wasn't that it had slipped my mind. I had no money. With four bar shifts the coming week I wasn't panicking. Problem was suddenly the last three years felt like I hadn't been paying attention to a lot of things. Realizing it then and there was as bad as a coughing fit from chain smoking the night before at a bar and trying to remember every time you lit up for an accurate count. I didn't have enough cash for a pizza. Instead I grabbed a pen and a paper towel for notes and for the first time in three years I was going to stay home and focus on something other than partying and calculate how much money I had earned and blown.

The math was not that complicated, $173,000. On my itemized list of cost consumptions, services and entertainment the biggest item was the roughly 13 pounds of cocaine I'd purchased an Eight Ball at a time. There was the cost of my drinks. Casual sex with woman and the thrilling times with multiple women had its steep price; prostitutes would've been cheaper. There was dancing and taxis and after-hours spots, and me always the big shot buying drinks for anyone. I also lent out a lot of money that never came back. I bought new clothes maybe more than I did laundry. Socializing is expensive in New York City, that's a fact. But this town is filled with transients. Most nightlife faces I'd only know for two or three months until they were fired or quit or I changed jobs or until they decided to go back home or just disappeared. Even nominal friendships had minimal costs and requirements and they'd disappear if you slipped up. Sitting at my kitchen table it was confirmed, I'm broke and I have no real friends. It felt like somebody threw a blanket that had been soaked in warm beer over my head. I slouched and desperately wished I had a bit of cocaine. Positive energy even artificially induced would help sort out the negative information.

My roommate Abigail was gone for the night sleeping at her girlfriend's apartment in Park Slope and she always kept a bottle of vodka in the freezer so I helped myself. I also had two packs of cigarettes so the world was not completely cracked open. My plan was to weigh the value of my favorite things against useless things. But the possibility that I could be a veritable loser

65

was making it difficult to settle into a critical thinking mode. I kept pacing from one end of the apartment to the other as if I was coked up. Back and forth, from the kitchen to the small living room chasing down a free ride to salvation and in a step or two more an entire life could be resolved without missing a beat. I noticed the little red light on answering machine in the living room blinking and keeping rhythm with me. I never got messages. It was really Abigail's apartment and it was definitely her phone line. I was thinking maybe her mother back home in New Jersey left a message about her Aunt's new car or her older brother's new baby or her Father's new heart condition or her little sister's new pimple. I didn't want to hear it. Only pacing, smoking cigarettes and taking swigs of vodka seemed engaging. Every return to the living room the answering machine kept its end of the dance going. After two hours when I still couldn't settle down at the kitchen table I figured I'd play the phone messages. I had no other entertainment in the apartment because the television and stereo had recently been stolen and the only books in the apartment were Abigail's and all she read was feminist poetry.

"Hey, this is Poe Poe. Long time, bro. I asked your mom what's up with you. She didn't know anything but she had this number. Maybe you'll be up in the Bronx for Thanksgiving. Your mom says you won't. I hope you do. Let's hang out. You can meet my wife and my son." Poe Poe's voice sounded different. It wasn't the quality of the answering machine either. He sounded like a stranger. He finished, "If Thanksgiving don't work maybe you can try Christmas." He wasn't mad in the least. It was hard recognizing his voice but I clearly recognized his heart. Poe Poe wasn't a kid anymore. Neither was I. Like drinking from someone else's glass at a bar and it wasn't what you expected I realized that I hadn't seen him or talked to him in over seven years. Worse, I hadn't had one thought of him. Then like a cab slamming into the back of a bus I realized I hadn't seen or thought of anyone significant in my life for a very long time. I'd been living without a past, truly disconnected. Dread instantly overwhelmed me. I tried to stop it fast, desperate to get my head straight before the shitty feeling settled under my skin.

I stumbled back into the kitchen and took another big swig

of vodka and lit up a cigarette. The smoke felt great in my lungs. I took another big swig of vodka. I heard my neighbor Tito and his mother fighting upstairs. She screamed and cried a lot and liked to throw things. As usual Tito was unresponsive. The distraction was welcome. I tried imagining his mother marching all over the apartment bitching at him. Then I remembered Tito sells dime bags of weed on the corner and there was a good chance he'd have some coke. I stormed out of the apartment and went upstairs and knocked a bunch of times on Tito's door. His mother answered. She hadn't liked me ever since the day she caught me using the third floor toilet, her toilet, because the second floor toilet was busted. Unlike the lousy toilet I shared with my neighbor, Tito's mom kept the third floor toilet immaculately clean. "He's in his room," she said, flashing me a dirty look. Tito was in his tiny dark bedroom that looked more like a DJ booth equipped with Christmas lights, two turntables, a mixer and milk crates filled with records. He was making mix-tapes and smoking a joint with headphones hanging around his neck. I asked him if he had any coke. "No man, I'd kill my mother if I did that shit at home." I jumped into an explanation about my financial situation. He knew I had a good job and I'd get the money to pay the rent and assured me that Mister Flannery, our landlord, wouldn't kick me out. "You got to chill, bro. You gonna get a heart attack. Take a hit," he said while trying to pass me the joint. He didn't know about my lost history. Instead I told him, "No…" "I have to think…" "I have to get sharp…" "Time is ticking…" "Gotta come up with a plan…" "Things need to get done…" "I need some coke…" Tito was tired of me being in his bedroom. He reached next to his bed and opened a drawer. "Take this. Buy me another one before Sunday." He passed me a Quarter bag of dope. I told Tito, "I don't shoot." He laughed at me. "Just snort it. It'll cool you out," he said, "It's good for thinking." I pretty much gave up on a plan right then because I felt like I was up against a wall. "Fuck it," I said and cracked open the bag and in two snorts it was gone. I thanked him and left. His mother trailed me to the staircase and eyeballed me until I was down the flight of stairs and in my apartment.

I was beginning to feel a bit nauseous but then great, very comfortable. I took another big swig of vodka and lit up cigarette. I wasn't thinking about my money woes or Poe Poe or my lost history. With an easy confidence I looked at the paper towel on the kitchen table with all the numbers and items I had scribbled out. I can fix this, I thought. My relaxed plan of the moment was just to fall apart and see what abandonment could come up with. No more blowing all my money or wasting my time. I'm going to do something with my life. I started wondering if there's a law of attraction written down somewhere. I heard people talk about it. It must mean you simultaneously attract from the outside what you resonate with on the inside. Be open. Be positive, that should work, solve everything. Bring into your life what you strongly focus on, that's what I was thinking. I took big swig of vodka and lit up another cigarette. I tried and failed at peeling away at a few girl band record promotion stickers my roommate had been slapping all over the kitchen table. The vodka was like water. I like pretty women more than plain women, that was a big thought. A warm sluggishness poured into me, weighing me down into the chair. "I like drinking more than drugs," I mumbled it out loud. I really enjoy the club scene, especially because I'm a good dancer. I leaned back in the chair and a fantastic laziness took over as I figured it out; there was something to be happy about, it was dancing. I took another big swig of vodka imagining what was going on in clubs right at that moment. My head was lilting. Slow, warm, glowing amber thoughts were coming. There would be plenty of people working right then and plenty more dancing. Working and dancing is often the same, that idea filled my head with radiant importance. Being in a club, in a big club you can connect to something free, some sort of free energy. It had to be true. It's not abstract or out of reach. It could be understood with words. Words like physics. But it's not in our mindset to think we can get something for nothing. "That's the problem," I said it to the walls of my kitchen and they appeared to respond with billowing gestures. The universe, the three dimensional universe that we see and the dimension of time we know are dependent on the laws of fluid mechanics. Slower or faster, things move all the time. It was clear.

The vodka was going down effortlessly and I noticed I had a lit cigarette in my hand and another two were lit in the filled ashtray and another lit one slowly rolled across the table. I was thinking, in a club you could handle many things at the same time. You deal with harmonics. You deal with empathy. You deal with telepathy. You deal with resonance. If you put two guitars together and you strum one the other starts vibrating. Minds do that with each other. Bodies do that. The universe must be an ocean of energy and a dance club is a splash of that. But it's not just ideas of homogenous energy. There are fine grains of it. There are bigger bits, packets. All of it is moving about in an ethereal soup. Sometimes you can actually see it behind a bar collecting at the bottom of the sink with straws, smashed lemons, limes and cherries. The stuff we see is more concrete. Our eyes take in a sweep of things. But there's got to be stuff we cannot see and it's swirling about, dancing all over the place. There's a divergence and a convergence. Structure comes out of chaos. Stars are born like the pimple inside your nose after days of drinking, snorting and dancing. It's the red spot on Jupiter. A massive storm and in the eye of the storm there's a strange attractor, a structure. Chaos and emergence. Phenomonon. Structures and cocktails swirling and emergence and it all can be explained with music, harmony. It is ether. We cannot see that it is a hidden orchestra of violins, drums, records scratching, double basses bowing, blowing and thumping. We must be the notes continually playing, a moving ocean of things, pleas for help and resurrections. In the beginning life was without form, a void, darkness. Let there be light and things started to move. The music, then came matter, then a symphony of matter or fabric or concrete and steel and a plexiglass dance floor. Whatever we are, we have emerged. We are the notes in the background of the subatomic and chaos is playing. We are. The energy. Boundless. We can be tapped as easy as a plucked wire can hold a note in a song. And you can twist that wire and spin a magnet and watch the world change. Something is for free and you can dance to it.

I passed out at the kitchen table.

I woke up to the sound of Mister Flannery banging on my front door. He was looking for the rent. There was no getting around him because he lived on the first floor. I let him in and offered him coffee. He accepted. That was too bad because I didn't have any. He politely reminded me of the agreement we made when I first moved in with Abigail. No lease, each of us paid our share directly to him and if rent was late by more than two days I was out. He'd been living the neighborhood for more than fifty years and there were family members that could assure that. I told him he'd get his money. My share of the rent was $325 bucks and I could easily make it over the next two nights. That was good but it was also part of the original problem. Club jobs provided quick and easy cash and you never had to really worry about money until you had to worry about it. My landlord left confident that he'd get the rent. I wasn't confident with much else.

BON VOYAGE

"You'll never change," Carina told me that as kindly as she could even though I'd let her down awful. We were at Penn Station. She was waiting for the airport bus with her big backpack. She thought I'd have a backpack. She was on her way to the Amazon in South America. "I just have to take care of some things," is how I explained it. She was holding back a big burst of tears when I left her at the gate. I'd let myself down for bailing on an adventure with a sincere, sensitive, funny and caring woman. I thought I deserved more than one woman. That was lousy because Carina was a catch, wild without perversion, put together with decency and electricity. Making the situation ultimately terrible was we'd clicked like beer and summer from the get-go.

Carina was from California and had skin as soft as a stuffed animal. Her blue eyes and long and loose natural blonde curls easily caught your attention, and she wasn't flashy. You would never have guessed that she made most of her own clothes or that she sowed by hand. She'd gone to college on a scholarship, Claremont McKenna. She said it was a good school. New York City wasn't her type of town. It took her less than two years to figure that out and that means a lot because some never do. We met and worked together at Indochine, a new high-end place downtown on Lafayette Street. We both lived on West 47th Street a half a block from each other and we realized it the first day after

71

our Indochine staff training when we took the subway home together and we both got off at 50th Street. I had my own studio and she rented out a comfortable bedroom from an older woman.

I got fired less than two weeks on the job. Carina stayed at Indochine longer than she needed to. We both agreed the place was odd. "It's a fabrication," Carina explained, "it comes from a money goal as opposed to an organic happening." She meant the food was a second thought or a third thought after profit and atmosphere. I simply thought it was too much. The place was properly swank. The food was great even if it wasn't the first thing on the boss's mind. The tips were amazing. The employees were first rate. The owner, Brian McNally, a great and incredibly talented guy put together a place that was beneficial for everyone working there. The clientele just rubbed me the wrong way. They were all beautiful, too beautiful, and rich, too rich, and famous. You can't imagine how many movie stars and models and Wall Street moneymen were in the place night after night.

New York City in the middle of 1980's was experiencing a mutation. People had been pouring into town for the past couple of decades and adjusting their way of life to the City's entrenched methods and mondo madness. The entire town was growing denser by the day sinking into the bedrock and splitting open arteries. Fissures were exposed to the elements and people and organic matter accumulated in the cracks. Predictably the town had begun to spoil as if the tons of garbage piled up in noisome heaps on sidewalks and in the gutters and alleys and clubs and restaurants and theatres had all gone foul. Hip cockroaches and cultural rats rummaged through building blocks of refuse. There were germs and bacteria growing all over everything that had once been the rage. An abhorrent epidemic could've broken out anytime of day. The town was beginning to stink and the fermentation was nearing combustion. Good and big things were going on for a few in the city while most of the rest of us lived under a subliminal threat. Wall Street was booming. The corporate city flush with money did no good, only increased the cost of housing. There were more jobs but no better jobs for most and inflation rose but your money stayed the same. A middle class penny pinch transpired to a lower class hunger punch. The city was infesting with resurging race tensions; the police were practicing badges-off brutality; we had a subway vigilante; derelict and criminal homeless competed for air with hard working folk confused by the whole affair. The glut of the population were bumping their heads into each other while a small, select and inbred group held a towering amount of wealth and power above everything and were exempt from it all. Indochine must have been desperate to bottle all of that, every ounce of everything dripping and leaking in New York under that pressure in hope of selling it as something you could actually swallow. The problem was there wasn't a person alive who could stomach that poison.

Indochine had to sell something so they came up with a life-sized blend of good wine and champagne in a chic French Colonial Vietnamese colored bottle with a faux label picturing the heart of the urban wilds. They made a good choice with the banana leaf wallpaper and the South East Asian motif with tropical wicker chairs helping you along with your fantasy of a haute dinner amidst a tasteful civilization smack in the middle of a steaming megalopolitan jungle. I'm sure they were hoping for the most interesting set the City had to offer, the center cut. But the group that represented the best of individualism and creativity must have run into a wall or couldn't get a reservation. Authentic personalities, thorns and all, were not on the menu. Fame, money and "with it" manners was the new attire and the only group welcome. Most worthwhile people were kept out. Even if the real deal showed up on a given night it was as if they were being paid to be there and put on display, much like all of us on staff. Regardless of its shortcomings Indochine was a giant financial success, incredibly popular and trend setting. The place proved to be the spot in New York City creating something new in a town fainting and desperate for fresh air. Indochine mastered the notion of a club scene and transplanted it to a fine dining joint. Bottom line, Indochine was an exceptional venture and New York City's exempt-ional customers loved it.

I might've looked the part when I was hired at the new hot spot and I was plenty capable of handling the same old work but I didn't know a thing about biting my tongue or keeping my dick in my pants. Not two weeks behind the bar when some world class, dark haired Italian beauty managed to turn Indochine upside down. That says a lot about her because the place was a dumping ground for beautiful women. She had been sitting at a table with a small group. I'd noticed her when she first came in, as did everybody in the place. The older man she was with was arguing with another old man at their table. They'd been going at it throughout their entire dinner. I guess the Italian beauty just grew bored, which I interpreted as a clear sign of her intelligence. She must have picked up on my mental antenna figuring on her because she came right up to the bar, caught me in between serving drinks and sat directly in front of me as I stood straight and narrow in my perfect Indochine staff form. Her English wasn't so bad. It was mixed with Italian but I managed to hear, "dammi... vetro... whiskey." I guessed she wanted ice and poured her drink. "Perfetto," she said and gave me a deep and serious smile in case I hadn't noticed how flawless a face could be. I was 24 years old and I'd learned by then when a girl was interested in me. The Italian beauty motioned for me to lean closer. I did. She managed to get out a few more words, "Guess you, numero ...things I wear now ...then you and I for you." She pushed her shoulders back and her chest out and put her finger into the glass and stirred the ice and then stuck her finger in her mouth. She liked the whiskey and arched her eyebrows in a moment of concern as to whether I understood her proposition. I smiled and took a quick glance to my right and then left to size up the situation. My boss was nowhere to be seen. I noticed Danny Devito getting up from his table on his way to the bathroom. He was taller than I thought he'd be. He took a look at the girl and then a look at me leaning over the bar and flashed a knowing nod of pleasure and approval as he walked on by. It didn't make a difference. I looked her over fast and figured she was tricky and the answer wouldn't be obvious. She was wearing a short, red, strapless one-piece dress. The dumb answer would have been one. I leaned a little further over the bar and tried to get a better look at her lovely bare legs. She was wearing high heels, two shoes. I could see her nipples pressing through her dress so there was no bra to count. It came down to whether or not she was wearing panties. The answer was as clear as her having the gumption to come up to the bar and ask the bartender if he wanted to have a quick fuck. I smiled at her and held up my right hand with three fingers and said, "Tre." She smiled and pretty much popped off the bar stool and told me in giggling whispers, "Veloci... Veloci," as she headed for the bathroom.

I was laughing along with Carina later that night in our neighborhood over late night vodka martinis that she liked on the rocks with extra vermouth because she said they went down easier. She really meant faster. She was giving me the cardinal details about what she saw go down at Indochine earlier that night. After I had punched the Italian girl's old-man-boyfriend in the nose after he had barged into the woman's bathroom not a moment after the Italian beauty and I had settled our bet, and after the old man had slapped her hard across the face, and then after I threw him through the bathroom door and followed him out to the dining room prepared to lay into him some more, and after I was told to leave before the cops would come, after all that, Carina explained the place nearly erupted with a jumbled uproar. Half the customers were appalled and the other half were thinking it was the true mark of a great party. The fact that I was standing in the dining room with one leg out of my pants in my worn out filled-with-holes fruit-of-the-looms and standing over the old man ready to pounce on top of him, well, the whole thing had Carina laughing pretty hard. "You're killing me.., unreal," she kept repeating and laughing. "When you yelled at him, 'You look like an old fool wearing a young man's tie,' while they were dragging you outside in your underwear, your underwear, I almost peed in my pants," she said. I tried making the excuse that I needed to do laundry and that I was wearing my emergency briefs. "What does a young man's tie even mean?" she said it while laughing and spitting out some of her drink and clumsily burning me with her cigarette. Carina was having a good laugh and I liked it. I ordered another round of drinks for both of us. Carina confessed, "I can't blame you, she was gorgeous and it's not like you forced your way into the bathroom." We drank and smoked some more and she laughed plenty more. We eventually went home. I walked Carina to her apartment, all the way up to her door on the fourth floor. Afterwards I walked down the street to my place. I hadn't even tried to kiss her.

Carina went back to working at Indochine the next day and I had to look for a new job. I got a one fast enough at the Film Center Café on 9th Avenue a few blocks from my apartment. There were only two shifts available, Monday and Tuesday nights. That was too bad because it was my type of bar with the right type of regulars serving the right type of food and drinks. The place had been around since the 1930's and it was pretty much in original form. The regulars were comfortable with me from day one. Behind the bar felt like a well-made shoe. I would've liked working there seven days a week. The Film Center Café was the place I learned that my trade was more often filled with stars in waiting as opposed to career bartenders or waiters. Everyone who drank at the Film Center Café, aside from pursuing a film and stage careers as entertainers or technicians were also waiters and bartenders somewhere else. Broadway theatres and all the Talent Agents in New York City were only three blocks away. Talk about a room filled with song, dance and personality. The bar money wasn't the best but I was beginning to realize that there are other values to a job.

The Film Center Café regulars were proud to eat and drink there as often as they could afford to. Declaring the Film Center Café your bar had to be an easy decision, if it was your decision to make. They didn't have to be at the bar everyday to be considered part of the gang, only the majority of their drinking needed to happen there. Any money they spent in the place had to be looked at as an investment. The owner made his profit, guaranteed, but a routine customer could count on insider benefits. For starters, the actors, singers and dancers had a base camp included in the price of a drink, a home turf, the place where they'd tell friends and associates to find them. They could use the bar as a message center and the old phone booth was free office space. When a newcomer came into the place a regular could act as an aficionado or an admirable guide, which fueled self-esteem – a priceless commodity for an actor maybe more valuable than the cost of acting lessons and therapy sessions. Hanging out consistently at the bar put you in a circle of New York professionals, gave you infamous "Contacts" and some credibility even if you weren't hitting the mark on stage or in front of the camera routinely. Unlike their auditions, they had a confidence-reassurance-place where they could relax and be their wonderful selves without worry over miscued projections. They had a free stage to practice entertaining others. They could get away with offending someone once in a while without being bounced out of the joint. Pursuing a career like acting is tough and you'd be hard struck for anything remotely considered an honest friendship but if you were a familiar face at the Film Center Café you had a clan. There was more grace allowed and more drinks considered whether you were receiving or buying, and best of all, a communal understanding that you were a very talented individual who is not getting the proper recognition you deserved because it was the world that was turned upside down on the days you didn't get the part. Stiff drinks and smokes helped ease everyone's struggle. You couldn't just walk in off the street and be accepted without something to offer, some talent or maybe another valuable entertainment network affiliation. If you were lucky enough to be one of the regulars you could count on better service and any drink mistakes or excess shots would magically land in front of you. By the time you rolled out of the place your tab would be considerable less than a lost tourist's check or anyone else caught slumming in Hell's Kitchen. You'd even have some say on business decisions, like who needs to leave the bar or maybe who should be considered a new regular. Ultimately you received an added element to your identity; you were part of something established in New York City.

Sadly the Film Center Café job wasn't going to pay all my bills. Ye Old Windmill on West 53rd Street turned out to be the place I mostly earned my keep. Unlike the Film Center Cafe filled with the right amount of interesting, fun and talented people you dream of knowing in New York City, the Ye Old Windmill was pretty much the under side of that bar top. Ye Old Windmill provided plenty of entertainment and cash flow but they served cheap beer and cheaper booze, and that's saying a lot about the place. You'd have to be careful sitting on any one of the bar stools for fear of one of the legs coming out from under you and crashing you on a floor that you had no business looking at let alone find yourself sitting on. Lights were always low for a reason, for two reasons; the owner never had concern for new bulbs and it was

77

better that no one ever got a clear look at the place. In a good light you might want to give up on drinking after seeing how bad things can really get with a look at the shambles, roaches and the dregs drinking alongside you who'd be looking into the cracked mirror behind the bar that made all faces look the same, wretched. The joint wasn't so much like a whole in the wall as it was more like a whole in the ground where everything just settled. There was no ventilation and the smoke was the same smoke from the week before or longer and in no short supply so smoking your own cigarettes wasn't necessary. The chipped paint on the walls was like that for a lifetime just like many of the rummies who practically lived in the bar sustaining their sponge drunk on 50 cent short drafts of Meister Brau all day long. The jukebox was even affected because everything coming out of it sounded like the Rat Pack with a two-day binge hangover. The best and brightest thing about the Ye Old Windmill might have been its undoubted darkness. The days I was miserable being there the cinched dimness was just what the doctor ordered. It was probably safest to not see and know everything that was going on. A guy could walk in and order a drink and literally disappear. The darkness was a draw for people up to no good, criminals. They weren't there to rob the bar, just needed a reliable spot to have drinks and tend rackets and scams. You'd also have plenty of men bringing their hookers in for a quick drink to loosen up before spilling their seed. I often had to uphold the house policy of no hand jobs under the tables.

Because Ye Old Windmill was in Hell's Kitchen you would've learned of a special breed of criminal who were famous for their joyful brutality and left body parts all over town and up and down New York's waterways, the Westies. A New York gang based in Hell's Kitchen on their last leg while another notorious gangster, the Federal Special Prosecutor, Rudy Giuliani, was near the end of cutting them down on his march to political fame. The Westies' reputation lingered vicious and shadowy all over the neighborhood so in a dark bar like Ye Old Windmill not many would easily talk about them for fear that one of the remnants might be sitting next to you. Big John McCarthy, my boss, might've been one of the Westies. He was Irish and the Irish are capable of anything good or bad. Ye Old Windmill was noted for cocaine dealing and I can't imagine Big John didn't get his cut. Once while working there a lowlife out of his right mind tried to rob the place. There was a Louisville Slugger behind the bar that I was supposed to use in dire situations. Happily I didn't have the opportunity to swing it. When the guy pulled the gun it barely happened. Before the hammer cocked or the thought of squeezing the trigger occurred there were at least fifteen guns drawn on him and not one cop in the place. It most likely spelled the end of the road for the dumb thug because a few of the guys dragged him outside and threw him in the trunk of a car. They came back into the bar afterwards and demanded free drinks for the next hour before four of them rolled out of the place talking about driving up to the Catskills before dawn for an impromptu hunting trip.

The better memories of Ye Old Windmill came mostly from other bars and restaurants. By 1:30 AM the place would be filled with cooks, bartenders and waiters just finished with work. They'd mix with the regular degenerates and pick up their supply to get high. That portion of the crowd meant a steady flow of late night flush tippers and by closing time a reliable supply of nearly empty bags of cocaine pulled off the bar and an endless circle of early morning apartment parties. There could be a dozen people crashing some chef, bartender or waiter's apartment at four-thirty in the morning. Party girls were always in the mix to keep you awake if pot, cocaine and booze failed. I enjoyed those early mornings seeing how my peers lived and how generous they could be with their living space. Many of them were glad to have their bed close by to collapse on after getting loaded. Others were seeking approval; get you back to their place to see a dumb Samurai Sword mounted on a wall or to look at their ugly drip and splash paintings or hear what they believed to be the best music in the world. Others only wanted someone to listen to them talk. Most of it would be happening as the sun rose to the alarming noise of blunder and devising cocaine banter. With the morning daylight coming through the windows I was most stunned by the common denominator of stolen restaurant supplies filling the apartments. The fridges would have full-length beef tenderloins, lobsters, pounds of shrimp, bags of french fries. The kitchen drawers and cabinets would be filled with stolen liquor, glassware, linen napkins, amazing sets of utensils and expensive knives. One waiter had a few of us convinced that a pencil drawing on his living room wall was an actual Picasso sketch lifted from a posh restaurant on the Upper East Side. No matter what apartment we ended up at I did notice something different about me from the rest of them. Aside from a keg of beer and a bottle of Dewars ten years earlier I never stole anything from a job.

The nights and early mornings that I wasn't at apartment parties with New York's thieving restaurant class were better because those nights I was with Carina. She didn't like cocaine but she did like to have drinks two days a week. It was part of her golden rule of moderation: five days of mindfulness and productivity and two days of mindfully celebrating production. If she were drinking she'd smoke cigarettes and occasionally some pot. On allotted days no measure was allotted so she would keep up with me elbow to elbow. I guess we evolved to be boyfriend and girlfriend but that idea was pretty much a misnomer for me. I had balls of fire and was craven to any female with prurient designs on my loins. That meant astounding passion plays with Carina but it also meant I was having sex with any girl willing to open her legs. Carina wasn't nearly as pathetic or anywhere near as unsanitary. She had control of herself and she really liked me and when she committed to something it was the end of it. The most I could commit to was the fact that I was a New Yorker incapable of putting on a false front. "You're undiscerning to a fault," Carina had told me.

Carina loved to hear stories of my younger years, stories of delinquency. She'd even get touched by some of them. "When I was fourteen my friends and I would play Acid Chicken," I told her, "We'd swallow acid tabs and surf the tops of subway cars uptown on the Bronx elevated lines." The game was supposed to prove courage, done in the spirit of destroying any modern view or any future vision of the world as we were supposed to come face to face with a monster called Crazy in the moment. It certainly destroyed the future of Nicky Fuentes. He won the game but lost his head, the last man standing that hadn't ducked and dived down fast and flat enough before the #4 train went underground and entered the tunnel at 156th Street. Carina's heart was in pieces. She wanted to know, "Why would you kids even want to take that chance?" She cried over Nicky and it had me wondering why she was so different than me. I'd only thought why wouldn't you want to ride on top of trains. I didn't have an answer for her about Nicky and a lot of other things. But I didn't do all the talking. As long as there was drinks and cigarettes Carina could sit up all night telling me everything worth knowing.

Whenever we got bounced out of a bar at 4:00 AM we'd head over to the Market Diner on West 43rd Street and 11th Avenue and go through cigarettes and pots of coffee talking and watching the dramas play out at other tables filled with late night bar hoppers, riffraff, transvestite hookers and their traditional colleagues while everyone ate pancakes, bacon and eggs and Turkey Club sandwiches. Carina knew things about history, philosophy, society, the stars and heavens and more. She was discovering a path to enlightenment. "I'm a Buddhist," she told me, even tried her best to explain it to me. I tried making a dumb joke about her not being from the Himalayan Mountains with all those obvious valleys and peaks and how she'd never grasp the religion. "Come on," she said, "I'm being serious." Most nights I couldn't keep up with her but I wouldn't dare say anything because I had no reason to. Listening to the tone of her voice and the slow and passionate way she spoke kept me in the moment like a content block of wood. She could tell me about what happened at Indochine or how much ice cream her roommate could eat or how to be mindful of your action and its consequence - it all sounded great. Buddhism was important to her and I liked that she had something important because it made me feel connected to something important.

"It's like you're at a bar," she explained, "but suddenly all the people disappeared. All that would be left would be drinks and 'things.'" I understood the part about drinks easy enough. Carina told me, "It's the weird idea of "things" you should try to understand." Something about "things" and your thoughts as being some sort of measure, a unit, a 'thing." An idea is maybe like a shot of booze, that was the gist of it. "Imagine," she said, "it's as if you're looking into a dark bar with a flashlight and tracing out the

81

entire place with the narrow beam and reconstructing all the 'things' you saw in your memory. You know the place, but you always know it as something after the fact, and as something that was assembled from bits and pieces, from tiny 'things.'" She explained how you could also see everything in the bar by just turning all the lights on in one shot like you do at the end of night when you want to clear out all the drunks. Everything still gets processed and assembled from bits and 'things' but all in a shock of bright. No matter what you always see the world after seeing the world in bits and pieces strung together or thrown together. She told me. "Either way there is an enormous amount of bits and pieces, 'things' we barely keep track of yet those 'things' are reality." I asked her if it was similar to when someone comes into the bar and asks if Jane Doe was in the bar yesterday and I say yes she was; but if they ask me what she was wearing I might not remember. "It didn't matter that I couldn't remember everything," I told Carina, "The dress was still part of reality and I missed it." "That's it exactly," she said and smiled and kissed me. She absolutely loved when we connected. "Why didn't you notice Jane Doe's dress?" she asked. It was because I was interested in her face or her breast but I gave Carina the polite answer, "It wasn't notable for me." She went on to explain: "Our minds record only the 'things' that we've been conditioned to know as important so we can stick a label on it." Apparently our preconditioned minds are very limiting and labels are supremely important so things can be prioritized. Those labels are words or symbols of some kind or a number. Carina explained how we wrongly break apart the reality of the world into "things" represented by noun labels and "events" represented by verb labels. Nouns and verbs is everything for the prioritizing mind. Even when we're not thinking we still manage to see the world as separated into nouns and verbs, "things" and "events." "It's sad," she said, "Our method of thinking about the world tries to be efficient and useful for predicting what will happen by remembering only bits of what really happened hoping to predict what will happen again by using limited parts of what had hardly happened in the first place. None of it completely deals with all of reality itself." She let out a sigh and lit up another cigarette. "It's mostly a mindless snowball that has run away from us." She went on about how all of us as a species are seriously in danger of being completely fooled by our deeply conditioned thinking process. "Our ability to think has gone to our heads," is how she put it. Equating all sorts of symbols in the world causes you to think there are clear lines of separation. It's blunder, delusion. Reality is intrinsically whole, not separated by the "things" and "events" or nouns and verbs. I told her with half a sense of uncertainty: "The process of understanding the world is not the world." She was tired and told me, "Enough processing. Let's go back to your place and unify all of our things."

Carina loved coming by Film Center Café on Monday nights because she was off and I was working. She'd be sitting at the bar by 8 o'clock ordering a beer, garlic bread with melted cheese, fried zucchini sticks, a blue cheese burger with bacon and an Apple Cobbler with vanilla ice cream for dessert. She did a fasting every Saturday and Sunday so come Monday she was starving. The Film Center Café is where we hatched the South American plan. The two of us were planning a meandering journey along the Amazon that would be waiting for us to discover strange plants and insects or maybe a lost tribe or a new way of life. After the jungle, slow boats, trains, planes and buses would bring us the world. For me, it didn't get deep because it was more like a fantasy trip. Carina had a different plan dead set on the road to enlightenment. "Purevana" is what she called it. The deal was going to be so cheap and easy you wouldn't imagine staying in New York. Our stand-by airline tickets could be as low as a hundred dollars and we'd be camping or staying in hostels for about $2 bucks a night. Food was going to be practically free. She had saved up over twenty-five thousand dollars for traveling that was already deposited into an account she could access from locations in Central and South America and all over the world. How she saved all that was beyond me. She was planning at least a couple of years on the road. I was just shy of four hundred bucks saved. "It doesn't matter," she told me. "We'll just go and see what happens."

I'd never been comfortable the times I might've taken two or three days off in a row. The idea of not having a job and not working for months or longer was scarier. Imagining wandering

83

the world to "see what happens" had my stomach in a state war and imbalance. Thinking about years aimlessly floating through third world countries was a welcome impossibility. I'd never left New York City. I never had a single thought about going anywhere before I met Carina. Most of the time we talked about traveling I thought we weren't being completely serious. After all, we were drinking. Maybe we'd end up taking a trip to Miami Beach or something, that's what I thought. But it was only me that hadn't been serious and that's because I wasn't serious. I was afraid. The dim wit deep down inside me wanted to know why Carina would take such a chance. You might get lost, that was the purest thing to know. I never asked directly but she got around to the topic and did her best explaining life as an adventure. "We're on an enormous rock spinning around a gigantic ball of fire moving through infinite space. Before you know it what you think you know about life's experience will be over and you might end up never knowing anything about it."

That night after she got on the bus with her backpack the giant spinning rock came to a stop. I was hit hard with the flu, probably caught it in the filthy Port Authority toilets. I was alone in my apartment for a week. Big John at the Ye Old Windmill didn't believe me when I tried calling in sick for the third day in a row and told me that if didn't show up I could pack my bags. Seven days locked away in your apartment, sick or not, can give you a lot of time to think. Carina was on my mind. I was imaging she made it to the airport and was probably somewhere south of the equator. I had episodes of anxiety about her safety. But she was smart, smarter than me. She had an incredible sense of direction and a bunch of Lonely Planet travel guides for everything from Mexico to Patagonia and beyond. She had maps, bus schedules and train timetables. She could speak Spanish and German. She had spent as much time in the library researching the places she wanted to see as I spent partying and screwing around. I had a moment of calm when I finally realized that more than likely Carina would find her paths and shelters without missing a beat. It was myself I should be worried about.

Lying around my dumpy apartment in the dirtiest part of town without one learned experience to show for anything had me feeling like a starving stray dog ready to drop. Carina was the best thing that had happened to me and I let her go like an empty bottle of beer. All I do is work and then try my best to latch onto anyone who wants to party like the toilet paper that gets stuck to your shoe when you're drunk and stumble out of the john at any old bar. I tallied up the last few years and tried to see a trajectory down the road. I was stuck on a lousy carousal that had no right to spin round, should be condemned. Grown up, stupid and going nowhere in the middle of New York City, I had to accept that. I'd been in the same party-life predicament before only this time around the party-life was honestly not the same. I'd been going through party motions and faking incredible commotions like an dunce hoofer stumbling into a mirrored wall on a dance floor and hoping no one noticed. Under scrutiny my cohorts, the late night cooks, bartenders and waiters were duplicitous and conniving. I'd been projecting a good light on them just so I could be welcome. Compare that to the nights I'd hang around with Carina that hadn't been so much about how much we drink or any real need to do drugs, it was about listening to her, making love to her. I looked out my window down on to 47th Street and saw the same old garbage cans dented and over filled with trash and the rats dragging their feet along the worn out sidewalk.

How many mistakes could I continue to make and still have a chance for anything? I had a compulsion to grab a kitchen knife and carve that cry into the walls. But I didn't have a kitchen knife; only a cheap frying pan, two spoons and one fork. Seven days simmering in a shit hole apartment will reduce you down to some resolution. I decided to read a book for the first time; one of the books Carina had given me. She'd said it was a book she'd like her son to read if she ever had one. I think one of the reasons she gave it to me was that it wasn't big and it had pictures, Jonathan Livingston Seagull. The first reading I had no idea what was going on, thought it was maybe some never ending lunatic poem; which could've been the case because Carina read a lot of poetry. The second reading went much better once I got my head around the fact that I was listening to the story of a bird's life. The third time was a charm. A story about flying higher than you imagined you could or where maybe you thought you should not go. It was about learning newness in life, about bettering yourself. It was about paying attention. It was about finding a place or returning to your place and sharing and teaching others what you learned about without getting mad at them if they hadn't learned what you had learned. It was definitive about learning to forgive others and yourself. I had trouble making sense out the part where I'm supposed to forgive myself when harsh punishment leaving an indelible pain marker to stay correct made more sense.

It was a warm and early Sunday morning, 3:00 AM. I was awful and half emboldened, and seriously needed to get out of the apartment. I headed over to Time Square. Lights were on as usual. I walked the crossroads in big circles trying to figure things out but there was a blinding glare in my head big enough to compete with the neon and flickering lights flooding the street. No matter how many rounds I made from 42nd Street to 47th Street along the junction of Broadway and 7th Avenue there was no escaping the familiar foul smell of rotting pavement and grime and the homeless asking me for a quarter and miscreants and urchins leering at me with disturbing looks and postures and prostitutes looking for a date. One guy tried selling me a 38 Revolver. It didn't matter what day or what time it was Times Square was always that tacky, gritty electric token reminding the world that New York is the city that never hides. I stood on the corner of 45th Street and Broadway in a stupor as all of it suddenly felt unnecessary. They should turn the lights off because the same fracas would still be there in the dark. They could add a million more lights and the reality of New York couldn't ever be known or completed. This never-ending town doesn't need me. It'll make noise and glare and foul up the air even when I'm dead. That much was clear but I wished for a sign just the same. Of course being in Times Square there was no shortage of signs. I decided to make do with the first thing I laid eyes on. A giant billboard, a large white rectangle with some text and blank spaces like you see when playing the word and phrase guessing game Hang-Man on a piece of paper where you have to fill in the blanks with only few mistakes allowed before being hung from a noose.

The 4 Great Designers For Men are:

R---- L------
P---- E----
C----- K----
T---- H-------.

The Great Designers For Men, it was simple and direct. Who has been putting their scheme on me? It had to be someone because this isn't the life I planned. I was about to turn 26 and still had the same helium pumped into my head that I had when I was a teenager. Maybe this is the end of it, the top of the mountain, proof of who I am. There was something to be remembered from being a small child that everyone must have, a blind and brazen courage to find a purpose. It was built in, just waiting for you to find it, to take it and run with it. How did I lose it? Subconsciously I must've started making predictions, wondering about a timeline for when and how my life would play itself out, estimating danger, the degrees of the risk, all while I was out drinking and dancing. My preconditioned thought process must've assessed a piecemeal reality and foretold bad outcomes. Mindlessly I learned about all the troubles and pitfalls that lay in wait for me and I decided to stay safe and stay put, or more to the point, stay at the party. Now I was an ass left on the edge of a curb at 4:30 AM trying to assemble more bits and more pieces, things and events that should lead to a purpose. But having never grasped reality or ever accepted it, and always denied my existence in it, the only thing I could figure out at the moment was a true purpose couldn't be slapped together. Things can and do happen spontaneously sometimes like an avalanche, it's undeniable. You can watch champagne glasses pile up in a pyramid on New Year's Eve and all that it takes is one crack and the whole of it will collapse. So what does it matter that you calculated the moments of your life, watching it build in bits and things and events when it all can come crashing down in an instant. You'd be stuck the same as the rest of the chary saps at a minute to midnight without a glass of champagne in your hand and the New Year rolling in just the same.

There should be a piece of me, at least a stain still on the sidewalk of the southwest corner of 45th Street and Broadway. That's where I came apart, self-destructed, nearly disappeared. It wasn't slow coming. A glitch, the pedestrian signal began flickering Walk and Don't Walk, and my brain deteriorated, hemorrhaged and everything inside of me liquefied. I couldn't read any billboards, or recall one bit or thing of my squandered life. The glitz of Times Square and more, all the sky above and everything below was as an energy streaming through my senses at an incalculable speed until bursting into an enormous collage of color, concrete, glass, neon and stars. The entire universe ripped through that street corner and I was in touch with it all. What it looks like. What it smells like. What it tastes like. What it feels like. What it sounds like. I was an energy beam connected to all the energy around me. My consciousness was perfect. I was whole. I was beautiful. Then in less than a minute, if I could even calculate time, I was transformed again. Everything that I was at one with suddenly imploded, bursting in reverse and then reassembling into something different. Reality was no longer omnipresent and magnificent but laid out in front of me like a subway line with hundreds of cars or more, one behind the other. But they weren't subway cars, they were smaller mounds, sloppy titles, lumps and clumps, the things and events of my life. All of it methodically pushing and pulling like a drunken caterpillar climbing out of the sewer and across the gutter bending and inching along, a quiet rhythm of moving muck. I could see in two directions along that slime line, the past and the other way to a future. I was at the center picking out details, and details about the details. Everything in the universe that had been in that enormous explosive collage of the present moment was spilled out. I was categorizing and slicing and sorting and shuffling in place all the mounds of me and making associations with everything in the past with everything I ever learned. I wasn't wiser. I could project that line into an enormous amount of new directions with new possibilities. I desperately tried to get my head around the entirety of it but it didn't last. Sludgy me transformed to a sound - my voice. The same voice I hear that will endlessly chatter away in my head when I might've been wishing for silence or sleep. The voice I recognized as the part of me that determines things and reminds me of things I need to do like buying toilet paper. It was the voice that connects me to the external world as a calculating intelligence.

The very same voice that says, "I am." It was clear and I said it out loud, "I am." The moment I did I became definitively separate from anything on Broadway or anyone else found walking around Times Square. Then the voice was gone fast. I lost my balance, stumbled. I was going through the ringer. I looked down at my hands and they didn't resemble any hand I'd ever seen before, more like paws or fleshy clubs with squiggly bumps were fingers might've been. I looked over the whole of me and didn't resemble anything that I'd looked like before. I couldn't define the boundaries between the world and myself. I blended with the sidewalk, the walls of the buildings, the garbage in the gutter, the lights, the smells and the noise. There was nothing whole inside of me. Then the voice spoke, what is this? But before that question finished the voice lost the desire to speak. I was petrified by the sudden and complete silence. Then fast I was something new again and captivated by everything that was around me - that collage of energy flowing faster than before. I was enormous and expansive. All was beautiful and growing incomprehensibly. Then the voice revolted and I talked with incredible speed blabbing out loud like an everyday lunatic in Times Square. Desperately I had to sort out a real life. If there was a hammer as big as any of the buildings surrounding me it would've been the perfect size to understand what it felt like when I was suddenly struck hard on the top of my head, smashed and splattered onto the sidewalk with a sense of permanence. Normalcy returned with vengeance.

Big and slow breaths began to open my lungs. I continued walking in circles around Times Square until the sun beat out the neon. I needed to exhaust myself. I eventually found comfort in front of Barnes and Noble Bookstore's expansive window display done up to look like a tropical paradise with a load of sand, beach chairs and a few plastic palm trees pitching books about cruises and tropical vacations. I knew bartenders who had worked on cruises. There was even an entire circuit of bartenders and waiters who would work down in the US Virgin Islands for a couple of months in winter every year and return in the spring. I'd heard you can make good money working on a Cruise ship and you don't have to spend a dime because your room and board is paid for. A guy could save a lot of money and manage to see the world. If you add the fact that I'd also watched plenty of episodes of the television show The Love Boat, what more did I need to know?

The Winners Circle

"You're in the wrong place," that was the first notable thing Tommy Saloon said to me. Imagine that as a good advice. Tommy Saloon was having drinks, seeing friends and associates, and making bets. It was Thursday, the only day he drank at the bar and the only day he made bets. Like clockwork, three Triples, Straight Trifectas, and three Johnny Walker Reds straight up, in the door at three and out the door at six. He'd squeeze in an oil sponged portabella mushroom or maybe a frumpy shrimp cocktail and wash it down with a half a glass of water before scooting out of the place. Tommy Saloon was the type of man you easily imagine lived in New York for a very long time - gruff, square jawed, strong bald head with some hair left on the sides clipped tight, a racing form under his arm, a cigar faithfully in hand, always wearing a sports jacket from a different era with an aged white dress shirt and a loosened tie. He was old, slim, had a bounce in his step and could still turn on his toes. You'd be pressed to guess his age because you would think anywhere from 60 to anything. Shockingly, he was 88 at the time. He'd told me I was in the wrong place after I put his Johnny Walker Red in front of him without ice and a lemon wedge laid out on a beverage napkin next to it. My blind stab at his drink was a jolt, made him gripe, "What the fuck!." He glanced around the room looking to spot a setup.

I guessed his drink by keeping an eye on him as he made his way to the bar through the rabble like a pigeon walking head-on into traffic on Broadway with confidence in his wings. I noticed how he threw his racing form on the bar top and the way it landed with a small spin that left the text lined up perfectly for him to read as he stepped up in front of it. The racing form was folded horizontally, neat and tight to highlight and center one race. He hadn't looked at anyone in the room but was certain some of them were clocking him. They were guys he knew and he'd get around to greeting them after he settled in with no chance of anyone getting between his great mood and the sip of his first drink. You could practically see a halo of independence above his head. He was like guys who drink their coffee black for the purpose and taste of coffee and don't like to depend on anyone or get hung up if the sugar bowl turns up empty or the milk spoiled. Guys like Saloon always drank booze straight up and they usually preferred scotch like too many men over 50 years old. The bar's scotch selection was slim. "Johnny Walker Red is good enough and not expensive. If you're smart enough to know that and you ain't rich enough to care, you drink Johnny Walker Red," that's what I told him. "So you're a wise guy…" he said, "What about the lemon?" "Your tie has a little pizzazz, some class to it despite the stain," I told him, "I don't think you'll use it for your scotch but you might bite into it to excite your palate before a drink, or maybe you just like the look of it sitting next to your glass." He gave me a double take and then a big glad smile as he smacked the palm of his hand on the bar top. "You're in the wrong place... When the carnival hits town I'll call in a favor and get you a new job, Carnac the Magnificent." Needless to say, we were instant pals.

I was working at 515 7th Avenue on the corner of 38th Street, on the second floor, The Winner's Circle. It was the bar and restaurant with betting machines connected to the gigantic OTB betting parlor on the ground floor. The place was built in the early 1970's. You would guess the design of the place was too much in the modern moment when it opened and oddly it must've been old the day after it was new with an awkward appearance unable to keep up with the tumultuous times. By 1988 it was a run down, doleful teal-toned space half-heartedly brightened by some fake flowers and blasé watercolors of stable scenes. The floor was carpeted and it was worn out, ripped, filthy, and plain ugly. They had televisions at every table broadcasting track and harness racing from all over the country. How anyone could keep up with it all was a mystery to me. If horse racing wasn't your thing and you wanted to be there for some incredible reason you could just as well sit down at a table and watch cable television. You had to pay a cover charge to be in the Winner's Circle but unlike the lack of a cover charge at the OTB downstairs that imposed a surcharge on bets the upstairs had betting prices in line with the track. The spread between upstairs and downstairs was even but the entrance criteria sorted out dregs from those who had heard of civilities.

Baring Triple Crown crowds or gambling junkies on vacation in New York, the faces at the Winner's Circle were mostly the regulars, routine and humdrum gamblers. Real degenerates in New York City gambled down on Wall Street. Occasionally when one of those braggarts was unchained from his desk and caught near midtown you'd see them at the bar drinking hard, barking orders and making big bets. If you didn't like horse racing you wouldn't want to stay in the place for too long. It'd be lucky a day if you ever found a woman there, save the occasional hooker on the prowl. Mostly it was a place for remnants, old time New Yorkers still interested in being part of a scene while eking out pension and social security checks into parlayed dreams of a better life at the end of life. Men who had lived in this town long enough that if you tallied up the years amongst them you'd have over 5000 years of New York City experience in one room. The old men would scour over programs shuffling back and forth from booth to betting machine, moaning and arguing over the best bets to be made or the ones that should've been made or the best formula for a guaranteed ticket. Most of them managed to survive on religiously committed budgets with one shallow pocket for routine bets and the other shallower pocket for habitual drinks. That was good for maintaining their equanimity but it created a bar lousy for tips. Grandstanders and lucky winners on occasion would save the day with generous gratuity. Most of the geezers sat at the tables but a small group of old men preferred the bar and they pretty much ran the place like the cool kids in High School. That was fine by me because I was one of the barmen and I liked the cool kids right from the start.

The Professor was the most consistent regular at the bar every day of the week betting every race he could get an angle on, and consistently managing to never appear drunk after polishing

93

off nine or ten cognac Stingers. He was tall, groomed and well built. He wore a fine jacket and a silk ascot everyday. The Professor didn't base any of his bets on a horse's reputation. His bets were based on gathered intelligence. He was an inside man with connections at Belmont, Aqueduct, Yonkers, Meadowlands, Saratoga, tracks across the country. He'd be on the pay phone on and off all day long and sometimes meeting with strangers in the bathroom or at a corner table, sometimes he'd go downstairs to meet someone in a parked car out front. The Professor's info was based on racetrack players. Shakespeare had players and a racetrack has its own: jockeys, trainers, horse owners, track judges, bookies, Honest Johns, betting clerks, veterinarians, Clockers, stable owners, Good Fellas - the list goes on. The Professor said it best, "The table is tilted, the game is rigged, by hook or crook all races are fixed and a conspiracy of players make easy money everyday of the week." The Professor would gather his networked intelligence and coordinate information with skilled guesswork while keeping his mind on as many players as possible to figure on who is fixing which races. Then a guy in his network would try his best to stay hot on the trail of whoever was making the sure bets and then copy those bets while staying wise to the fact that the guy making those bets might be a sucker's decoy. The Professor lost and won bets all day long and by the end of the day he'd either win enough to pay for his drinks and food or he'd end up losing the cost of necessities. By my measure he'd cover his routine more than having to pay for it and once a month he'd win a load of dough. "Young man, life is not about money, it's about being engaged in action," the Professor often explained. Easy for him to say, the Professor had money to spare. Though he never let on to it the Winner's Circle grapevine had it that the Professor had written a string of successful Romance novels under a pseudonym and also held a profitable patent on a super glue used by the US Army by the truckload.

The Professor's younger brother, Rabbi Odds On as he was known in The Winner's Circle, loved showing up on Thursdays. It was the day of the week he'd have to be in the city to take care of whatever business he couldn't take care of in Brooklyn. As he put it, "A little bit of work, my brother, horses and free lunch,

94

bakvem." The Professor always picked up their bar tab. Rabbi Odds On was more interested in seeing his older brother than playing the ponies. He was vaguely involved in the Garment industry but you would never have guessed it by the shabby condition of his clothes or his reckless head of hair and beard. The Winner's Circle was in the middle of the Garment Center so you'd find plenty of guys who worked in the industry drinking and betting at the bar. Rabbi Odds On appeared to know all of them, or better, they all knew him, or at least his reputation. Rabbi Odds On only drank Seltzer and only bet on horses with odds on favorite to win, ergo the nickname. He'd bet eight bucks to win two bucks and make at least twenty bets like that and usually win between $5 bucks and $50 bucks by the end of the day. He'd never collect on the winnings. He'd cash in a few tickets to cover the cost of his bets and then pass the rest of the tickets around to the barmen, waiters and busboys as tips. Occasionally he'd slide a winning ticket into the pocket of some poor sap down on his luck. As things were at the Winner's Circle there was never a shortage of saps.

Rounding out my Thursdays was my new pal Tommy Saloon who only bet on long shot Triples and it appeared he never won. He played Triples exclusively because he believed: "A Pinhead cashes in small on luck when you could just as well win big." The Professor certainly agreed with Saloon about the notion of "luck" because he had produced a dissertation back when he was earning his Doctorate at Berkley about the notion of luck with a number of case studies that concluded some people experience very real and actual streaks of luck. Apparently a few individuals had been able to hone the timing and good use of their luck and made a fine living from it. Even without considering windfalls, Saloon, the Professor and Rabbi Odds On always came across as lucky to me, lucky to be alive.

They genuinely liked me, thought I was the best barman at the Winner's Circle in years. We had pre-measured pouring spouts on the liquor bottles so pouring drinks was easy enough for a monkey. It was my attentiveness and my open, friendly demeanor that had them keen on me. Rabbi Odds On said I was born that way because it shined through naturally and it was a blessing. "Shining through naturally" meant I was not just being nice for tips. The Professor liked my demeanor because he was sure it was the main reason I'd done well with women. Anytime his brother wasn't around he'd want to hear any tale about chasing tail I'd be willing to share. Saloon simply thought, "You're a good guy to chew the fat with." Plus, as he put it best, "If you're a Yankee fan, all faults are accepted."

A great change of pace to listen to guys with something relevant to say and maybe teach me a thing or two, or three, or four, or more. Rabbi Odds On was the smartest guy I ever served in a bar. He was a mathematical savant with a vast set of interests and could speak a dozen languages, probably more. He was good for everyone who stood around the bar because he'd thank you for anything and everything and always offer you help with whatever you needed. Come tax season he'd sit at the end of the bar and go through three or four pens in a day while ripping through long form tax filings for anyone who asked - for free. You could count on the biggest return possible. Only you did have to let him call you Genzel and listen to him explain while he did your taxes that you shouldn't pay Income Tax in the first place. "Genzel, Income Tax is modern slavery.., di avle." He explained it by pointing out that on average Americans are forced to pay about 35% of their wages in taxes and that means 35% of the year you are working for free and any man forced to work any amount of time for free is a slave. Voluntary tax was justified, and points collected on imports and exports. Rabbi Odds On knew more than taxes; he could answer mechanical problems with ease for all the building engineers working in the area coming to the bar for bets and drinks. Elevator troubles, air conditioning, steam heating, water pressure, electric, he knew it all. One afternoon an old timer was drinking away his sorrows over his sick dog, his life companion for the last 14 years. The pooch had been suffering gravely and was ready to be put down. Rabbi Odds On suggested a load of chopped carrot tops and minced ginger mixed into raw lean ground beef for the dog's meals for a couple of days instead of canned dog food. The following week the dog was back to chasing squirrels in Central Park. One time I'd forgotten the combination to my lock stuck on a locker at the YMCA and Rabbi Odds On prompted me with a few strange and trivial questions about my early childhood and sure enough I remembered the lock combination better than my phone number. He could pretty much translate anything for anyone that might come in the door from China to Cuba. Those were his shining abilities. Other times you might walk into the place and find him with a great ability to blow his lid. The times that happened he could still be considered intelligent but the notion of being kind would be challenged. He could scare you to the point of tears if the topic of Judaism ever came up.

Rabbi Odds On wasn't necessarily a Rabbi. He had been in his younger years. That was after the time he denounced Orthodox Judaism as a teenager and embraced Reformed Judaism and subsequently became a Rabbi. He was no longer a Reformed Jew or a fully recognized Rabbi. He'd returned to a true Jewish principle and tell anyone asking if he was really a Rabbi, "I uphold a Torah perspective in the service G*d and an age old hope of heavenly redemption. I denounce false redemption. I heed the Holy Scriptures and the G*d of Abraham, Isaac and Jacob, the Living G*d, the ancient paradigm of enlightenment. I have an open heart and mind and I know a lot of things that are helpful for others and their troubles." He'd have a firm hold of your shoulders and look deep into your eyes while telling you all that and it'd rattle out of you any notion of challenging him on his legitimacy. Apparently Rabbi Odds On was infamous in the world of Reformed Judaism having pissed off the whole hierarchy from New York to Israel. Often he'd spout the same speech verbatim at the bar that likely created his non-kosher reputation. "In 1966 I was swept up in the anti-war movement. The American invasion of Vietnam was a heinous injustice that discredited everything the US pretended to represent, freedom, justice." He'd clear his throat after uttering freedom and justice and get very loud, "Jewish revolutionaries like me were useful idiots. Illuminati Jews, Rockefeller and Rothschilds engineered the Vietnam War in order to alienate a whole generation... I was socially engineered. My mind was molded. They used my youth and distorted my idealism!" Tommy Saloon said Rabbi Odds On was either a prophet or a friggin mad man. The Professor explained his younger brother's enthusiastic way of speaking as a decades-delayed result of a self-inflicted head injury as a child. As it goes Rabbi Odds On at 8 years old was reciting the pattern of Pi for eleven hours straight until he finally lost control and ended up smashing his head a hundred and one times against the sidewalk on the corner of 16th Avenue and 54rd Street out in Borough Park. Rabbi Odds On came across straight to me and I hadn't noticed any peculiar bumps or dents in his head. There were no contradictions in what he was passionate about and, if anything, he provided a great way to break up a boring afternoon.

"I'm not interested in the distinctions between a Luciferian and a Satanist," Rabbi Odds On once blurted out while grabbing onto the bar as if we were all on a ship in rough seas. "Until almost 40 years old I was another confused liberal, socialist, kibbutz dirt digging feminist loving fool. Lucifer and his Kabbalah Jews are metaphysical outcasts. That is why they are restless. They are alienated from G*d and their soul and a decent sense of Being. They're desperate, constant and craving to justify their existence by asserting dominion over others." My booze slinging Rabbi Odds On schooling taught me that Kabbalah centric followers of Lucifer aren't real Jews. The Kabbalah is a 12th Century fraud produced by a con man and, more importantly, Kabbalah teachings deny and defy G*d by overturning His design, the natural and moral order of the universe. Rabbi Odds On explained, "They're at best hypocrites, at worst categorically sufferers of dementia, cracked minds, black magic astrologists, hustlers and numerological gypsies slipping into a dark fissure plummeting into the core of the physical world of diverging densities and trickery and living in denial of the pure truth of reality, the Eternal." Sometimes out of the blue and at his loudest Rabbi Odds On would belt out, "True religion renounces the world and the pursuit of sex and money and embraces the one and only non dualistic eternal G*d... You cannot square a circle!" The Rabbi would seemingly levitate for a second or two in the middle of a conversation if someone ever triggered the "Do Jews run the world?" button: "The money trading elite have designed the modern world which they insidiously built on the ruins of prehistoric religious superstition." During some of Rabbi Odds On's episodes my boss would flash a look at me as if it was my job to contain him. Even if it were possible it wasn't my job to restrict free speech. I served drinks, listened to people and asked questions or talked if there was a call for it. If he wasn't hurting anybody who am I to stop him.

If a new face appeared at the bar Rabbi Odds On would pounce on him with a lecture on the contemporary history of Jews. Some would ignore him but plenty paid attention. I heard it a hundred times how 17th century Sabbatean Frankist Jews from Poland set their plans for world domination and they've since infiltrated the European power structure and hijacked institutionalized Christianity and paved over organized Jewry with their unprecedented wealth and behind the scenes influence while the throngs of the western world have been out of touch and without a real and leading belief system since then. The Kabbalah Jew believes in a god of materialism, a god of earth and exoplanets, astrology and geometry, and his interplanetary space based context and will is expressed through them exclusively. According to the Rabbi, "They plan to destroy every last remnant of decency and authentic humanity in the world and rebuild a new reality in their own image." For the master planners, the slate must be wiped clean. The fanatics have been carrying out this devilish plan by unleashing the ideals of nihilism and atheism in order to provoke a great social cataclysm, a momentous horror show of absolute atheism that will culminate with the masses experiencing the origins of pure carelessness, of savagery and bloody turmoil when everyone eventually will turn desperate for survival. Rabbi Odds On five alarm warning: "It will be a dog eat dog world and mankind will give up on the G*d given moral code which has been the harmonious sustenance for humanity for eons. The devotees have undermined wholesome virtues and are breaking down all sexual restraint and unleashing perversion into the culture in order to weaken an individual's good use of his righteous will that is quintessential for social harmony. When the state of humanity has been deconstructed to useless parts of faithless atheism, failed Christian values and annihilated Abrahamic traditions then the doctrine of Lucifer will finally be brought into public view as a naturally occurring manifestation, a mass reactionary movement to destroy failed-Christianity and atheism at the same time, and to establish a new world religion with Lucifer on its throne. With this dark and masochistic belief system embedded subliminally in the culture the masses will accept a Sabbatean Frankist fabricated reality and all will be integrated into a vast conglomeration of mongrelized humanity when people will embrace a slave identity."

That was a lot to take in while I was supposed to be pouring drinks and keeping the action flowing for a bar full of old men betting on four legged prayers. Extraordinarily there would always be a deathly moment of silence after Rabbi Odds On belted out his public service announcements, and then with an incredible sense of timing the sound of the televisions would return and rise and all the geezers would warm up to cheer the track announcer's call of the horses coming round the final turn. Moments like that felt like time slowed or missed stride. I'd get through it. I shared with Rabbi Odds On some of my hopes for a righteous world and my questions about sleeping with loads of women and whether or not it was good for my soul. "They call it sexual liberation," he explained, "They've breached the collective adolescent mind and implanted an obsession with sex determined to tear down traditional marriage and family. You are a victim. You should have a wife and children by now. How else will the world carry on?"

Rabbi Odds On was taken out of the bar by ambulance after he shouted down everyone in the place with his escalating tirade on Satan's agenda. An off duty cop came up from the OTB downstairs with his gun drawn because he'd seen people running out of the place. Rabbi Odds On's voice was hitting every corner of the room like a trained opera singer. "The Kabbalah cult and their Freemason accomplices have the intention to degrade the masses to livestock and concentrate wealth and power in their hands. This satanic cult is hidden within Judaism masquerading as a modern and reformed religion and they've put the entire Gentile establishment in place!" It was a good thing the Professor was at the bar that afternoon because he intervened before spontaneous combustion, did his best to settle Rabbi Odds On down by holding his hands. The Professor seemed loving when he did so and he was brought to tears when Rabbi Odds On finally collapsed. Some of the patrons were put off by it but they had no where else to go for drinks and bets so they put up with it, and it finally gave them something other than horses to talk about. As it turned out the Rabbi didn't have a heart attack. It was the bowl of lousy Pasta Bolognese he ate.

Before I started working at the Winner's Circle I'd set off on an urban vision quest to pound out a desperate formula for a deeper life. Having just come off a heartbreaking and familiar stretch of road lined with drugs, drinks and negligent sex, the Winner's Circle was going to be life anew. The daytime/evening job combined with avoiding the nightlife was the necessary shock. 'Above and beyond' was my new incantation. Instead of being aroused by life I was going to jump in and make a contribution. I planned on paying attention to as many things in my daily life as I could and fill in any and all possible shortcomings in the events I witnessed. I wanted to learn how to treat others with fairness, compassion and especially without judgment; to be that simple person answering the needs of others. It was the opposite of being a half ass chasing cravings and party circles. Because I'd had trouble sustaining any long-term convictions in the past I reckoned it was time to try out a day-by-day approach. I didn't want to waste the effort so it also made a lot of sense to put my heart into it. I showed up for my first day at the Winner's Circle in an absolute and eternal form of a bartender. With the prospects that come naturally with a new job I also sharpened my wit and began my journey to being the best customer care representative New York City had to offer. I did it all with a valued sense of humility because I was grateful to finally realize doing something well is living the good life.

My attention was poured mostly on the old men at the Winner's Circle. It was less about being an adept libation mixer and more about being capable of elevating a customer's casual bar experience by watching and listening for cues to answer their public house needs. Being an invisible hand was new to me, had me feeling substantial; knowing when a customer was going to need a glass of water before they asked for it; delivering a pen and a beverage napkin to someone to scribble down a note before the idea was complete in his head or the phone number forgotten; or directing a customer to the bathroom the moment before the urge to take a piss took hold. Body language was obviously helpful. More valuable was remembering experiences with people and matching similar patterns with others in new and different situations, from topics of conversation to the way they present themselves with their clothing and hygiene, or with their vocabulary and use of phrases and the many tonal variations a voice is capable of. Listen carefully to how a guy will say, "This round is on me," and you'll know if he's really broke and desperate for a dose of good will even if he has to pay for it, or, he's got a pocket full of cash and he's riding high anticipating greater fortune by spreading some. Tidbits of information that when accumulated give you a great lead on a person's inner thoughts and needs. You know when a guy is uncomfortable being new at the bar and hopes to impress by ordering expensive scotch when he'd honestly prefer a cold beer after telling you he schlepped all over town, and his bloated face and the size of his gut tells you he loves beer best. Sometimes you can notice a defensive front in a voice of a guy ordering a drink with a chin pointed sharply at you and contradictory slouched shoulders. He either just got fired or had his heart broken and is truthfully interested in finding someone to agree with him that today is a good day to drink a barrel of whiskey. Without fail, looking directly into a set of eyes while your eyes are open and honest will always be the best tell. I tracked my empathetic progress by the number of surprised customers asking, "How did you know that?" or "That's right!" or the countless and bewildered, "Thanks." Cheerlessly, I discovered too many people are simple cutouts that are as predictable as 124 pints of beer in a keg.

My success wasn't garnering any more money than my fellow bartender Carl who was mastering his skill of getting shit-faced everyday without the boss noticing. Fortunately money was a distraction, an offensive nuisance to my sensitive goal of perception. Unfortunately, New York City was blasting off in its climb to becoming a ridiculously expensive city to live in just as the cheap lease on my sublet studio expired. Without skipping a beat I moved into Tommy Saloon's place on West 38th[st] Street between 9th Avenue and 10th Avenue next to the Lincoln Tunnel conduit that brings nine-to-fivers in constant slow motion in and out of the city for work everyday. The instant he suggested the living arrangement planted a smile too wide on my face. The short open air walk to and from the Winner's Circle was going to be an inconspicuous reward for not surrendering to an ordinary life. I'd explained to Saloon my day-by-day life plan of mastering empathy and honing customer service skills in a bar fixed with geriatric spending plans, which was at heads with my hunt for an affordable place to live. He told me, "It'll be practical peace of mind... Go climb a mountain or sit under a tree if you want to become an Ascetic. There's no escaping the cost of living."

I was honestly surprised when I carried my bag of clothes over to his place and discovered he was letting me have a basement apartment rent-free. I'd thought I'd get an affordable deal sleeping on his couch or maybe in a spare bedroom. He never mentioned it before but Saloon owned the entire five-story apartment building I was moving into and the building next to it. The basement apartment was for the superintendent at one time but the superintendent next door took care of both buildings. On the door leading to the basement Saloon had hung an engraved wooden sign that read, Prosperous Books. I cracked a lame joke, "Am I gonna be sleeping in an underground business school?" He laughed and told me that it was play on words, a reference to an old Greek who liked books as much as him. "As if reading books can be prosperous," I told him. He let out a forged laugh and then stopped mid staircase, turned and jabbed me in the gut and told me seriously, "Books are as important as food. There are books about everything imaginable." He wasn't joking because when we walked into the basement it looked like he owned every book imaginable. The living portion of the apartment was crammed. There was a very comfortable Lazy Boy alongside the back wall where the only windows in the place faced a backyard; there was a small table and a very uncomfortable wooden chair; an old record player and an older radio on a small shelf; and a single bed in the corner under one of those windows. The bathroom was old but it worked, had a mini sink and a shower stall. There was a small refrigerator and a hotplate for heating up food. Most of the basement was bookshelves lining the walls floor to ceiling and a double row of shelves running in the middle of the room. He had bookshelves crammed into the boiler room. "Saloon, you're nuts," I told him, "You gotta have over ten thousand books down here." "Closer to twenty," he told me, "not counting magazines and records." It was a good thing it was all in the basement because the weight of those books would crash through any of the floor joists on the upper floors. Saloon could've easily operated an underground bookstore and made a good living from it.

On the lighter side the backyard was big, open, had vegetables planted in a number of raised beds and there was a small apple tree sitting in a gigantic wooden barrel. That knocked my socks off because at the time I hadn't really thought sustenance could grow on the island of Manhattan. Because the Lincoln Tunnel conduit and a bus parking lot for the Port Authority terminal were next to us there were no buildings alongside so the garden got plenty of eastern and southern exposure. It was great for the basement's atmosphere, as sunlight poured into the back windows in the morning and most of the afternoon. I did have to get used to the noise of cars and buses rolling in and out of the city all day. But sitting out back with the way the sun's radiant heat can quiet your mind sure helped drown out any noise the city could drum up. It was spacious out back because Saloon owned the building next door and both backyards were open to each other allowing room alongside his urban homestead for a small shed, a makeshift patio and gazebo with an old picnic table and a bunch of random and rundown chairs scattered around. All together Saloon was a landlord with 28 apartments between the two buildings yet he lived in a tiny studio apartment on the first floor of the building I was staying in. Part of my free-living deal was that Saloon would need access to the backyard through the basement to tend his garden and he usually started early in the morning. Also, many of the tenants in both buildings had free access to the library and the backyard and they were known to grab a book in the middle of the night if they weren't sleeping well. It made no difference to me because living and sleeping in a basement can easily conjure up loneliness so I was always glad to see anyone.

In exchange for the apartment Saloon asked me to re-sort all of his books. At first it seemed overwhelming until he told me that I could start whenever I felt the urge and take as much time as I needed, and not to worry if I couldn't finish the job. He told me, "It'd be best if you read a few books first, get a feel for the place." At the moment the books were alphabetically organized by subject matter. Other times Saloon had them sorted by date of publication, or by listing the authors. This time he planned for me to organize by size, book cover dimensions first and then thickness. I thought it was odd but he explained that he had read most of them and changing the order on the shelves made reading them again more interesting. Half-heartedly, he said, "Shuffle the deck. The book you pick and read right after you finished reading another book can have its own effect unrelated to the books." I figured he thought I wasn't smart enough to sort books any other way than size. Or, most likely, he wasn't as interested in re-sorting all of his books as he was in helping me out with a place to sleep and giving me something to do so I didn't feel like a free loader. I never questioned whether he read all of those books because I wasn't in a position to do so. He'd read plenty of them. I'd read only one.

I enjoyed his company and he enjoyed mine so all was good in basement. Even the neighbors coming downstairs for books or to sit out in the backyard turned out to be nice, though a bit meek and weak in the knees. Mostly it was old people with a common placidity that took a couple of weeks to get used to. Maybe it was all the reading and fresh vegetables but at times it felt like living in a tenement sanitarium for people who had recovered from some sort of trauma. Another thing they all had in common was that everybody thought Tommy Saloon was an exceptional guy. I agreed. After a few midnight talks in the basement with my mellow neighbors I discovered plenty of them barely paid any rent, a few paid nothing. Saloon was floating them based on their situations and some were far worse off than me. I also discovered that Saloon had accumulated all of the books because many mornings he'd peruse trash heaps on the Upper West Side or in the Village; two neighborhoods he figured read more than the rest of New York combined.

One morning Saloon was out gleaning books and I was in the backyard helping Demetri, the superintendent living next door, slice in half an old oil drum. He was making a barbeque grill out of it as a gift for Saloon's birthday, which was April 5th, a week away. Saloon had been incredibly generous with me so I decided I wasn't going to let his birthday slide. Best was I knew what to get him without even thinking. A couple of tickets to the Yankees' home opener against the Twins that coincidently and perfectly landed on his birthday. I gave him two tickets wrapped nicely in a racing form cover and explained to him, "I'm not being cheap, I went up to the stadium and could only get a hold of some bleacher seats." He loved the present and loved it more that I was going to the game with him. "The bleachers are the only place to see a game," he said, "We can go on a toot out there." I wasn't sure about the drinking part because I'd been doing my best to curb partying. But after he convinced me drinking in the afternoon is different than drinking at night I couldn't help but smile and tell him, "Let's go Yankees!"

Saloon filled two flasks with bourbon, handed me one, stuck the other in his pocket and we took the D Train up to the Bronx and watched Rick Rhoden pitch a great game and the Yankees clobber the Twins 8 to 0 under sunny skies and temperatures in the 70's. We washed back the bourbon with Stadium beer. It doesn't get any better. "This is my favorite bar in all of New York," Saloon told me during the seventh inning stretch with a smile that made him look younger than he already looked. It was a great place to drink, an open-air bar like a church devoted to the audacious. Smuggling in your own booze made the cost of drinks manageable, meaning you'll manage to drink more, and everybody has got a seat whether you need it to sit on or stand on or dance on. Best is the general freedom from anxiety because you're sure you are welcome and the more noise you make the better. The hooligans sitting in the bleachers are Yankee loyalists and everybody drinks and it turns the game into a slapstick experiment on stadium fun. Saloon knew a lot of the guys at the game, even got a birthday hug from super fan Cowbell Man, Ali Ramirez. I told Saloon how remarkable it was that we both had been to so many Yankee games and we must've been sitting in the bleachers together many times and just never knew it. "New York can be a small town," he told me while looking at me like I'd lost my mind, "Don't get mushy or no more booze for you."

After the game we jumped on the train. Saloon wanted to get off at 125th Street and walk the rest of the way. The sun was still shining and he needed an extra dose of Vitamin D because, as he put it, "The winter is hard on old people." We stopped at a

Bodega on Amsterdam Avenue and bought Cubano sandwiches and a couple of Tall Boy Budweiser's and then headed over to Broadway. At 116th Street he wanted to sit on a bench on the median in front of Columbia University to watch girls going in and out of school while we ate. "I'm entitled to a few fillies," he explained, "it's my birthday." Like a baby with a belly full of milk his smile was honest, and his eyes were bouncing, keeping up with the trot of the college girls as they crossed Broadway. Who could blame him? With Spring fever in the air and blooming females enjoying the unseasonably warm afternoon in their spaghetti strapped t-shirts and skirts and their bare legs and sandals, they're impossible to resist. The world can be perfect sometimes and most of the time it's in the spring.

We were in no rush to go anywhere so we didn't. Saloon pulled out a cigar. Normally at the Winner's Circle he'd only have three drinks and talk simple and direct. But the late afternoon sun shining warmth down on his head had him open and glib. The loose talk had me relaxed and curious. One thing had been burning a whole in my tongue since I'd moved into the basement so I asked him, "Why do you live in that tiny apartment?" He owned the building and I figured he could pick something larger than the 100 square foot studio under the stairwell. He turned gruff, "How much space does a guy need!" I apologized fast and serious before our good vibe pissed away. After a big sip of beer he let it go. I learned the micro apartment was choice because he'd spent a long time in a jail cell. "I like having things at reach," he explained. "You're kidding me," I said, "I had no idea... Geeze! 32 years?" Of course I asked how he landed in jail. "I killed two pricks," he told me easy enough, "And the police and courts in this town are crooked and malicious." The news had me screwy. "I never would've pegged you as an ex-con," I told him, "Unreal." Temporarily at a loss for words and noticing our beers were empty, I offered to make a run to the Bodega. He agreed without hesitation. "Grab me a pack of Garcia Vegas and a bag of pretzels," he yelled as I crossed Broadway.

Saloon and I had a slow city block rhythm working under our feet stopping every ten blocks or so to sit on a bench on Broadway, maybe have a beer and a cigar and then move on

107

yapping all the way downtown. It was already dark when we reached Columbus Circle, still plenty buzzed and had to piss like racehorses. We relieved ourselves in the fountain because it was the right thing to do. Saloon was extremely proud that he held his water for as long as he did and even prouder when he was able to shoot it into a high arc competing with the fountain. By the time we crossed the Circle and sat down in front of the USS Maine Monument at Merchants Gate to Central Park I'd learned a lot about Tommy Saloon's life in jail and out, and while we sat there watching New York City finally let go of an impeccable spring day I learned more.

The Winner's Circle wasn't his only watering hole. He made routine weekly visits to Billy's Topless over on 6th Avenue for the free buffet and cheap drinks. On Sundays he'd go next door to Demetri's basement apartment and watch football or baseball and drink Demetri's homemade wine and order pizza with all the toppings. Afterwards, they'd head out to Jackson Heights, Queens, to the illegal immigrant strip clubs and, as Saloon put it, "the most affordable prostitutes in all of New York." On summer evenings a couple of times a week he liked to drink white wine with a few neighbors while standing in front of his buildings. "It's the best way to keep tabs on the neighborhood," he assured me. I also learned that he bought the two buildings in 1974 for cheap after hitting the jackpot on horse races twice on the same day with his famous long shot Straight Triple bets. His windfall coincided with New York City's real estate market crash and he laid out huge down payments on both buildings. I discovered he picked up the reading habit in jail where some days if he started early he could read three or four books by lights out. Tommy Saloon's real name was Tommy Solendera and he got the nickname because he was a barman back during prohibition. "I liked it so it stuck," he told me as he flicked his cigar butt into the gutter like a bullet out of a gun and then reminded me that we were going to need more beer soon.

"I worked in a number of speakeasies here in the city," Saloon started to explain. It was while he was tending bar back in 1926 when he killed the two pricks that landed him in jail. "They had it coming," he said. He was working on Gay Street in the West Village. "16 Gay Street," he told me, "A class spot to have a drink and enjoy the night side offerings." That meant no bathtub gin or intoxicating poisons in the house liquor and the beer was always fresh. At that time the Speakeasy-tolerant Mayor of New York City, Jimmy Walker, owned the building on Gay Street where Saloon was tending bar. "All the papers called him The Night Mayor," Saloon explained, "And the Night Mayor kept one of his girlfriends in an apartment in the building because he liked the idea of having a nightcap downstairs from his girl's place before heading home to his wife." Saloon told me how Gay Street back then was different than Gay Street of the moment. "The Village wasn't filled with queers. It was for bohemians, open minds, revelers. It's where the Negroes came to play New Orleans jazz," he said, "What a sound!" Saloon was telling me this and bobbing his head to an imaginary rhythm that wiped away any common stiff sheen he might've had. "There were underground breweries and Speakeasies scattered all over the Village," he said. The way he described the old time nightlife was almost like a movie being projected onto Columbus Circle and the walls of the giant Coliseum in front of us. "I loved the life and I was going to live that life until that prick Capone came along."

Al Capone and a few of his henchmen barreled into 16 Gay Street. "Dirty Sicilian oil and clean water don't mix," Saloon told me with a dead serious look, "You have to realize, kid, we had a well-bred, connected crowd. Capone and his soldiers locked the door. We were trapped." The gangsters were in the bar looking for a Police Captain who was a regular at the bar that failed to keep up his end of a deal between New York and Chicago. Saloon told me, "They found the dirty copper sitting at corner table in the back. The brutes held him in a chair while Capone bashed his head open with a hundred blows... He must've done something terrible to make Capone leave Chicago. Or Capone had good reason for sending a personal message to the New York syndicate. I never imagined that much blood inside a man." Afterwards Capone and his henchmen sat at the bar and drank leaving the dead man with his head smashed open on the table. "Vulgar animals," Saloon griped, "Two of the gorillas singled out a debutante, dragged her out back and spilled their filth on her while Capone just drank his beer leering and smiling at the customers huddled up in a corner."

109

Saloon's eyes were bulging and his forehead sweaty. "I still had to serve the sick bastards," he said, "By the time Capone ordered his fifth beer I was jumpy. Standing behind the bar I'd halfway filled a mug with piss and I topped it off with beer and that barbarian got what he deserved, a mouth full!" Saloon slapped his knee hard and laughed even harder. "Somebody had to do it," he barked.

The mug of piss might've been a noble idea but the fallout was bad. "Capone was disgusted," Saloon blurted out, "He stormed out of the place and left two goons behind with orders to drag me along." Saloon was grabbing a hold of my shirt to make sure I knew what he was going through. "I saw the back of Capone's fat head in the car in front of us pull away while the two grease-balls tried to throw me into their car." Saloon took a big swig of beer and then a bigger breath of air. "You gotta understand, kid. They were going to take me to a place where they could do unspeakable things to me. Something like that will transform you." He stood up and showed me how he kicked and twisted his way out of their grip. He'd run back into the bar, the two thugs followed, the dapper gang was still huddled in the corner. Saloon let out with a sigh, "Not one of those chicken necks helped me." But Saloon didn't need help because Saloon was scrappy and on top of that he was smart.

He went on and explained how the beer pump was low behind the bar for leverage and a lower counter sat underneath it for the clean glasses. That's how he managed to piss into a mug unnoticed. "We used to pump the pipes back then," he said, "Bartending was real work." There was a box of arsenic handy behind the bar to sprinkle the floorboards every night after work to kill the mice. Saloon had done his best to sprinkle some of that poison into the beer. He told me, "I was trying not to look down while I did it. I didn't know if any of it was in the beer." Fortunately for Saloon most of the arsenic landed in the mugs of the two guys who were trying to drag him out of the bar for a second time that night. "When they finally got a hold of me they started puking," Saloon said, "One guy was bleeding out of his nose. I had the upper hand and I used both of them to smash them to smithereens with bar stools and full bottles of gin." Saloon face drooped and he shook his head with a look in his eyes resonating a bad dream. By the time the police showed up everybody had scrammed and the place was a bloody mess and the only one still standing was Tommy Saloon. He was arrested for the murder of the Police Captain. The DA discovered the truth but it made no difference because the bad publicity of Al Capone doing business with one of New York City's Finest all inside of the Night Mayor's building in an illegal Speakeasy was too much for the City's establishment to handle so they threw Saloon in a cell and forgot about him for 32 years.

"I could eat a roasted pig," Saloon told me. The streets were dwindling down. I told him, "Let's head over to PJ Carney's and grab a couple of burgers and a piece of cake for your birthday." "Burger sounds good," he said, "I don't eat cake." We squeezed into a corner table up front next to the window and placed our order with the waitress. I knew the bartender Dermott and he sent us over shots of whiskey with our beers. We didn't need whiskey. When the burgers arrived Saloon was quick to order a side of potato skins. He was staring out the window onto 7th Avenue with ketchup on the side of his face. "Get a look at these two tomatoes," he said, gesturing with his head for me to take a look out the window. "I know those girls," I told him. One of them caught a glimpse of both of us and fast enough recognized me. She didn't waste time and came up to the window and wrapped on it hard and flipped me the bird. We both heard her clear through the glass, "Fuck you asshole!" The two of them turned in a huff and strutted away. "What gives?" Saloon asked. "That's Ann and Angie," I said. Saloon asked while eyeballing them out the window, "Which one is the redhead?" "Angie," I told him. Saloon was smiling and told me, "Angie has the finest behind in midtown." I said, "You should see her tits." Saloon was upset, hoping they'd be squeezed in at the table with us to celebrate his birthday. He said, "Opportunities with two Bearcats just don't happen for old men." He was more upset after I explained to him how I'd been trying to stay away from girls like Ann and Angie. "What's the matter? An affliction?" he asked, "Or are you a dandy?" After I guaranteed him I wasn't he took a guess at my reason for pissing off a pair of Bearcats: "I hope she had a nicer caboose than Angie." "Who?" I asked. He shook his head as if I was the biggest party spoiler of the year, "The girl that made you lose your mind."

I ordered a brownie sundae and asked for a candle. I didn't sing Happy Birthday but I asked Saloon to make a wish and blow out the candle. "Get a grip," he made his point. He ordered another beer and being courteous asked me, "So how did you end up tending bar for old men?" I gave him a bit history of drugs and drinking and stumbling my way to The Winner's Circle. "It's all connected to the greatest girl in the world that I let slip away more than a year earlier," I told him. I continued explaining with all the fluff and puff until a look of impatience grew on his brow. I summed it up, "Carina was a one of a kind." "She doesn't sound like the rest," he said, "You get a girl like that, you tie her down with chains, never let her out of your sight." I explained to him how I'd gotten a job on a cruise ship right after Carina left because I was heartbroken and needed my life ship shape and how on the first day as the captain made the call, anchors aweigh, I jumped ship. "I was spooked by a very pretty and fully blossomed teenage girl traveling with her parents after she offered me a blowjob and the opportunity to fuck her as much as I wanted to for the next ten days as long as I made sure her coca colas always had enough rum." Saloon gave me a confused look. I told him, "I was trying to set sail in the other direction." I also told him how I rented a dirt-cheap smelly room down on Barrow and West Street and started working for a corporate catering company. "I worked as much as I could," I explained, "Breakfast and lunch conference buffets and then serving Vodka Cranberries and opening bottles of Heineken at after work cocktail meetings for tools and stiffs... I worked as many shifts as they would give me." He told me, "Work can be good medicine." I said, "I managed to save forty-three hundred bucks in ten weeks and then took off for Mexico without a plan." "Sounds like fun," he said, "I've been to Mexico. Beautiful country... Hard to find Ghost peppers here. I tried growing them. You need the right sun." I explained how I begrudgingly hooked up with a hippie chick as soon as I landed in Mexico City airport because she could speak Spanish and I didn't and if I would pay for her cheap bus tickets and meals she could show me a million fantastic places and she'd share her big bag full of psychedelic mushrooms. I told Saloon, "She was slim, her hair was long and wonderful and her eyes were green and the two of us ended up screwing in a taxi and then jumping on magical mystery buses all over Mexico and Central America in search of jungle pyramids with a pie in the sky plan of digging up relics while putting down mind-trip mushrooms for thirty days straight." "You can't get away from yourself," Saloon said. "We made our way to Coban, Guatemala," I told him, "She had plans to meet up with a friend there and pick up another load of mushrooms and I guess she did because she took the $300 bucks I gave her and I never saw her again."

I explained to Saloon how on my own I tried to chart a course in my broken Spanish up north to the Tikal Temple because for some magic-mushroom-residue-reason I thought it'd be a good idea see a couple of jaguars in the jungle. Along the way at a bar down the street from my hostel in San Benito the CIA tried to recruit me to travel with some older lady posing as a doctor promoting vaccinations. I was supposed to carry and deliver packages of cash for bribing a list of local officials all across Guatemala and the rest of Central America. Saloon believed me when I told him, "They didn't like it when I refused and they threatened to have me arrested for smuggling drugs unless I complied." "Never work with genuine criminals," he told me, "At least willingly." I told Saloon, "I made it out of San Benito fast enough but didn't make it to the Tikal Temple. I did, though, get off the bus in the middle of nowhere and manage to walk down the wrong road then the wrong path then around the wrong tree and ended up misplaced in the jungle for three days where I nearly lost my mind." Saloon was looking at me in disbelief. I told him, "The idea that I might never be found had me scared out of my skin like a hysterical spook. More frightening was the pitch black nights alone with a million strange animals that I was certain were conspiring to eat me alive." With real concern Saloon asked, "How did you get out?" He was looking at me and trying to flag down the waitress. "A local hunter carrying an old rusted rifle searching for monkey meat stumbled on me," I explained, "I was dying of thirst because the only water I had was the morning dew I licked off a thousand leaves each morning. I was covered in a million bug bites and it turned out that likely I really was out of my mind because the hunter's nephew spoke a speck of English and translated the fact that I had a nasty and inflamed snakebite on my calf and for some reason I survived the poison when I shouldn't have." Saloon ordered two shots of whiskey and told me, "Snake bites can kill you. Some of them down there will swallow you whole." I told him, "The hunter and his nephew were certain I experienced nightmares and hallucinations." "It's a wonder you're still in one piece," Saloon said. "Not so sure about that," I told him. I went on about how the hunter's mother helped heal all of my scratches, bites and snake poison hangover with some concoction of leaves and dirt and bark smashed up in a wood bowl with spit and how the entire family eased my mind by letting me sleep on the floor of their hut alongside all nine of them for four days until the next bus came along. It turned out that for the three nowhere to be found days that I was alone in the jungle tripping my head off on snake juice I was only five hundred yards from the tiny village I was looking for in the first place. Saloon told me with a wink and smirk, "I guess the Jaguars were going to have to wait for their white meat."

I explained to Saloon how I still had a load of money sewn into the straps of my backpack so I headed back up to Mexico, to Merida. "The hippie chick I started the magical journey with had spoken about it often," I said, "I thought I'd find her. I wanted to unload on her." "That was dumb," he said. "I made it to Merida," I told him, "And fortunately I didn't find her. I did find a great little bar with a bartender capable of speaking crappy English where beer cost a dime and for twenty bucks a night I was king buying cans of Montejo for anyone who walked into the place." I went on about how I met a Mexican girl in that bar. "An earthy beauty with eyes a shade of brown that could only exist above the clouds... I made love to her for five days straight with barely any food or sleep until the sixth day when she had to leave to take care of her kids that I didn't know about and asked me for 800 pesos for the sex." "How much is that," Saloon asked. "It's like fifty bucks," I said, "It was the dumbest I ever felt in my life. I'd fallen hard for her... It was the end for me because of all the drinking and all of the mushrooms and all of the bug bites and snake poison and

114

miscued sex." Saloon told me, "Sounds like a good time to head home." I told him, "I was on it until I met a sympathetic backpacking couple from Germany who appeared to have their act together and they promised me a full recovery. All that was needed was a trip to the untouched beaches of Tulum." "Never liked the beach," Saloon said with a complacent look on his face, "Too hot, sand in your shorts, sunburn." I told him, "Tulum was beautiful, littered with spirited backpacking chicks from Italy, Germany, France, Denmark, from all over Europe."

I went on about how a grass hut on the powder white sand beach cost you three bucks a night, the ocean was turquoise, beer and food was cheap as dirt, marijuana and nighttime bonfires with guitars and topless girls was the routine. The licentious life appeared endless. By the ninth week there I still had plenty of cash but my crotch was overrun with crabs and a bad case of clap and my head was clouded from way too much marijuana, sustaining a large colony of fleas and sponged with an ocean of warm beer. I had asked a friendly beach bum dude from England if he knew what could be done about the crabs and clap and he told me to go into town, gave me an address of a doctor. The next day when I got out of the taxi and stepped into the house expecting to see a specialist I met a group of banditos. I was pretty sure the English dude was standing in a back corner. They walloped me with baseball bats and took everything I had. I waited a week in the bus terminal all banged up sleeping on the floor and eating out of the garbage until my mother could wire me money she didn't have for a ticket back to New York.

"I want you out of the basement by tomorrow morning," Saloon told me with a suddenly ugly face. For a second I thought he was going to pick up the knife and take a stab at me. I was confused. It had been a long day and I'd had a lot to drink. Maybe I should've kept my mouth shut about my fuck-up journey through Central America and Mexico. Before I could try to explain myself better Saloon grinned wide and laughed. "It's a good thing you're working at the Winner's Circle. It's the only place in the world you won't hurt yourself." Joke aside; he was looking at me differently. "I guess we're both filled with surprises," he said. "And mine barely compare to yours," I told him. With a new tone in his voice

115

Saloon said to me, "Kid, to live without an ounce of shame or two ounces of gratefulness or regret is dangerous. Unless maybe you are one of those rare and perfect people I've never met." I told him, "I don't understand." He said, "It sounds like you're looking for something or trying to figure something out." He was right. "Isn't that what I'm supposed to do?" I asked, "Isn't that how you make your life better than expected?" He told me, "I spent a lot of time locked up in a concrete and steel cage thinking about what should've been expected out of life." I suddenly felt bad, realized my lapsed commitment to empathy. It was Saloon's birthday and I was blabbing, bringing him down. "You had it hard, harder than most. 32 years," I told him apologetically. "Forget that," he said, "My life is great... What I'm telling you is that unless you've carried out some heinous sin, you have to accept yourself, put your feet on the ground, have a plan for life." I said, "I am doing something. I'm a bartender." He told me, "I'm not talking about your job. I'm talking about what's in your head." I wasn't sure what he was getting at. "Tell me straight," I said, "What should I do?" He suddenly sounded like he hadn't had a drink all day, "I've read a lot of books by guys who know a lot of things, and books like that have been written for thousands of years and more come everyday and not one of them can give you the answer to everything you need. The best you might come to learn is you become what you put your mind to, whether it's a revelry, violence, self-pity, greed, lust, hard work, adventure, customer service, plain happiness, or even confusion. The most intelligent thing a man can recognize is the futility of life. Some problems just can't be solved and maybe the best thing to do is to quit before you destroy yourself." I asked him, "Are you saying give up?" He shot me a sympathetic look. "I'm telling you that you can exercise your intelligence but maybe quit trying to answer all the questions that will be impossible to answer." I told him, "That's depressing, Saloon. Call it quits. I'm only 26." He opened his eyes wide and spoke sharply: "I'm telling you to start living your life because you're already 26." It felt like a punch. The words had my head bobbing around. It was late and I hadn't had this much beer and whiskey in a long while. All of it had me sluggish and probably explained the dumb slack jaw look on my face. Saloon lifted his nearly empty beer and finished it off. He put the bottle down on the table grimaced and told me easy like, "Snap out of it, kid. You don't want to end up a loser."

Wealth, Abundance and the Last Wild Human

"'Ever since I was a child I've had a fear of someone under my bed at night. So I went to a shrink and told him: 'I've got problems. Every time I go to bed I think there's somebody under it. I'm scared. I think I'm going crazy.' 'Just put yourself in my hands for one year,' said the shrink. 'Come talk to me three times a week and we should be able to get rid of those fears.' 'How much do you charge?' 'Eighty dollars per visit,' replied the doctor. 'I'll sleep on it,' I said. Six months later I ran into the doctor on the street. 'Why didn't you come to see me about those fears you were having?' he asked. 'Well, eighty bucks a visit three times a week for a year is an awful lot of money. I found a bartender who cured me for the cost of a few drinks. I was so happy to have saved all that money that I went and bought me a gold watch!' 'Is that so!' With a bit of an attitude the shrink said, 'and how, may I ask, did a bartender cure you?' 'It was nothing, he told me to get drunk, go home and cut the legs off my bed!'"

This guy Kevin just sat there staring, not even a smirk despite every red headed, red bearded guy I ever knew would've cracked glad half an inch for anyone simply trying to tell a joke; especially if he's the one who asked for it. Kevin was more interested in the nasty razor nick on my chin from shaving too close in the morning while I was pressing too hard to look my cleanest for the interview. Maybe it was a lousy joke. It came straight out an old book I pulled out of Tommy Saloon's basement. I thought it applied. I also thought it was tactful that I came prepared with a joke because I was certain most of the booze

118

slingers lined up for the job didn't.

Telling jokes behind the stick was never one of my bartending virtues. I'm not against funny. It's more that some bartenders usually have nothing worthwhile to say or are too lazy to sincerely contribute to the atmosphere around a bar so they tell jokes like a workaday gimmick. That's not anything honestly worth complaining about. It's just that if you get stuck with a bartender that's got head full cornball jokes, if he's gets a hint of encouragement, he'll end up telling you sorry jokes for hours and make you think it would've been better to stay home. In a jam I could pop out a joke, a limerick or an anecdote. But my job was to serve you drinks. If you were in need of company or if you were feeling down, I'd do my absolute best to be there for you and listen. If you needed me to talk, I could talk, tell you whatever, especially talk good about the weather: stay cool if the world's got you down because things always get better, it may be storming today but the rain can't last forever.

Drippy jokes aside, ginger man Kevin interviewing me for the job wasn't there for me. He had a boozy glaze in his eyes and it was only half pass twelve in the afternoon so maybe he didn't have his mind right and wasn't capable of a laugh. Or he could've been wondering what it'd be like if he shaved off his red beard and it left him with a gash on his chin and a funny face he hadn't had a good look at in years. I got tired of looking at Kevin looking at me so I looked around and watched the carpenters putting the finishing touches on the tabletops and a few of the booths. The place looked nice despite the overkill of blonde wood the color of baseball bats. The bright milieu was helped along with the load of great sports memorabilia, paintings and classic photographs up on some of the gleaming walls already. The designers must've been swinging for ceaseless promise, something bright and new about something old and lasting, making a luminous statement by going against the aged grain associated with the traditional reputation of the bar's namesake. It was the last thing I expected in a Hall of Famer's sports bar. Instead of a classic hard wood bar there was a polished black granite top wrap around bar, which I figured makes for easy tending and cleaning but guarantees more broken glasses. I noticed that they only had four beers on tap and a sports bar should have

119

more. A couple of stylish steps and a big glass wall separated the front of the place from a sunken dining room in the back that was filled with more great photographs, paintings and sports memorabilia laying up against the walls in the spots where they eventually would be hung. There were a bunch of televisions throughout the place sitting on customized shelves matching the polished blonde wood paneling and flooring. The overall look of the joint had me guessing the owners were more interested in serving cocktails than beer, which had me wondering about a possible new type of sports fan emerging in New York.

A hundred people might've been lined up for the job stretching out the door. It was a two-tiered interview: Kevin or one of the other assistant managers first, then the General Manager. Kevin was probably hired about a week earlier and I was thinking he wouldn't be there in another week because he can't take a joke. My head was already preparing for tier-two with the General Manager. Alas, getting in front of things is as bad as lagging behind. As with baseball, if you swing in front of the pitch or slow behind it you're going to strike out. It's always best to take a crack at it in the present moment. Like the present moment of the interview when Kevin didn't have any more questions or joke requests and told me straight, "We'll give you a call." In other words: Get the fuck out of here.

It's not that I needed the job because I was still working at the Winner's Circle and living on the cheap in Tommy Saloon's basement. I was interested in making more money but it was more than that. Pulling beer and pouring booze for the Yankee legend would've been a lifelong fantasy come true. As bad as I felt about the lousy interview I knew Saloon was going to be more let down because he'd found out about the job and encouraged me to get it. He was waiting in the cold across the street leaning against the stone perimeter wall of Central Park South anticipating good news. "I struck out," I yelled to him as I nearly got run over by a taxi while crossing the street. "Impossible," he said, "Did you tell them you were born next to the stadium? ...Nincompoops! ...You're perfect for the job." "No kidding," I said, "Did you get a look at the minor leaguers I was competing with?" Saloon was shaking his head and told me, "The world ain't right, kid." He tossed the nub of his cigar in the gutter and pounded his fist into the palm of his hand. "You're going to have to try again," he said, "You were meant for that job." We didn't want to be girls about it and it was too cold to harp so we tucked our chins and decided to move on. Saloon kept shaking his head and mumbling grumblings as we walked along the south side of the park toward Fifth Avenue.

Saloon had wanted to come along to the interview for good luck but he also wanted to track down an associate, English Steve, a Horse and Buggy driver. Those guys always pile up near Fifth Avenue and Central Park South across the street from the Plaza Hotel waiting for tourists with money. English Steve owed Saloon a hundred bucks from the Holmes vs. Tyson fight. He was worried that English Steve might get arrested and deported any day of the week because of a bad habit of getting drunk in Irish Pubs and belting out "Hooray for the Queen!" as many times as he could before fists and fury sorted things out. Saloon asked around and it turned out English Steve just took off in his buggy with an older couple under a blanket and they were making a loop run in the Park. Saloon suggested we get out of the cold, step in the Plaza Hotel's Oak Bar for a drink. He had friend who worked there; a bartender he hadn't seen in a while and hopefully was there today. Saloon also thought it was about time I see a classic New York City bar. "I remember when they built this thing," he said, raising his voice and looking up to the roofline of the Plaza Hotel as he crossed the street out in front of me. "My father helped put in the toilets." Being that we were in the swank part of town and because I was already dressed well for the interview I figured why not see the place. I told Saloon while keeping up with him zigzagging through cars and taxis, "Only if you really want to." Normally I was against going into a place like the Oak Bar because of a shoddy working class principle stuck in my head: Eat the Rich; a cultural maxim I heard too many times and the caste assumption was too catchy to forget. Obviously it wasn't embedded deep enough to hold down my curiosity. "Just one drink," I told Saloon as we stood on the sidewalk getting squared away before we entered. Saloon smiled. "I'm pretty sure they ain't running a Happy Hour," he said, "Unless you're buying, one drink is all you get."

121

Like all New Yorkers I was familiar with the Plaza Hotel and all of its haughtiness that cost an arm and a leg if gaudy marble, shiny brass and an ornate facade are a requirement for spending your vacation dollars. The Plaza's glitz is what makes it an icon of Gotham's high society. Like it or not, the Plaza is a striking and clear cut part of New York City's history having been around nearly as long as fire hydrants. The place is a hulking eighteen-story symbol of warranted elegance and at the present stage of New York City history, if you look pass the opulent adherents, it's an impressive place in its own structural right as a growing rarity in a town slowly transforming into a grid filled with communist styled buildings of no notable dimension other than being tall glass rectangle blocks of efficiency. The Plaza is from a bygone era of baroque art in building design and it's set back from an open square on Fifth Avenue; the best location in all of New York for a rich man's hotel. The exterior is lavish with a marble base three stories high and above that tiers of huge windows symmetrically and tirelessly rising one above the other leading to balconies, chimneys, dormers, and insets with two-story-tall columns on the upper floors, and then a roof out of a fairy tale with a steep aged green slate shingled crown stretching five stories tall on top of it all. If you've never seen the Plaza Hotel you can easily imagine it by thinking about what the most famous hotel in the world might look like, or maybe think of one of those charming houses on Cherry Tree Lane from Mary Poppins on steroids. Saloon and I didn't have to imagine because we walked right in the front door where I discovered the obvious reason for the bar's name: dark oak paneling everywhere and of course a long and enduring solid oak bar.

I was quietly hoping the room was either worn out or maybe spruced up to the point of being uncomfortable but it was undeniably old and staunchly beautiful. One in the afternoon and the place was filled with tailored suits drinking and smoking their lunch. It was a long storied place for men in New York with loads of money so of course guys like that demand a bar that is comfortable; unless they're perverse or bored. But as far I could tell none of them drinking and puffing away looked bored. The only thing perverse about the lot of them was the amount of talking going on. If you closed your eyes and changed the pitch you might imagine yourself in a ladies' beauty shop on a Saturday afternoon. None of the clean-shaven chatterboxes looked at us twice. I looked around and Saloon looked for his pal Mike. He told me as we elbowed up to the bar, "You fit right in, sharp, like a man in charge."

Saloon introduced me to Mike. He was probably in his early fifties, had a great head of thick jet-black hair combed straight back. It went well with his uniform, a white shirt and black pants, white clubroom jacket and black bowtie. He had a manful face, handsome, but looked tired. Not so much from a bad night's sleep, more like a laborious life that left him with a solemn good look. I noticed his fingernails when he put my beer in front of me, cut professionally short, easy to keep clean. Nobody wants a drink from a barman with gunk under a set of overgrown nails. Excellent sized hands, big, not bulky, he probably hadn't dropped a glass in years. "I did time with his old man," Saloon said to me, referring to Mike. "No, no, no, it's the other way, my old man did time with him," Mike replied. He broke his professional Oak Bar stance and leaned over to give Saloon a squeeze on the shoulder. It opened broad smiles on both their faces. "You hit on a pony, looking to spend a few?" Mike asked, "Or are you just slumming?" Saloon let out a laugh. "Not today," he told Mike, "Not with these prices... We're out trying to get this guy a better gig than the one he has bartending at the Winner's Circle." Mike looked at me halfway guessing I might be desperate. "We stopped in at Mickey Mantle's new place down the street," Saloon told him. "I saw it," Mike said with a shot of excitement, "Looks great. If I was twenty-five years younger I'd try to get a job over there myself." I told him, "If I was 25 years older I might've had a better chance." Saloon was shaking his head expressing our combined sorrow. "Too bad," Mike said, "What was it? You're not a Yankee fan?" "Careful Mike," Saloon told him, "this kid's a real Bronx Bomber." I told Mike, "The manager was a stiff, doesn't like bar jokes." Mike had to step away, tend to customers with bigger tabs than ours. Saloon and I relaxed, proudly sipping our beers and smoking like ad hoc gentlemen. Saloon went on about how nice it was to be in a bar nearly as old as him. When Mike came back over to us he

123

apologized for not being able to talk more. The place was busy. He was excited. "Listen," he said to me, "I don't know if you're interested but one of our bar backs got fired yesterday for swiping a wallet off a table. I could set you up with the manager before he goes looking for someone." Saloon popped off his stool, "Lucky day, kid," patting me hard on the back.

      The opportunity caught me off guard. Not so much because it came out of left field, but more because I never once thought about working in a classy spot. Plus the job was for a bar back. Progressing with life at a normal pace hadn't been my thing but I didn't want to intentionally start taking steps backward. "Iron in the fire," Saloon told me, "You kickoff with a job like this and you'll end up working here for life, a made man." Mike was waiting for an answer while looking over my shoulder at some of the customers who might need service. "What do you think?" he asked. I didn't put any thought into it and told him, "If you think I got a shot." Mike told me, "Just tell him you have a lot of experience." Saloon answered, "He does, a lot." I did. It should've given me confidence but instead I felt all clamed up. "Anything else he should know?" Saloon asked. "Nothing," Mike said. He paused, drew a blank look on his face, then continued, "Yeah, tell him how much you like the murals we have hung on the walls, especially the one behind the bar. He wets his pants over it." Mike told us to wait five or ten minutes before Fred the art loving manager would be back at the bar when he'd set up my interview.

      I wondered if I was serious enough to be considered for the job. My brand new suit felt too big and I was dawdling with Saloon's yapping about how I might make a career for myself. Working a job for a lifetime suddenly felt like I'd be serving a prison sentence. Plus I didn't know anything about paintings or murals. Making matters worse I'd only brought along one copy of my resume' and the laugh-less ginger man down the street at Mickey Mantle's place was most likely making no good use of it by now. My gut was telling me to go for it. It was also a good thing to have Saloon along because being as well read as he was he knew a thing or two about the paintings hung in the Oak Bar. "Everett Shinn," he told me, "The guy loved slapping out gritty pictures of New York City. Ashcan School ilk." Saloon swung his head around the room and then swung back around and settled his eyes on the giant mural behind the bar. "That's the Pulitzer Fountain with Pomona, the goddess of wealth and abundance," he said it to me sharply making sure I took a good look at it, "It's the fountain right outside the Hotel." I thought it looked like a stage set from the Academy Awards or a bad rendition of one of the pyramids in Egypt but after giving it a look over I did recognize it. "Why would you hang a picture of the fountain outside when you got the real thing steps away?" I asked. Saloon said, "It probably makes it a lot easier when you're drunk, maybe can't stand and clamoring for a fountain." He let out a laugh. "It doesn't matter," he said, "All the murals are from scenes right outside the hotel. We better just figure out something good for you to tell Fred about the Pulitzer behind the bar."

I had to be at work by 11:00 AM, which was perfect. I finished by 7:00 PM, which was also perfect. 11:00 AM to 7:00 PM is the most civilized shift in the entire western world because leisurely mornings and evenings is the wax for a polished mind. I had a locker in an employees' room in the hotel's basement, as well as access to a break room with a couch. For the life of me I couldn't figure that one out. Breaks while working was odd enough but seeing a couch that some waiters and bartenders took naps on had me wondering what kind of boss would ever let his employees sleep on the job. Then I learned about the Union and how employees can sometimes slack off as long as their dues are paid. I wasn't in the Union being that I just started out on the job. It made no difference to me because I liked square deals and the good hourly wage and a piece of the tip action from a pool collected and distributed at the end of shifts was more than enough.

The bartenders were all older men, pros that knew how to make any drink imaginable, including fashionable cocktails prior to prohibition for nostalgic drinkers. Their best trick was martinis, which was the most popular drink in the place beating out scotch by a gallon or two everyday. You'd be shit out of luck if you were on the cheap looking for a drip of rotgut. We served a lot guys working in the General Motors Building and advertising men from Madison Avenue and they'd go through premium gin, pearl onions and olives like going through premium gin, pearl onions and olives. They'd also smoke at least two cigars or an entire pack of cigarettes to balance out their lunch. Every day was incredibly busy and my work was to hustle and stock the back bar and clear tables without a peep out of me or appearing flustered because the art loving manager didn't want the place to come across like a madhouse. "We have a legendary reputation to keep up," said Fred. That was the day shift. I figured nighttime was different because every morning I'd have to reload cases of champagne and when I'd empty the linen bag in the laundry room there was no shortage of napkins with lipstick kisses.

My clearest assessment after only one week on the job was that the Oak Bar regulars drank more and smoked more than any bar crowd I'd ever seen. They also held their liquor better than any other crowd, or at least with a more practiced and put together way of embodying their drunkenness. Maybe all their cash helped sop up alcohol. It helped with tips, which were at least 20% across the board along with a couple of huge tips every day from some of the suits celebrating a big deal that was approved, bought or sold. I was only a bar-back but consistently I made great money. I also enjoyed my fellow bar keepers right from the start. Everything was near perfect, better than expected. It probably could've gone on like that for a lifetime. The thing that changed it all happened near the end of my third week at the job.

Every morning I'd walk to the Oak Bar. I'd climb out of Saloon's basement library and head east on 38th Street to 6th Avenue and then north to Central Park South. I went that way because it was the fastest way to get to work, but more because I'd developed a curiosity about 6th Avenue, the Avenue of the Americas. Living in Saloon's basement for well over a year without a television and avoiding bars and chasing girls left me to reading. I'd keep my head buried in a book so long as it was something that grabbed a hold of my nose. Inexplicably the history of transnational corporations pulled me in. Go figure. Maybe it had something to do with seeing loads of people in this town who I considered dumbbells with money and I was wondering how that was possible. Or maybe it was fascination with a stumbled upon history of something I never knew existed. Or maybe it was because anyone living in New York will eventually become curious about corporations because you can't spit without hitting one of them. There are probably more corporations in New York City than rats. Though getting that count correct would be a mess.

My corporate history reading fit started out easy by randomly grabbing a book off the shelf about the infamous British East India Company and the original multinational corporation that tried to conquer the globe with their gigantic sailing ship organization, the Dutch East India Company. Admiralty law, tall ships, Captain's logs, soaked investments, salvaged manifests and the sea faring trade held me captive. I dove in with a cargo hold of books about early European corporations and the divisive early American corporations and their principle differences that in part led to the Revolution. I made trips to the library for books I couldn't find in Saloon's basement where I bulked up on reading about how in the newly formed States, unlike with corporations abroad, citizens' authority clauses limited capitalization, debts, land holdings, and sometimes even profits, while also limiting corporate charters to a set number of years. I read how the power of large shareholders was limited by scaled voting so that large and small investors had equal voting rights, interlocking directorates were outlawed, and shareholders had the right to remove directors at will. Adversely, on the other side of the pond European charters protected directors and stockholders from liability for debts and harms caused by their corporations. American legislators explicitly rejected that corporate shield. Eventually differences sank to the bottom of the Atlantic and a sea monster arose, the Anglo world order of multinationals and charters and their UCC, Uniform Commercial Code - the holy scripture of international business.

Imagine how empty-headed I felt after randomly discovering the vast and virtually invisible history of global corporatism only to realize most of the world is run by it; like mindlessly working a lifetime on a ship and finally figuring out how water displacement floats the giant box made of 200,000 tons of steel that you're standing on. More than dumb I felt like a sucker. I pressed on, gobbling down a couple of hundred pounds of books. By the time I got the job at the Oak Bar I'd come to the conclusion that a simple walk up the Avenue of the Americas on my way to work would display nearly every fat cat corporate conglomerate this side of the Atlantic. I also could grab breakfast at a Deli I liked on 6th Avenue and 58th Street.

Where the Avenue of Americas flows into the park and becomes Center Dive there's a small square built to honor western ideals and principles and a few of the historical Pan-American liberators from Royal Spanish business domination. I'd sit there on a bench for an hour and mentally review my previous night's reading before hopping over to the Oak Bar. A trio of giant bronze equestrian sculptors set the contemplative perimeter as I ate my bagel and drank my coffee. I'd try to figure out if there was any irony in the statues or was it just a triumphant tribute to an age old parade of cooperative business interests rising up and replacing kings and their feudal system with contemporary corporate rules, settlements and hierarchy. Most days I sat under the hoof of a giant Simon Bolivar on his horse. It was the best seat for taking in the late morning foot traffic with a keen and pivoted view looking pass the Saint Moritz Hotel down the Avenue of the Americas into a canyon of corporate skyscrapers, our supposed modern day world liberators.

Because I'd been pretty much off booze and drugs for well over a year combined with the fresh morning air and the massive amount of whirlwind reading and the incredibly good sleep I'd been having, my mind was in a period of remarkable sharpness and creativity. My metabolism experienced a major intake of vegetables. My old habit of waking up after noon and getting an hour at the YMCA pumping weights had changed to waking with the sun no matter the weather and doing calisthenics like a kung fu monk for a two or three hours in Saloon's backyard. The new regiment enhanced my mind's focus as much as my physic. All pistons were firing, all synapses were supercharged and all senses magnified before most people punched their work clock. Topping off my mornings with a walk up the Avenue of the Americas altered my daytime mental state in the most positive way calculable. Instead of processing my thoughts in a mechanistic, linear and tactful manner I began seeing things through the process of imaginative reckoning. Like the way a heretic ship captain might not rely on charts for his destined port of call and just point his ship in the direction of his nose.

From my Simon Bolivar park bench with the morning sun climbing higher in the early March sky the image of the Avenue of the Americas stacked to the hilt with corporate skyscrapers was vibrant and would easily morph from hundreds of separate buildings into an overwhelming double-sided, unified behemoth business front. I could practically read their common commercial code etched into the asphalt twenty blocks long. The whole of it would awaken with shining newness and then quickly turn fierce and intimidating. I'd stretch my imagination and squint my eyes trying to connect the colossal image to my bench in the small square with its nod to corporate history. When the figment would near burst my skull I'd open my eyes in a flash trying to catch a glimpse of what we might expect from big business in the future before the idea scattered above the trees of the park behind me. The best I gathered was an ever-expanding empire growing rapidly until the globe was entirely theirs.

In the wake of that vision, as predictable as a stone dropping out of the sky, was the visible fear that the empire possessed: the threat of a true free market! I could see the history of their investments in high risk ventures and acts of piracy and espionage coupled with the inelastic demand and relatively elastic supply of ideas and products that were needed and not, and the mass of it was unbalanced by the great many things latched on to the closing balancing act of an unrigged free market capable of leveling all of it to its cheapest margin and setting prices bent on making second rate companies tumble while also ruining all prospects of overreaching growth and unjust profitability. In the low level clouds I could see the empire's panicked decision on how to deal with the unavoidable and adversarial free market. I could hear the historical board room call to form a cartel to confront it and shine a light quicker than the sun on the absolute control of all supplies and all ideas good and bad, right and left. The formation of a global market monopoly was playing its hand above my head.

The Avenue of the America's skyline drew out an inconspicuous plan for a holistic system interconnected with multi variable dependency on their invented dollars; petro dollars, nuclear dollars, war dollars, Fortune 500 dollars, welfare dollars, drug dealing dollars, television dollars, blackmail dollars, big medicine dollars, indulgence dollars, endless dollars. A corrupt international system of money contracting the sum of life in an unnatural order of the world from point blank programming charts and statistical decision algorithms driving silicon solutions for price cost probabilities of multinational transactions and investments. Laid out from Central Park South to the edge of Times Square was a double paned glass, steel and brickwork of corporations ferociously determined by sacrosanct bylaws of a crooked craft and a rigged market. It was an apparition of a one world corporate tower laid on its side like a jagged obelisk being slowly hoisted into an upright position with every common man entitled to one measly share of it and brutishly bound to work for it and the larger share of profit and dividend delivered to a crony hierarchy fueling their wicked dream of eliminating the human ability to decide what is needed, what should be bought and sold, what is right and wrong - all while quelling merit and the spectrum of free human emotions to white noise yearnings and lobotomizing the consequential boredom with the production and heavy handed use of big corporate media.

The Avenue of the Americas was alive, breathing and angry, an advancing leviathan that would leer its sites on me sitting on that tiny park bench with a rabid intent of devouring me for daring to look at it. I'd have to turn my head away fast otherwise I'd be overwhelmed. I'd be caught looking toward Fifth Avenue and I'd stare and begin wondering about the clan of old wealth that occupies that part of town: the monarchs of money, the Astors, the Vanderbilts, the Morgans, the Rockefellers, the Whitneys, the Carnegies, the Fricks and the Dukes. The two parts of this town were related not only by the proximity of Fifth Avenue and 6th Avenue but by knowing one part was old money and the other end was the total production of new. They were connected by investment, insight and the age-old purpose of usury, crooked business, profit and unsubstantiated growth, control and utter disdain for free markets. You could see their palpable connection in the sky when clouds blocked the sun; a shadowed string and lacework of money, smog, grime, crime and glut connecting old and new. It was accessible, bold, disturbing and it had me thinking about climbing up the side of a building and grabbing a hold of the capital strings of revenue and maybe swing through the streets of New York and be a part of it all.

In the broad daylight I was sitting on a bench eating a bagel with cream cheese before heading to a job to clean a bar while so many others were cashing in. I looked down at the back of my hands and noticed the hair was thicker than it used to be. I wasn't sure if it was because I was getting older or maybe I was closer to being an unworthy ape not capable of getting a piece of the establishment's pie. Maybe I was one of the last of the wild humans unable to connect to the materialistic world. Before letting it turn me queasy and filled with rage I'd settle my eyes on pedestrians walking between Fifth Avenue and 6th Avenue. There was relief from the convoluted moving mass. I'd breath deep and slow until I was normal again. That was my routine for three weeks: heavy reading at night; wake up very early for a few hours of hyper calisthenics; a walk up the Avenue of Americas; then drink my coffee and eat a bagel while going through the intense paces of the birth and rise of corrupt corporate gloablism nearly to the point of an anxiety attack. On the twenty-second day I saw Mickey Mantle.

If you can get pass the fact that Central Park is unnatural, its original root system dug up and the land carved out, redesigned, cultivated and manicured to be an idyllic representation of wild nature at its harmonious best, and accept it as a proxy for the realm of nature, you'll have half of what's needed to understand the unasked-for-religion being projected onto all New Yorkers. For the full picture of that faith you need the realm of the city that surrounds the park like a brute's hands wringing a lady's neck. The realm of the brute is also unnatural, carved out of the bedrock and dutifully refilled with brick, mortar, steel and glass and designed to represent what metropolitan man a few times removed from nature is capable of at his harmonious best. Both realms are fabrications standing in for the dualistic vision of the men who built this city; high priests of the establishment with money and the gall to push their spiritual beliefs in opposing forces on the rest of us. If you live in this town it's probably best to come to terms with their stamped out adversarial view of the world. You might think you have no use for it but a black and white perspective will help you properly judge this town and the men who built it. For them, the park represents all that is free, alluring, enduring, wild and unpredictable; while the city blocks surrounding the park represent everything that is planned, organized, admirable, rising and triumphant. Opposing forces, day and night, ying and yang, above and below, beauty and the beast, Dionysus and Apollo, circles and squares, trees and skyscrapers; a religious canon of dualism right under your nose in the middle of New York City. The swell brim of that canon is Central Park South.

The top of a midtown skyscraper would provide an ideal look at the bombastic divide but sitting on a Central Park South park bench was enough for me. A smack of green leafy nature butted against a corporate owned and operated fortress wall reminiscent of castle walls of yore defending against natural incursions of unadulterated freedom. Imagine sipping your morning coffee while sitting on that sacred threshold after a night of reading about the history of pedigree groomed crooks, conspirator business and bloodline money. Flood your head with the opportunities a dark kingdom like that might have if only you could slip through a crack or a small whole in that wall. Imagine you hear a loud call from the top of Rockefeller Center, "Take what you want." It spooks you. You ignore it best you can but you debate the sincerity of the words and it leaves you with shivers. Now also imagine you've been a Yankee fan for your entire life and raised to believe Mickey Mantle was not a mortal being; imagine the only material possession you've held onto throughout your starry-eyed life was a Mickey Mantle commemorative t-shirt from his farewell ceremony at the stadium twenty plus year before; imagine only two weeks earlier you read about Mickey Mantle's Grand Opening Party that had a line of famous people running out the door all the way to Fifth Avenue but since that night the place had remained closed. Was it because they didn't hire you? No matter what you were planning on making it a regular spot for a beer after work. Now imagine sitting on that bench on Central Park South while the corporate history of the world has you choked up with fear, doubt and blistering possibility when suddenly you see the living legend Mickey Mantle walk right pass you.

I could've reached out and touched The Mick on his arm. Instead I watched him cross the street and go into his bar as easily as it was for me to get up from my bench. I stood there looking across the street into the large plate glass storefront trying to keep track of him inside but the sun's glare made it impossible. Then as if wishes were heard and answered Mickey Mantle's storefront transmuted and appeared to be a wide opening in that wall of establishment wealth. A lure, an opportunity to step inside and shake hands with dreams and success. Instantaneously I realized I'd been sitting on that bench for the past three weeks with a true buried intent of seeing Mickey Mantle. It was only a matter of time before I did. The only thing I didn't know was what I'd do after that. I hesitated at the crossroads of Central Park South and the Avenue of the Americas neither here nor there as the pedestrian signal was haywire displaying both Walk and Don't Walk, as if I needed to make a deal in order to move on. I did and landed at the front door of Mickey Mantle's Bar.

I was inside the first compartment of revolving glass door with my forehead pressed up against it trying to get a look inside. The Mick had disappeared into the back. There was a woman standing at the hostess desk talking on the phone. Next to her was a very large portrait of Mantle standing on the steps of the Yankees' dugout with his bat over his shoulder and an easy knowing-I-am-the-best smile on his face. I looked over at the bartender as he was stepping behind the stick. He was wearing the same thing as I was, black pants, a white button-down shirt. He was sorting things out, pushing bottles and glasses across the bar and onto shelves. I could see a few waiters and mostly waitresses buzzing around. When the hostess finally noticed me she put the phone to her chest. "We open at noon," she said it loudly. I wanted to ask her if Mickey Mantle just walked in the door and maybe share some of the excitement but it was a pointless. I was happy to hear the bar was finally going to open. I looked at the bartender again. That was supposed to be my job, that's what I thought. My fists clenched up. I was standing firmly inside the locked revolving glass door like a big menacing rock; it caught the attention of the hostess again. She put the phone down and came to the door. "We will be open at noon," she said as if she was too far away the first time she told me. She was petite and very pretty, a dark haired doll really, and my instinct was to smile, which quickly shook the tension out of me. It also filled my head with words. "Kevin called me, said to get here early." "Kevin?" she asked as she reached to unlock the revolving door. I pushed my way in with excitement. My vision expanded taking it all in fast before I was told to leave. I got a better look at all of the waitresses setting tables, reviewing menus, twisting and turning. With their hair tied back in ponytails and buns, dressed in their short black skirts and white shirts tucked in showing off their thin waistlines they were like a company of ballerinas with the prima gone missing. It was finally opening day and everyone was trying to get organized down to the last minute. The delightful chaos had me salivating.

It dawned on me that I had a real opportunity. They had to have hired more staff than needed because a smart boss doesn't want be left short-handed at the grand opening, and he'd want to see how an untested crew performs on their feet, sort them out. In all I was looking at twenty bartenders, waiters, waitresses and busboys. Five of them, at least, would be cut, sent down to the minors by the end of the day. The manager would need backup. "Kevin doesn't work here anymore," the petite hostess told me with a sympathetic look. I did my best to look confused. I wasn't. I was prepared to face Kevin if I had to, play it off that I received a phone call from someone pretending to be Kevin and he told me to show up; I'd apologize, blame it on a wise cracking friend and then leave; and if I were lucky I'd get a chance glance at The Mick muscling up to the bar with a beer and his lunch. "But he called me two weeks ago," I said, "I interviewed with him. He told me to come today." The attempt at professional concern with tragic tension in my voice was over the top. The dark haired doll didn't notice. Instead she looked over my work attire, black pants and white shirt and tilted her cute head and said, "Oh, well... just have a seat. I'll call the manager."

I sat down on a three-seat row of old Yankee stadium seats that had been salvaged from the real House That Ruth Built. It had me remembering that last game at the old stadium in 1973 when the Yankees lost to the Tigers and how afterwards all of us fans razed and clawed the place to shreds for souvenirs and how my piece of Yankee history was ripped out of my hands on the subway ride home. I looked at the display case behind the hostess stand filled with memorabilia. Number 7, Mantle's team jersey was the centerpiece of the cabinet and it looked amazing behind the glass alongside autographed baseballs, bats and gloves. I swung my head around and took a hard look at the bartender who was bopping around trying to look professional. When the manager finally came up front I snapped to my feet, chin up, chest out, shoulders back, stomach in. He had his hands full with a clipboard in one arm and a bunch of gray flannel baseball uniform styled tops under the other arm. He looked like he had a lot on his mind. I'd been working in bars long enough to have a professional smile and I didn't let it go to waste. Having just had a glimpse of The Mick along with the bevy of beautiful waitresses flying around also meant my smile was foolproof. "I'm Bart," he said with his own reliable smile, reaching out to shake my hand with his clipboard then stopping and smiling again trying to hold onto everything. He halfway looked over his clipboard as if referencing my name but then the effort suddenly didn't seem worth it. "Do me a favor. Kevin is no longer with us," he said it to me while leaning toward me, fumbling, gesturing for me to take the load of gray flannel tops from under his arm before he dropped them. "Pass these out to anyone that doesn't have one already," he said. "What are they?" I asked. "It's your uniform," he said.

An old doctor with a plundering taste for Port wine once told me that every seven years nearly all cells in your body are replaced, practically life anew. By Port standards I spent more than a lifetime at Mickey Mantles. Because of my enthusiasm I did whatever was needed, washed dishes, cooked food, took reservations, strong-arm duty, waited on tables, and for the most part I tended bar. All together, and without an easily swallowed explanation, my Mickey Mantle life was a tragedy without hope, a clichéd' Dickensian experience: "...the best of times, ...the worst of times, ...the age of wisdom, ...the age of foolishness, etc... etc..." I landed at the front door on Central Park South compelled by destiny, permitted entry on false pretense and floated on dreams of arrested youth, parties, heroes and delusions until finally leaving the place years later broken, embarrassed and guilty on my knees diminished by the despicable truth of who I really was.

In early1988 Mickey Mantles opened and was belted out of the park becoming the unpredictable hot spot on that enigmatic Central Park South strip between the St. Moritz and Plaza hotels where a square meal and an amazing bar was a gathering place for anyone in New York notable or worth their spit. Mickey Mantle's was also a tourist's Mecca and I got to meet America and much of the world there. I tended to, joked with, and drank with storied athletes like Muhammad Ali, O. J. Simpson, Reggie Jackson, Don Mattingly, Wade Boggs, Evander Holyfield, Wilt Chamberlain, Patrick Ewing and Michael Jordan; as well as considerable encounters with Donald Trump, Bill Murray, Julia Roberts, Mel Gibson, Billy Crystal, former the Governor of New York, Hugh Carey, and Vice President Dan Quayle. The list goes on. Mickey Mantle didn't own the bar. He was a front man, held a nominal and symbolic 7% share and was under contract for his namesake and a certain number of appearances every year. My real bosses were Bill Liederman and John Lowy. What those two guys did by careful plan or unadulterated delinquency was sit on top of a hugely successful business that became the greatest sports bar in New York City's history. Most of the credit should go to Bill Liederman and the General Manager Bart Alexander. Give John Lowy credit for being lucky enough to be friends with Bill or getting a discount price on bar rags. Bill had the looks, the personality and the brains, along with a magnificent sense of timing to know exactly what New York was looking for in a new sports bar.

I liked Bill right off the bat. Aside from his generosity, his openness and having a great sense of humor, Bill's hands-on approach to restaurant ownership was unheralded. When a place rakes in four or five million bucks a year most owners assume a sort of celebrity status, especially with the ranks of their staff. Bill seemed to reject that notion, at least not embrace it. If you walked in on a busy night there was a good chance you'd see him bussing tables, expediting food orders, or fixing toilets. For a stint he was the toast of the town and there were important people and countless classy gals lining up to meet him, a few trying to corner him. He obliged most them with a sense of duty. But he seemed to prefer waitresses to silk stocking Town and Country socialites. It was no secret that he enjoyed partying with the female end of the workforce, which explained the shamelessly larger portion of the staff made up of the kinder, gentler gender. I, along with the rest of the bartenders, waiters, busboys and cooks greatly appreciated that. Any guy walking pass the giant storefront window appreciated that.

There was a certain prestige to being a Mickey Mantle's waitress and because of that it drew the best the City had. Bill attributed as much of the business' success to the waitresses as he did to Mickey Mantle. Maybe Bill's best talent was putting together the most covetable group of young women ever assembled. They were the type that guys fall in love with instantly; "the beautiful girl next door" as opposed to painted porn stars. That doesn't mean the kittens were missing their claws. They knew how to party as hard as they worked. At one point there was a plan to make a Mickey Mantle's Calendar with waitresses as models. It never happened because there weren't enough months in the year to make good use of all of them. I could've used that calendar because they had me staggering, unable to keep track of the days of the week.

Not many can handle a waitress job, especially at Mickey Mantle's. Taking care of tables requires complex abilities and raw talent. The stress load is up there with brain surgeons and air traffic controllers. An obligatory amount of magnetism and charisma is crucial to approaching countless tables over the course of a workday. Each and every time a little stage show is performed. "Hello (big smile), my name is (Maureen, Paula, Ann, Libby, Sharon, Christine, Katherine, Sherry, Debbie, Fiona, Liz, Bethel, Melissa, Betsy, Zoe, Siobhan, Natalie, Susanne, etc…) I'll be your waitress tonight. Let me know if there is anything I can get you." She's got to deliver that snappy line and hit her mark at every table, every night. A waitress doesn't have to be happy but she better look happy. She can't look too happy either because a flaky waitress can scare away customers. But flakes don't last too long on a job that requires you to bend and twist and pick up plates and drinks all at the same time and not drop anything or let anyone get a good a look up your skirt. Did I mention her obligatory smile?

She needs to be a good listener. Not so much about hearing people's troubles but knowing whether that steak was medium rare or was it Black and Blue or blue cheese dressing on the side or crumbled blue cheese in the salad and extra mayo on the side and no tomatoes and find out if the chef can slice that steak in strips, and if not, cancel everything and make it the lobster ravioli but no cream in the sauce and if there is fresh basil please add it unless you charge for it. You cannot believe how many otherwise normal speaking people suddenly mumble or whisper when it comes time to ordering food. The waitress needs to act as if everything is in perfect working order at all times and the processing of drinks and food orders will fly without a hitch even if the chef is sticking a knife into a line cook's back and the bartender is drunk and the busboy is high on nitrous oxide from whip cream cans. The world is made up of billions of people and apparently each of us is somewhat unique and set in idiosyncratic ways, which means a complete set of unique problems and complications could arise at any given table that the waitress will have to deal with. There are only so many portions you can divide a Cobb Salad into and the waitress needs to politely explain that to the group of six young ladies out to dinner who have a real intention of meeting men who might be able to pay for a more substantial meal. She has to figure out at least four or five different congenial ways to explain to stubborn and relentless customers that it is impossible to serve food that the kitchen does not have. Every time there is a new table the entire set of potential troubles repeats itself, and on busy nights those troubles can be compounded; yet every table still needs to see that same original pitch perfect nod of assurance that you can sit back and enjoy your lunch or dinner because your waitress is in charge. I mentioned her obligatory smile. The waitress has a duty to create and maintain the illusion that the customer she is taking care of at the moment is the only customer she truly cares about, and she needs to repeat that at every table, and at some tables with thick-headed and mollycoddled customers she needs to reinterpret and repeat again and again that affectionate affirming performance. Mickey Mantle's waitresses were masters at communicating with a grin to a customer that he will lose that hand resting on her ass if he doesn't remove it quickly. Some would play the tip angle and

138

THE LAST BAR IN NYC

allow a hand to open enough to get a feel and then she'd slip away with grace before anyone noticed and before he thinks the caress was free. Certainly a waitress is human and can make mistakes like the rest of us but it doesn't mean she's entitled to live with her mistakes like the rest of us. One way or another she needs to fix problems and fix them fast lest it disrupt the great rhythm of her service, which would be hell to pay for because once the momentum of waiting tables slips behind by a minute or two the entire shift may come undone. She'll spend the rest of the night catching up to that rhythm or jeopardize tips on every table after that like a wobbling set of dominoes collapsing one onto the other. She has to be the banker collecting the equitable dough or processing the right credit card for the actual grub and drink at the correct tables. She has to move customers in and out of the restaurant quickly without making a customer feel rushed. She only has two hands but needs to figure out how to carry five plates of food with sides of ketchup, Tabasco, mustard, two extra sets of utensils, extra napkins, a glass of water with no ice, and toothpicks, and serve it all. A waitress needs to make all of her customers feel their personality is magical and witty when you can bet money most of the time those customers are pretty much dull and ordinary. If she's heard one joke over and over and over, i.e. "I'll have the halibut for the hell of it," every time needs to be like the first time. Good waitresses have the hidden ability to maintain a half a dozen deep virtual love relationships with different male admirers on any given night and still not remember any of their names. Mickey Mantle's waitresses needed to manage double that. A waitress has to deal with customers with strange allergies, or stranger food requests and has to answer questions about whether the chicken was farm raised or from a factory or was the salmon free to swim a long, healthy and happy life in the pollution free part of the ocean. Chefs are generally out of their minds and some of them have a sadistic delight in demanding a waitress know every ingredient of every daily special right down to how many grains of fine sea salt was added to the actual dimensions of the tuna carpaccio slices. There are customers who like hearing those diminutive descriptions and they like hearing them so much they'll ask the waitress to repeat them over and over. There are customers who have so many problems with so many types of foods it's a wonder they're allowed out of the house yet the waitress needs to take care of them as if it's the most ordinary restaurant experience in the world. You have customers who say they're ready to order yet when the waitress stands ready at the table the entire decision process will start again as if having the waitress bear witness was required to finally pick a burger and fries. The waitress has to open bottles of wine with care and professional style whether it's Château Lafite or twist-off swill, and the better the bottle the more backbreaking it is to pull that fucking cork out. A waitress cannot complain because there's really no one for her to complain to. Restaurant managers are notorious for disappearing when they're needed most and an owner doesn't want to hear it. If a waitress has any troubles she has to leave them at home, even if her trouble is that she lost the lease to her apartment and doesn't have a home. A waitress can't really get sick because she won't get paid, and if she calls in and can't cover her shift she'll lose her job. To top it off she needs to stay late until all of her closing side work is done, work she doesn't get paid to do. It's a good thing she has that obligatory smile.

All-Star waitresses closed the book on my near two-year effort in Tommy Saloon's basement. My natural drive for booze, drugs and girls was violently reawakened. Compulsively, I tried to bed every one of the young ladies at Mickey Mantle's. The laundry bags filled with table cloths and napkins piled up in the dark corner outside the women's locker room was as good as a mattress sometimes. The ridiculous toothy smile perpetually on my face was evidence that I'd lost all control. I might've been dreaming during my time working there. After all, what are dreams? Each night we close our eyes and slip away from the waking world and enter a richer one. Who isn't fascinated with dreams? They're outrageous events in our lives, bewildering, terrifying, inspiring, and most often downright unbelievable. Try to get your head around the reality of a die-hard Yankee fan from the South Bronx with barely a High School diploma and a longtime ambition of being a bartender getting thrust into the limelight of the greatest wonderland sports bar in New York City. It was rocket fuel for delusions.

140

I'd always idolized Mickey Mantle, at times as a kid I questioned if he was real. After the first couple of weeks on the job my childhood hero knew my name. I was meeting and hanging out with more sports heroes and celebrities than I ever knew existed. The cash flow was incredible. I moved out of Saloon's basement into a nice apartment on West 96th Street. I bought a new motorcycle, new clothes, a new television. Routinely after work I'd hustle my way into the midtown hotel rooms of young ladies visiting New York City for a weekend of fun. They'd stop in Mantles for a drink and I'd masterfully play the part of a real sweet guy waiting for the one and only special girl to fall in love with, and I'd mix it with shots of whiskey and couple lines of coke for the perfect formula for getting laid. The times I might've come up short on excitement the staff at Mantle's was large enough that you'd always find someone to have fun with. To state the obvious, I was no longer sitting on a park bench examining what New York City had to offer. I'd come into my own and took a bite out of the big poisonous apple.

Even with a creeping stagger in my walk I got accustomed to the pomp and circumstance along with anything or anyone Central Park South had to offer. Howbeit, the one individual that kept me in awe was The Greatest, Muhammad Ali. He levitated in the kitchen one night. He was making an appearance at a private party of high-end pharmaceutical executives in the back room. Imagine how much they paid. He arrived an hour late. It was understood because he was Muhammad Ali, and he was disabled - Parkinson's Disease. After a lickety-split appearance he made his way to the front door to leave. Word about Ali being inside Mantle's had already gotten out to the street and the place was packed to the rafters. It would've been the biggest let down in sports bar history if Ali slipped out the back. Instead he shuffled to every square inch of the joint mugging his famous fists-up-I'm-boxing-with-you pose two hundred times or more.

After getting a wagonload of dough to mingle for twenty minutes with the well-mannered corporate drug dealers in the back he'd given away the same goods for over an hour to the plebs up front. When he finished the gratuitous round he grabbed a hold of my arm, pulled me closer, peered into my eyes and struck his I'm-going-to-knock-you-out pose and asked in a broken voice, "Where are the dishwashers?" I told him, "Right this way." The entire restaurant was on pause. There must have been seventy-five people packed into the narrow kitchen and two hundred more spilling outside the door. At the top of the stairs leading down to the dishwashers I yelled, "Get ready, Muhammad Ali is coming." I saw the Ivory Coasters, Boulaye, Mamdou and Abdoulaye pop their heads out taking a look up the stairs and rubbing their eyes in disbelief. Ali waved them up. We shuffled to the other end of the kitchen and cleared out some space near the salad prep table because Ali wanted to address the crowd. "Watch my feet," he said with effort. He repeated it again though he didn't have too because everyone's eyes and ears were peeled.

No other athlete, American or foreign, and certainly no other boxer in history could claim such global popularity as Muhammad Ali. He likely was the most popular man in the world. In parts of Africa he might've been considered more a god than a man. In the kitchen of Mickey Mantles he was the only thing that mattered. With everybody's eyes locked on his feet Ali stood stoically for nearly a minute then began trembling. I wasn't the only one thinking his Parkinson's was in play and he was about to have a convulsion due to all the excitement. But as smoothly as October 30th, 1974 at the Rumble in the Jungle when Ali delivered his famous left right combination and knocked out Foreman in the 8th round, The Greatest levitated in the kitchen. He was two or three inches off the ground. The crowd burst into cheers. The Ivory Coasters had the closest front row view of him and they were in spasms. It was amazing. Though my interpretation of amazing was different than everyone else. At the end of the kitchen where Ali sprouted wings I had the worst seat in the house. I was jammed up against a sink, the only one at Ali's side. From my angle I could see his trick. He'd shifted his weight onto the backside of his right heal and then lifted both feet in a level fashion, save the right heal point holding his balanced weight. No one else could see it. Add the near hysteria of being in the presence of Ali in a packed and hot kitchen and it's easy to understand the heightened mindset for magic. It was truly incredible. Not because Ali levitated, but the way I saw it, he took the entire restaurant with nearly three

142

hundred people and lifted everything above it all.

Charity events were routine and some nights we'd have Star bartenders swinging booze and beer to raise money. If you were a big giver you'd have a genuine Yankee serve you. Mostly it would be me making drinks and the players would be behind the bar joking and posing for photos. As fun as a night like that might sound it was mostly difficult. Ballplayers are generally big and because of that I wouldn't have space to work, and most athletes played ball better than serving drinks. Out of all the Yankees who could find bar work if his baseball career had ever fallen apart was Wade Boggs. He was a better bartender than me. That's saying a lot because most of his career he played for the stinking Red Sox. Boggs had remarkable dexterity. He was grabbing four bottles of beer out of the cooler in each hand and popping them open in a flash with the opener attached to the side of the cooler. He could pull four different drafts into mugs at the same time with perfect heads and not spill a drop. A busy bar with drunks screaming for drinks and autographs didn't stress him one bit. Steady hands, a batter's eye and the hugeness of being a Major League All Star probably explained it. I told him what a good bartender he was, a real natural. He told me, "If you think I'm good at serving beer you really need see how good I am drinking it."

In 1989 the NBA Eastern Conference Playoffs were at the Garden. Michael Jordan was in town playing the Knicks. The Bulls won the first game on a Tuesday night and on Wednesday night Jordan was at Mickey Mantles. He was sitting in the back with a small group. I was so desperate to see him up close that I jumped from behind the bar and rushed into the kitchen when time came to serve his party's dinner plates. I was putting down a bowl of chile for the blonde bombshell sitting next to Jordan and I guess between the easy view of her cleavage and His Royal Airness under my chin I was distracted. The piping hot bowl of chile slipped off the under-plate. Jordan's reflexes were fast and he caught the bowl mid air and saved the blonde's red dress and a trip to Roosevelt hospital's Emergency Room, and probably my job. The chile had come straight from the oven in the bowl it was served in so it had to have burned his hand. Jordan shook it off and didn't say a word about it; though out of the corner of his eye he sized me up as a real doofus. The calamity happened so fast no one made a fuss about it. I was embarrassed and stayed out of Jordan's view the rest of the night. The following night the Bulls lost to the Knicks and Jordan only scored 15 points. I didn't mention anything to anyone at the time but I always thought I should have made the NBA record books for being the only guy in history to hold Jordan to 15 points.

A certain unnamed NFL Defensive Coach who wears a Super Bowl ring and has two others at home was in town with his team playing the Giants. He was getting drunk on single malt scotch at the bar. He'd had a dozen and was completely taken with me. Apparently I was the spitting image of his father in his younger years. He so enthralled he promised to return with his brother so the two of them could drink, smile and reminisce about their childhood. Between the booze and the fatherly look of me he was wide open, blabbing with glee. I asked him a bunch of questions about football players, stadium crowd energy and all sorts of gridiron queries. He answered everything. He also set me straight about the NFL. He was retiring at the end of the season after a long career so I suppose spilling dirt didn't have him concerned. He made me promise to never say where I heard it and assured me there were real tough guys who wouldn't want NFL secrets out of the bag. A father should never break his word with his son so I agreed. "It's all fixed," he told me, "A ring of top owners draw out the Conference champs and the Super Bowl winner before the season starts." I couldn't believe it. "It's impossible," I said. ""It's true," he said, "Sometimes they'll change plans midseason or right before the Super Bowl for one reason or another but it's fixed." I asked him to explain how all the players could be coerced into such a scam and how is it that nobody ever blew the whistle. "I watch the games, guys get hurt they play so hard," I told him. "Owners, refs, some coaches and two or three quarterbacks. Nobody else knows anything," he said, "Those boys do play hard. Some of them will break your heart they play so hard. All you need is a few bad calls, the wrong play called by the coach, or an intentionally bad pass." He had me scratching my head. He asked for his check and paid it, and left me a hundred dollar tip. As he struggled to get up off his stool and turned toward the door he told me, "There's too much money to be made fixing professional sports. It's too easy... Still fun to watch."

The most unassuming celebrity who frequented Mickey Mantles was Bill Murray. His only problem was being a Cubs fan, and not any Cubs fan but a baptized Cubs fan. Once you get pass that baseball blotch, he was a great guy. He'd pop in to watch a game. He'd sit at a table by himself not trying to draw attention. If a customer noticed him and had the gumption to say hello, Bill would chat back baseball banter. If he got along with you he'd invite you sit down and pay for your lunch. If the waitress was busy, he'd come up to the bar and fetch his own beer and remind you to add it to his check at the table and still peel off a couple of bucks for a tip. One time he helped out a waitress by grabbing a tray of beers and carried it over to a table and nobody noticed it was Bill Murray serving them. Often he'd point out a family at a table and pay their check for no reason. One time I ran into him outside of Mickey Mantles on the 57th Street cross-town bus and he recognized me, asked if I was on my way to work, asked what I thought about the Yankees loss the night before. I was baffled seeing him on a bus with him being a rich celebrity and I asked him, "Why are you riding the cross-town bus?" Of course, with a straight face, he told me, "To get across town." He paused and then gave me a look like I was a loon and asked, "Why are you on the bus?"

The biggest twit celebrity at Mickey Mantle's had to be Julia Roberts. She'd come in on Saturdays, early evening. Families took over the place on Saturdays and if you didn't like kids you'd probably do best to stay away till they cleared out. She was fresh from a Pretty Woman box-office breaking week, which had put her on the map as America's new sweetheart. As bright and sparkling as that sounds we all know fame comes with a price. People are going to clamor for an autograph or a chance to say hello. Julia Roberts had her back to everybody. One little girl, maybe eight or nine years old, had planted herself about ten feet away behind a column trying to get the nerve to say hello. Julia Roberts had to have noticed the kid because she was poking around the column like a heavy headed spy for half an hour. When the little girl finally took a deep breath and walked over to the table Julia Roberts

145

snapped back, had the little girl crying as she skedaddled back to her parents. Sealing the deal on meanness America's Sweetheart tracked down that little girl's table and delivered a five minute tongue lashing, an out of place lesson on etiquette. I never watched another Julia Roberts movie after that. Word has it I haven't missed much.

A direct confrontation with categorical rudeness that had real consequence was the night I served New York Governor Hugh Carey at the bar. The place had emptied out before midnight, front door locked, staff gone and the manager busy in the office. I was alone at the bar when his honor slipped in the side door connected to the lobby of the building Mickey Mantle's occupied. The only people that used that door were those who lived upstairs or someone who knew someone that lived in the building. The Governor had been in before for parties and charity events always shining populist to the crowd. Tonight he was wearing a tuxedo, a cigar in hand and his nose was red. He moved to the nearest spot at the bar. I didn't mind staying late because I figured he spent much of his life serving the people. I put down a fresh ashtray and he put down his cigar. He ordered a Martell Cordon Bleu with an aimless smile, took off his jacket and carefully laid it over the stool next to his. The bottle was on the shelf above my head. Wise to the monkey suit I asked, "Park Lane closed early tonight? Or a party upstairs?" Good chance he had friends living in the building and the Park Lane Hotel Bar next door was where Central Park South aristocrats rested elbows for nightcaps. He hadn't responded, smiled obliviously. I put a snifter in font of him and made a stiff pour. I had cleaning to do but I didn't want to give him the impression that he needed to rush so I stood there politely as he settled in. I looked him over, unsure if he was troubled or hammered. "Did you have a nice night?" I asked. "Right," he said with another useless smile. He wanted a menu. The kitchen was closed but there were things I'd be able to run to the back and prepare. There were other things I couldn't make but I figured I'd wait to hear his order before frustrating him. "Here you are, Governor," I said, handing him the menu. He took it out of my hand without looking at me and told me, "Let's keep the chit chat to a minimum, will you." It felt like I got hit with a curveball that failed to break, and I tasted blood. I'd bitten my tongue. The Governor ordered French Onion soup. I went to the kitchen to prepare it for him.

My head grew heavy fast as I went downstairs to the walk-in to pull out the pot of soup and Gruyere cheese. I had to hunt down a leftover slice of a baguette for the floating crouton. My tongue was hurting and for the first time in all my years of bartending I was embarrassed about my position. Hugh Carey was a prestigious Governor of the Empire State at one time and ran in affluent circles, probably had a lot of dough. But up until then the line that divided me and him, us and them, was nothing to me. 'We all put our pants on one leg at time' and all that jazz, that's what I believed. The Governor shooed me away while I wasn't in his face, when just the opposite was the case. My shift was over and I was going beyond to serve him. He might as well have grabbed a baseball bat out of the display case and cracked open my head and jammed the words inside, 'You are a servant.' That lower role between bartender and slave, somebody compensated to be under someone else's thumb, definitively unequal, somebody who could only speak when commanded to do so, a little man. "Let's keep the chit-chat to a minimum," it echoed in my head. I put a piece of ice in my mouth because my tongue was hurting and dripping more blood. I threw the soup in the microwave and slammed the door hard. I fired up the broiler and peeled off a ready slice of Gruyere preparing to melt it over the top of the bowl. The idea of bartending was transforming. The microwave beeped and I took out the soup, stirred it up. With my head over the bowl I breathed in the heat. I was dumbfounded, watching drops of blood drip, disperse and slip into the murky brown slow moving whirlpool of softened sliced onions and speckles of black pepper. I could've fallen into that bowl.

Screw you, Governor, that's what I was thinking. Despite what I thought I should say I was preparing his soup. The man inside my head was not the same man manifesting in the world. That thought sunk to the bottom of the bowl. Why didn't I tell him the kitchen's closed? I picked up the slice of Gruyere to put on top of the soup but quickly realized I can't serve him blood. I wondered if it was too late to rectify my actions with my thoughts, go to the bar and tell him pay up, go home snob. But I couldn't do it. I had a half a thought to give him the bloody soup; a silent, Fuck You! But it'd be pointless, anger pitted against the reality of the Governor happily slurping tainted soup none the wiser. If I wanted to be a real man, not a little man, not a servant or a slave, I should do as I say and say as I do. Duplicity and delusional dissonance is for con men and cowards. Maybe take the high road, I thought. Make a fresh bowl of soup and throw an extra slice of cheese on top. I'd be aligned, thoughts and action, better than him. But I wanted to bring the bloody amalgamation out to his majesty and let him choke on it. "Let's keep the chit chat to a minimum," I couldn't let it go. I also couldn't decide what to do so I didn't. I put two hot bowls of soup on the bar in front of the Governor. "I ordered one," he said with a deer-in-the-headlights look on his face. Like an exaggerated sap with a swollen tongue and dopey grin on my face I said, "Oh! Dat's right. Chef mistake. Pick one. I eat udda one." My impaired speech had the Governor looking at me as if I was a special needs person. I drummed up all the politeness and sincerity I could and told him, "I eat far away." He finished his soup alone. He ordered another Martell Cordon Bleu and drank it. He asked for his check and paid it. I cleaned the bar and went home.

Swallowing your pride can go down as easy as a warm bowl full of beef stock, onions, blood and cheese as long as you pretend it was your intended recipe. Even with a swollen tongue you can learn to gulp down yellow-bellied swill. Continue to improve on the lies you tell yourself and you can start spitting out trouble and vice with velocity and lift to replace your missing spine. When the pile of lies topples and you can't stand straight then tell yourself a whole new set of lies about why it's good to be crooked. Drinks and cocaine will support your baseless cause. Unfortunately, wrong choices will eventually show you who you are. It didn't happen over night but I figured out I wasn't the happy go lucky party guy I thought I was when I first started out at Mickey Mantles. I worked hard, and I was good at my job, but I wasn't more than that. Mostly I was a friendly-faced bull-shitter, a kiss ass doing stupid and nasty things when I should've known better. I stepped on people, used people, let people step on me.

Long ago I had sex with women because we were young, horny and fell into each other's arms. I'd moved on to bedding women with a split tongue whistle, a snake singling out the troubled and desperate. I went as far as securing a wanton girlfriend thrilled by my foulness. Misspent energy, self imposed importance, cheap laughs, boozing and the proximity to fame, heroes and the fortune of others was the theme of my growing cowardly life.

A need for real change was highlighted near the heartless the end of my tenure at Mickey Mantles. Central Park South was dark and desolate. We were closed. Customers and staff had cleared out. The night manager was downstairs smoking a joint. I was already out of uniform waiting for Mabel to finish changing out of her uniform. The replay of the Knick's game was on and I was drinking a beer alone at the bar. I knew the Knicks had lost. Regardless, I watched. Mabel was the red headed older than usual cocktail waitress. A former ballerina for the Cincinnati Ballet Company transplanted to New York City on a passion play for the main stage years earlier. Her leaps came up short and she moved from the dance bar to cocktail bars. It probably made more sense than going home to face a hometown she promised never to return to. She was simple, forty-three years old and alone. She'd kept up her dance routine over the years, which kept her limber, lean. She liked me, a lot. We had sex, a lot. She didn't care if I was a flimflammer. She didn't care if I lived with my perverted girlfriend. She didn't care if I forgot to call her or if I had to change plans at the last minute or if I had anything better to do. Mabel needed affection, hated being alone. Older single woman in New York are desperate, that was my thinking.

The Knicks were in the lead and I was about to go and drag Mabel out of the locker room. My plan was to take her back to her small studio apartment on West 55th Street for a quick fuck and try to make it home to West 86th Street in time to watch the end of the game, and then see how many vibrating things my girlfriend and I could stick between her legs. But that plan wasn't going to work out because someone was rapping on the storefront window with no good intention. I made my way to the front. "Open this god damn door. Drinks! Drinks! Dinks!" Mickey Mantle was chanting. Billy Martin was smiling. I opened the door and they rumbled over to the bar making noises only the two of them could understand. They could barely stay on their stools. I'd seen Mickey drunk before but this time they reminded me of old rummies you'd find curled up on a curb more than Yankee legends out for an infamous good time. Billy ordered a whiskey and Mantle ordered a brandy with kaluha and cream. I asked Billy if he wanted Jameson's. With a debilitated sneer he told me, "I said whiskey," and then asked, "You know why god invented Jameson's?" I'd heard the joke a thousand times. "So the Irish will never rule the world," I told them. They laughed. I laughed. I got them their drinks and thought we'd be having some sloppy fun. I told Mantle, "Real ball players would never drink Kaluha and cream no matter how much brandy you put in it." Mantle took my joke the wrong way, sat up on his stool, put out his chest. He said, "Listen queer don't ever tell a ballplayer what to drink." Billy chimed in, "Get it right!" They both laughed. I tried apologizing. They didn't want to hear it or couldn't hear it. "You wouldn't know a ball player if he was sitting at this bar spitting in your face," Mantle told me, "I ought to fire you." I thought he was going to spit in my face. I tried again to make light of the situation and told them, "If you fire me you'll have no one to serve you manful drinks." Billy laughed but Mantle was grim. "Tell me the top five ball players in history and you can keep your job," he demanded. That was easy. I told him, "Not counting pitchers, you got Babe Ruth, Hank Aaron, Ted Williams, Willie Mays, and you." Billy was shaking his head sort of agreeing with me, sort of not. Mantle told me, "You're fired. Willie Mays couldn't play ball. Without Red Juice he's a minor leaguer. Now get a big dick shoved up your ass." They both laughed loud and hard. Red Juice is old time slang for Crystal Meth and I had to ask, "Willie Mays drank speed?" "I'm saying you're fired queer." He followed that with a loud belch. The two of them laughed more. Billy reminded Mantle how they always drank beer during a game and fair is fair so he had no right to send Mays all the way to the minors for Red Juice. "The Mets are low enough," Billy said. They laughed some more. I laughed; pretty sure Mantle was ribbing me. "Do you want another round," I asked. "Give me another one," Billy said while struggling to keep his head up. Mantle told me, "Why not, you won't be the first queer to serve me a drink." He then barked, "Give me a god dam menu, we're hungry." I gave them menus and stepped down to the service end of the bar hoping to avoid more trouble.

Mabel was finished changing and came over to me. She was upset that I was stuck with Mickey and Billy but saw the shape of them, knew I had my hands filled. She was pretty in her pink chiffon tube top with her bare shoulders glistening, reflecting the soft red from her hair. Mantle recognized Mabel and shouted aggressively, "You're one of my waitresses, come over here!" She smiled and politely followed the order. "Get her a drink," Billy slurred. Mantle immediately grabbed her around the waist, halfway pulled her onto his lap and knocked over his drink. Mabel was startled, struggled out of his slushy grip. Her top was soaked with brandy, kaluha and cream but she didn't say a word about it. I poured her a glass of wine even though she didn't ask for it. She wanted to leave but was caught standing there, obligated. I asked them, "What are you guys gonna eat?" Mantle turned to Mabel and playfully asked, "What's good here?" "Chicken Fried Steak is the house special," she said nervously, "and the Chicken Pot Pie is popular." Mantle then grinned and reached for her again with both arms, nearly falling down, got a hold of her, pulled down her top, had a hand on her tits. She squirmed out of his arms for the second time. In a blink he was on her again. She was looking to me for help. Mantle yelled out, "I want some pussy pot pie." I pretended it was all fun and games despite the honest look of fear in Mabel's eyes. She managed to get lose, though her top was down to her belly. She was pulling it up as she ran to the front door. Mantle barked at me, "Get her." I yelled, "Mabel, loosen up, come back." She was gone.

Billy had his head on the bar. Mantle stumbled to the bathroom. I cleaned up the broken glass and wiped down the bar. I sat on the stool next to sleeping Billy Martin and waited. After ten minutes I went to the john to check on him. He was bent over on his knees beside the urinal leaning up against the wall. It was terrible. My hero, the guy who hit 54 homers in 1961, had hit 536 homers in his career and a record 18 World Series homers had his face planted in vomit and piss. He was covered in it. I wanted to give him a swift kick in the ass and I could have. My ideal vision of him was destroyed. The worst part, instead of giving him a good kick in the ass I bent over and helped him to his feet. I walked him out the bathroom and laid him in a booth. I sat down across from him, buried my head in my hands, too easily pushing back a lame urge to cry. I smelled scud in my palms as I wondered who was more pathetic, Mantle or me.

The First Baseball Game and the Last Prostitute

By 1996 old notions of New York City were near death. The exhausted character that put this town on the map was about to be razed, buried and built upon. A thousand years from now they'll dig up the area and discover that the nineties was a prodigal layer in the family of periods explaining this city. A heroic archeologist in the future might go out on a limb and claim that the nineties was the decade that New York actually died and the times that followed where only years of glossy decomposition when scavengers rode into town in coach seating gliding on jet streams contaminated with servile spores spilling into the streets helping spawn a new population of dimwitted denizens, suckers and saps. Our archeologist will try to illustrate the City's death by revealing the contradictions of lifestyles old and new in the decade with the split seams of debris and retarded antiquities discovered that would appear to have come out of nowhere. If our archeologist is a drinker he might go as far as to suggest aliens from outer space infiltrated city life during this time. He'll ask his peers to better explain the nineties' break away from natural progression and the disturbing developments uncovered in the landscape. One example will be Trump's Riverside South Complex, which will baffle minds for generations as they debate whether it was a housing experiment or a prison complex for white collar criminals or an extravagantly over-budget movie set depicting a faux finish dystopia from the era when people yearned for density and confinement and television was more desirable than life. If our hero is laudable he might explain the nineties as the time of the

153

Great Sickness, a period when men with diseased minds were in charge and began redesigning the city and its culture to reflect a control freak's mindscape. They'll discover that our people, our dignity and our couth had been commandeered and the remnants that refused to take orders were swindled and prodded to vacate the premises and if you didn't the disease settled in no matter how resilient you thought you were. It'll be known as the time when the genial struggle of the City's everyday man was decidedly replaced with a new breed of out of town Disneyworld babies with credit ratings and rip-off college diplomas in hand, and when a marked rise of simple minded identities based on race, gender, sexuality, and willingness to join the corporate collective overwhelmed the mass of unique and diverse individuals throughout the five boroughs. Established cultures, immigrant heritages, a diversity of religions, and people colored from light pink to deep purple were snuffed out and replaced by a new and strange people amalgamated not from roots all over the world but forged from a new world technological concept. In the future they'll decipher a fabricated and orchestrated rise in anti-capitalism sentiment while along the way the town contradictorily transformed into a one-dimensional multinational haven for monopolists and no one caught the grift. The nineties, the decade when New Yorkers lost control, unable to regulate autonomously the living standards and simple creative needs of our population. Computers replaced nuts and bolts and enabled trumped up fiendish money from banking and insurance derivatives rooted and pegged to a floating global exchange to propel absurd financial speculation and greater risks and greater delusions with increasing rapidity across oceans in response to currency valuations while the accumulation potentials extinguished the lines of capital assets of our localized economies. The man-on-the-street's traditional plan of diversified, slow, steady, dependable and earned growth was cancelled and gave way to the birth of 'flipping' apartments for short sale profit. Sending an email became the fabric of our lives and an impersonal force began eating away real identities and undermined truthful individualism and genuine New York character while mass-produced kinky-cool became the new black and chemical flavored vodkas replaced immaculacy. A thousand years from now they'll laugh at the fools who surrendered their input for the greater transnational commercial good and the backwards bizarre world of a supposed and impossible to sustain new normalcy; an uninformed, empty, confused, dazed and finally numb normalcy when a graphic design of life with a vibrant and 'sexy' look was on every corner for the taking. The time when exhausted spirits gave in to the bombardment of reversed truths, cognitive dissonance, denials, omitted information and financial-state propaganda selling a techno-hell of manipulated and weaponized information that was driven into seduced minds with a creeping paralysis. Unforgivable depravity and complacency was born of it.

"If you don't like it leave," that's what Jodi told me. She wasn't looking at me, just sucking on her straw and staring at the two longhaired blonde women licking and kissing on the dance floor. Others were watching the same show. "It's Saturday night," she said and then huffed, "Enough whining." Jodi and I were downtown drinking and trying to dance at Nanny's. Jodi was my girlfriend. Nanny's was a lesbian bar. They had a DJ. We lived together, had been since soon after we met at Mickey Mantle's a few years earlier when she was a waitress there. It was summer and it was hot and Nanny's was packed with aroused and sweaty woman not at all happy about me dragging my feet in their club, obsessing and being a nuisance. My Jack and Coke was missing the rub and I was pretty sure it was intentional.

I was trying to tell Jodi that I used to think we were like Bonnie and Clyde cruising, on the lookout for mischief and carousing with femme fatales for fun in the sheets but now it was clear we were like dogs in heat roaming the streets. I badly wanted her help in explaining why almost a year had gone by and I still couldn't get Mabel's bathtub drowning out of my head and why did it barely seem to faze her. I wondered if she could explain why we treated Mabel like a pornographic experiment? We both knew she was over trusting, too casual with her pride and desperately lonely and if taking on both of us meant a minute of attention or an ounce of affection of course she was signing on. We hurt a woman who did nothing wrong except yearn for her lowly share of tenderness and loving companionship in a City that had outlawed those notions for simple, passive women over forty. I didn't have it

155

in me to ask Jodi if she loved Mabel for a minute during the whole affair? I wanted her to tell me how we could jump right into another three-way with fresh-to-New-York wide-eyed Lana while we were still sorting out Mabel's personal belongings and the grim water was still pictorially in the tub. I never told Jodi how poisonous I felt when Lana disappeared in a panic after learning about Mabel and the fact that we failed to mention suicide. I was worried about Lana and how was it possible that we have no way to track her down when we had sex with her for months. I wish I could've told Jodi that I was a creep and thought she was creepy, selfish, shallow and I didn't think either one of us were meant to be like that, and we should stop.

Jodi wasn't hearing any of it because she was desperately into Madonna and Erotica was blaring over the speakers. "Let's finish these drinks," I told her, "I want to go home." "You go," she snapped, "I'm staying." Finally - I might've said it out loud. It was an immediate, immense and terrific relief not to be needed. I made my way to the front door trying to avoid the intense stares I was getting from the bulls after they saw how pissed off Jodi was. Lesbian bars are obviously different than other bars, they're filled with females, many of them quite pretty, some of them tomboys and a lot of them bulls. Some bulls are bigger and meaner looking than a lot of dudes. The bulls were especially territorial and a straight dude in their bar prodding a bodacious female across the dance floor was like pushing a porterhouse steak in front of Rottweiller. Just get to the door, I thought. When I stepped outside onto 7th Avenue the hot and stinking muggy night slapped me in the face hard. I had it coming.

I moved out of Jodi's place into a tiny, incredibly low priced studio on West 81st Street. We remained friends because we both had our breakfast a couple of days a week at the Columbus Avenue Bakery. There were other places for coffee but I guess we didn't mind running into each other, and more to the point, Jodi was in need of a stand-in for her parents' routine visits to the City. A craven and forlorn ex-boyfriend on her arm was less complicated than having one of her new girlfriends along. Her parents were good-natured and her younger brother Sheldon was goofy, a bit backward, but not a bad guy. Confused guilt about whether or not I was responsible for Jodi's crossover passion mixed with free high-end restaurants and Broadway Shows made joining her ruse a troubling yet palatable obligation. By that time Jodi was no longer a waitress because she'd finished Law School, which was right before we were finished. I'd quit Mickey Mantle's soon after that because going to the place where the three of us had worked turned from an eight-year good time routine to agony on my own. My fellow bartenders and the waitresses were shocked by Mabel's death, it had them looking at me as if I was covered in open sores. Everyday was progressively humiliating. I crawled out of there.

Timing couldn't have been worse. I got word from my old friend Demetri that Tommy Saloon was dead, killed in a strip club out in Jackson Heights. He was sitting at the bar when the place was robbed, had mouthed off to one of the punks, got punched hard and knocked to the floor. He was 96. A broken rib punctured a lung, dead before the ambulance arrived. Demetri also informed me that Saloon left me three grand in his Will, which had me feeling like I'd been knocked to the floor. I hadn't visited the old man or called him in over six years. The money was a you-are-a-loser confirmation. The light in my head suddenly dimmed and my life path of growth hit the end of the road. I began experiencing myself as being neither wonderful nor downright evil but as a low and struggling, too often confused, inane and blasé human being. I was able to perform life's basic tasks of feeding, sparse cleaning, and minimally tend social interactions but below the surface my heart was out of action, filled with rancid guilt and grief. Normally when you fall into a rut it's practically impossible to find new work, and work was the medicine I needed. Instead of looking for a job I spent a couple of weeks holed up at the Holland Bar or Rudy's in Hell's Kitchen drinking my inheritance, trying to retrace my roots to see where I'd gone wrong, hoping someone might remember me, remind me of who I was. Eventually bad timing played out again the other way when I missed an uptown train and stumbled on the platform into a young lady I once had pursued and failed to catch. Some women are natural saints and Sarah Fabricatore was one of them. The shape of me compelled her to hook me up with a part-time job a few nights a week at the Park

Avenue Country Club. The hint of pity in her eyes was disturbing but she was so pretty my pride was distracted. Saloon's dough was also gone and I couldn't turn down the work.

In the past whenever slipping into the Blue I'd respond aggressively by chasing down as many women as I could and ejaculate my way out of the sad sack. The hint of confidence that the new bartending gig put under my belt helped me devise a radical new plan that was going to act as shock treatment to put me on the up and up again: a life altering sex fast. I was going to hold out until my botched head was screwed on straight, years if I had to. It'd also serve as penance for wronging Mabel and put an end to my ripening perversion. Kill the root so I could get back to normal pleasures between a man and a woman and back to drinking for fun instead of gloom. In a mortification ritual I changed my Hell's Kitchen drinking location to the bars surrounding NYU were the naïve scholars famously drank a lot of woozy shots of willingness flavored with tequila and got naked faster than average. With my constraints loosened I'd see how long I could go without hitting on any of them and reject any offers that might've come my way. When temptation was too much to bear I'd disable myself by getting fall down drunk. I thought it was a good way to build myself up. If I were up for a dose of hostile punishment I'd go to The Westpark Hotel bar.

The Westpark was Mabel's bar. It was far from fashionable. In the past whenever Jodi was at her parents' home for the weekend Mabel would drag me there for drinks because she was always on the lookout for her old time friend, Patricia, who frequented the joint. Ballerinas from the Cincinnati Ballet Company partnered up to make the journey to New York with Lincoln Center in their sights. The times Mabel might've had a dream about Patricia she'd be frantic for me to take her there. "Patricia will never be tied down," is how she was explained. That meant she didn't have a permanent phone number or home, always had to be hunted down. They had been best friends but by the time I entered the picture they mostly led separate lives. According to Mabel, Patricia was the better dancer and it confounded her as to why she didn't make it to the big stage. After finally meeting Patricia one night I tried to explain how cocaine changes plans all the time and if you throw heroin in the mix it should be easy to understand how she opened the wrong stage door and stepped onto a stripper's platform and then onto Midtown corners luring strangers for $100 bucks a throw instead of grand battement with pirouettes at the MET.

The Westpark Hotel Bar was a hooker bar. Not a strip club but a bar in the lobby of a hotel across the street from the Coliseum on Columbus Circle and its business was primarily based on the shows, events, and conventioneers hosted there; which brought in the Professionals working the nighttime corners between 57th Street and Central Park South. Considering I was ramped up with a sexual impairment, had cash in my pocket and a passionate promise to myself to refrain from screwing you might think I was nuts for going to The Westpark to get drunk. But I was living a vacuous martyrdom and the bar was the best wet-repository for expelled pain from love lost memories with the added challenge of easy pay-for-sex sitting on the stools next to me. I wasn't completely out of my mind. I'd only drink there on Sunday nights because conventioneers were back home with their wives and kids and hookers usually took the night off leaving more space for sad contemplation.

A few ladies worked on Sundays but it was not a routine for any of them, which meant a random selection of Professionals on view. They'd sit at the bar and have a drink to rest their feet or duck out of the rain or kill time between johns or try their luck with me. One night I was nearly alone drinking and manic about what I could've and should've done to change Mabel's mind about emptiness, kinky entanglements and a bathtub filled with sleeping pills and vodka. Before I ordered my fourth Whiskey Soda the bartender out of the blue grabbed his cigarettes and tips from behind the register, a bottle of Smirnoff from below the bar, and left with the blonde in purple fishnets and eight-inch stilettos that had been chatting him up for the last half hour. I sat solo finishing my drink, chain-smoking, obviously cheerless. When I was ready for another I poked my head through the side door connecting the bar to the hotel lobby and asked the desk clerk for help. The hotel's night manager, not too happily, stepped in to serve me my drink. She asked me what had happened and I told her what I knew.

Instead of blowing up about it she changed her attitude and laughed. She then asked me, "Do you know any good bartenders?"

Working Sunday nights boiled down to me behind the bar and a number of Professionals on the other side attempting to communicate their troubles to me. With any luck a bit of variety would walk in the door; maybe a salesman who missed his flight and wasn't keen on getting drunk alone upstairs in his room; or a husband from one of the apartment buildings down the street sneaking in and explaining to me that his wife was away till Monday morning and he needed to act fast and discreet. I'd buy the lonely hotel guest a round to keep him for company and I'd tell any husband that he was in the right place but I wasn't a pimp and if he liked I can sell him a drink and because I was a real bartender everything is discreet. The only Sunday night regular at The Westpark aside from the rotation of Professionals was Sister Mary Hugh, an honest to goodness prioress. She'd pop in for a minute or two about once every three or four weeks.

Sister Mary Hugh didn't wear a black and white habit. She wore dark slacks, navy blue blazer one or two sizes too big, and a white dress shirt buttoned up to her ears. Her hair always tied up in an ungraceful bun as it likely had been for half a century. Old enough for retirement but she was still running a halfway house in Chelsea for teenage prostitutes. She'd make the rounds throughout the city at night looking for lost girls. Typically she'd order a coke, maybe bum a cigarette, eyeball the ladies around the bar and then ask me if I'd seen any underage girls. I tried my best to explain the difficulty in determining a girl's age when they come in dressed to the hilt with heels and all the makeup and their hair done. She had told me, "You'll know them when you see them." She'd hand me a business card hoping I'd call her if I saw something and then leave.

I made chump change for the bar shift but I was going to The Westpark to drink my bereavement in the presence of hookers anyway so why not make a couple of bucks and get a load on for free. Also, the way I landed the job felt like destiny, made it more meaningful, had to be the only place with a chance to unwind my screwy sexual practices and my bad doings with Mabel. I didn't have support of any sort to help me think otherwise. Walking to and from work was the only grateful and sober act I had going for me. Because I'd bottled up my libido tightly whatever oozed out of me must've been less toxic. Something should explain why the Professionals felt safe around me. After I guaranteed them I wasn't gay, which was challenging after turning down their steep bartender discount, and after hardly explaining my triangular-heartbreak redemption plan, they warmed up to me. One of them, Odyssey, a skinny Puerto Rican girl named Chacha from Spanish Harlem who wore electric blue contact lenses that looked painful, she told me, "You're weird but cute."

I was very good at standing behind the bar drinking, smoking and appearing attentive. The Professionals obviously liked the practice because they kept returning more and more regularly to vent. Though "vent" barely describes it. Venting would describe something sensible, as aggressive as it might be, it'd be something you could get your head around. Between regional accents and their erratic mode of speaking it'd be tough to say any of them spoke English. They'd throw fits in the middle of delivering their complaints as if the villain of their story was standing in the bar. They had no gage, opened up with every last detail of their wronged lives. Some nights I'd have to break up a fight because more than one girl at a time wanted my attention and they had trouble figuring out that I was going to be there until 4:00 AM with plenty of time for all of them. As weeks went by they only grew more demanding. I'd keep an eye on the clock if they were lined up to state their grievance and give them about a half an hour each.

I wasn't happy with the routine. Take eight or nine cats and douse them with a gallon of lousy perfume and grab them by their tails and swing them around as fast as you can while standing in a very small room without windows and a locked exit and then let the kitties fly. It was worse than that. You can never honestly say that you've heard it all until you've stood behind a bar lined with hookers yapping freely about the unjust world for hours on end week after week. Unfortunately I made a commitment for punishment and change and I was going to ride it out until I dropped. All was not lost. Sunday nights at the Westpark helped me realize some lives are mind blazingly more fucked up than mine. It also extinguished any trace of a candid view of the world I might've had, left a grimy and gritty perspective after hearing how many of the hookers were abused by the men in their lives that were supposed to honor and protect them; fathers; grandfathers; uncles; family friends; teachers; rabbis; priests; neighbors; and a bus driver. I'd say it was a direct correlation to their careers.

The world according to a gaggle of midtown prostitutes drunk on phony champagne and cheap, sweet, colorful drinks was ultimately puzzling with layers of complex and hyper-vocalized nonsense illustrating how incredible it is that some people can survive day to day when everything in the book says they should be dead. If I could break down the character of the Westpark Professionals for easy consumption I'd say overall they were overloaded with stress and it had caused serious defects. Aside from their traumatic upbringing and their present drug and alcohol addictions and the fact that they permit complete strangers to deposit feasible toxins into their available orifices, I can sum up all their troubles and their inability to solve those troubles as lacking basic communications skills, primarily communication with themselves. For starters they possessed a strange and irrational way of dealing with fear. They'd jump in a taxi or car or go to a hotel room with a potential psychopath after repeated instances of getting beaten, raped and robbed, but they couldn't face their mothers to sort out parental mistakes or make a phone call to their fathers to tell them to fuck off and die. Moving on from general childhood traumas and accepting responsibility for the adult portion of their lives wasn't in the works. They were brimming with exaggerated emotions and concepts connected to all of the wrong things. They'd react to stories in gossip magazines about Royal families luxurious troubles or a Hollywood star's tumultuous affair as if they were in significant relationships with those tabloid faces. They lied constantly, unless it was possible that Bruce Willis and Denzel Washington were having loving, passionate affairs and private jet trysts with at least a half a dozen West 58th Street hundred dollar hookers.

A very large breasted and very blonde Professional flagrantly named Lucky who only wore every shade of blue from her eye shadow down to her heels strung out an excited yarn one night about her true calling in life. "I am going to become brain surgeon," she said as a matter of fact. Inside her platinum head simple concepts like time was too much to grasp, today could be yesterday or tomorrow. She had the game Operation as a kid and won often because at 8 years old her hands were steady. She explained, "As soon as I get some money saved I am going to Medical school." She was oblivious to finishing high school or a attaining a pre-Med college degree. All of them were completely unable to sustain their attention or manage appropriate physical reactions to emotions. A not so pretty Haitian girl, who likely was a man, occasionally spoke in tongues. She spelled out on one of her more grounded nights that woman are more inclined to being possessed by demons, and beautiful women even more so. Fleshy magnetism and voodoo might've helped explain why a strikingly pretty black girl named Diamond who could wear a leopard print mini-dress with a more natural fit than any big cat imaginable would routinely burst into tears after talking lovingly about her sister and then begin punching the sides of her head and the top of bar until her knuckles bled. She'd scream with a desperately sad tone in her voice, "I don't want to jinx my baby sister's life. I don't want to jinx my baby sister's life," over and over until she petered out to a quiet sobbing facedown on the bar. They were always coming down with a cold or just getting over a cold, and they all had chronic constipation. Their massive anxiety explained why most of them were drug addicts. "My mind flips faster than I can keep up with," was a common self-evaluation. They all shared bad childhood experiences with other children. They had a poor ability to regulate their mood, never on target, either too excited over silly things like new shoes or unconcerned with things with real consequence like their babies being raised in abusive institutions and foster homes. They had a grave inability to generate solutions to interpersonal conflicts other than vendettas. There was absolutely no willingness to explore and take on growth challenges. They lacked insight into themselves and others. The rare chance they did observe themselves they'd remain on the fringe like watching a hockey game from the rafters with a beer in each hand. Without fail they all questioned their bar-tab at the end of the night and every last one of them were lousy tippers.

Mabel's friend Patricia would come into the bar every

month or so. I'd have to reintroduce myself every time and remind her who I was. She'd always ask how Mabel was doing. I'd tell her that Mabel passed away and she'd respond with a far out look in her eyes, "That's too bad." Track marks must've caught up with Patricia because she eventually stopped showing up. I guess it goes with the degenerate territory. I was far from a shining example of anything much better but there I was sticking with my punishing plan because I needed to expel my demons, and the truth is that as much as the Professionals drove me nuts my demons still wanted to screw at least half of them. So I drank. I smoked. I listened. Word about my free grievance sessions had gotten out and on some nights regular New York City women that for some inexplicable reason were associated with the Professionals would come to the bar. The friend would be dressed as conservative as possible lest I mistake her for a hooker and she'd order a white wine spritza and say, "My friend says you're good guy to talk to." She'd then gripe about her frigidity or her suspicions about her boyfriend or husband, or most often why she doesn't have a boyfriend or a husband, or why does she need to have a job when deep down all she really wants to do is have babies and move to the suburbs and bake cakes.

The curious thing with all the ladies, Professionals and their friends alike, I didn't talk. Nothing. I wasn't playing the part of a Zen monk or anything like that. I just didn't know what to say to them. I'd listen with a serious and glum look on my face because I was depressed. If it reached the point where I couldn't listen to it anymore maybe I'd nod a few times with a changed look of concern. The times it was too much to bear I'd tell them something simple like, "You're going to work this out," or I'd ask, "What sign are you?" I didn't know squat about astrology but you cannot believe the overwhelming majority of hookers and New York City gals who live by it. It always blew my mind when one of them would tell me, "Thanks, you really know how to talk to a woman." The Professionals and their friends' real problem was they didn't have anyone to listen to them. I filled a void like a block of wood with ears carved into the side of my head. It was something but I should have had more to offer. Underneath it all they were beautiful woman simply coming undone from a crooked and abusive world that left them without legitimate relationships and it was wrong and obvious. Had the world been honest, they wouldn't be suffering; they'd be bonded with standout men.

One of those standout New York gals, a lady who worked for Mademoiselle Magazine, sat down at the bar. She had me baffled because she had it all: intelligence, sense of humor, looks, beautiful body, humility, success with a career, a Gramercy Park apartment, the works. I was amazed that she was associated with one the hookers but with all her mouth-watering qualities I was more shocked that she didn't have a husband or a boyfriend or a lover. That's what she was griping about, loneliness. She ordered a white wine but didn't touch it. I lit her cigarette but she didn't smoke it. I was compelled to finally speak and ask her, "What do you want out of life?" She exploded with every answer in the intellectual, hard-edged feminist handbook; female empowerment and accomplishment sliced and diced and served up loudly. It was exhausting listening to hundred different ways of saying, "I am woman. I am strong." My next question to her was, "What do you need?" Silence, not a single word, no smart answers, no answer at all until finally she gave a reluctant and quieted, "I have no idea." It started her crying. It felt like I screwed things up. I thought if she could come up with an answer for anything it'd help. "What do you know about men?" I asked. "That's problem," she said, "I have no idea about them either."

I didn't have anything else to say. I failed horribly. She was despondent. I might've asked her out for a date if I wasn't a weave away from being a basket case. If I had it in me I should've given her some dreamed up, ideal spiritual view about how women are intelligent, compassionate creatures who can be amazing mothers, sisters, wives and partners to good men. I should've been able to give her simple and humble down-to-earth advice and explain the human bond between man and woman, love, intimacy, compassion, gratitude, acceptance, respect, commitment, integrity, trust, modesty, care for another. I should've told her that carving out a career in New York City makes no difference at all when the bottom line is men and women are supposed to be together in loving relationships and anything other than that is unnatural, a setup, a delusion, a con. How in the world can anyone think power, domination, earthly material success, selfishness, competition, fear, hatred and suspicion toward each other will produce anything other than emptiness and unhappiness?

Loneliness is hard on everyone. Despite what you might think about pouring drinks for a bar full of yapping Professionals Sunday nights were always the loneliest night of the week for me. The rest of the week wasn't much better. My silent Sundays were mostly attributed to being dumbfounded and other times fearful of saying what might've been on my mind. All of it dug a deep hole of solitude. Add what I learned about the onerous and steeped road too many women have to travel on and just how close Mabel likely came to living her life as a prostitute, and the fact that I played no positive role whatsoever in her moving away from that direction or toward any positive direction, all of it was moving me closer to being a forgotten cause. The nearly year and a half that I'd gone without sex was mental and physical torment. I'd developed chronic Charlie Horses in the back of my thighs that were unpredictable. The pain was welcome. I deserved it. It's just that I'd suddenly have to spring straight up on my feet and quickly bend over reaching for my toes to stretch out my hamstrings and too often the screwy Professionals thought I was bowing down to them in some surprising and honorable moment. They were that ridiculous and I was too stymied to explain otherwise. I was drinking all the time and I'd turned exclusively to brown liquor. I was smoking three or four packs of Marlboros a day. I'd lost weight and it wasn't planned. On the upside I was beginning to fantasize about a life spent with one woman, a sane woman, a woman who I could hold in my arms and care for, any woman who could hold a sensible thought in her head for more than a minute. It felt like progress.

I needed to remind myself routinely that I wasn't giving up on sex forever, only till I was normal again. I was backed up with buried heat. Aside from the fever of puberty, I'd always felt going a cappella, pulling on my joint in huffs and puffs till I creamed was peculiar, odious, something monkeys and apes do. Nothing compares to women's hips that'll leave you feeling like you contributed something original to the world, no matter how you ended up there or how long you lasted. Every aching week I

166

thought about peeling off some doe for a roll with one of the Professionals. Any release of my manhood, a wet dream or maybe irresistible true love finally walking in the door would've been a prodigious painkiller. Those chances were slim and nil. Nights when thunderstorms hadn't been forecasted were especially excruciating. The Professionals, without umbrellas, would come crashing in and fill the bar. Their silky, skimpy, candy colored outfits drenched and clingy. Some would strip off their dress to dry on the radiator and stand there in spiked heels and a G-string. Crudeness would swell in my crotch and thrust head first into a hoard of complaints, pain and nonsense.

The miracle happened on a miserable rainy night. Almost a dozen Professionals were yapping at the bar. A blood vessel in my left eye popped just as I heard the front door open and close with a thud. Sister Mary Hugh was standing there, wet. She had a hesitative look in her eyes, like she might sit for a while. That had always cleared out the ladies in the past and this night rain made no difference. The substantial wooden crucifix always around the good Sister's neck probably explained it. She was taking off her raincoat and inspecting them up and down as they grumbled in unison filing out the door. A quiet conversation about anything other than dumb hooker jive had me salivating. Earlier in the week I had a short and hectic conversation with myself on the subway and it scared some straphangers. It scared me. I knew it was from a breach in routine speech. I quickly considered lying to Sister Mary Hugh, tell her I saw a thirteen-year-old with a black eye wearing a short school skirt and red patent leather pumps. A wind gust pushed open the door, sprayed some rain inside and hurried the good Sister over to the bar. She ordered a coke and delivered her usual, "Have you seen any underage girls?" She was pasty, nearly as white as her starched shirt, had to rest her hands on the bar to settle them from trembling. "You feeling okay?" I asked. She told me, "I'm fine." I said, "You catch a cold? The flu? ...You don't look 100%" She told me, "Migraine. I've had it since this morning." I brought her a glass of water. I wondered why she hadn't stayed home. "Isn't there a pill for that?" I asked. She said, "The side effects are worse." I said, "I think they have an operation now." She told me, "Once in the rare while I'll have a Rob Roy." I

167

told her, "Then you should have two." I jumped to it. The Professionals' grievance committee had sent a scout pass the front window to see if Sister Mary Hugh was settling in at the bar. All of them were probably down the street huddled under some scaffolding. "A small one, please," the good Sister said, "I still have to take the subway up to Hunts Point."

I took special care making it for her and told her it was on the house. "No, no I can pay for it," she said. "Believe me," I told her, "it's for a good cause." She was smiling like I'd seen a lot of people do when they honestly appreciate their drink. "Rob Roys are tasty, especially on a rainy night." I told her. "Oh they can be good any night," she said. She took a big sip and let out a sigh of relief. "Works that fast?" I asked. "Anticipating the comfort," she said. A big gulp and it was nearly finished. I made another one and poured it before she could finish saying, "No... Oh, well, maybe I'll just have half... Until the rain let's up some." She then straightened herself on the stool and adjusted her shirt collar and told me, "I have miles to go before I sleep." She giggled and then informed me, "That's a Robert Frost quote." I told her straight-faced, "Is that the night train conductor up to Hunt's Point?" She laughed again and told me, "Oh, you're funny." The good Sister was tipsy, having a little fun. It was the most fun I'd had in the place since I started working there. She was simple and pleasant. It brought out more of the Jane Doe in her, less of the nun. I offered her a cigarette and lit it up. She proceeded with her Rob Roy in tiny sips. I smiled. She smiled.

Considering she was out on a horrible rainy night with a migraine doing a payless job I started wondering if she was like me in some way, carrying out a penance, doing something we don't like to make up for earlier wrongs. Maybe Sister Mary Hugh was once an easy lay with a penchant for the party life and a progressively dwindling concern for others and consequences. Or maybe the good Sister was chasing down underage prostitutes because she'd been one and was trying to save lost girls from the misery she lived through. Maybe her mother was a Professional. Maybe it was something else altogether. Trying to make polite conversation, I asked, "Sister, what do you do in your downtime?" She arched her eyebrows and straightened her look at me.

"Downtime," she said, "It's not like I'm in the Union." Of course, it's not a job, I thought, it's a calling. "Even in a thunderstorm when you got a migraine?" I asked. I was honestly interested. How often do you get to talk to someone who does what she does? She smiled and told me, "You have a compassionate heart." She went on about life for her is not divided into downtime and uptime. She said, "Everyday is Judgment Day." Aside from the brief time she spends eating and resting she's carrying out good deeds, or as she put it, "The work G*d has put me here on earth to do." I told her, "That's incredible." I'd come to a similar conclusion, though with far less devotion, and not really connected to good deeds. "My purpose is to serve drinks," I told her. I didn't tell her I hadn't consulted G*d on the matter or that I'd always made sure to carve out a healthy portion of time for carousing. Though the last year much of that allotted time slipped into the scenario of me crawling home to watch television till after sunrise in a heartless trance with a pack of cigarettes, a big glass of Jack Daniels and a joint or two.

Hearing the good Sister's creditable affirmation mixed with her Scotch Whisky, Sweet Vermouth and Bitters had me wondering about what motivates people like her. I had to ask, "When did you know you wanted to be a nun?" Without hesitation she happily exclaimed, "When I was five years old. Christmas Eve." I told her, "How poetic." She agreed. "I'm from Saint Charles Borromeo Parish in Detroit," she said, "I was sitting in a pew between my mother and father listening along with everyone as Sister Gayle McCormick sang The First Noel." I told her, "With a name like that I bet she was a good singer." The good Sister smiled with her eyes and told me, "A very good singer." She continued, "Our church was full of grace, white marble, Cathedral ceilings, an uproarious pipe organ. Sister McCormick was our Parish pride, kind, generous, a very pretty woman. By the time she was halfway through The First Noel I couldn't contain myself and started to sing along." I told her, "I know the feeling. Joining the fun is hard to resist." She told me, "Yes, that's true. In fact everyone in church couldn't resist and started to laugh, lot's of laughs." I said, "Fun is contagious." She told me, "Sister McCormick 's laughter resounded most. It was different, unlike anything I'd ever felt... Of course I cried." I told her with a dug up tone of seriousness, "I could imagine." She told me, "The entire congregation quickly hushed in unison." I said, "Probably trying to save a bashful little girl from embarrassment." The good Sister told me, "I wasn't embarrassed. I was touched by all of it, Sister McCormick 's voice, the organ music, the caring community, the laughs, our splendid church, my loving parents. The solidifying silence was a divine affirmation giving my heart a hug." Something was wrong with me, a broken drum, depletion, it was something more than my sad state resulting from a lifelong run at parties. I told her lifelessly, "So you knew just like that." The good Sister lowered her eyes some to a humble glare at the bar top. "It was a personal experience," she said. Unintentionally a doubtful tone resonated in my voice as I told her, "Absolutely, Sister."

The thing is I appreciated hearing her story. It was generous of her, and soothing on my hooker-pummeled-ears. My heart was simply worn out. I wanted revival and didn't want to miss a beat so I told her with quickly stirred up enthusiasm, "You can't imagine the routine talk that goes on here, Sister." Her eyes brightened a bit, she took another sip of her Rob Roy and another drag on her cigarette, and then like an old chum of mine she asked, "When did you know you were born to be a bartender?" I hadn't connected to the good Sister's Christmas rapture but regurgitating my life would've interrupted the griefless female voice at the bar. I kept it brief. "I guess I just ended up a bartender." She said, "Well, you're a very good bartender. Your Rob Roy is sincerely delicious. And you've always been very professional and polite to me. Not like other bartenders in similar establishments." I told her, "That's nice of you to say Sister but the bigger difference between me and those other bartenders might be that they probably like their job." She lifted her head. "Oh," she said, "You don't like bartending?" I told her, "I love bartending. This place is the spear in my side." She was about to take another sip of her drink but stopped and slid the glass away an inch or two as if she'd maybe had too much or decided to change her pace. "Is it the money?" she asked, "The hours? Is your boss difficult?" I explained to her, "It's the customers, Sister. The ladies." In her line of work she'd come to know more Professionals than me. "They are challenging," she said.

170

It dawned on me that the good Sister was authentic, being open and honest. I hadn't been able to recognize it because comradery had been long missing in my life. She was extending a real invitation for straight talk. I started to wonder about explaining myself. Who knows? I thought, maybe this was my chance. If I heard myself yap simple and direct about the muck I'm stuck in it could clear my head, speed up the self-repairs and I'd finally have the reason to get out of this bar. Normally it wasn't my style to open up to customers but I'd done my fair share of listening. More excusable, Sister Mary Hugh was less a customer and more like a Game Ranger in a Catch and Release program trying to corner underage prostitutes at the bar. Plus it was her calling to deal with others' troubles. With a fast rising sense of enthusiasm I told her, "Sister, I actually don't need this job. I could work somewhere else. My work here is penance."

I went on straight to explaining what had happened with Mabel and Jodi and Lana and a lot of other women and how I needed to right myself with sex. "Sister, I hope I'm not offending you. It's just that you come across as a nice lady and I thought it be best to be honest instead of beating around the bush." She had one hand on her raincoat hanging over the stool next to her like she was getting up to leave and told me, "It sounds like you have a medical issue. You should visit a qualified doctor. Soon." I quickly tried to defend myself as she turned to the front door, "I'm trying to get straight, trying hard. Isn't confession the protocol?" She hesitated, her head rolling with thoughts, and then slowly turned back at me. She took a small breath. "If you refrain from graphic details," she said not so happily, "we can discuss it further." I told her, "I'd love that because the thing is I realize what's wrong with me. Immaturity for one." She said, "I'll say." I went on, "I like women plenty, always liked them, but the older I got the more I just wanted sex with nearly everyone of them I laid eyes on, and not just regular sex but ridiculous sex. It's like I was coming down with a fever that took a years to boil over because I wasn't always like that, Sister. It started as playful impulses but turned into a gripping compulsion. I let go, acting out sexual whims, twisting the idea of pleasure to be at odds with myself, imagining that violating my conscience would be the maximum thrill, even heroic. It has to stop. I just don't see how the world could carry on with warped inclinations like mine."

The good Sister looked up like she had a belly full of me, and it wasn't mixing well with her Rob Roy. I was wondering if she thought her migraine had taken on a human form and was serving her drinks and telling her dirty stories she didn't need to hear. I would've bet she wanted to get off that barstool and walk out regardless of the wind and rain. But she was a nun and already committed to charitable attendance that was clear. I told her, "Sister, I figure suffering through sorrowful memories and serving nutty hookers that I'd like to screw is the best way to get straight. Balance out one sufferable thing with another sufferable thing. You know, crime and punishment." She took a breath and squinted her eyes, figuring things in her head, seriously confused or seriously concerned, or both. I was blustering, "I'm old school, Sister. An eye for an eye' and all that." She reached for her Rob Roy and took a sip of as if it was more important than all previous sips and looked up at me from her glass, staring. I thought I should calm her in case she was thinking I was a nutjob. I asked her, "What would Jesus do in my shoes?" I must've said the right thing. She laughed. After hearing what I said about Jesus I laughed too. I don't like sandals and certainly he has bigger feet. "What I mean, Sister, what would Jesus tell me to do?" She perked up with a clear look in her eyes, finally confident with something to say. "That's simple," she said, "Turn the other cheek."

Having gone to a Catholic School I was familiar with the Christian credo. I couldn't say I really agreed with it. I always thought Jesus was a great guy and I always imagined if he ever came into a bar I was working at he'd definitely be the nicest guy in the place. Here's a guy who would give you the coat off of his back; the guy who turned water into wine just when the party was about to flop. Who wouldn't want to buy Jesus a drink? I'd make a toast with him. "To the good life," I'd say, and likely be saying it to the best example there is. Still, Turn the Other Cheek, it always sounded to me like you'd be enabling the bad guy. I told her, "I don't know, Sister, sounds cowardly. Not a real solution for the trouble that got your face slapped in the first place." She told me, "Well it's not cowardly. It's the opposite. It's about being a human instead of a brute. It's about the action you contribute to the world. It's about justice." I didn't want to get uppity and tell her she was beginning to sound like one of the screwball Professionals. I wanted to remain sincere. I told her, "Turn The Other Cheek, it sounds like abuse. You let a bully get away with slapping people around he's only going to hurt more people. A brute needs to be stopped. Besides, what does it have to do with me having a healthy relationship with a woman?" The good Sister sat back on her stool and tugged a bit on her shirt and jacket. She said, "Turn The Other Cheek doesn't mean defenselessness. It's a metaphor!" There was a surprising new sharpness in her voice. She told me, "It's a Christian's duty to defend yourself and to defend the innocent. Jesus told his disciples to sell their cloaks and buy a sword if they did not already have one." I would never have guessed that one. "The Prince of Peace?" I asked. She explained that Turn the Other Cheek is the way a human should respond to mindless, brutish acts. "I don't follow you Sister," I said, "how is it defensive?" She told me, "It means you do not repeat the savage act of an attack." She looked me in the eyes seeing that I was still confused. She said, "There's a saying you're probably familiar with, 'You don't kick a man when he's down.'" I told her, "Yeah, only a scumbag kicks a man when he's down." She said, "That's it. That's what Turn The Other Cheek means. You defend yourself but you don't act, as you said, like 'a scumbag.' Rise above gut instincts and earthly forces of material balance because it does not apply to the human soul. Eternal justice is a human need and understanding it is attainable. Praise the Good Lord for showing us the light." Well how about that, she's right, I thought. Something so simple and I'd misunderstood it. It's a shame it took so long. "I understand, Sister. I get it," I told her. "Do you?" she asked. "Don't kick a man when he's down. Of course," I told her, "Someone attacks you and you defend yourself. But once the scumbag is contained you don't start torturing the bastard. You only put an end to the fight. It can't get any straighter than that." She then told me, "You know that applies to yourself as well." I asked her, "What do you mean?" She said, "Kicking yourself while your down over the mindless things you did in the past will not accomplish anything except more grief, pain, and more confusion. You need to be sincere with yourself, completely truthful about the life you're living and the wrongs you've committed, take responsibility for your actions and your thoughts. Ask for forgiveness."

My Sunday nights at The Westpark came to an end and I caught a glimpse of my old copious self. There was a shot or two of me left in the bottle. Not much but being distilled in New York City and packing a punch at 160 proof meant there was enough of me alive to keep an edge. I could move on from wrongs and imperfections, strive to better. I decided to throw a little bit of my born again weight around and get the rest of my week in order. Having been labeled the sad sack bartender by the staff at The Park Avenue Country Club forever excluded me from relationships with them other than charitable ones. That wasn't going to work anymore because somehow Mr. T's motto, "Pity the fool," had become a succinct chime in my head. My shifts were paying my bills and then some but I no longer considered it gainful employment. The place was simply too much to embrace.

A glorified sports bar and banquet hall and radio and television studio. We had satellite dishes on the roof and two dozen giant screen televisions and about 60 plain large televisions throughout the place. There were televisions in the bathrooms that guaranteed there wasn't a bad seat in the house. A seating capacity of 600 people, twenty-foot high ceilings and a long and wide corridor separating the back from the front with a game room in the middle for virtual golf and shooting basketball and a pool table and darts. Too much to drink and you'd swear you saw a small roller coaster somewhere in the joint. On Friday nights tables and games were stowed away and the Park Avenue Country Club turned into a Hip Hop nightclub. Stiffs in suits lived vicariously through televised sports stars during the week and Friday nights were packed with everyone from housing projects pretending to be rap stars. Close your eyes tight, eliminate the pay scales, iron out the vernaculars, switch back and forth from scotch and beer to gin and juice and you'd swear you were serving the same delusional customers. I was finished with delusions; and the necessary drive to blend in with a room of sports feigns had faded to zero. I couldn't fake anything anymore.

Sarah Fabricatore couldn't fake things either but didn't

need to. A bartender, our shifts matched one day a week. With her being so pretty, all heart and never one to pity the entire time I worked with her she'd been the only glimmer of what I could be if I kept right with the world. I'd met her two years earlier when we moved in and out of a small circle of overlapping friends. It hadn't taken long before I was ousted from that round for being a hound. Like everyone else she'd heard the stories about Mabel and Jodi and other women. She cut me slack when others cut me lose and set me up with the job because she wasn't the type to string a noose. There was no romance between us, at least no intrigue on her part. I wished I had my act together at the time because I would've liked to be her boyfriend. She was precious, a good drinker, a talented poet, a great bartender, and best of all she saw right through me. The idea of not seeing her anymore was the only hard part about leaving the Park Avenue Country Club.

I gave my notice the evening a guy came in wearing a replica of a vintage Chicago White Stockings baseball jersey. His cheeks were round and the shirt was tight. He ordered a Coors light and told me he was from Naperville, Illinois, outside of Chicago, and his name was Jim. He'd read in a tour guide that we had Best Time Sports Trivia Game Consoles and if it were true he'd like to have one. We did and I gave it to him. It was an electronic sports trivia game system that worked by flashing questions and a multiple-choice selection of answers on one of our televisions at the bar. I set him up with the game console, turned on the television and went back to cutting lemons. It was about two minutes past 5 o'clock and I still needed to get the bar setup for the night. Within a minute round face Jim called me over again and asked me to adjust the color of the television because the lettering of the trivia game was yellow and it was supposed to be neon blue, and he knew that because he'd played the game in many other sports bars across America. I fixed the blue and went back to my lemons. Within another minute Jim called me over again because he thought it was essential that I know why he has played the Best Time Sports Trivia Game in sports bars all across America. "Why?" I scantily asked. "I've just finished visiting every Major League ballpark in the country," he said, "I drank a beer and ate a burger at sports bars in every city with a ball club. Every respectable bar has Best Time Sports Trivia Game." Park Avenue Country Club was the last stop on his odyssey. I told him, "That's great," and went back to my lemons.

Within a minute Jim called me over again because he wanted to tell me exactly why the Park Avenue Country Club was the last stop on his trip. It wasn't because Yankee Stadium or Shea Stadium was the last ballpark on his itinerary. "Did you know the first official baseball game under the established rules was played by the Knickerbocker Baseball Club of New York in Hoboken, N.J., on June 19, 1846?" he asked me. "No," I told him, "I didn't know that." I tried making my move back to my lemons when he interrupted again: "You know that only means one thing." I had to give in, "What is that? Jim. What does it mean?" He went on, "The earlier Knickerbocker Baseball Club of New York must have practiced somewhere else, almost certainly using the same official rules." I told him politely and with a bit of enthusiasm I could drum up that it was quite amazing that Knickerbocker Baseball Club of New York must have practiced somewhere else and then went back to my lemons.

Because the necessary focus required for cutting lemons was now floating around ballparks across America and through the annals of baseball history I cut my finger. As many people know lemon juice in a cut stings like a fucker. "You'll probably want to rinse that," Jim shouted from the end of the bar. My hand was pretty much under the faucet already. He hollered again, "I bet you're wondering how I know all that." It was clear Jim needed attention and he wasn't going to let me slice lemons and it was my part of my job after all so I sucked it up and went over to him. "Tell me Jim," I said, "How do you know about rinsing a cut covered in lemon juice?" He opened his eyes wide as if somebody had woken him from a nap. "No," he said, "I meant the baseball information." I told him, "Relax Jim, I'm pulling your chain. Tell me, how do you know all that stuff about baseball?" He shined and laughed over the fact that he was getting on with me, and happy that I finally gave him center stage. "Rare Book Division of the Chicago Public Library," he said, "You'd be surprised about all the stuff you can learn in the library." I told him, "That's what I hear. We have a nice library here in New York. It's worth a visit if

176

you're up on Fifth Avenue and 42st Street." He said, "Maybe I will. But at the Chicago Public Library I found a another interesting reference in the 1885 edition of Appleton's Annual Cyclopedia, which said that the forerunners of the Knickerbocker Baseball Club of New York played on a lot on Fourth Avenue as early as 1842, which is four years before the first official baseball game in Hoboken." I told him, "Well how about that. Baseball has some deep New York history." He said, "Well back then it was called Fourth Avenue but today it's called Park Avenue South." The smile on his face was pure; happy about what he discovered and even happier that he could share it with the world. "That's right," I told him, "Fourth Avenue now blends into Park Avenue South after Union Square." He swallowed what was left of his Coors Light in one mouthful. "Oh, there's more to know," he said, "I found an old book by a sports reporter who wrote for a few different New York newspapers. It was published in 1866." He then reached into his pocket and pulled out a piece of paper with a photocopy of a page from the book he was referencing. "In the book it said that 'during the years of 1842 and 1843, a number of gentlemen, fond of the game, casually assembled on a plot of ground on 27th Street.'" He was smiling brightly at this point. I told Jim with a genuine surprise in my voice that we were on 27th Street. "I know," he said, "This morning I was downtown checking real estate records and the Harlem Railroad was built right down the middle of Fourth Avenue. That means that the forerunners of the Knickerbockers were playing on the only available lot on 27th Street and Fourth Avenue. I found that lot. I'm not sure I could prove it in a court of law but I don't think everyone will disagree with my logical assumptions that baseball started at 381 Park Avenue South. The very spot that this bar is located." I told him, "Well ain't that something, Jim. You're a regular baseball gumshoe. You just won yourself a beer." I reached into the bin for another Coors Light and did my best to dig down under the ice for the coldest one I could grab.

I was happy for Jim. It was something else to realize we were in the spot were the very first baseball game was played. But I wasn't fooling myself any longer – sports were truly trivial to me. More meaningful was Jim's persistence in telling his incredible story. He put me over the top. Here's a guy pursuing what he wanted out of life and he did it with passion and proficiency. I was about to turn forty years old and there was still some passion inside of me and I was professional. I put the Coors Light down in front of Jim and told him our burgers are great and I usually order one with everything on it and if it was okay with him I'd like to buy him one. "I've never turned down a free meal and I see no reason to change my ways now," he said. His face resembled an eight-year-old boy on his birthday getting a great present, it gleamed a light on me, made me smile, think of something genuine, a crystal clear purpose. It was time I opened my own bar.

DRINKS, SMOKES and the COOL WAR

"I bet it's like throwing blade," Immanuel offered advice on opening a bar. He had his black pearl handle Stiletto out, switchblade folded, showing it off, wheeling it between his fingers with a piano player's dexterity while he talked. Immanuel was an old friend of mine. I say friend lightly. He was one of those guys built out of iron and testicles and "I'm gonna rip that guy's head off" was his maxim. I was one of the few guys he didn't want to murder. We didn't have much in common other than in the eighties we'd often stumble into each other at 3:00 AM at Rudy's in Hell's Kitchen and snort cocaine in the back corner booth, and both of our mothers were named Constance. I hadn't seen him in over ten years. Earlier I was down at the Rector Street DMV renewing my driver's license and Immanuel was on line in front of me. He looked the same, the same monstrous scar on the back of his big hard bald head, same hulking back and shoulders, same barrel chest, same crooked nose and slippery glass eye not quite the right color. I'd guess he was over fifty at the time and still looked like he could run through walls. He suggested we have a drink. I suspected he'd already had a few. It wasn't quite noon but I thought why not. It was August. It was hot. I had a lot of work to do but an afternoon drink sounded like an energizing break, and if I remembered correctly Immanuel didn't like it when somebody turned down a drink with him. We walked up to Puffy's on Hudson Street because we were both headed that way. We were sitting at the back end of the bar near the dartboard. I was drinking a beer because I had to work with power tools later on. Immanuel

179

was drinking vodka neat because he had a job interview for a laundry company in an hour and didn't want to smell like he'd been sitting in bar all day. I didn't say a word about his new sense of responsibility.

"If you want to kill some cocksucker," Immanuel explained, "and not just piss him off by getting your knife stuck in his leg, you gotta know what the fuck you're doing. You know, concentration shit." He was right. Since my partners and I picked up the keys to the front door and with the amount of shit that needed to get done concentration was quintessential if I hoped to open the bar by the end of October. "You gotta know how to hold on to it," Immanuel said while gripping the knife a few different ways, "know how terrifying it looks in your hand, the power." He tossed the Stilleto back and forth a few times from hand to hand so fast that you might've thought you saw two knives in the blur. He shouted out for another vodka and then asked if I was buying. "You gotta know where you stand," he said, "How you gonna pull it out." Put it away, I was thinking. We were friends but I was hoping he'd stop playing around with the knife because switchblades and Immanuel had a history of popping open at inopportune times. The bartender was looking at the two of us like we were crooked. Immanuel shot back the vodka in one swig and quickly asked for another one, a double. "You gotta use your imagination," he said, "Think about the blade in flight, how it's gonna penetrate. You gotta size up your target, get'em in your sights. Sometimes you gotta hit moving targets. If you don't know the lethal spots you're fucked and you'll end up losing your knife. Or your bar!" He popped open the switchblade to make his point and held it up in front of both of us as something immeasurably more valuable than the $25 bucks he probably dished out for it. "You getting me?" he asked. I told him, "Sure. If you want to run your own business you have to be 100% prepared, experienced and you need to go for the kill otherwise your target might turn and run at you with your own knife and maybe slam it into your chest." He smiled and laughed. I easily noticed he was missing a number of molars in the back of his mouth and I hadn't remembered that about him. He stopped short of laughing too hard because either his mouth embarrassed him or he remembered that he built his whole life around not laughing too hard. "Yeah," he said as he folded back the blade, "But don't worry if you fail. Just empty your liquor room and throw a party for your friends and declare bankruptcy. Or make sure your insurance is paid up, give me a call and we burn the place to the ground."

It was strange, in the past sitting anywhere near him felt like you were sitting next to a volcano, but sitting with him in Puffy's there was a newness about him, something humble, maybe a bit of tenderness had seeped in. Subtle but noticeable in the tone of his voice and the way he sat back on his stool. I'd remembered him more stone faced, elbows on the bar, and always pissed off at someone. He sounded like he had real hope for me. "You got it right, plan for the kill, fight to survive," he said, "Make use of all of your knowledgables. There are things you know just because you gotta brain, like no matter what no nobody gotta teach you how to open a bottle of beer if your thirsty for one. And then other things you know from experience, like what bottle of beer to drink. You gotta use everything in your head."

He pushed his stool away from the bar giving himself more leg room confident that he had given me good advise. The half smile on his face had him looking like somehow he paid off a debt even though for the life of me I couldn't tell you one thing he owed me. Immanuel was the type of guy who didn't owe anybody anything. I was picking up the tab for the drinks but it didn't match up to his unusual delivery of what seemed to be an obligatory life lesson on bars from the heart. He stretched his arms above his head like he was ready for a yawn and maybe ready to get up and leave but instead he flicked open the switchblade, twisted around quickly and violently threw the blade at the dartboard behind us and nearly fell off his barstool in the process. Helter-skelter. I nearly fell off my barstool because he scared the bugaboo out of me. He completely missed the dartboard by a foot or more and had thrown the knife so hard the blade was buried into the sheetrock midway up the handle. The bartender yelled immediately, "Throw that knife again and I'll have the cops in here!" Immanuel was laughing to himself as he went over to pull his knife out of the wall and told me his last bit of advice: "Drinkers lose their bars. Critical thinkers hit their target."

I was critical about a lot of things related to opening a bar in New York City primarily because most of them fail within the first year. The one thing I wasn't critical enough about was partnering with my ex-ménage-a-trois playmate Jodi Dingleberg and her little brother Sheldon. Diverging means of coping with life's dramas and sexual dispositions hadn't prevented Jodi and I from staying connected since our break up. My stand up time as her stand in boyfriend for her parents peace of mind coupled with her knowing my ability to get any job done was enough for her to be drawn to opening a business with me. She was perceptive. She was also potentially ruthless, and, to put it nicely, she didn't have an even-tempered attitude. She had money though and I didn't have enough. Sheldon didn't have a reliable ounce of bar experience, appeared to still need somebody to wipe his ass at 26, and hadn't a clue about New York City. Recklessness aside, me, Jodi and Sheldon, or as I refer to them, Team Dingleberg, we opened Circa Tabac in November of 1998. The bar was homage to the culture of smoking, drinking, harmony and mature ambiance. It was a critical and adversarial venture from the start.

We ended up in SoHo on the conduit to the Holland tunnel concealed in an exhaust filled shadow two blocks north of Canal Street, a ridiculous location to open a bar. I originally scoped out a juicy spot in the Meat Packing District. The 1998 going rate for rent in that neighborhood was a steal and I was betting the area was going to be developed into a legitimate nightlife district worth its weight in gold. You could see the changes going on as the City enforcers began clearing out the S&M Clubs, cracking down on drug dealing and transsexual prostitution, and when a couple of high end boutiques catering to deluxe trendies began staking their claim in the whereabouts of 14th Street and 9th Avenue. Getting word from a buddy of mine who tended bar at Balthazar that his boss Keith McNally was going to open a place in the Meat Packing District was like getting insider-trading information. Team Dingleberg had no way to comprehend changes in New York City ahead of the curve because they were from the supple part of New Jersey, from the persuasion that makes up that slow, sheep-minded curve. I was shot down and horn blowing, car fumes, road rage drivers heading home to New Jersey, and a small army of stealthy squeegee guys was our new doorstep outside the Holland Tunnel. It almost didn't matter because everything nearly fell apart before we opened the door.

Jodi had started the corporation without my name on the charter and signed the lease on her own. Team Dingleberg pulled a fast one, had a meeting on the QT and the original corporate papers with my name on them were never filed because they secretively felt the bar I'd named and was in the process of erecting should be a family business, their family. She informed me after I finished demolishing the old store and laid out much of the work for the new bar at the cost of supplies. They no longer wanted the agreed upon 1/3 share for each of us and offered me a 5% stake. When I rejected the offer and left Sheldon in charge of finishing off the construction, final design and potentially the future management of the place Jodi changed her mind in a sorry minute. So did I.

Team Dingleberg's double dealing and their true capabilities in being productive partners in what I was hoping to be a swank bar in SoHo were far from favorable. I didn't want to risk anything other than my time because odds were against us getting along let alone succeeding in the uber competitive New York City bar business. Figuring on giving it a year for the experience I settled for 20% take and not a dime more invested, along with the important stipulation in the agreement that Sheldon and I would always have equal footing. I wasn't going to get stuck with a pampered dolt who didn't know the first thing about bars barking orders at me inside a liquor stocked half ring circus with the tent collapsing on everyone. Jodi had professional capabilities and bar experience but considering she was already practicing Law and the Team Dingleberg investment would be hinged on the boy incapable of paying his phone bill on time or navigating the subway from 96th Street to Canal Street I should've demanded my full 1/3 share just for having me on board, maybe more.

We had a haughty Opening. I thought it was a bad move. Spending thousands of dollars on a publicist's fee and the cost of staged popularity parties with limitless booze and food for a group of the publicist's friends who would never become regulars was a ransom for fictile smiles and a promise to get the word out that our bar was the hottest new spot in the City. Promise was the key word and all expenses paid nights of fun for hyper-trendy yes men and women was the only guarantee. It made no logical sense because our publicist, along with all other publicists in the City, in order to sustain their business need to say the same thing about all of their clients' glistening new bars. We paid big money to get screwed with a chintzy blurb in a New York magazine and the deadweight of a professional support group of moochers and ass kissers. I didn't like having my ego stroked and trumped up promotion went against what I believed. Just build a great bar, provide appeal and customer satisfaction and you wouldn't need the polished publicist's ploy that'll only get you lost in a glossy wash. I put together a standout drinking hole and even though our location on the Holland Tunnel conduit was maybe as bad as it gets my plan was for my curious SoHo neighbors with their built in influence to inevitably discover an honestly comfortable place for drinks. The money spent on a publicist and Opening parties would've been better spent on an unprecedented and guaranteed-to-be-influential buy-back policy of every third drink on the house until we built up a loyal customer base.

With Team Dingleberg stacked against me I learned fast that my way to operate the business was going to have to struggle and/or manipulate for its right. That approach was tolerable because my partners, especially Sheldon, liked to have hot air blown up their ass and that made the cursive craft a breeze. I was compromised but everything was less complicated. I'd make the boy wonder-less think any good idea or practice came out of his hollow head instead of mine. Things went swimmingly when I started referring to the man-child in a playful way as "Genius." It was easy for me to surrender things like that because I wasn't going to let my pride get in the way of Circa Tabac becoming a memorable New York City bar. A throwback to the bygone era of jazzy indulgence, a mahogany, gold toned and tobacco stained art deco bar and lounge with classic palm motifs, flapper girl iconography and smoking-culture memorabilia beautifully appointed throughout the joint with a hint of tasteful tiki, and all of it dedicated to the spirit of liquor and smokes with friends and affable strangers sitting in plush clubroom chairs and cushioned full back bar stools while being served stiff drinks with

184

unpretentious service at an incredibly fair price.

The first 30 days after opening a bar you'll identify some of the major mistakes you made. I guarantee you at least the heat or the air conditioning is screwed or the computer system is on the fritz. Our first minor trouble was storage space. We didn't have any. After I struggled to convince Sheldon to try out his great idea, wink wink, to use the little closet in the back of the kitchen for storing dry goods, liquor and the 150 types of cigarettes we stocked rather than a pointless micro-office with his nameplate on the door, our storage problem was relieved - not solved. Our first real and ruinous trouble was our staff. Because Jodi actually bought into the publicist's hype that Circa Tabac from the first night it opened was going to be a packed with high end fashionable drinkers running up outrageously large bar tabs we'd hired about 35 cocktail waitresses, bartenders, busboys and cooks; 25 more on staff than I thought we'd ever need even in the best of business times. After our coming-out publicist's parties we were left to fend for ourselves inside an empty bar with 35 employees getting paid an hourly wage. The only good thing about not having customers meant no tips so most of our staff problem solved itself within the first three weeks - they all quit. Startup money evaporated just when rent and every other bill were due. We sat down and reevaluated everything. Sheldon, wink wink, came up with an emergency bare bones approach. I was going to bartend and take care of tables seven nights a week and we decided to fire the cooks and stick Sheldon in the kitchen. We wouldn't draw a salary because there was none to be had and we'd do our best to live on tips I collected and shared. We kept on one busboy, Rudy, to help out on Friday nights with the rare chance of getting a rush and because he worked for a pittance. Sheldon and I ran the joint top to bottom and Jodi popped in at the end of the week to go over the barren books.

Sheldon turned out to have a knack for cooking. The problem was he was the filthiest chef in the city. He'd spill, slop and drop everything and chain-smoke while preparing food. He'd defy gravity with mess because there were repeated times when for the life of me I couldn't explain how dense and heavy gobs of honey mustard sauce and fist sized hunks of butchered meat scraps

185

and chicken fat ended up stuck on the 11ft high kitchen ceiling. Somehow he turned out a spiced filet mignon on croissant that was worthy of praise along with other tasty bites and he did get all of the food out while it was hot. The new setup added to my responsibilities because I'd have to hop out from behind the bar every hour or so and run into the kitchen to empty Sheldon's overflowing ashtray in case the Health Department stopped in and also perform a whirlwind cleanup whenever he made an order of crab cakes or spinach dip or anything just so the pile of mess by the end of the night could be more manageable.

More than saving money on a cook, Sheldon was exiled to the kitchen to keep him out of the public eye. He was not horrifying to look at, just far from delightful. If you're familiar with Charles Shultz's Peanuts cast of characters then imagine a tubby, balding, kosher version of Pig Pen with overgrown tobacco tinged fingernails wearing an unbelievably crumpled and sauce stained black sports jacket, stretched out faded black t-shirt and filthy jeans with ripped up black sneakers, and a perpetual cigarette in his coffee stained mouth. He didn't shower. He was the last thing you'd expect to see when thinking of a young buck 26-year-old downtown Manhattan bar owner and more like a forty-year-old porter working in a greasy spoon out in Newark. Still, the most important reason for his back of the house sentence was his lack of couth or any real life experience and personality. Sheltered by his mother for too long with his namby-pamby New Jersey upper-middle-class life of privilege, which he hadn't made good use of like his barrister sister had, and instead of having real friends as a teenager and attached himself to a group of suburban kids who'd only have him along for fun as long as he was the one paying for the fun, well, all of it resulted in Sheldon's mental and emotional outlook having an air of peculiarity.

The times Sheldon would get up the nerve to come out of the kitchen and happen into a conversation he would feign an amalgamated personality forged from late night R-rated cable television shows. If there were woman in the mix, he'd turn on a crass and bizarre Catskills' comedian shtick cracking the same uncomfortable joke out of nowhere about how every woman's best friend should be a foot long dildo named Dr. Strangelove, and then go on and on over and over about how he's really into necrobeastiality. "What's that?" some unassuming young woman would inevitably ask. He'd reply with a poor attempt at a Humphrey-Bogart/James-Dean impression that unfortunately ended up sounding like Mae West: "It means I like having sex with dead animals." Everything out of his mouth revolved around foul and pubescent exposition. Fortunately, most of the time it went in one ear and out the other because people often enough don't listen. Once in a while an attentive customer would hold back a surprising look of shock, roll their eyes, bite their tongue and realize they were talking with a juvenile schlemiel.

1999 finally settled into a slow grow year of 90-plus hour workweeks and hardly a dime to live on. I could've bailed on Team Dingleberg but I was committed for one reason: running the joint I put together turned out to be working ecstasy. I was motivated for exceptional service and discerning drinks. The few after work regulars were quality patrons seriously pleased with what they discovered. It was mostly those working in the area or anyone finding their way in SoHo and in need of a drink and smoke without feeling like persona non grata. A mix of struggling artists and successful artists, small shop owners, a sampling of fashionistas, architects and designers, entertainment lawyers, a few Union hall members, and a couple of office girls. The late night scene was more curious. It was strictly SoHo inhabitants. There'd only be three or four tables and a handful of people at the bar, the lights were low, candles were lit, and nobody worried about a job. A cool cat named Loic affiliated with the music industry donated music CD compilations and it made it easy to get into the swing of things with bootleg tracks of Thelonious Monk and classic jazz sets from inside small venues in Kansas City and tape recorded Big Apple jams from inside uptown apartments along with the complimentary and rounding out sound of indie soul, funk, rock and smooth hip-hop that hadn't been annihilated by thugs.

The bar was on the down low to start so you can imagine how easily it turned into an invisible universe for a select circle of late night chums when the Holland Tunnel traffic died down after 11 o'clock and our little street disappeared from the map. The night owls loved the nonchalant atmosphere, the drinks and service, and mostly the intimacy and privacy of the place. That soon led to downtowners like Kate Moss, Heath Ledger, Michael Stipe, Carmen Kass, Bono and The Edge, and their famous friends discovering a comfy spot free from gawkers. The nocturnals' mood was no fuss so I stuck to my bartender's code of ethics and gave them what they wanted. They enjoyed cigarettes, drank beer, cocktails and Martinis, not as much champagne as you might think, and they smoked a lot of marijuana. They were mellifluous with zero risk of a snitch calling the cops so Circa Tabac held up a laissez-faire attitude: Smoke'em if you got'em.

Our powwow-puff-puff circle of famous-face friends became a late-night marijuana routine for those in the know in SoHo. The only flaw was the late night gang wise to weed wasn't large. In 1999 and 2000 our average drink price was $6 bucks and with anywhere from ten to at most thirty limelighters sitting around till 4:00 AM each having only two or three cocktails and smoking four or five joints and drinking a dozen glasses of water we weren't making much money. It was nothing compared to what a cocaine crowd could drink and spend. The celebrities did eat food but not as much as you'd expect from marijuana smokers. I suspect it had a lot to do with keeping slim for the spotlight. The bit they ate did mean more work for Sheldon. He wasn't happy about that because for his whole life he generally was unaccustomed to moving his limbs. Plus, after longer than a year of endless work hours under his big belt, Sheldon was coming undone; especially anxious over the idea that our patrons were thinking I was the sole owner of Circa Tabac. Sheldon should've rested his nerves because I never volunteered bar ownership information to celebrities only caring about a convenient and comfortable high outside of their living rooms.

By early 2001 we did our best to keep the penumbra over the glow of our late night weed scene but as the old saying goes, "If you tell two friends and they're high, and they tell two friends and they're high, and so on and so on and higher and higher," eventually the moonlight spills out. We pulled off an outlawed magic trick; Circa Tabac became a bona fide Celebrity Marijuana Club. The group still wasn't large but consistent seven days a week. We should've charged a membership fee because no one would've argued. A handful of nickels in my pocket weren't much but I felt like a great success. There are not many things I've yearned for other than a comfortable pillow, three squares, and the opportunity to be in a bar with mostly good people. I could've been happy if things kept on like it was for a lifetime. Putting a drag on my merry, however, Team Dingleberg wasn't as cheery. They were drooling and desperate for big money and a taste of fame and thought blowing the whistle to the paparazzi about our celebrities would be the best way to blow up the Circa Tabac image, cash in and get the Team Dingleberg name on Page Six. It took a lion tamer's effort on my part to hold them back. I thought it'd be best to continue with the slow and solid growth in the shadows we'd been experiencing as a SoHo hideout. If we kept at it for a year or two more Circa Tabac's destiny would be an iconic New York City bar with a priceless reputation. After I convinced Sheldon that his way of thinking, wink wink, about how we'd lose our celebrity clientele if the paparazzi caught wind of the situation and without fame we'd be finished, Team Dingleberg dummied up.

Tending a tight group of bigger than life personalities drinking and mostly smoking in the recesses of SoHo was something I never expected to be doing when I was forty. Getting greeted nightly from Karmen Caas and other supermodels with a warm soft kiss on the cheek was preposterous. Telling Madonna's head of security that we had no room at the Inn for her incredibly large and loud entourage was brash and scary. David Bowie, anxious and goofy, asking me if I thought early-20th-century German expressionists were fascinating was off the wall. Directing Willie Nelson to the bathroom was a life achievement. In the past I'd want to join in on the fun with as much enthusiasm as was required to tend it. Now I was following my knife throwing buddy Immanuel's advice about bar owners and drinking. Cocaine had completely worn out its fun factor and my days of smoking marijuana were gone except for a sunny summer day or two. I was obsessed with customer service and maintaining the bar and no longer worried about embarrassing drunkard behavior, getting in fights, hangovers or STDs. Other people's good time fit the bill. Out of the gutter, sitting curbside understanding enough is as good as a feast.

Being the most sober person in a bar full of breezy celebrities high as mountain goats had its thrills. A provisional drink now and then had no effect on me being on top of everything delivering the best service of my career, practically a candlelight mentalist or a rapt speed-reader and everyone was a pulp fiction paperback at my fingertips. With a loose air of confidence in the room competing with spellbinding smoke I could see traceable currents above their heads: talents, strengths and camouflaged vulnerabilities. A few stars had residue of innocence. It helped me know when someone wanted to see a big smile, no smile, or the straightaway look of a bartender on my face. I knew where to seat everyone. I could make dead on stabs in the dark at drink orders and knew what songs to line up to keep the touching tempo in the room moving. I'd magically appear at a table of super egos in jeopardy from a ganja labyrinthine of far out ideas, cursed agents and drink orders and sort things out in a jiffy leaving each of them with an intact and crystal clear sense of humble superiority in their heads and brand new business contracts. Nearly forty years of practice had paid off; I was the genuine article, a crackerjack barman. All of it was playful, like an odd gang of strangely tall and fashionably dressed children talking, laughing and dancing in my small bar sitting on the edge of a mythical canal that could easily drag them east or west into hazardous waters if they fell in and I was solely responsible to keep them safe and let nothing disrupt the puff-puff drink-drink game they were playing.

Blithesome times began to affect my sleep with a recurring dream where I'm in an empty Circa Tabac, the way the room was when it was gutted with plywood floors and unpainted sheetrock walls in preparation for building the bar. Bottles of booze begin rolling in the front door one by one and then faster and faster until a hundred bottles surround me. The walls change right before my eyes and are suddenly coated with lustrous paint and beautiful textured coverings and the floor is hardwood and polished so perfectly I catch the glimmer in my eye shining back at me. I'm very happy and feel the need for an observant drink so I reach down for a bottle of Smirnoff at my feet but I can't do it. I can't find my arm. I begin feeling stiff as a board. I struggle to turn my head to the right and left and it's hard to see any part of me. The only thing apparent is a beautiful oak bar that is the centerpiece of the room. I take a closer look at the bar top's wood grain lines and the arrangement oddly appears to be a face with a forehead, cheeks, mouth and chin. It's my mug and grin embedded in the wood. Mercurial metamorphosis. I am the oak. I am the bar. I can't hear music but I sure as anything can feel it. There is a crowd of the best people sitting around having a grand ole time, resting their drinks on me, spilling their drinks on me, laying their hands and elbows and slapping their open fists and leaving money on me, guys and girls crossing and touching their legs and pressing their knees against my side, feet are resting on my rail. There's even a young woman with healthy legs in a short skirt dancing on top of it all. Too much fun would wake me with a big smile and I'd try desperately to go back to sleep to chase down that dream. The slumber land figment could be explained by the fact that I'd started making mid-life self-evaluations and justifiable comparisons of my experiences in and out of bars against everyone that came into Circa Tabac while avoiding heavy drinking and all of it helped paint a vivid metaphor of my existence. Or maybe it was the more obvious fact that I was working seven long nights a week submersed in a cloud of marijuana coupled with exhaustion.

I was tired but at long last I'd reached the top of the rock. I knew more about people in bars than ever before. Past misconceptions, illusions and projections were extinguished. A history held together with moments of drunken epiphanies and catastrophes died. Social gravity vanished and kinetic glue melted away revealing the cold hard reality of anyone caught ordering a drink: on our surface, a veil of deceit and compromise - two boundaries maintaining a necessary void in the middle. Sometimes wiggle room is handy when you want to buy some time, shrink or expand, appear as something you're not. But mostly the space is for respectable weakness. Being face to face with another, completely revealed, on a collision course with our unassailable tendencies brimming with feeling, enthusiasm, celebration, joy, wonder, abandon, tenderness, the experience can be stunning. Difficult. Staggering. Avoiding the pure elation of being ourselves is perfectly normal and the more drunk and stoned you are, whether famous or not, the more apparent it becomes. Tucked away in those inebriated voids are simple spirits bent on fun, appreciation, generosity, kindness. Glimmers coming through seem to be enough. It's the name of the game. If you ever walked into Circa Tabac and the only thing you had was a trying-smile on your face and a taste for drink on your lips and you didn't mind smoke in your eyes, and had no plans on autographs or fussing, you were welcome. With famous faces mixing with downtown commoners in the midst of a late night pool of liquor and a cloud of marijuana inside a business that should've failed, a perfect normalcy poured into the place. A dream bar was born.

September 11th 2001, everything changed. I was getting to the bar early for deliveries, ready to pull up the storefront gates just before 9:00 AM. I saw a large group of people on the corner of 6th Avenue and Watts Street. I walked over to see what's up. The World Trade Center was about fifteen blocks south and smoke was pouring out of the top of the North Tower. After about twenty minutes of collective concern for the people affected by what we thought was an office fire there was a monstrous explosion and a massive fireball at the top of the South Tower. For all of us New Yorkers standing there we knew in 1993 a famous sting operation went afoul when the FBI set up a dupe with a van packed with explosives and it actually blew up in the underground parking garage of the World Trade Center. The idea back then was the towers might've tipped over. That idea resonated years later and sent a shock wave through all of us on the corner and had some running north up 6th Avenue.

I went into the bar and turned on the news and learned planes had crashed into the buildings and terrorists had attacked us. I rushed back out to the corner and told everyone what I knew and we watched as black smoke poured out of the tops of both towers and more and more fire trucks, ambulances and cop cars with what sounded like every siren in the City blaring raced downtown. I stood there with the others for 45 minutes until finally it looked like the fires were dying down when out of nowhere the South Tower exploded as if in a startling special effects movie and then disappeared behind Tribeca's buildings within seconds. I immediately looked up searching for our fighter jets because I assumed we were on a battlefield and a cruise missile strike must've blown the South Tower to smithereens. I looked downtown and I could see an ominous pyroclastic cloud of dust swelling and slowly moving uptown devouring anything in its path. I ran back into the bar and watched television news in a frightened stupor for an hour when then the North Tower exploded on live television and disappeared within seconds in the same exact way the South Tower had. It rattled me. There were no cruise missiles. The attackers must have pre-planted and detonated massive sets of explosives in order to take down those giant buildings, that's what I thought. But how could that be possible when security is crawling the walls in the financial district? After sitting alone frozen in confusion for another ten minutes I realized there must be chaos downtown and a great number of my fellow New Yorkers were hurt and in desperate need of help.

I made it to the corner of West Broadway and Barclay expecting to see the massive remnants of two-mangled steel towers maybe fifty or sixty stories tall with the floors above that bent over, twisted and maligned but there was nothing. The two towers 100-plus stories tall made up of hundreds of thousands of tons of reinforced grid worked steel and concrete had been leveled to the ground. I couldn't figure how it happened like that and it heightened my fear and anxiety. There was gray dust dense in the air and inches deep covering everything all the way up to Chambers Street and further. The color of everything was gone, a massive monochrome scene. None of it looked real. There were cops and firefighters randomly appearing and then disappearing into the cloud of dust. As I moved along I noticed cars, trucks and buses that were burnt to the core as if a nuclear inferno had ripped through the street. It looked like a war zone and nothing like the result of buildings on fire. Coming through the dust were countless haunting digital beeps repeating like a small flock of exhausted birds scattered, lost and stupefied in a fog. I didn't know what it was so I asked a cop. "Distress signals," he said with urgency, "Firefighters wear them so if they're laid out on the ground for an amount of time they go off." Unseen heroes were amongst the rubble and their ominous alarms were as much a part of Armageddon as the destruction of the buildings. FEMA was already organized at the scene. I wondered how they could be so fast when our supersonic fighter jets still hadn't arrived. I tried doing anything I could to help but there was a quiet confusion mixed with cops and others waiting for orders. People were leaving the area and others were arriving. I was coughing my brains out like everyone because of the pulverized concrete in the air so I decided to head back up to the bar.

I washed up best I could in the kitchen sink, caught my breath, tied a bar rag over my nose and mouth, stuffed a handful more in my pockets, grabbed two cases of Evian and headed back downtown. The water was gone in seconds. Ground zero was more apparent, an incredible sight, hazardous with no real way of getting near the jumbled steel heart of it. I looked around and saw people consumed with concern and a fierce duty to help yet there was almost nothing that could be done. I was standing in front of Saint Paul's Churchyard cemetery that was blanketed with dust and a million pieces of paper from the thousands of file cabinets that were inside the exploded buildings. The cemetery was directly across the street from the World Trade Center yet it was free of any debris larger than smashed pieces of telephones. Strangely there were tiny patches of green grass behind a few of the tombstones. I was thinking that at the time of the explosions anyone fortunate enough to be in the cemetery would be alive.

The dust cloud was still settling but I could see the buildings surrounding the perimeter of the World Trade Center were unscathed. The colossal disaster was remarkably contained to the boundary of World Trade Center complex. Taking a closer look at the core of the disaster it was unmistakable that the massive skeletal steel grid work of the Towers appeared to be haphazardly disassembled into two relatively neat piles of girders were the buildings had stood and absolutely everything else that was the buildings had vaporized or exploded to dust. By 4:00 PM the area was being organized best it could. A bunch of us had been moved a couple of blocks to West Broadway and Chambers Street to unload and pass out water, dust masks, hazmat boots and other random emergency supplies. Everyone anxiously waited to hear word of anyone being rescued from the Towers but all day long there was no one. The only reports were of still missing firefighters and cops that had gone into the buildings. There was an outspoken group mystification over the fact that no bodies were being found anywhere near the scene when there should have been thousands.

All of it was a horrible and unexplainable and just when things couldn't get any stranger word began to spread quick that we were all going to have clear out fast because the Emergency Response Commanders were going to implode Building 7 of the World Trade Center Complex. No plane had hit Building 7. The building was a good distance away from the Towers and was undamaged aside from broken windows and a few small office fires slowly burning out. Regardless the bosses in the midst of the chaos decided it was unsafe to leave the building standing so they were going to blow it up. We moved another couple of blocks north and gathered around listening to the countdown over a fireman's radio: five, four, three, two, one – boom boom boom boom boom rapid and thunderous explosions while we watched Building 7 come straight down into its own footprint, a picture perfect controlled demolition. I couldn't handle anymore and I left the scene in a hurry because there were more reports that other buildings were wired with explosives and I wasn't sure what the authorities were planning on blowing up next. I made my way back to the bar and washed up best I could, poured myself a shot of Jameson's and slammed it back. I poured another one quickly. The rest is well known history.

A lot of people throw the word complexity around sort of as an all purpose descriptor of things when they're kind of hard to figure out. They use complexity and complication interchangeably. That's not close to correct. Some things can be complicated but not necessarily complex. For example, a Mojito embodies every reason a bartender hates to make a cocktail. It requires a bunch of fresh mint, and fresh means sorting out the dank and rotten leaves from the prime, and in order to release its flavor the mint must be muddled with a special tool, the muddler, and all this takes time. Then you have to deal with an excessive amount of sugar and squeeze a small harvest of limes, two sticky ingredients that require immediate cleanup otherwise every drink made at your prep station afterwards will taste limey and sweet. You still have to measure and add the correct rum and soda water. To finish it off Mojitos must be shaken like a rat bastard so all the ingredients coalesce to the perfect icy consistency; and still it's up to the customer at that point to decide whether it's just right or not; and if not you'll have to remake it all over again. To the point, Mojitos are complicated; and considering they usually cost the same as an uncomplicated gin and tonic you can also understand them as a pain in the ass. Complexity, however, is a different drink altogether with a set of properties that go beyond complicated. The most important thing that stands out with anything complex is that unknown things can emerge, come out of nowhere quickly and still need to be assimilated into the workings. Like figuring out how to make a Mojito when you've run out of the most important ingredient, Puerto Rican white rum. Hopefully the bar stocks cachaca or maybe a spiced rum; if not, a shot of vodka with a bit of honey and a splash of tequila to confuse it all and a big dash of hope that your Mojito drinker is tipsy enough to not notice.

Suffice to say, from the days after September 11th and throughout the decade that followed Circa Tabac was not complicated. Transformative scenes unfolded and brought with them unpredictable properties that resulted in my life bewildered, too often struggling for satisfaction, and unmistakably complex. Circa Tabac's original little late night crowd of famous-face, happy and high creatures of lounging unconcerned with the outside world were pushed out of the bar by a new spectacle more akin to a marijuana coffee shop in Amsterdam filled with tacky American drug tourists. Cloudy eyes, slack faces and rubber necks made it clear the big new crowd was unsure about what they want out of life, let alone what to drink, so getting the required read for compassionate service made tending them frustrating. They also lacked an obvious yearning for libations. More recognizable was a slight cultural scent of patchouli and a hazy air of religion like a loosely connected urban marijuana cult faithful to throwing wishes into the wind. The bar had turned from a secret SoHo hangout to a cannabis pilgrimage site; like someone told all of them, "You ain't nothing in New York till you smoke a joint at Circa Tabac." I had no real reason to complain because they were mostly good people and business was good. We acquired the basement below the bar for desperately needed storage, a walk-in beer cooler, and a small office. Sadly, because I was busy managing a whole new load, I wasn't behind the stick anymore. On the upside Sheldon was no longer making a mess in the kitchen. Instead he had extra time, more cash in his pocket, and the added attention the owner of a popular bar receives; it unleashed his aimless purpose in life with abandon.

My main barman was Leo, a talent from Brasil with a great sense of humor, charisma and as good fortune would have it he looked like a mix between Clarke Gable and a young Marlon Brando. Best, he was honest. Together it meant Leo had a collection of very attractive women constantly standing around the bar and that meant a larger group of guys with money constantly standing around them, and by closing time all our sales constantly stayed in the register. Leo was nearly a faultless contribution to the bar aside from the fact that he was territorial with women – they were all his. It made no difference to him even if you were with your wife because he'd display some sly and friendly enough gesture to have her notice him. He might not make a play for your woman but he'd do his best to have the romantic notion cross her mind and slip into her subconscious where he'd wait until later that night to appear in her dreams to seduce her.

I was standing at the service end of the bar with one eye on all the ladies keeping all their eyes on Leo and my other eye was on the lookout for customers in need and potential trouble. Scarlett Johansson tapped me on the shoulder and asked if I knew where the bathroom was. "Lucky you, I do," I told her, "But at the moment they're both occupied." The two tiny bathrooms were right behind us. She'd been in the bar before and I was sure she knew that. I was also pretty sure that she saw her girlfriend Natalie Portman just step inside one of them. Regardless, her tipsy smile was distracting. I'd seen her movie Ghostworld. She was a standout and possessed that timeless Hollywood look that meant she was destined for fame and I told her, "Your film presence is rare." She batted her eyes. "Thanks," she said, "I really liked working with Steve Buscemi."

Before I could compliment her further Leo noticed the two of us and practically jumped over the bar. Scarlett smiled. He had Lemon Drops shots in hand that must've been just prepared for someone else. "Let's make a toast," he said off the top of his head while passing us the shots, "Flowers inspire, uh.., music.., and uh... music inspires uh... beautiful women," he searched for an ending in the movie star's eyes and finished, "and you inspire everything." He smiled big, threw back the shot, laughed loud and nearly gagged on his cheesy toast. "Let's do another," he said with a loony smile while reaching for a bottle of Patron. The screwy act had Scarlett Johansson giggling. Before we could put the empty shot glasses on the bar Natalie Portman walked out of the bathroom. Leo couldn't have been happier. Natalie didn't miss a beat and slipped into Leo's glow and asked, "What's going on?" I told her, "We're happy you made it out of the bathroom safely." She nodded her head politely, unsure if I was joking and said, "Yeah, it's a tight squeeze in there."

Scarlett's need to pee must've dwindled because some girl stumbled into the bathroom ahead of her and she didn't seem to care. Up close I noticed Natalie Portman was a lot prettier than I thought. Though something wasn't quite right with her. She's not accustomed to bars, I thought, maybe she's slumming with a safety belt on in west SoHo. It was crowded and a few drunk guys were beginning to act sloppy, bumping, grabbing. The smell of marijuana was strong enough to be noticed in midtown. I took a good look at both starlets wondering if there was something I could do to make their night easier. With the two of them side by side my on-the-spot classifications of young women that I usually reserved for interviewing new servers was triggered. The way I see it you are either a cocktail waitress or you're not. Being a cocktail waitress doesn't mean you're below certain achievements or a particular stature in life, or vice versa. It has more to do with your heard-it-all cultivation and your tendency to roll with the punches, and above that your agility, reflexes and overall sense of movement that's not defined as graceful but something more in tune with able. Scarlett Johansson was a cocktail waitress. Natalie Portman was not. But with both of them being so friendly and incredibly easy to look at I wasn't going to mention a word about it. Instead I wanted to play their choice of music, get them more drinks, something to eat or a better seat, anything. I decided it'd be best if I jumped behind the bar to relieve Leo so he could entertain the two of them more judiciously.

Before anything happened Leo had tequila shots lined up. Natalie tastefully passed. The three of us tossed them back and then Scarlett said something to me about the Olsen Twins sitting at her table, something about shoes and a questionable dress and asked if I wanted to join them. As our circle chitchat started to roll my partner Sheldon walked in the front door. He quickly spotted us. I nearly didn't recognize him because he was dressed unlike I'd ever seen before. I thought it was gag costume, a hip-hop fanatic wearing a XXXL bright blue hoodie with a neon New York Knicks logo on the front of it, extra long and extra baggy denim shorts that cut off above his ankles, a pair of bright orange and blue high top Nikes with neon green laces and an awkward fitting baseball cap turned backwards on his head. For a second I thought he was wearing a fat gold chain around his neck but it turned out to be some sort of flashy backstage pass. The most eye-catching aspect of the outfit was how ridiculously oversized everything was, like he was under a small urban circus tent.

Sheldon quickly barked at Leo to get back to work and then forcefully introduced himself to Scarlett and Natalie: "I own the bar." Leo and I glanced at each other with the same what-the-fuck-is-Sheldon-wearing smirk on our face. The starlets weren't exactly attentive. "I thought you had plans tonight," I asked Sheldon while trying not to make a big deal about his get-up. "I had a meeting with my record producer," he told all of us seriously and loudly. New outfit, aggressive attitude, record deal, none of it was making any sense. "I write rap," he told Scarlett and Natalie. They hadn't asked. It was news to me. He noticed they weren't paying attention so he decided to be pissed off at me and talk even louder. "I told you to text me whenever the Olsen Twins come in. I had those two on my hit list since Full House and you gotz your finger on my trigger, Homey. Why I gotz to wait for one of my customers to call me with the 411?" Sheldon was shaking his head dramatically as if he was listening to some apocalyptic rap song in his head. There wasn't much I could say. He had come out of the blue with his whole new show. Dressed like a commercial street thug? Hit list? Homey? 411? Talk about body snatchers. I was in awe.

Clearly Sheldon had gotten his hands on some cocaine or someone had been feeding it to him. Somebody definitely dressed him like a wigga clown because dumpy Sheldon Dingleberg had no means for such a production on his own. He gave a last shot at Scarlett and Natalie, "I make movies too. Off the hook shit, I mix rap and porn. I gotz a meeting with Ice T and Coco Marie. I gotz to sign'em. We be droppin da bomb on ya. Yo yo yo yo!" he said it all hectically, without a trace of rhythm. It was scary and funny and I'm sure Scarlett and Natalie would've been laughing if they hadn't already walked away. "Sheldon," I said, "Take it down a notch. Let me get you a glass of water." He didn't want to hear it and waddled away like a knockoff hip-hop gangsta with sores on his feet to the back where the starlets were sitting. All I could see was Sheldon approaching their table and within a blink the Olsen Twins, Scarlett Johansson, Natalie Portman and their beautiful friends headed to the front door never to be seen again.

New York City is great town and everybody knows it. It's a place of unparalleled opportunity and a proving ground, so much so it's a cliché'. As the old song goes, "If I can make it there, I'll make it anywhere." The thing no one likes to sing about is that New York is a town filled with thieves, pimps, cutthroats and cheats; guys and dolls dressed in all sorts of threads with dark skills perpetually on the hunt for easy marks that are found on practically every corner. Sticking out like a sore thumb on my corner was another obvious cliché, Sheldon, a mark among marks, the prince of dupes. At the time Sheldon began looking like a jerky thug rapper he'd naively started carousing with a few of our new and out of place unsavory customers. It didn't take me long to find out they were porn producers and pimps for bottom-rung hip-hop artists.

Unbeknownst to Sheldon but clear as vodka for me was that he'd started the process of surrendering our bar to hustlers. They weren't threatening us with guns and violence from the outset. They'd simply moved in on the place night after night slowly filling my seats with more and more of their people. I'm guessing their plan was to make anyone outside of their ill tribe think twice before sitting down for a drink and then eventually they'd have the bar to themselves. Sheldon and I were already working different nights of the week so I had no way to consistently filter out the gruff element. They flooded the joint on

Sheldon's watch. It only took two or three months before an X-rated hip-hop gansta crowd was dominating the bar. I figured some schemer had taken over my role of blowing wind up Sheldon's ass; and unlike my plan which included gently crafting him a venerable and valuable personality and building him a thriving business, the enemy scammer must've been dressing him, shoving cocaine up his nose, indoctrinating him with a smash and grab attitude, and promising him a rap video pool party lifestyle in exchange for riding roughshod on our bar.

Sheldon's new crowd looked more infamous than famous, like they'd jumped the turnstile at Myrtle Street Station and rode into town on the J train straight from the Marcy Projects. The most common affinity of the new group was that they either worked for The Source magazine, wanted to work for The Source magazine, or knew someone that either worked or wanted to work for The Source magazine. One way or another they were all hip-hop music industry fanatics and The Source magazine was their bible. They smoked more weed than you'd think was scientifically possible. Drink orders disappeared because they all brought their own Hennessey, Alize or malt liquor. Our seats and booths were being shredded with razors and shivs, graffiti and tags were sprayed on the front door and in the bathroom, the music system was constantly hijacked to play nightmarish criminal gangster rap while lap-dances, Glocks and drug deals were on full display. Neighbors became fearful to walk pass the bar at night. Many nights I was scared to be in the place.

By 2003 Circa Tabac had crossed the line and became SoHo's unwanted Black Gangsta Go-Go Bar. I say Black in the most definitive way. Aside from the white hip-hop business handlers who were manipulating the entire scene for their own exploits and the varying colors amidst the mix of discount hookers, porn stars and porn producers hanging around that crooked hip-hop music industry scene, everyone in the joint was pitch-black. That was definitely not my thing because I preferred a non race-centric customer base, diversity. I wasn't against an all black bar, it's just that a bar like that should be owned and operated by someone black. To get where I'm coming from it's important to understand that having seen Kurtis Blow perform The Breaks at a Bronx

Block Party back in 1979 and Kool DJ Herc at the Executive Playhouse on Jerome Avenue along with having listened to many other legends of the poetic craft through the eighties, I was no stranger to hip-hop. The problem was that by 2003 I considered the genre a bastardization of its former self completely controlled by mafia record production teams operating under the thumb of global media conglomerates bent on bringing out the worst of my brothers of another color and silencing the true and insightful voice of the urban poet. Laid out simple, commercial hip-hop was nasty and passé and real rap had been murdered.

The Source magazine was one of the biggest commercial platforms for hip-hop in 2003. A darker urban element filled its base here in New York City but its bread and butter across the nation came from catering to young, middle class, suburban white male hip-hop fans who could actually afford the subscription fee and who unabashedly cared nothing about railroading the black artist's image. Black Means Thug might've been a more honest name for the reprehensible rag. Two white kids from Harvard started the publication and that should tell you something. One of those kids, David Mays, came from a family of establishment cronies straight out of the lily-whitest part of northwest Washington DC. Somehow he hijacked the last word on the rhythm that had originated in the crime-ridden South Bronx where kids with streetwise ingenuity and little cash forged a new style of music ramped up from a rougher spin on funk made from spare parts, extracted beats, breaks and melodies lifted from already existing records and majestically cross-faded it all and sealed it with blistering poetry chronicling ghetto life. The Source magazine burned that perspective to the ground and replaced it with glossy covers of Hollywood styled hood-mafia knuckleheads standing in as the best contemporary black artists of the day.

David Mays, or The Great White Hunter as I referred to him, was the ringleader of Sheldon's imbecilic black crowd that had taken over the bar. I was betting that either David Mays was the guy pulling on Sheldon's strings or a prick named Andrew Cohen, an entertainment-lawyer/porn-producer/drug-dealing/drug-addict creep. Because Andrew Cohen was merely a David Mays sycophant I figured it'd be best to chop off the head of the snake, severe Sheldon's debasing attachments so I could get my bar back in order. With the Great White Hunter out of the picture Sheldon would collapse back onto his former sloppy self and the rest of the undesirables would soon disappear. I made the decision to move aggressively with my plan after New York City's biggest hip-hop radio station, HOT 97, began talking about Circa Tabac on air as the best place to meet Rappers and smoke weed all day, everyday. I had no choice because what followed the radio play looked as if Riker's Island started running a bus shuttle to and from the bar. Either I was going to have to put an end to it or the police were going to get wind of the situation and shut us down.

It was a Thursday, around 5:30 PM, I was sitting at the bar, on the phone talking to my partner Jodi telling her about our new lethal crowd and what we needed to do about it. Because she only showed up on Sunday afternoons after a downtown brunch to grab her weekly share of the profits and go over the books and pay some bills, like her new Lexus car payment, gas and insurance that covertly started coming out of the bar's bank account, she had no idea what was happening with our clientele. She relied on what she heard from Sheldon over coffee once every month or so. Telling her details about The Great White Hunter and Andrew Cohen and drugs and Sheldon was a losing battle. She told me I was in an ego driven power struggle with her brother and to stop causing her trouble and to just take care of the bar. She screamed, "Get a life!" and hung up on me.

Four guys I recognized from the congregation of the rap cult band Dead Presidents walked in the front door and went straight to a table in the back and each of them lit up a blunt. One guy was extra large, more than 300 lbs of muscle; he'd brought his own jumbo bag of Burger King. Because of his size and the dead man look in his eyes that made you think he had nothing to lose which had me thinking I might have everything to lose if I got in his way, I pretended to not notice the greasy bag of food. According to my new plan I was supposed to go over to their table and inform them that no outside grub was allowed and we're now enforcing a no-marijuana policy. But I didn't do it. I just sat at the bar trying to build up some courage. I kept on eye on them as more members of their congregation showed up and all of them lit blunts and harassed the waitress every five minutes for water refills and glasses with ice so they could pour their own drinks. At 8:00 PM I saw a familiar Cadillac Escalade pull up in front of the bar. David May's best boy, Che Faker, a beige dude who also had gone to Harvard, hopped out of the passenger seat and walked in the front door and informed me that The Source magazine was having a private party later on that night. He wanted to make sure I saved the back corner booth for The Great White Hunter. I told him clearly, "There's no private party tonight." He told me, "There is. David cleared it with your boss." I grabbed a hold of my chin to steady the tremor in my head. I told him, "Che, I don't have a boss. And get it straight, there is no private party tonight." He was unconcerned and told me, "We'll be here by nine. Make sure that booth is saved." He turned and left.

Needless to say my night wasn't going well. But things were about to change because I got off the barstool, went over to the CD player, turned off Jay Z's Hard Knock Life and set up a collection of the Beatles greatest hits. I grabbed the CD player's palm-sized remote control and hit play. In unison, at the start of Love Me Do, the room already half filled with Dead Presidents and The Source magazine's minions all jerked their weed clouded heads with painful expressions on their faces as if a giant hand had come out of nowhere and slapped them upside the head. Before Love Me Do had finished one of the Dead Presidents' devotees was standing next to me attempting to change the music. I interrupted him, told him to not touch the CD player because it was my favorite song and it's my bar and that if he didn't like it there are plenty of other places he could go. "I'm not forcing you to stay here, pal." He was high and must've thought I was tripping because he just laughed and popped a Dead President's CD in, hit play and sat back down with his posse. With the little remote control in the palm of my hand, a most excellent power granting gizmo, I switched it back to the Beatles like a magician. There was a commotion but the waitress informed anyone who asked that I was indeed the owner of the bar and, as unbelievable as it sounded, I really did like the Beatles.

Everyone went back to smoking blunts and begrudgingly listening to the Mop Tops' greatest hits. By the time I Want To

Hold Your Hand was playing they all had earphones stuck in their ears. My confidence had steadily grown and by 9:00 PM with Hello Goodbye playing in the background I was running a zigzag pattern through the room to every table telling anyone who lit up a blunt that they couldn't smoke marijuana in the bar. The common response after they'd pop their earphones out was, "What? ...Why?" To which I replied over and over, "Because it's illegal." Every time I walked away they'd just light up again. It was a losing battle but I was getting total satisfaction by annoying the shit out of them. David Mays' Cadillac Escalade pulled up in front of the bar again and The Source magazine's inner sanctum finally entered the room. Without wasting time best boy Che let me know that David Mays was very upset because I hadn't reserved his back corner power booth. Someone in his crew quickly fixed the seating arrangement and just as The Great White Hunter sat down best boy Che was handing me a stack of CD's. He told me, "Turn that Beatle's shit off and play these in this order." He turned around like he just knocked me out with one punch and headed to the back corner booth. I left the stack of music sitting on the bar, went over to the CD player to stand guard and asked Leo for vodka neat, a double. By the time Hey Jude was in its first chorus Leo was handing me the phone, "Sheldon wants to talk to you."

Sheldon was in Las Vegas. It was a surprise to me. He was there with porn producer and super prick Andrew Cohen. David Mays had called him to chew him a new asshole over the Beatles. Sheldon followed up with a call to me. Within the first minute on the phone I concluded Sheldon was out of his mind. He had set up a deal for The Source magazine to have exclusive use of the bar for the night and part of the arrangement was The Great White Hunter could play any music he liked. John, Paul, George and Ringo were causing turmoil on the verge of violence. Sheldon told me, "David Mays is very upset. Do you know how bad that is?" I didn't. Sheldon told me, "He might stop coming to the bar." I told him, "That's the plan." Sheldon cried to me, "I finally have something going right with my life and you want to destroy it!" David Mays was the least of his troubles. With the crackling tone of Sheldon's voice and at the tantrum pace he was yapping it was clear he was at least two eight balls in front of the wind. I figured cocaine was

205

only a small part of a larger blabbermouth drug cocktail he must've swallowed. It was a bit pass 7:00 PM in Las Vegas and Sheldon was experiencing diarrhea of the mouth. I ended up hearing it all and it had nothing to do with The Great White Hunter or the Beatles.

Sheldon and Andrew had partnered up to produce a porn in Las Vegas. They'd rented out a 2000 square foot luxury penthouse suite at the Bellagio Hotel for the night, hired some porn actors and an expensive camera guy, filled the place with drugs and liquor and were just about to start filming an orgy scene when one of the porn studs announced that he didn't do gay scenes and took off. They had four girls and one guy left but the film's script, Scared Straight, called for two guys. "Two gay guys," that's what Sheldon screamed into the phone.

I hadn't asked for the synopsis but I got it. Four women with guns and knives break into a gay couple's luxury apartment and try to turn the men straight by threatening to cut their members off if they failed to sexually satisfy all of them. In the end one guy succeeds and the other fails. There's straight sex, gay sex, blood and gore. Honest to goodness sewer entertainment. Sheldon was upset because he'd invested a lot of money into the production. "You don't understand," he told me, "Andrew got me in on this deal as a favor and he already signed the contract with our distributor. We have to deliver." Sheldon's idea to film the one remaining dude and the four chicks didn't fly. He spewed, "Andrew says the deal was for gay guys. Scared Straight – get it!" Even if the distributor accepted the new heterosexual version he might as well throw the investment money away. Sheldon cried to me: "Andrew said there's no profit in one guy and four girls. It's an old storyline." I told him, "Whatever floats your boat, Sheldon." "You don't understand," he said it as if I cared. "Andrew says new porn demands twists and new angles. You have to stand out from the rest. Our script is great. We can't let it go to waste."

The whole enterprise sounded like staged sleaze. It also sounded like Andrew Cohen bamboozled Sheldon and probably dosed him with some bizarro-inducing drug on top of everything else because Sheldon didn't sound anything like the harmless, awkward and messy kid from New Jersey that I once knew. Plus it had to have been Andrew Cohen that convinced Sheldon to replace the missing porn actor because I couldn't imagine him volunteering. Sheldon told me, "We will have bigger market potential." He said it as if he were pitching the idea to me likely the same way Andrew Cohen must've pitched it to him. "More profit if I star in it," he said, "Fat bald guys watch porn more than anyone. It's added value for the porn purchaser. Don't you get it, they'll identify with me. I'll be the star." Sheldon was telling me everything so fast that he repeated parts of it without wasting much time. I figured Andrew Cohen must've planned Sheldon's starring role all along. When it came time to film the depraved video Sheldon had a panic attack and ran out of the room with a six-pack of Red Bull, his cell phone, his cigarettes, and the pink satin robe he was wearing for the scene they were about to shoot. He'd been prancing up and down the hotel hallway when unexpectedly he got the call from David Mays about those awful Beatles.

The Sheldon saga took a final and desperate turn when after unloading his pathetic Vegas situation on me he switched his attitude like someone with a multiple personality disorder and told me I was doing a great job running Circa Tabac. He begged me to call Andrew Cohen and tell him some cockamamie story that Sheldon couldn't possibly be in the video because of a contract with me regarding a ludicrous licensing deal connected to our bar. "Just tell him you need to sign papers before any filming begins. It'll buy me some time." Sheldon was in a pickle. I thought of calling his sister Jodi to see what she could do for him but most likely she'd tell me to stop causing her trouble. I suddenly felt like I was a large glass of water and Sheldon was dying of thirst. He needed his head clear from distractions if he wanted to survive the ordeal whether he starred in the video or not. Having The Great White Hunter call him every fifteen minutes about the Beatles wasn't going to help. I told Sheldon the best I could do was allow David Mays to have his private party but he was on his own in Vegas.

"You can listen to whatever you want," I told that to best boy Che while drumming up the worst smile I could plant on my face. "But the music can't get any louder than it is now." I was surrendering the bar to villains for the night but I wasn't letting it go without a hook. I also didn't think it was fair to include my neighbors in the base line drubbing. The volume was set to the halfway mark, slightly louder than normal; a nice level for a good time and less so for bar room conversation. Apparently it was nothing close to the amount of decibels needed for hip-hop numbskulls. Regardless, best boy Che was willing to accept the progress we'd made. I looked at the time, 9:45 PM. I still had at least six hours to go before the night was over.

The Source magazine's crowd was living up to their reputation. Every person in the place took turns telling me to turn the music up. I told them all the same thing, "No can do." The smoke was unbearable, mostly because they were smoking ratty blunts; cheap and bad smelling marijuana rolled into an even cheaper cigar wrapper that has more in common with cardboard than tobacco leaf. The air filtration system was on full force and every fresh air vent wide open. Had it been a different crowd I'm sure there could've been something redeemable in the air. Leo was displeased behind the bar as were the waitresses because the sales and tips were lousy and customers were crass and scary. Things started to get more ugly when Che finally ordered me to raise the music volume. I told him straight, "No can do, Che," and then turned my back on him. I peeked over my shoulder and enjoyed watching him walk back to The Great White Hunter and get chewed out for not trying harder. I reminded myself that I am in charge by grabbing a hold of the little palm-sized remote control in my jacket pocket.

A lot of people will eat a plate of rotten food so long as the portion is big enough. I imagine it's the same for hip-hop gangstas, any crap rap will do and as long as it's loud enough. Sure enough Che was back at me. "Dave will give you a hundred bucks if you turn up the fucking music." Being somebody's best boy is horrible. If he asks you to pick his teeth you scrape; if he asks you to carry a bucket of spit you lift; if he asks you to clean his ass you wipe. I told Che, "You're job sucks." Che whined, "Come'on! Sheldon plays it as loud as it gets." I told him, "Sheldon is not here." He stormed away. I looked back at the corner power booth and saw The Great White Hunter bobbing his head and mouthing off at Che waving his arms defensively. Next thing Che walked over to the table of Dead Presidents' devotees peeled off some cash and handed it to the Burger King giant with the dead man eyes. The giant got up from the table, put the cash in his pocket, walked over to the CD player and lifted his paw like hand to the volume control and cranked it up. The bar erupted into cheers. Before the momentum could take off and without anyone noticing my hand in my jacket pocket I fingered the volume control lower. The lost look on the giant's face overshadowed the crowd's loud complaints, "What the fuck..." "Booo..." "Turn that shit up!" The giant quickly spun around and cranked it up again with an awful smile. The crowd was back to hooting and hollering. I let the giant walk to his table feeling like a champ with a bunch of them patting him on the shoulders as 50 Cent's In Da Club was pumping. Just as his butt hit the shredded seat cushion I lowered the volume again. The giant looked over at me with his eyes blinking rapidly. I must've appeared to have magical power because I was nowhere near the CD Player.

It only took minute for Che to be back at me. "Dave will give you five hundred to turn it up." I told him, "I thought your big dog was in control of the volume." Che repeated, "Five hundred!" I told him, "Tell your boss to buy his own bar and then he can play anything as loud as he wants." He walked back to his boss and told him what I said. The Great White Hunter lifted his head up and for the first time he looked directly at me, eye to eye. I smiled. I had to. Not because I was trying to stare him down or connect with him on some mano-y-mano elevated stage but because fortuitously playing at a civilized party volume was I Made You Look by Nas. It was perfectly cute and I felt like turning the volume all the way up just for the one song. I didn't. Before the song ended Che was back with a new and very serious look. "Dave will give you a thousand bucks to turn the volume up right now."

A thousand bucks is a good amount of money, especially if it comes easy. Circa Tabac's business was paying its bills and then some but with only a 20% take on the profits and our new black hip-hop crowd mostly drinking their own booze I was far from rolling in doe. I looked back at David Mays and he was looking at me with a buried smile on his face. There was no way I could take the money, it would mean losing my bar. I told Che, "Please stop bothering me. I told you the rules." He didn't like my cordiality and went back to his boss. The two of them immediately went over to the giant. David Mays peeled off a portion of the thousand bucks that was supposed to be mine and handed it to him. The giant got out of his seat. I jumped off my barstool to meet him at the CD player.

"Gonna tell you one time," the giant said to me, "gonna turn da shit up and I know you ain't got nuttin to say. Sit your white ass down before I bust you open." Standing in front of the guy I could smell onion rings and I suddenly noticed a flicker of life in his eyes, not much but something. I was wrong about him because at first he seemed unearthly with his size and intimidating look but now up close and personal he was just a big guy with bad breath. Then a wild thought took over my head and reverberated: I'm wrong about a lot of things. Instead of 300 pounds he's lighter, only 275 or 265, and there's plenty of fat on him. Still, he could rip me in two but the thing ringing my head like a bell was my perspective had refocused closer to the vivid and gripping reality. I was bigger, stronger and smarter than I thought; at least smarter than the giant. I wasn't looking for a fight, it's just that cognizance was inflating my head. I'll fast-talk my way out of this, that's what I thought. I quickly explained: "The CD Player has a computer chip already pre-programmed with an algorithm matched at sonic tuned pitch levels resounding against predetermined sound samples factored from the room noise level setting the master level with no bypass permissible until coded sequences set in tomorrow at 9:00 AM when the volume control returns to manual operation." Like a flash inside a cloud I saw the urge inside of the giant to bang the top of my head with his fist like a hammer. "Whacha talkin bout," he said, and then turned around and cranked up the volume. Everyone in the bar cheered. He appeared to be on top of the world. With my hand already in my jacket pocket I fingered the volume lower again but this time it went so low it was hard to hear the music over the noise of the crowd. Sticking to my distraction script I snapped at the giant, "Now look what you've done. You broke it!"

The crowd had gotten up out of their seats at this point and piled up at the end of the bar making a dense circle around the two of us. Our mass shifted to the center of the room knocking over tables and chairs along the way. "Gonna bust ya ass then gonna put a bullet in ya head," the giant informed me. Others threw their two cents into the ring: "Hang the white motherfucker." "Bury his pink ass." "Put that cracka bitch on the ground." The devil was in the room and it appeared he had backup. I looked over at the bar, Leo with the two waitresses and the busboy were taking cover. I was scared but the truth is I'd been more scared before. I knew I was in the right. Maybe I'd get hurt, so what. I didn't want to die, that was true. Most important was I couldn't give up my bar. I didn't have any choice. It was a moment of invincibility.

As long as there are pricks with a compulsion to bully, cheat, rob and murder to achieve their ends someone needs to stand against it. It might as well be my turn tonight, I thought. With my hands still in my jacket pockets with fifty or sixty thugs surrounding me I must've looked like a real cool cat. My eyes were peeled wide open and I looked into anyone's eyes that dared to look back. There were no takers, only glazed over crazy eyes looking at nothing and everything in all directions reflecting the confusion and hate that was bouncing off the walls. I smelled a gross dose of sulphur fading and I wondered if someone found a carton of the bar's matches and lit it up in an attempt to burn the place down. I looked out the window and noticed The Great White Hunter's Cadillac Escalade pulling away from the curb. Something scared him off and he left me alone with the room full of unhappiness. I was worried about my staff. I could feel the sweat and tremble inside of me but I held it back because the entire group, despite the venom dripping from their mouths, seemed like outright dimwits to me. Then it dawned on me that total destruction was not inevitable.

The numbskulls were capable of dispersing. I fingered the remote control in my pocket trying to turn the volume up. With some rap song blasting they'd all be distracted like dogs with a treat. But instead of the volume I must've hit the CD changer button. The CD Player held 300 discs and we had nearly every type of music in there. I quickly fingered the control again because I wasn't exactly sure what happened after I blindly pushed the first button. I wanted the music playing before somebody threw the first

211

punch and the place erupted. With the volume accidentally set to full blast, Patsy Cline's Crazy started to play. It was the last thing they wanted to hear. It's a great song. Sadly I was the only person in the room smiling. The giant grabbed me by my belt and shirt collar and hoisted me up to his chest and carried me out the front door and tossed me. Roughriders followed him and for five minutes in front of the bar I thought they were going to murder me. I got away after a bunch of kicks and punches to the head and torso. I made it around the corner to Spring Street and Sullivan and called the cops from a payphone. Ten cars with lights swirling showed up and cleared everybody out.

Tumultuous times force big questions on you, like "Do you know what you want out of life?" If you don't it can only be for one of two reasons: you already have what you want, or, you don't know yourself well enough to figure out what you want. Maybe you think self-exploration is vain or uninspiring. After all, the true genius at the core of all of us lacks a natural drive to examine ourselves just as a drink doesn't naturally drink itself or a cigarette doesn't smoke itself. Life is to be lived, preferably lived right, visible and not boiled down to a static internal reality that you desperately try to trap under your thumb. It's the outward view of our lives in action that best explains who we think we are. You know it every time you cross your heart or make a toast to another. That genius at the inner core of you is a perpetual mystery, an acceptable mystery for good reason. Consider how many through the ages have pondered what churns deep inside and not one of them discovered anything finished - philosophers, theologians, gurus, priests, rabbis, monks, psychiatrists, and bartenders. No one is better for deeper thoughts and the shallowest are capable of profound acts that have lasting effects on the world. The bottom line on that mysterious internal you can be summed up with that famous group of words that define the infinite space in your head and always answers things that have no answer: "I DON'T KNOW." Maybe. I don't know. I do know those famous words stand for something you drink without a need for knowing ingredients and it allows life to proceed long enough to pull your nose out of your bellybutton and maybe enjoy the world a little. Regardless of residing in the grasp-less realm of "I DON'T

KNOW," that wishy-washy identity of "you" is sufficient because simple enough it'll have to do. Get that notion in your mouth, swish it around and swallow it. You'll stop clinging to yourself because you won't honestly say anymore, "I'm afraid to let go," because there's nothing definitive at the core of you to hold onto in the first place. Think of the energy wasted on trying to maintain a false sense of an absolute self, or trying to manage every detail in your life, or trying to keep everybody in line with you. Accept it and become a bona fide witness to the throes of your life and the process of your death that are equally upon you.

It's very fortunate to know you are something in the midst of that living and that dying and much more than what gets nailed down in a box and buried. It's the oomph, the animation of soul endlessly existing in the wax and wane of the sound breath makes passing through our chest and out pass a silence and with the light that goes through our eyes until the same light is in and out of the eyes of others while we sit together for a drink and watch ice cubes melting, cooling, transforming our scotch, or the drops of red wine on the side of our glass that seep to our fingertips and under our nails staining and eventually fading along with the vapor of breath condensing on the bottom of beer glasses emptied into our mouth and passed onto piss and into the toilet and sewers and rivers and oceans to the tips of waves rolling and tumbling and dispersing to spray then into the air and then gone until we order another drink. Order a double. Life does not know life. There is great hope in the ultimately unknown you and letting go with only faith in the eternal and that lively ride on the universal bend that mysteriously remains in the right. "I DON'T KNOW," if you get with that you might be surprised by the power of you. It's not power that you grab at. It's power that comes from surrender.

I came very close to surrender on a quiet Sunday afternoon while sitting at the bar with Jodi and Sheldon. I was done with the two of them and the stinking black brawler scene had a strangle hold on me. I needed air, wanted out of our joint venture. With a slack face and glazed eyes Sheldon liked my point of view. "You don't get it," he said sluggishly, "It's all about groove." He struggled for more words and energy to explain how Circa Tabac was a stepping-stone toward the global corporate empire he was going to build complete with a movie production company, hotels, a chain of retail outlets, nightclubs, private jets, penthouses and yachts. "It's about me. Me, me, me" his words collapsed on the bar. Jodi too easily accepted Sheldon's exhaustion excuse for the way he looked and sounded. She was also patient with his mushy mega business vision. But she was counting on me for her small venture benefits. Sheldon offered me twenty grand. I estimated the 2003 value of my 20% cut closer to fifty grand. Jodi tried hard using legal jargon to convince me that our business agreement stipulated that I have to stay and manage the place no matter what happens. Everything for her was hunky dory, extra cash that came easy alongside her legal career. If Sheldon were left in charge "easy" would be removed from her profit line. I called her out on her business doublespeak and plainly told her, "You're absurd." She told me, "Fine! Leave. I'm not paying you a dime." The look she gave me was scary enough that I scanned the vicinity making sure there were no sharp objects within her reach.

Sheldon was perplexed in slow motion by our three-way face-off and the fact his sister didn't get behind his low-ball idea of buying me out. Sheldon being perplexed had already become the new normal. He'd been hanging out night and day with super porn prick and drug fiend Andrew Cohen. Whatever had happened in Vegas hadn't stayed in Vegas and it was growing on Sheldon with an empty look and a jaw drooping closer to the floor day by day. I'd been tracking Sheldon's slide since a couple of weeks after Vegas when I found him downstairs in the office dozing off and on perilously balanced on the edge of a chair a micron away from falling over. There were a few small, empty wax-paper envelopes and a bit of rose-gray powder on the desktop. Sheldon's nose was into junk, saddled high on horse roaming the drowsy road to smack town. The drug cocktail Andrew Cohen had started Sheldon off on was finished and he'd successfully incorporated heroin into his daily regime. At the bar that quiet Sunday afternoon throughout our business buy-out meeting Jodi hadn't broke character and was oblivious to the welfare of others and Sheldon's listless persona. She was also impatient and finally barked at me, "What are you going to do? Are you going to quit?" I told her, "I don't know."

I was chomping at the bit to clear out but leaving the bar I built with only twenty grand was a painful idea. With the bit of money I'd saved and Sheldon's measly offer I wouldn't have enough to open my own place. I'd end up bartending or managing another spot. I'd probably earn more dough but being my own man was more important. I seriously considered my equal standing with Sheldon, wondering if half a black gangsta Go-go bar is better than nothing. Current New York City affairs of the day complicated my decision process. Mayor Bloomberg's quest to outlaw smoking could inevitably close down Circa Tabac because the joint was homage to tobacco and drinking and we wouldn't have much else to offer aside from a miserable location on the conduit to the Holland Tunnel. Taking Sheldon's twenty grand before Bloomberg killed the bar might be best. But I also had to consider a smoking ban could rub out the dirty black scene at Circa Tabac because enforcement is always strict right after bogus laws are enacted and Sheldon would go along with clearing out the blunt smoking thugs or risk losing the stepping stone to his global corporate empire. I'd be back to working 90-plus hours a week, back to square one going after trade the old fashioned way. There's always hope in that. Cash would be seriously tight but I'd have my bar. Then again, with Sheldon creating a mess of everything he touched, I could bet on him eventually making a mess out of me. Ultimately Sheldon's insulting offer of twenty grand had me thinking that if I walked away I'd be bowing down to a heroin-addicted schlemiel. That was almost too much bear. I resolved to prayers for an answer to whether I should stay or go?

For a couple months afterwards I kept up my end of the partnership by going about my normal routine. Filling my head were thoughts of earlier times when Circa Tabac was the best watering hole in town and elation carried me to the bar daily. Now I was surviving on the thrill of harassing hip-hop goofballs to get me to work on time. On Sheldon's watch you could buy marijuana, cocaine, heroin, crack, ecstasy, oxycontin or a gun at a corner table and the place could've been aptly renamed The House of Hip-Hop. When they returned on my nights I was miserably trying to stomp out the thug life and the bar could've been called The House of Flip-Flop. I stood over tables and played heavy doses of the standards, classic rock, southern rock, punk, Latin music, country, experimental music, new wave, even classical music and opera. The nights the bar was bum rushed by hip-hop knuckleheads I'd play Chinese mediation music and nature sound effects. I wasn't proud of myself.

After a month of no sleep you end up appearing very odd to others and even a stranger to yourself. I was drinking a lot of vodka and smoking a pack of cigarettes every night hoping it could keep my eyes closed. The times sleep came for a sparse hour or two my recurring metamorphosis dream where I turn into a solid oak bar with a party around had changed. Instead of being startled awake with a smile and the good feeling of wood still on me I was waking up with my fingers and toes digging wholes in the mattress. It'd leave me pacing in my apartment. In the dream, by the time I become the bar, there's no party anymore, just old drunks minding their own, nursing their drinks. There's not a woman in the joint. Everything is rundown and only cheap liquor is being served. Another month of indecisiveness and sporadic shitty sleep had the dream take a painful turn. Riffraff started scraping their initials and crushing their cigarettes out on me. So much beer was spilled I got a taste of it, spoiled, horrible beer that woke me in a gagging fit. Another week without sleep was going to permanently disturb my psyche. Buckling to Sheldon was going to have to be my salvation, that's what I thinking. Taking so long to make the decision probably meant I didn't know what I want out of life. I was so far gone that visiting a gypsy crossed my mind. Instead I flipped a coin.

I called Sheldon with my decision. "You took too long," he told me, "I'll give you ten grand." He knew I was hurting with the way the bar was destroyed and that I'd taken my time because Circa Tabac was all I had. He continued, "If you don't take the offer right now, I'm going to lower it to five grand." He was trying hard to sound like a tough guy but it came across campy and rehearsed. Regardless, the low offer was like a scumbag kicking a man while he was down. One of those kicks rattled me enough to remember the old adage that you never let a scumbag win, ever. I'll just suck it up. "Fuck it! I'll stay then," that's what I told Sheldon. The shock of it felt comforting, immediately snapping me out of the delirium I'd been in for the past two months. "Don't forget to order beer," I told Sheldon, and then hung up the phone. He followed up by leaving at least a dozen messages on my voice mail throughout the day explaining what a big mistake he'd made and that he'd give me the twenty grand after all. The last message was anxious rambling, going on about how terrible he felt and how he wanted to increase the offer to twenty-five grand and then thirty. I didn't return any of his calls.

I got to Circa Tabac early the next day because I woke up energized after an incredible night of sleep. I was drinking coffee and counting the receipts in the register wondering what I might be able to do with Sheldon's thirty grand. Opening a bar wasn't an option. Upset with myself for not having more money saved, I couldn't count straight and I spilled coffee into the register. As I wiped up the mess I experienced divine intervention. The fluorescent light built into the art deco column behind the bar flickered and went out. I was surprised to notice it because it was a very dim light and the afternoon sun was still in the bar. I'd changed that bulb only a month before and they normally last a year or more. I pulled out the register to get at the light and found an opened business letter. It was dated two weeks earlier. Sheldon must've stuffed it back there. It was a letter from the City informing Circa Tabac that a citywide smoking ban was going into effect but our bar was granted an exclusive and lucrative permit to remain open as a smoking bar - one of only a handful of places in New York City exempt from the new law.

In 2003 being granted a monopoly on New York City smokers who drink was like winning the lottery and receiving it in daily installments. The good fortune came with a hook, guilt. Opening the door everyday at 5:00 PM and having customers pour into the joint instead of competing for their money was not real business. The unjust smoking law punished bars around town, many closed down, illustrating the ugly difference between government-controlled trade versus free market enterprise. The overflow of patrons was enough to avert my capitalist conscious. It also resurrected my customer service mojo. I didn't have time to waste looking back at the scam Sheldon tried pulling on me. To guarantee a covetable bar for New York City's nightlife lining up for drinks and smokes I had to move forward quickly. Jodi agreed that continuing to permit hip-hop gangstas to smoke marijuana, not order drinks and swing a wrecking ball around the bar would be dumber than allowing it in the first place. She levied serious threats on Sheldon and he dropped the amateur gangsta persona and the oversized hip-hop duds and settled on a cleaner version of his old getup of black jeans, black t-shirt and a black sports jacket. I suggested we tap into our reserves to redo the floors, patch walls, remodel the bathrooms, fix booths and seats, fresh paint and polish, a new storefront, and jazz up the smoking culture feel to the place with more tobacco centric art work and memorabilia. Very fast the joint looked better than ever.

Drinkers citywide were so happy to have a legal place to smoke that very often I was greeted at the front door with hugs; a few female French tourists offered me more. Profitable times meant plenty had to be managed correctly and efficiently. Despite Sheldon's new attire his steadily growing heroin habit was slowing down a smooth operation. I ran the daily opening and closing responsibilities, the food and liquor orders, maintenance and repairs, staff trouble, scheduling, hiring and firing, customer issues, private party organizing, website build and maintenance, along with advertising and public relations. Sheldon seized the role of star bar owner who routinely rolled in the door after a late dinner. As a means to a winning personality he'd let any girl with a nice set of tits and a notable rump drink for free, pick up tabs on rounds for guys he wished to be like, and then get a sloppy load on. Once he achieved his premiere sense of self he'd struggle to climb on top of a barstool and then clumsily jump onto the bar top and yell into the room full of people dense with cigarette smoke, "This is my bar! This is my bar! This is my bar!" It was like a bloated and bogus theophany struggling to levitate through a smug cloud above the heads of apathetic worshipers. The bloated part was spot on and when he'd end up falling off the bar and crashing to the floor anyone who might've been paying attention would blow it off as drunken buffoonery.

Nightly, when the bar top stage show settled down and the boob was picked up off the floor one of SoHo's heroin dealers would show up and Sheldon would stuff a scribbled I.O.U. into the register to pay for a couple of bags and then head home to melt.

Jodi was going through her own changes. New money had her more involved in the business. Not so much as helping with the day-to-day operations but more by setting up a new business bank account and seizing absolute control of accounts payable. That was a curious and aggressive change that in retrospect I should've addressed. But it's common knowledge that you never notice a problem until it becomes a problem and when you have little time to examine details of seemingly unimportant things stuff sneaks pass you.

Jodi's authoritarianism was a knife in my side. Sheldon's smack habit was taking a toll on our cash register. Sorting things out would've required time and trouble with a cost more than heroin. I was simply too busy. Now and then I managed a minute or two to brood over my relationship with Sheldon. Our pairing was something out of a cosmic karma fairytale. It wasn't a symbiotic relationship because that would mean we both relied on and benefited from each other. I can't say parasitic because that would mean Sheldon was draining me of nutrients and making me weaker day by day when I was feeling stronger than ever. It might've been more like the relationship between a kite and a tail, a necessary weight stabilizing an otherwise accomplished wing that could fly up through the atmosphere up where the air is famously too clear. But even that couldn't explain it. The best I came up with was to think of Sheldon as my evil twin. Both of our lives were the opposite of each other yet directly related. He lived with the conviction: all or nothing. For me, the universe was limitless potential beyond a choice of only one thing or another; and my intake and mood had become moderation. He did no work; I did all the work. He was sloppy; I was a stickler for order and cleanliness. He told everyone he owned the bar; I only answered people who begged to know because the bar itself was the star of the show.

I wasn't imagining our dynamic oppositions. At the time we each had a celebrity pal. Sheldon belonged to Vincent D'onofrio, a Brooklyn born actor famous to moviegoers as the tubby halfwit, Gomer Pyle, who blows his brains out in Stanley Kubrick's Full Metal Jacket. I didn't like the guy. To be fair, I had a predisposition. The Cell, one of his shitty films, was an in-flight

219

movie and I can't sleep on a plane; the moving image of D'onofrio flamboyantly dressed like a disturbed showgirl from Cirque du Soleil in a endlessly long crimson velvet gown and sporting a queer horn head hairdo making him look like a big sore dick stuck in a unraveled bloody tampon was sadly seared on my brain. The big sore dick was a heavy smoker, a drinker, and according to Sheldon, a dubious drug dabbler with a penchant for eighteen-year-old cocktail waitresses. He was in my bar too often. One night he tried pulling me into his little domain by sharing his appetite for decadence, titillating darkness and perversion. A story about an Eye's Wide Shut styled party in a castle in Transylvania and how he spent the night with some old Duke's wife in the tower. He spoke to me in a pretentious poetic tone about moonlight on centuries old granite walls. "Warm pee from an old woman in the palm of your hand will open you to unknown pleasures," he explained. Worse than his icky story was the way he treated my bartender, Dixie. A Sunday school girl and a High School Theater player, nineteen, eager as a shiny new penny, from the outskirts of Savannah, Georgia. Broadway lights brought her to New York. She had star quality, the requisite thin waist, perky tits, round ass, long legs, big blue eyes, and a mouth you'd want to curl up to and sleep on. With the way she moved behind the bar I would've bet money she was a talented dancer. Vincent D'onofrio got one look at Dixie and struck like a viper promising her personal direction and acting lessons and a step up on her road to success. She was a sickly coke whore within three months. What a guy.

My celebrity was Sir Ben Kingsley – Ghandi.

The big sore dick was desperate to be Customer #1 at Circa Tabac - the guy who can walk in anytime of night, even if the joint is packed to the rafters, and be treated like Frank Sinatra. He indulged Sheldon with a private jet to Las Vegas for a long weekend of banal debauchery. Once there, Sheldon had to dish out his life savings to keep up with the big sore dick's extravagant bets and pleasures. D'onofrio wasn't as life threatening as my past hip-hop headache but the potential damage to Sheldon and subsequently my business profits was nearly as serious. A different night, he was sitting alone at a table for six while I had a line of people going out the front door. Much to my pleasure he got up and left. I quickly squeezed a group of eight in the same spot. He returned two hours later pissed off at me for not saving his table. "I'm reporting you to Sheldon," he said. "Sorry, buddy. I thought you left," I told him. The big sore dick whined, "My Camel Lights were on the table. You should've known I was coming back." Half empty packs of cigarettes were left at the bar every night and I told him that. I also told him, "If you wait here at the bar I'll have a nice little table for you in about a half an hour." My offer had him put his hand up, twisting his wrist and showing his palm to my face in some sort of baphomet contortion that I guessed was supposed to reject my bad energy. This guy is a twit, that's what I thought, probably an Aleister Crowley devotee or into Hollyweird kabbalah or some other school of delusional thinking. "When Sheldon gets here," the big sore dick told me, hamming up his superiority, "have him call me immediately." He stormed away. "And what world do you live in?" I shouted that at him but he was out the door fast. The next day it was in all the papers, Vincent D'onofrio collapsed on the set of his criminal-injustice-system-are-gods television show and was hospitalized. How's that for an energy blocker.

Half an hour after the big sore dick stormed out of the bar that night I went down to the basement for a bottle of tequila the bartender needed and found Sheldon passed out on the floor gagging on his vomit. I quickly rolled him over onto his side and pumped his gut clean. It wasn't pretty. He was breathing clearly again but remained catatonic. I thought about calling an ambulance but I didn't. I wiped up the mess best I could and discovered a hacksaw blade lying next to him and half a hole cut out of a crooked floorboard and a small wax paper bag filled with what I guessed was heroin at the bottom of that hole. There were four small emptied wax paper bags sitting on the desktop. Sheldon must've snorted the four bags and dropped the fifth into the gap of the crooked floorboard and then exhausted himself hacking away to get at it, keeled over.

I couldn't lift him up onto the desk chair so I fixed him on his side against a few cardboard boxes. My plan was to leave him there and look in on him every ten minutes or so. On my second checkup he'd rolled off the boxes onto his belly with his face smashed into the floor. I rolled him onto his back. I wondered if I made a mistake about not calling the ambulance. I felt his pulse and it was beating slow and steady like his breathing so I stayed calm and sat in the desk chair looking down on him at my feet. With his mouth slack and his eyelids closed like a tossed blanket on a bed he looked fantastically peaceful. Some of the vomit I didn't manage to get off his face had dried and it painted a funny, crackled smile across his chubby cheeks. Between his roundness and slow breathing he had me thinking of one of those statues of a fat Buddha that maybe got knocked off a table and laying there on its side it would have you thinking that being horizontal or vertical made no difference at all when you are one with the universe. I couldn't help but notice the remarkable smoothness of Sheldon's forehead and a few cheerful red hairs highlighting the arch of his eyebrows and some of his eyelashes. A slight undulating appearance on his face made it look like Sheldon had nothing to hide. It had me remembering the first time I met him when he was eighteen; a messy, awkward kid who always wanted to be part of whatever was going on. As he lay there on the floor maybe not a part of anything something inside of him was coming lose, shining through like a noiseless laugh, the good hearted aura of someone who wanted to be liked.

Sheldon had always been uncomfortable with his physical condition but grateful to at least have a puppy dog gleam in his eyes. I was thinking about what a bad turn he'd taken in life. Maybe because it was late or I was tired but tears swelled up and gushed for a moment when I realized what was going to happen to him if things didn't change. I'd seen my fair share of people hooked on dope. Plenty of them died. It can happen quickly. There's always an exception to the rule but Sheldon wasn't one of them. He was missing a tolerance gage. Plus it'd only take one bad bag of junk and he'd be done. I was thinking how a bottle of tequila saved his life. I was also thinking about Jodi and how she trash talked Sheldon all the time. I wondered why she didn't like her brother. I looked down and could see all his loneliness on his big milky white mushy belly spilling out from under his shirt. Despite nearly the whole of him having come undone and sprawled out on the floor I noticed his fists were clenched tight and no matter how much heroin he snorted they were never going to let go. It made me think something wrong happened to Sheldon and it wasn't his fault. Maybe he was seriously sick as a child. Was he abused in any way? He could've witnessed something a kid should never see. I sat there watching over him for a while wondering about what he really wanted out of life because I didn't think anyone in the world had ever done that for him. Sure his mother pampered him but it was likely she tended to him like a little girl deals with her doll projecting her vision of life on him unconcerned with his outlook, his vision and dreams, what he thinks about anything. It wasn't long before Sheldon was coming out of his little coma. His eyes were fluttering and beginning to look around. He caught a glimpse of me sitting above and it spooked him. I left before he completely woke up because I didn't want him to feel embarrassed. I also didn't want him to see that I'd been crying over him because it'd be hard to explain. Half an hour later I went back down to the basement. He was sitting up on the desk chair slowly swaying back and forth with his eyes closed while a lit cigarette nearly burned to the end dangled from his lip. I grabbed the butt out of his mouth and smashed it into the ashtray. I looked down at the hole in the floorboard; the bag of heroin was gone.

Brutal arguments ensued between Jodi, her mother and me over next couple of weeks. For them it was impossible that Sheldon had a cretin's habit. I told his mom there was a good chance he'd be dead sooner than later. She told me: "You should grow like an onion with your head in the ground." After Jodi exhausted herself calling me a liar and every foul name she could come up with she turned unresponsive, hoping feigned ignorance would defer responsibility. She could be ice cold on demand. It was during her grandfather's funeral a few years back when her barbwire heartstrings nearly strangled me. Sheldon and her were bickering and she threatened to not attend the service because the stamp collection her grandfather left Sheldon was worth more money than the book collection he left her. I knew the old man; he was a standout guy, generous, smart, funny and loving; a businessman on point with a long list of grateful employees with grateful families; the provider for three generations of his entire family's comfort and lifestyle. I spent the day of the funeral in a shaky Shiva, upset that Jodi and Sheldon couldn't recognize the contribution their patriarch made to the world. At the funeral the sad emotion inside of me was strong and gaining momentum. I grabbed a hold of it best I could but the more I tried the pressure to escape built up until it popped out in a loud squeak that pierced the eardrums of the three hundred mourners packing the synagogue. I should've been embarrassed but heartbreak was all that resonated.

As dopey and cumbersome as Sheldon was he didn't deserve to die so I kept at Jodi. The lump of ice buried in her chest finally cracked when I had our bartender Leo tell her about Sheldon's heroin dealer making daily visits to Circa Tabac and money coming out of the register. Cash caught her attention and the corroborating witness forced her plausible deniability to fall apart. Blood would be on her hands if Sheldon died. She accepted the situation but wasn't capable of a serious and truthful talk with him. It hardly made a difference because Sheldon was pretty much lacking a brain at that stage of the game. "Get professional help," I told her. I told her that daily for three weeks before the ball started to roll. Sheldon was home for the weekend and his mother snooped around and found a small bundle of heroin packets in his jacket pocket. The family staged a half ass intervention. After a week of kicking and screaming they checked him into a fancy Rehab Center in sunny south Florida where he stayed for months.

My time alone at Circa Tabac can be summed up easily, tops. It felt like a fresh coat of grease on the tracks of my storefront gates every afternoon I pulled them up. The good natured stench of cigars, cigarettes, beer and booze sitting inside the bar patiently waiting for my afternoon arrival to open the windows and let them out for a few hours was like having a beloved pet waiting to go out for a piss. Opening the mail and checking the bar's voicemail everyday was like a proud family member anticipating news of a baby's birth. Wrangling out food and liquor deals from salesmen became child's play and my cost of goods shrunk dramatically. The place was tidier and shinier than ever. My employees were thrilled because the split-personality two-headed boss they were used to was gone and they were left with the one head that always helped them with work instead of threatening to fire them every other shift. A growing list of new and satisfied customers along with climbing sales had me feeling like I'd gone through a late-in-life growth spurt.

I took one complete day off every week, Mondays. I'd ride my bicycle from downtown to the George Washington Bridge and across it to the end of Palisades Park, spend a peaceful hour or two surveying Hudson River currents, and then back home for an incredible night of sleep. The rest of the week I'd only leave the bar for a few hours at a time to get things done or see people. I squeezed in charity work for 9/11 First Responders and ran a free of charge political film series on Sunday afternoons at the bar that had people talking about government corruption, crony capitalism, the bogus two party political system, the central banking syndicate, the evils of internationalism and global corporatism, 9/11 cover up, immoral wars, geo-engineering, libertarianism. With some new friends and associates I started a citizen muckraker group, We Are Change. The only thing that irked during my time alone running Circa Tabac was one conversation at the bar about health with some male customers my age. I was the odd one out having never seen a doctor in my life. The single malt consensus was: "You're nuts! Get a checkup." Hearing that I might have Coronary Heart Disease the following week from a doctor with only the help of a stethoscope stuck in his ears had me thinking he was getting a piece of the action on the drugs he was pushing on me. I felt great, left his office, never followed up, and remembered why I never went to a doctor in the first place. With the way things were going I could've done anything. Best, I was back into the swing of things having extras drinks and smokes on Friday nights for the fun of it.

When Sheldon finally returned to work he was stinking with a new sense of humbleness. He'd lost weight and had an obvious look of maturity that brought out some of the hidden handsomeness in his face. He took up a habit of introducing me to new customers at the bar as his business partner. He was smoking heavily but eating healthy foods and not touching a drop of the spirits. That's what worked for him in Florida. I tried selling him my practice of smoking only when drinking, and not to drink everyday, and every other month or so go a week or two without any of it. Sheldon was sticking to his guns. I was happy for him. I suspect the family periodically had taken weekend trips to the

Sunshine State to participate in Sheldon's therapy sessions and it turned out good for all of them. Jodi was now having lunch with Sheldon once a week like a normal brother and sister should be able to do. She started being respectful and appreciative toward me. A bunch of times she brought the topic of how Sheldon was tracking down people in his life that he might've hurt or offended while he was on drugs and how he was supposed to apologize and reintroduce himself as new, improved and thoughtful Sheldon. Jodi kept bringing it up to me as if it was her therapeutic duty to make sure he did it. I told her he apologized even though he didn't just to get her off my back. Only Sheldon could know the truth about anything new that might reside inside of him. Apologizing to all of humanity wouldn't make a difference if honesty were absent from your heart. Sheldon hadn't overdosed, that was enough for me.

Things went swimmingly for a long, long while after rehab. With our state sanctioned monopoly on drinks and smokes, along with Sheldon taking on work responsibilities, the bar turned clockwork. I had money and time in my pocket. Dough accumulated because my routine was cheap and I dove back into reading. Righteous liberty, stateless societies based on voluntary associations, and the history and goings on of the abominable Central Banking system were my favorite topics. I didn't have to sweat business so any time the urge arose I could appreciate cocktails and tobacco alongside friends and strangers at the bar without desperately looking out the window every three seconds anxious for customers. There might not be a better combination of ingredients in existence than the rich and elevated sensation of people sitting around a bar drinking, smoking and yapping. It's the optimistic and combustible mix of booze and smiles that'll immerse you in the moment while smoking prevents hot and empty air from being blown at each other. Everyone becomes acquainted and reciprocal under a genial awareness as lofty as the smoke above our heads as we casually figure out we love each other as much as a good time.

Douglas "C-note" Haus-Sachsen IV was built for good times. He stood 6 foot 6, weighed over 300 lbs, and any night he walked into the place he'd peel off crisp $100 dollar bills for the bartenders, waitresses and busboys. A small and excited group of customers familiar with his routine would quickly form a protective circle around him at the bar. Anyone within his long reach got free tequila shots all night long, as much as they could handle. That's what C-Note drank, shots of Patron. He'd chug an Amstel light after every other one to clear his pallet and before the empty bottle hit the bar top he'd reach into his shirt pocket as if his arm was spring loaded and pull out a small ziplock bag of cocaine, rip it open with his teeth and snort the entirety in a blink. Making a trip to the bathroom for drug privacy wasn't necessary because he was head and shoulders above everyone and his practice was so hammered into his movements you'd be pressed to know what he was up to. Four bags of coke and eight shots on the hour was my best estimation.

C-note was more than generous with cash and tequila. He liked my bar, our crowd and me, and decided I should have a lot of money. Instead of $100 tips he managed a stock portfolio for me. My $162,000 dollar stake multiplied like rabbits. Fast enough my net worth, though far from a Rockefeller fortune, was easily more money than I deserved for no effort. I didn't do anything with the loot because my balance sheet exploding on the computer screen every day made it look more like play money; and the only thing I ever mindlessly blew cash on was partying and those days were over. It piled up. Every once in a while C-note would ask me, "Do you want own a helicopter?" I didn't but I'd simply tell him, "Let it ride." Of course the evil that runs the world wouldn't let lucrative times remain airborne. The leviathan reared its ugly head in 2008 with the criminal financial crisis and my booty vanished faster than it accumulated. I cashed out with less than twenty grand. C-note lost his job at Lehman Brothers and his drive to party. My big customer was gone along with many medium and small sized ones. Like so many businesses in City, the financial crisis smashed Circa Tabac.

Summer evening sunlight was hanging around the bar with a handful of customers. My bartender had called to say he'd be an hour late and the waitress was wiping down menus. "Money is not everything but it's a lot things." I was explaining things to Tony Masaccio, taking my time making his Whiskey Soda while the craving on his forehead cringed. He was a long time regular.

Though using the word "regular" anywhere close to a description of Tony Masaccio was misleading as many in this town will attest to. An old artist who came up in the sixties and seventies with the reigning New York School that included his friends Andy Warhol, John Chamberlain, David Budd and the gang that forged the City's infamous nightlife culture. Tony always appreciated our jab and smile style of talk, free drinks and a hassle free place to rest his feet, as well as a corner in the basement to keep a bag of belongings for safe keeping. He didn't have a reliable place to rest his head at nigh but knew enough people in town for a shower and a shave every week that helped maintain a happening appearance that never would have you think he slept in doorways. Bad breaks hadn't destroyed his charisma which meant a bar character well worth the price of five or six house whiskeys.

Tony had been a notable painter but experienced more success as a forger, a master de Kooning forger. He claimed to be so good at it because one night back in 1969 at Max's Kansas City on Park Avenue South while sitting at a table with de Kooning and consuming vast amounts of gin and unknown substances he was able to shrink himself to the size of a martini olive and crawl inside of de Kooning's mouth and shimmy down into his gut and grab a bit of what made him what he was. For longer than twenty-five years Tony's forgery career amounted to routine times when he and his hustle partner, Ken Perenyi, could move fakes through compromised New York and London dealers and get ten to fifty grand a pop and downtimes that could last for months when dealers didn't want to gamble with their knockoffs. When Tony was flush he'd burn through twenty-five grand or more in less than a week at the Carlyle Hotel with an expensive room, prostitutes, champagne, cocaine, fine new threads, and his biggest thrill, throwing crumbled-up fifty dollar bills at people.

I told Tony, "Money can be magic. A guy with a lousy personality but a couple of bucks for drinks can always find company. Money decides who eats, starves, or wins a war and rewrites history. Money disappears, only reality is sustained." I wasn't telling him anything he didn't know by heart. He patiently listened to my jabber because he was dead set on the bottle of whiskey in my hand. The tension in his forehead was getting close to imploding and I didn't want to taunt him anymore so I poured. "It's because they're Jews," he said as he reached out and grabbed the drink before I could slide it across the bar top and then had most of it down in one gulp. Tony was referring to my business partners with one of his trademark in-your-face proclamations.

We'd been discussing serious fiduciary matters connected to my bar. 2007 through 2009 were years marked by economic crisis and an overall 35% reduction in sales. Having grown accustomed to easy times, the fading profits had a tense, meaner reality settle in deep like heartbreak for Jodi and Sheldon. Other than a pricked concern for business cash flow not much changed for me. My rent was affordable and I wasn't going hungry. Best, I could still share a drink and smoke with my regulars and talk about money or anything. Conversations with Tony Masaccio were choice because he was experienced with complicated situations and relationships and he'd been around New York City bars and bar owners his whole life. He was also from Flatbush and that made our line of communication tangle free. I needed to hear what he thought about my business partners and our bank account being run down to nearly zero every month and how the bad economy didn't half explain it.

I laid it out for Tony: "The last ten years Jodi has been slowly adding her personal expenses to the business ledger. She tells me it's the best way to take her share of the profits and still get the most out of a tax write off. Her business Amex card is a complete mystery to me. She keeps three sets of books and the more she adds and removes from any of them over time the more it looks like crossed wires with enough mumbo jumbo to confuse everything down to nothing, zilch, zero." Tony was drinking the last bit of his cocktail. I told him, "I think she's scraping off the top." He put the glass down and gave me his routine, fun and confident smile and shared his wisdom. "The price of doing business. Accept it." I told him, "Easier said than done." He then flashed his life hardened smile and told me, "It's probably not as bad as you think. If it makes you feel better keep a record of everything and stay in touch with a good accountant." He reached across the bar top and gave me a fatherly pat on the forearm that quickly turned into a strong squeeze and a dig into the muscle and then a big fun again grin on his face and shouted, "Now give me a cigarette and another Whiskey Soda and make it four fingers you cheap bastard!"

In 2009 there was a price of doing business. In 2010 there was a bigger price of doing business. By the end of 2011 the price of doing business superseded my cost of living. It was the Cool War era at Circa Tabac. Unlike the hot wars WWI and WWII, Team Dingleberg wasn't launching violent attacks or telling me directly that they want me out. They telegraphed their intent by giving me less and less of the profit every year. It was unlike the Cold War with its indirect struggle of proxy battles resulting in a zero-sum geopolitical stalemate because a standstill was next to impossible with the crooked set of books acting as a time-bomb ticking when eventually someone was going to be blown up. It was a Cool War because to the clueless observer Team Dingleberg and I were getting along fabulously while behind the scenes a smiley-face game of poker was being played and in the pot was a hammer and a nail. Unfortunately, after a lifetime of disparity, Jodi and Sheldon were finally working together to dominate me with an 80% shareholder stake and being the nail meant I'd eventually have to stop complaining about the emptied bank account and the crooked books and accept whatever money was thrown at me, or, I could just walk away from it all empty handed.

I had a scant, one-dimensional strategy: keep my bar. Their strategy was tension; complain and complain about not having enough money to run the operation and infer we could go out of business any day and hopefully I'd start to look for some other work. Jodi was the crafty comptroller with a set of records split up between the basement office and her apartment making an easy view of our finances impossible. Luckily basic math showed rent, salaries, the cost of goods and essential bills were easily below what we took in sales. The truth about being in the black was comforting and I could hold my head up everyday because our shareholders' agreement stipulated Sheldon and I stood on equal ground as far as day-to-day operations go. He and I also drew an equal salary before any profit sharing. It wasn't great money but survivable. By late 2011 all profits vanished into the singe and ash of overcooked books and Jodi and Sheldon started threatening to burn my paycheck. I was facing a brick wall on a dead end street. The only thing keeping me positive was following my friend Tony Masaccio's advice best I could. I dug up and slapped together a decent record of every penny we ever collected and where it was supposedly spent.

"I want to buy your bar," that was a very popular thing I heard over the years. It usually happened at two or three in the morning when heads were wet with wild visions of their own wealth and how a bar owner's life must always be New Years' Eve with a girl for every guy and the boss takes his pick and there's never a hangover or a lick of work to be done. It was easy enough to smile at whoever made the boozy proposition and tell them that I'd call in the morning to discuss the deal because it's bad to mix business with pleasure. They'd usually agree and order a round of shots to celebrate the inebriated venture. One late night things were different when Zoe Duchensne came rolling in the front door with some friends. She was an exceptional regular at Circa Tabac; a talented painter and lingerie model. But a virtuoso with colors, canvas and lacy panties was nothing compared to her being a natural lover of the bar life; the drinking; the talking; the smoking; the shimmy - all of it. It was in her blood, her perfect bones, the corners of her martini glass smile and the souls of her pretty dancing feet and it radiated out of her nighttime blue eyes like the bright lights tracing out the show-time scene on Broadway. Her magnetism would have people randomly walk in off the street and tell me they hadn't intended to but were compelled to enter and order a drink. They'd inevitably settle their eyes on Zoe, men and women alike, and ask me, who is that girl? I'd tell all of them the same thing, "She's the Giver of Nightlife." This night the brown haired dynamo was looking like a long-legged funhouse in heels, a short pleated denim skirt and a tight pink midriff t-shirt that said Unthinkable Party in sparkled lettering that made it appear to be blossoming from her heart. Her pack of professional long legged girlfriends in tow were stinking up the joint with charm and bruising beauty. A happening, pug looking English dude was buying bottles of Cristal for the gang of darlings and having a shitload of fun doing it. At $400 a bottle I was having just as much fun opening them. By 3:00 AM he was telling me, "I want to buy

231

your bar." I gave him my usual: "Let's not mix pleasure with business. I'll call you in the morning." They drank more, smoked, laughed and danced and on the way out the door at nearly five in the morning my English chum had enough wit left in him to pass me his card and tell me, "Call me tomorrow about the bar."

Paul Kensley, Football Chairman and Property Developer, that's how he was listed on the easily found Internet profile. I drummed up a tremendous effort to contain my excitement and called Jodi and Sheldon, told them, "I might have a buyer for the bar. Are you interested?" I gave them his name. Later that night, "We're open to it," was the Team Dingelberg response. "He's worth a billion dollars," Jodi told me. Sheldon tried a laughable paternal approach with me: "Let me have his phone number and I'll take over from here." They were easily capable of cutting a shady deal that could leave me on the outs so I told them, "Just tell me your price." For me the price was simple because a friend of mine was in the business of selling businesses and according to industry standards calculated against our bar sales and bottom line costs and the remainder of our lease and the potential of lease renewal Circa Tabac in 2011 was worth upwards of $650,000. Not a fortune but not bad for a little joint sitting on the dirty lip of the Holland Tunnel. You might add a price premium because Bloomberg's anti-smoking law supposedly guaranteed Circa Tabac solid business. Though a steady decline in our official sales reports for the previous three years would say differently. You'd also have to consider people only obey an unjust law when they're afraid of getting caught and enforcing the anti-smoking law by 2011 was hardly heard of. There were plenty of bars you could smoke at after 11pm when the Health Department is done for the day. Any businessman worth his salt would also know there was a chance the smoking prohibition might not last much longer than the prohibition of booze. Without the slanted law Circa Tabac would be just another small bar in a lousy location competing for business. I figured with Paul Kensley worth as much as he was he must know a thing or two about business so he probably wasn't going to pay more than the real value; maybe he'd go as high as $700,000. Sheldon and Jodi came up with their number, $3.5 million. "I can't tell the guy that price He's going to laugh," that what I told them. They told me, "That's what the business is worth."

I thought about not calling Paul Kensley to avoid the embarrassment but I picked up the phone because I was desperate. Thievery had me leery in Team Dingleberg's company, unable to look them in the eyes anymore. The idea of years more of business together was odious. Dante's Inferno has the ninth circle of hell reserved for treacherous bastards who betray. I would never condemn anyone to hell, especially to the bottom ring, but it helps explain how I felt. A Paul Kensley cash return for my years of sweat and devotion and the opportunity to get on with my life was the remedy I'd been praying for. I made the call. He was very happy to hear from me. He was leaving town by the end of the week and wanted to close the deal before he left. "How much for the bar?" he asked. I explained that I have two partners and coming up with a price was difficult and it was far from what I proposed, and blah, blah, blah. "Three and half million," I said. The laughter was brief and polite. He said, "It was very nice to meet you and thanks for a memorable night at the bar." Click. I tried throwing my phone through the wall. I didn't call Sheldon or Jodi with the news and my smashed phone had nothing to do with it. I'm pretty sure they called me a hundred times. The next day I went to work as usual and both of them showed up with dollar signs in their eyes and asked me what was his response. "He said what I told you he'd say."

"How can you smoke here and not anywhere else?" I heard that more than people telling me: "I want to buy your bar." An older, heavyset couple from Knoxville, Tennessee nursing diet cokes and smoking Merit Ultra Lights 100s asked me that question in early 2012. You might think it'd be nuisance to answer the same question a thousand times a year but due to my partnership quandary diverting my interests away from the bar over the last few years along with my skyrocketing curiosity into the unchecked power and the gluttonous, murderous ways of the DC establishment running amok since 9/11, I always used that tired question as an opportunity to give a civics lesson on corruption originating from a growing government force. "A Grandfather Clause," I told the Knoxville duo, "When the anti-smoking legislation went into effect the powers that be simply made up a new rule exempting any bar that had at least 10% of their sales tobacco related and had been open for business before December 31, 2001." The old man said, "Oh, I see." The blank look on his face had me thinking he didn't. He was nervous, as some tourists are when they first start talking to you. I told him, "Mayor Bloomberg made an exception for a few businesses that operated with a clear intent of catering to smokers." He was still perplexed. I said, "This is Circa Tabac," with emphasis on Tabac. His wife said, "I get it." She did.

With the conversation suddenly open I didn't miss a beat and jumped into a routinely practiced explanation of how Circa Tabac was the perfect example of government's unjust power to bless certain individuals or groups with guaranteed businesses while at the same time outlawing normal competitive opportunities for other hard working entrepreneurs. "A lot of bars went out of business when the law went into effect because plenty of their customers were smokers," that's what I told the Knoxville couple. "That's dumb," the old man said, "Why don't they just make it the proprietor's choice if he wants smokers in his bar? Nobody force'n you to go inside if you don't like smoke." I told him, "It's about cultivating authoritarianism." The woman told me, "You don't sound happy about the law even if it gives you a living." Honest and competitive businesses are supposed to provide a living. I was pointing out the contradiction my business posed by being a government-privileged business. I told them, "Just because it's good for me doesn't make it right." People always loved hearing that part because it was the truth and people simply love the truth. "Ain't that the truth," the woman said.

The truth, as always, led to a deeper conversation. We talked more about big banking and big business and their control of our big government, and the Federal Reserve's monopoly on money that gave them control over big banks and big business. "Central Banking is the root of all evil and inherently anti-American and anti-human. Crony capitalism is not real capitalism. It's not what our founding fathers had envisioned for all of us," I told that to the Knoxville duo at the tail end of our conversation. When they finally finished their diet cokes and got up to leave with smiles on their faces they grabbed a handful of souvenir matchbooks and the woman told me, "We're gonna tell everyone back in Knoxville about Circa Tabac and those scalawag Central Bankers!" I loved that part, like eating the whiskey soaked cherry from your emptied Manhattan.

Whenever delivering my money-monopoly-government-corruption diatribe, or other talks on essential life topics, the volume of my voice would be up a notch or two in an attempt to draw others into the conversation. The technique worked often and always encouraged a lively talk around the bar. During the back and forth with the Knoxville couple one of Circa Tabac's premium styled customers was sitting alongside us; a middle aged, pleasant looking guy wearing an expensive suit drinking 18 year old Bowmore and smoking an Ashton VSG cigar. The fact that this guy was sitting at the bar as opposed to a discreet table in the back meant he was my type of customer unafraid to mix with the denizens and villagers elbowed up, drinking beer, house pours and blowing Marlboro Lights. He reached out to shake my hand and introduced himself, "Charles Antoninus. It's a pleasure to meet you." I told him, "The pleasure is mine." He told me, "If you weren't a bar owner you could have a great career in Law."

Charles Antoninus was impressed with how I delivered the loaded conversation to an older couple that probably hadn't thought much about the workings of the marketplace or money creation or the foundational principles of the United States. I'm not sure how he would've felt about my screed if he had to sit through the previous thousand times I delivered it like my bartenders have had to. He then told me, "I love Circa Tabac. Not only for cigars. I like the odd mix of people hanging around and tonight marks the third time in a row I heard a great conversation. I can't tell you the last time I was in another bar and the talk wasn't centered on sports, television, movies or celebrities. Your employees are great. That Sally Anne is exceptional. You should teach a class on how to treat customers." I told him, "I love my customers." I also thanked him for the kind words and for his business and I bought him a drink because you buy drinks for people you want to see more often in your bar. I ordered vodka for myself. Without anyone else sitting near there was no need to raise my voice and Charles

Antoninus and I had a more deliberate talk about nouvelle colonialism, crony capitalism and how disastrous it is for the true free market system and the world. Both of us had read Murray Rothbard's books and considered Ludwig von Mises' Human Action a seminal work that should be on everyone's must-read-in-your-lifetime list, the sooner the better.

Charles was more informed and better spoken than me. Franchise Law was his work. "Fortunately," he said, "my Firm's growth has been as consistent as a chain reaction." Because we were like-minded we got into a talk about my business. I had a couple more vodkas along the way and gave him the skinny on Jodi's cooked books. Displaying the mark of a good lawyer, his opinion on how I should handle the matter was clear and brief: "Press criminal charges and sue them." "Can I do that?" I asked with an awkward spike in my voice. "You can," he said, "I make a lot of money doing that. This stuff happens all the time. The worst is in a family business when they start stealing from each other." Of course to be absolutely sure about my case he'd need to review my shareholder agreement and have one of his accountants look over financial records and anything else that might be incriminating. Charles was coming on like gangbusters with jail talk and a lawsuit; none of it had been in my line of thinking. I wasn't sure I could afford his services and told him so. "Just call my office tomorrow and make an appointment for Friday afternoon," he said, "We'll go over a few things and I promise you won't be billed for the meeting. I'll treat you to lunch."

In three weeks time I was in Charles' office for the second time, the accountant's report was finished and he made me an offer I was finding hard to turn down. He could prove embezzlement and successfully bring criminal charges against Jodi and very likely against Sheldon. He could start a civil suit against both of them that in the end would force them to turn the bar over to me in a settlement. He told me, "They've stolen a serious amount of money from you." It was more than I thought. His accountant suspected they'd been skimming from the beginning but the last few years were very concerning. Charles told me, "I checked on your business partner Jodi Dingleberg's law background. Aside from filling out a skirt and a tight blouse nicely she's a hack. If she plans on handling her own case she'll be in jail before you get a chance to change the locks on the front door." He explained that Jodi likely would get a real lawyer and that could drag things on for three or four years, maybe more. "Rest assure," he said "when it's over, the bar will be yours." To prove his confidence in my case he offered his services in exchange for a nominal percentage of the bar. "3% percent," he said, "You can keep the profits. Just greet me at the door as your partner. I'll even pay for my own drinks."

I didn't believe in guardian angles, and if I did I never could've guessed mine would be a sharp suit wearing, hawkeyed libertarian-loving lawyer. How do you explain something like that? Some might consider that we are part of the infinite universe and that if you wait long enough eventually everything happens. But considering the fact that I was fifty years old and in the scheme of things with how old stars and planets are it had to be something more like an intentional blessing. My heart was beating loud and fast I'm certain it could be seen through my shirt. "If I ever have a child I'm going to name him or her Charles," I said with a smile nearly ripping my cheeks apart. He told me, "I don't need to know your answer today so please take a breath before you have a stroke in my office. Also keep in mind that if you decide not to press criminal charges and only want out of the business I'll handle the corporate settlement for you. If you need me too." I wanted to hug him but of course I didn't. I told him, "I'm indebted to you." He told me, "The case isn't complicated, mostly court filings, we have the evidence. Besides, helping you will be a pleasure. Believe it or not, the more good you do for the world actually makes the world more good." Before I left I took another look at his Law Degree hanging on the wall to confirm what I just heard had come out of the mouth of a lawyer.

Imagine the feeling inside of me after learning my criminal partners were going to get what they had coming to them and the bar was going to be mine. It was the end of February and luckily it was warm outside, reaching the fifties. All for me, I thought, a perfect opportunity to stretch my legs and get my head straight after having my world turned around. I was downtown near the bottom of Broadway outside Charles Antoninus's office, salivating, walking and wondering if it was a piece of the burger I had for lunch stuck in my teeth or was I craving Team Dingleberg blood. The new situation was way beyond the reach of my earlier grim expectations, had my thoughts racing as fast as my legs were moving. Before I knew it I was on Broadway and Canal Street. I thought of stepping over to Circa Tabac for a smug mug of beer in the afternoon to look over the whole joint, knowing in my head that it was my bar. Then the idea of maybe running into Sheldon cramped my brain. I was too ramped up to slow down anyway so I kept up a good stride. Bipedalism can be an enthralling experience; it's like low level flying mingled with a thousand or more controlled crashes with every step you take and an instant spring return from your heel and soul that wakes up the buried you inside to come out and partake in the fresh air and action, buoying you in the face of the world. Somewhere on Broadway between Houston and 14th Street I must've skipped along for a half a block or so.

By the time I made it to Times Square my bluster had mellowed. I was facing a chunk of confusion, as if I tripped and smashed my head into a lamppost. My mind was off Circa Tabac and lawsuits. Times Square was missing its lifelong tally of a hundred million New Yorkers' primal connection to the universe. Sure, there were more billboards than ever before, more flashy computerized signs, bigger projections, a bunch of gigantic and practically nude images of models everywhere, but the bottom line that nearly knocked me out was the Crossroads of the World had been converted to a dime-a-dozen pedestrian plaza. The warm afternoon in February had drawn out all the wrong sorts and crowded them at the center of it all. I'd heard about Bloomberg's transformation of the area back in 2008 but I hadn't been above 23rd Street in years to witness the carnage. It was hard to believe the intersection of boom and bust was closed to the traffic light pulse of taxis, buses and cars. The pavement was painted a queer blue that had me wondering if it was a color at all and the place was filled with clownish toned tin tables, chairs, benches and shade umbrellas. The low spending tourists from all over America and the world were camping out for the day side by side with a rainbow army of life sized Sesame Street characters, Batmans, Spidermans and Supermans fighting it out for $2 tourist photos.

238

"Where the fuck am I?" that's what was pounding in my head. A simple and absent look was obvious on all the faces but there was more to them that was hard to put your finger on. Looking at everyone was maybe like being in an outdoor meat market with price slashed commercial grade steaks on a table waiting to be eaten by choice or consent. Though with the way all had their heads were tilted up at an awkward angle it was more a space age cult waiting for the mother ship and the word on the street was the most asinine get on board first. Or maybe they'd all heard there was a new roller coaster in Times Square and the mindless get free rides, and any second now we'd see and hear a bunch of buffoons strapped into coaster seats screaming as they dipped off the side of a skyscraper. After Bloomberg's ridiculous vanity projects like Central Park's orange Gates and the millions of taxpayers' dollars he spent on Waterfalls constructed out of scaffolding all over the city's waterfront anything was possible.

Bloomberg's goofy new Times Square was making me nervous, nothing like the nervous I remembered from standing there in the past. The best I could guess was that the heart of the City was replaced with an artificial pump moving fake blood through surrounding streets filled with replica people dressed in a splash of plastic colors and patterns that I'd always thought were forbidden in New York. They appeared to have been drawn together for a sacrifice, kindle collecting, waiting for the spark to ignite the inferno for the coming New Age Baal. All of them selfishly having slow minded, off-the-shelf fun while stumbling around in a smiley face stupor snapping the same unnatural pictures a thousand times over and sending the lame experience and images to each other in a SmartPhone/iPad/WiFi circle jerk. Times Square was undoubtedly still alive but it appeared to be a life not worth the cost of living. I had to keep walking to shake the heebie-jeebies that were crawling up and down my spine.

The bad feeling didn't leave. By the time I was at Broadway and Columbus Circle I was feeling pretty fake myself thinking about what it was going to be like to run Circa Tabac on my own with Bloomberg's anti-smoking law in my favor. "It's a dishonest business," I admitted it out loud. The pure bar competing for trade I opened back in 98 was long gone. As if spitting into the wind it hit me: I'm not a real bar owner. What partner percentages were written on a piece of paper had nothing to do with it. I'm simply managing an operation licensed into existence by the powers that be. Everyday I pull open the storefront gates of a calculated business producing smoky, boozed up shits and giggles for the system's benefit. Sure I get a cut of the action but it's not guaranteed; unlike the gentry that get theirs, their taxes, their jobs report, their nook on a downtown street keeping locals and tourists addicted to New York City and tobacco in line while their guide book routine puffs up bogus establishment authority. Ultimately I'm another native surrendering my life over to the crowned heads without a fight. An aristocratic mind game, that's my bar. A joint where the City is boss, the final word on whether I stay open or closed. One day they'll tell me who I can serve, what ingredients to mix, and how much to charge; always changing laws, drawing their lines, lines that have no right to be drawn because they're only billionaire purchased prism lines capable of changing angles on forceless colors that don't give a fuck whether you call them red, orange, green or blue. Colors that are like people that would rather be left alone with their born right to run a legitimate business or drink and smoke anything they damn well please.

Punch-drunk from the walk up Broadway mixed with my staggering thoughts and a wall of buildings surrounding me had me seeing the City as a bruising and infectious quadrillion-dollar maze. I crossed their line. Thirty-plus years at it and I'm not my own man anymore. Looking up at the enormity of the Trump International building and the Time Warner Center reflecting all sorts of unasked for colors butted against the old stonewall of Central Park and the trees and the sky, it had me thinking something behind the scenes is going on, something not right. Invention and effort was painfully obvious. It spotlighted how truth is the only thing that doesn't require trying; which means this town is stacked with fallacy and struggle. The skyscrapers in front of my nose were plain ugly and terrifying with glass seventy-five stories tall that made them seem like gigantic shimmering, tacky knives thrown from the moon aimed at Columbus in the middle of the Circle in order to keep him on his toes. It had me looking up to the heavens fearful that another global corporate dagger was on its way and I better watch out before it buried me into the granite of New York for a more permanent and painful position. I cleared out of Columbus Circle in a hurry, straight up Broadway.

Knowing that troubles and surprises can come on their own accord had turned my long walk into a defensive prayer. Step after step I filled up with distraught faith and my heart begged to know what to do about the ever changing City and my bar and my partners and my life. Above 110th Street it became too much to bare, I had to stop. I bought some chips and paper bagged a couple of big cans of beer. I found a familiar bench on the Broadway median at 116th Street outside of Columbia University. I sucked down half of the first can in one shot and belched. It helped. I was breathing normal again, relieved to be out of midtown and happy about the long walk I'd taken. At fifty years old, even though it took some of the wind out of me, I was able to do it. I had an alive again attitude. An attitude that chugged what was left in the can of beer with gusto and an outspoken, "aaaaahhhhh!"

A college girl popped out of nowhere and was immediately sticking a translucent clipboard under my nose. "We have to stop them. It's too big and tall for the neighborhood's character." She demanded I sign her petition. I looked at her long and wavy jet-black hair, the bright whites and the green of her feline eyes and her thick eyelashes, tender skin, a flawless smile. She must've been out all day because her cheeks were rosy. Her hips and round rump in tight jeans and a short, tight fitting faux fur jacket accentuated her thin waistline. A knockout. But instead of a cheap thrill it felt like a work assignment to look at her. Listening to her earnest glee was worse, nauseating. I couldn't help but think of her as a tall child with premature bumps and a whole life in front of her and she didn't know crap about anything, and she had a petition in her hands, a petition to define New York City, its character, its pride, its height and strength, whether it should live or die.

I realized on the spot the Big Apple is an enigma, a versatile religious vision surrounded by millions wrapped up with diverse and discriminating blind faith in concrete, glass and steel. I should've told that to the college beauty. New York has its past, parts of it that I was involved with and loved and wondered too often about where it's all gone. But even the past in is incomplete because they're still digging up archeological finds in this town. No matter how many global corporate pirates try to ring her neck with towers these streets are truly capable of anything good or bad. Like a rose that grows its story goes. I opened up my second can of beer and took a big gulp. I told the girl, "Go back to school with your twat clipboard." I did I my best to be rough and rude in case she thought all of New York was peachy and keen and a petition could fix everything or if she didn't know the City can cut it the other way and tell you to get the fuck out of my face. I'm not going to change this town or keep it the way it was. I was just born here. "Keep walking!" that's what I barked at the girl with a snarl. She shrieked and moved away quickly.

The sun had some shine left. Finishing off the second can of beer in three or four chugs invigorated me. I wondered if I could make it to the very end of Broadway, to the Bronx where maybe I'd find something worth seeing again or maybe something I left behind. The temperature dropped at sunset and the brisk air was like having a friend along. I walked and walked and by the time it was plenty dark it was cold. I was up in Inwood, the top of Manhattan. I easily gave up on crossing over the Harlem River to the Bronx. Instead, I thought about going into an old neighborhood bar, maybe run into a long ago friend. But I guess I'd walked a lot and I really was fifty years old, my dogs were done. I couldn't remember which bar was where anyway so instead I walked over to the 215th Street train station to catch the #1 train back downtown.

Being tired had my thoughts simple. I stood away from the platform edge because my head was hung low. I had to piss like a racehorse and I didn't have the energy to go back down to the street looking for an alley or a doorway. There were others waiting for the train but they were far enough away for me not to care. I turned my back to them, unzipped and put one push into starting a flow that immediately took on a life of its own. It flooded out of me with a thrust lifting me back on my heels and making a pool at my feet that ran a trail to the platform's edge then spilled over in a pale yellow waterfall onto the tracks and then the cars and 10th Avenue below. Two 24oz cans of beer is a lot to hold onto. The relief was continuous and exaggerated as if my entire life was passing through me. Everything I'd ever drank or witnessed or been a part of flowed at a perfect speed only piss is capable of. It had me thinking how everyone has their way, their timing - their own speed. I could feel the nerve endings from the top of my head to the souls of my feet connecting to a sense of achievement in an endless stream of splash and purpose. Circa Tabac was amidst that drift, a life experience, an authentic portion I could live with, learn from, remember and take with me, a beginning, an end, and wet all the way through. What comfort. I shook off and zipped up.

I stood on the platform wondering about Jodi and Sheldon, what jail would be like for them. Likely they'd get a year at a low security prison, prison nonetheless. Jodi was capable of landing on her feet but practicing law would be finished. Poor Sheldon would never recover. He'd learned a lot about running a bar and how to appreciate customers as much as I do. He'd grown out of his Pigpen stage, knows how to manage employees and can keep the bar clean and appealing. Add the parts of my identity he stuffed in his pocket along with a natural appreciation for a good laugh, he'd assembled a decent personality. But with a felony on his record and the debilitating experience of being locked up compounded with the many years of not having a boss, what could he really do? Maybe he'd go back home to his mother. It wouldn't be stretch to think he could go back to heroin. Either way it seemed clear to me that sending Sheldon to jail would not be the best thing for the world. Could I even live with the fact that I destroyed his life? Anytime I think of Sheldon the picture of his mug in my head always has a cigarette hanging from his mouth and after nearly fourteen years the bar had become his new appendage. Who am I to send him to jail? Or Jodi? I knew her long enough to guess that she put a lot of thought into figuring out her version of fair distribution of profits. Jodi's intention, wrong as it was, was like a little girl at her birthday party wanting the biggest piece of cake. Is jail time what she deserves? What is money anyway compared to what I learned and experienced over the years and the people I managed to meet and the contribution I was able to make. Who in the world of billions gets to do things like that? I can still eat. What do I deserve? The only thing I really want is to run a bar without loopholes or slanted laws from some goofy Mayor or anyone breathing down my back. The last bar in New York City serving necessities to mostly good people happy to be nowhere near the center of the universe.

I stepped to the platform's edge and looked up the tracks for my train, nothing but cold air blowing. I thought about how the last three years have been a very different part of my life. More often than not my thoughts hadn't felt like my own. The secret tallying of financial records and ever growing mistrust have had me looking over my shoulder like a bad habit. I stopped evolving. Too often my approach to people changed from being honest and communicative to playing a part in a conversation, using false drama to coax things one way or another, intentionally misunderstanding people to cut off communication or a better understanding. All my energy directed in a perpetual strategic mode of thinking and talking. Worst of all, I was bored, and what boredom means is a dying consciousness. That's not who I am. I know right from wrong. I have a craving for truth, justice, beauty, goodness, harmony and love, in a word, bliss. Letting calculations take me over and squeeze humanity out of me was like taking the proof out of booze.

Circa Tabac was Jodi and Sheldon's bar as much as mine, and on paper it was more theirs. The two of them were guilty but they were dumb to it. Forgive them, that's what I thought I heard in my head but it turned out to be my ride rolling into the 215th Street station reminding me it's time to go home. I got aboard and was happy to find a seat. The #1 runs local and though I was tired I didn't care how long it took to get downtown. I needed to shake lose the thick thought that had jumped on the train with me, about how a victory in war means survivors on both sides emerge battered and crippled. I didn't want to be entangled with brutal outlooks any more. Then and there, I only wanted to look at my fellow New Yorkers on the train and remember the part of the bar business that I love: knowing most people work and struggle to eek out a bit of comfort and more often than not we love each others company.

"We'll give you $35,000 – CASH!" that's what Sheldon had to say to me. This was after he pointed out how unhappy I looked. We were in the kitchen in front of the dishwasher. He was smoking a cigarette. I was looking for Tabasco to dose my tequila sitting at the bar. Sheldon's price offer was wrong but he was correct about my attitude. It'd been almost two months since my long walk and since I told Charles Antoninus that I need a little time before pulling the trigger on Team Dingleberg. He gave me until the end of May otherwise his workload would push my case back to the end of the year. Charles had no idea I wasn't sending anyone to jail, or that I'd decided to leave the bar. Glum, dumb and sluggish was my approach to how and when I was going to tell Jodi and Sheldon. From February to nearly April I let drinks and smokes direct me. Normally that's not such a bad thing considering you'd be doing that in a bar where others could share your pain, highlight the humor of it all, or maybe help find a better solution. But there wasn't anybody I could open up to because the regulars were also friendly with Sheldon. My friend Marco, a confidant, was a good guy to talk to. He was an authentic artist and a talented sign painter. That meant he was a wild card who knew how to get a message across and his simple advice to me was to tell Team Dingleberg: "FUCK YOU!" Not bad advice but I'd already sided with leniency.

Showing up late to the bar everyday, skipping on duties, drinking and smoking as soon as I arrived and then leaving early was my routine. Some days I wouldn't show up. The lowest part of the doldrums was sleep sucked and my recurring dream where I'm transformed into a bar was no longer weird, imaginary or scary. I'm standing in Circa Tabac like always, the way it was during construction before the bar was built with only plywood floors and sheetrock walls. Instead of a hundred bottles of booze rolling in the door nothing comes in. The solid oak bar that I'm normally transformed into with a crowd around is nothing but scrap-wood. There's no party, only an old man up against the wall nursing a beer, smoking his cigarette down to the nub, hanging his head low. The saddest part is I'm no longer transformed into the bar and when the old man finally lifts his head, cheap surprise, it's me. Dreams should never become predictable.

"$35,000 - CASH!" Sheldon told me again. "CASH!" was supposed to do the trick. What it did do more than anything was have me wondering where Team Dingleberg got that cash. Most of our business was credit/debit card payments. We handled cash but it was spent fast on off-the-book busboys' pay and off-the-record liquor supply runs. Team Dinglberg accumulating $35,000 or more only reminded me that they were thieves. "Cash?" I asked. "Yeah," Sheldon said. "$35,000," I said. "Yeah," he said. He cleared his throat as if he was doing me a favor and elevated himself to a more benevolent, know-it-all tone, "You calculate the kitchen equipment, the booths and tables, the beer lines and coolers, the inventory and the rest of it, everything is getting old, our lease may not be renewed, the business is worth at most $200,000. In a buyout the partner leaving always takes less," he said. "Always?" I asked. "Always," he said.

Sheldon was trying his best to be more substantial than me, tipping on his toes some to stand big and tall, tilting his head down to his cigarette as if leverage was necessary to draw on it hoping to create the impression of control, intelligence and strength. He must've picked up the routine from an old Bogart movie. The amateur act made me smirk and that made Sheldon blow smoke with a cough. He shuffled a bit back onto his heels and grabbed a hold of the dishwasher to regain his black and white couth. "I don't know Sheldon," I told him, "Six months ago when Paul Kemsley was interested in buying the place you and your sister told me the bar was worth $3.5 million." Sheldon nearly swallowed his cigarette, started bumbling and mumbling. "Well the price is different for him because he... uhhh, different... I mean a different use for the bar and, uhhh, costs... He would have to remodel... You have 20%... I'd have to cut the deal... and legal fees... that price would include everything... you have to consider costs... uh, you know most of his money is in euros..."

Sheldon was caught with his pants down. More than showing what a prick he was it showed just how out of touch he'd become. He lived his life within the framework of his delusions and had no real understanding of the people around him or their perception of him - truly lost. I felt sorry for him. But it didn't matter. Not so much about the $35,000 offer because I wasn't taking it. Bitterness had nothing to do with it either because aside from feeling down about the situation I honestly had no hard feelings for him or his sister anymore. I wasn't going to carry that stuff around and be pissed off my whole life. Bad things happen all the time. I got screwed, that's that. With Sheldon standing next me in the kitchen mumbling on about $3.5 million being a similar number to $35,000 I cheerlessly disconnected from him. After nearly two decades of life experience and business together, and with his face only two feet away from mine, I couldn't recognize him, a stranger. "Whatever," that's what I told him before I left the kitchen to sit back down at the bar with my tequila. Sheldon left straightaway.

A week later Jodi arranged an afternoon meeting at Circa Tabac. She didn't mention it but the get-together was to negotiate a buyout price. When I walked in the door the two of them were huddled at the end of the bar in front of a gigantic, disheveled pile of paperwork as if they'd been going over fourteen years of reports and records in the last half hour; an impossible prop for a staged intelligent business price evaluation. I casually made a coffee and joined them. "What's going on?" I asked friendly like because drummed up drama only complicates things when making life-altering moves. They must've decided Jodi was going to do the talking because Sheldon was sitting back on his barstool with his arms folded and a tight lip. She had a look of sincerity on her face that only she could've thought was natural. "We know you've been very unhappy and we want to help you," she said, "We've tried to get as much money together as we could and we can give you $40,000."

For the first time in months I felt excited. Not about the $40,000 offer. I was happy they got my message. Two days earlier I left copies of some of Jodi's condemning accounting records on the desk downstairs in the office that she had no clue were in my possession. The following day the papers were gone and I could feel the heat leftover on the desktop from the fear that must've boiled instantly and spilled out of her the moment she realized I had the drop on her. As I sipped my coffee my claws were retracted; it had them confused about the exposed books; probably had them hoping for a chance the accounting records were overlooked; maybe I'd picked up some lose paperwork off the floor without looking it over. The $40,000 was to feel me out. I'd already decided what the price was going to be and I was more interested taunting than halfwit negotiations. I asked Jodi, "$40,000? For what?" Unsure why I was unsure she said, "For your share of the bar." I caught her off guard but Sheldon knew I was being a wise ass. He did his best not to respond. "Don't you want a buyout?" she asked. I told her, "I hadn't really thought about it. I love our business." Sheldon struggled to remain quiet. Jodi asked, "What if we offered you a little more?" "More?" I said, "How do you put a price on a place that lives in your heart." That was enough for Sheldon. He interjected with hammy authority, "If you're not leaving, we are going to make big changes." I told him, "Change can be good."

They both looked at each other for confirmation to move on to the next step of their gimpy plan. Sheldon told me, "The new name of the bar is Café Tabac." He said it like he was throwing down a straight flush in a poker game. He'd been talking about changing the name for years because I came up with Circa Tabac. It drove him nuts anytime somebody told him, "What a great name." I could care less about who named the place. Bottom line, it was a good name and a rose is a rose by any other name and Circa Tabac was definitively not a café. "Café Tabac?" I asked and winced, "Are you sure?" They both responded confidently. Sheldon said, "It's the only way to increase sales." Jodi shot me an affirming look. They must've thought I wouldn't be able to live with the name change, force me to accept their $40,000 offer. Trying to pretend the bar was something different would be like trying to convince Sinatra that he'd have more fans if he wore a dress. It'd be too much to stomach even if I weren't going to be around much longer to gag. "You know best," I told them, "But you're letting a New York City reputation fourteen years in the making go to waste. Sort of like changing the name of the Empire State Building, a lot smaller in scale, of course." Jodi's jaw dropped like I slapped some of the silliness out of her. Seeing her crack while hoping to salvage a drop of dignity for Circa Tabac I told her with a remnant of sympathy and not a hint of irony in my voice, "If a name change is necessary, why not something simple, uninspired, but at least direct, like, I don't know... Downtown Cigar Bar or something like that. It'd be a new direction and more on point than Café Tabac. Cigarette smokers are an endangered species anyway. And cigar smokers are timeless. Plus they spend more money."

Sheldon panicked, quickly explaining away any identity confusion by delivering details of Circa Tabac's transformation into Café Tabac. I'd heard it all before: a vague and loose fitted vision of a post WWII version of a Parisian/Viennese café guaranteed to be filled with pseudo intellectuals likely wearing berets, goatees and thick black-rimmed glasses who spend all day drinking coffee and reading newspapers and blabbing existential jabber and writing never ending poetry and monumentally important works for the benefit of civilization. With the way he'd wholeheartedly go on about it like a school girl planning a slumber party the Holland Tunnel outside our door ceased to exist and we suddenly had a roomy and sun drenched sidewalk café wrapped around the corner of Boulevard Saint-Germain. Sheldon was obsessed with an elaborate newspaper wall rack stocked with every major rag and paper from the US, Europe, South America and Asia. It was going to be the centerpiece of the new Café Tabac. He never considered the subscription costs of a hundred magazines and newspapers would be more than you'd make from the coffee you sold on a street with no foot traffic. He also didn't realize we weren't living in post WWII Paris or Vienna, nobody read newspapers anymore because of the internet, people had jobs and couldn't sit around drinking coffee all day, and sad but true, there is a Starbucks or a want-to-be Starbucks on every other corner in New York. "Listen," I told the two of them, "I have to take off. Let me know when the café is set to go." Nine o'clock that night Jodi called me and asked, "How much do you want?" I told her, "The bar is worth six or seven hundred thousand. I'll give you the deal of your life and take a hundred thousand and be gone fast." There was a minute of silence, likely consulting with Sheldon. "We can offer you seventy," she said. "That's too bad," I told her, "You have a good night." I went back to making my rice and vegetables. About ten minutes later Jodi called me again. "We can do $100,000."

Three days passed and Jodi stopped by the bar before five o'clock wearing a perfectly short and tight fitting gold and silver sparkled dress showing off enough come-hither cleavage to bury mankind's hope for world peace. She was a sight to see but having seen it all before and knowing everything that comes attached was enough for me to not give her a second look. What had every follicle on me aroused was her perfume, Hermes Caleche, my favorite; it helped me realize she was committed to put an end to our partnership with a vengeance. Before saying hello to me she put her Burberry shoulder bag on the bar, stood straight and yanked on and shimmied in her dress, then reached into her bag and pulled out a huge manila envelope. Even with her looking like a million bucks I knew she wasn't carrying $100,000. She looked at me with a cheeky, celebratory smile, which had me thinking how there'd be no reason to go out on the town to commemorate a hundred grand or fantasize about opening a new bar. That's a hunk of dough for many but for a 50 year old without a career path in New York City it's more an emergency fund to get you through the shit. Still, Seeing Jodi in gold and silver had me feeling like somebody who had been lost at sea and finally got his sights on a shimmer of land twinkling over the horizon. I greeted her with a genuinely thirsty smile. She greeted me with a fifty-page buyout agreement that nearly sunk my boat.

She'd moved very close to my side, brushed against me as she handed me the stack of papers. She told me, "I made you a copy in case you want to take it home and read it before signing." I got dizzy breathing in cheery citrus and floral hearts of rose, jasmine and irises floating on a newborn woody spirit as she started pushing a very strange idea of me co-signing a loan for the $100,000 she was going to give me in the buyout. She added, "It'd be best not mention your departure to the employees or the regulars to avoid any disruption. And if you sign the papers right now we can arrange everything quickly, maybe close the deal by the end of the week." I flipped through the agreement and told her, "What have you been drinking?" I'd done my research with New York State Division of Corporations. I told her, "The deal is simple. You give me money and I sign off on the Liquor License and my Stock Certificate." I figured I wouldn't even bother my lawyer. She told me, "No. It's more complex than that." I told her, "It's not." She said, "It is." I told her, "I'm going to have to speak with my lawyer." She flinched hard shaking loose gold and silver sparkles from her dress and then barked, "What do you need a lawyer for?"

I called Charles Antoninus the following morning. He hadn't heard from me in a while so I gave him a brief update, how I wanted out the business ASAP with something in my pocket and how I didn't have it in me to send Team Dingleberg to jail. I tried explaining the fifty-page buyout agreement and the strange loan Jodi wanted me to sign onto. He said, "Wait till my partners hear this one." He was concerned about my decision not to press criminal charges,. "Have they made threats of any sort?" he asked. I laughed. He pressed me, "Are you sure it's the right thing to do?" I told him, "It is." He then assured me the deal was not going to happen the way Jodi would like. "Sit tight," he said, "It'll take a couple of weeks and it'll be cut and dry. You won't be signing any fifty page agreement or any loan."

"It was the best of times, it was the worst of times. It was also my last day of work today. And now my dear handsome angel of mercy we find ourselves nestled on your doorstep with an unforgivable need for drinks," that's what the older woman was telling me after I opened the front door to let her and her friends inside. She had a head full of straight and thick charcoal gray hair, striking, beautiful to look at. She was svelte, wearing a very tasteful, snug black sweater dress. She was maybe ten years older than me; one of those ladies that holds onto a girlish prettiness her whole life. "I like a gin martini," she continued, grabbing a hold of my hand as the group of them stepped inside, "Two at the very most. Three and I'm under the table. Four and I'm under the host." She added an exaggerated photogenic smile, feigned a dreamy look and then battered her eyes at me. "Dorothy Parker," one of her younger friends said for my benefit. Another one told me, "Careful, Judith will either break your heart with quotes or have you dizzy with an aversion to books." The oldest woman in the bunch told me, "Whatever you do, don't encourage her." They all laughed.

Six women, the youngest was in her twenties. They'd been standing out in front of the bar while I was in the kitchen making honey mustard sauce for our Chicken Tenders. I heard them knocking on the door when I stepped out of the kitchen for a quick look at the reservation book, which happened to be empty for the night. It wasn't close to five o'clock but I opened the front door for the ladies because I hated to see customers standing on the sidewalk waiting for a drink. Though after getting a closer look at them walking in it was easy to see they hadn't waited at all. Turned out that it was Judith's last day of work. I didn't bother telling them that it was my last night at Circa Tabac. They were downtown carrying on from Judith's retirement/farewell party at their office in midtown, publishers. Judith's face didn't seem old enough for retirement but who really knows about those things. They were new faces to me and I liked their attitude. A great reminder of the most obvious quality a New York City bar offers: the any day chance to meet glad heads handing over free smiles and unpredictable potential. I sat them in the back and then turned on the music. Ella Fitzgerald's I'm Beginning to See the Light started things off.

I poked my head in the kitchen to check on the pot of honey mustard simmering on the burner. I still had to make spinach dip and cut a bunch of lemons and limes. Things were hectic before I let Judith and friends in the door because my busboy called in sick and his backup wasn't arriving until 8:00 PM. That meant I was getting the bar ready for the night, carrying up beer, wine, liquor, food and dry goods all out of the basement, cleaning the windows, polishing up the tables and the bar. To make things perfectly demanding the waitress had called to tell me she was locked inside her Bushwick apartment because a doorknob broke and her superintendent couldn't save her for another hour. By 5:00 PM my bartender still hadn't arrived and I could always count on him being ten or fifteen minutes late. None of it normally would've been a problem but aside from Judith and friends getting in the bar early another group of twenty were five minutes behind them.

I was getting a drink order on Judith's table and listening to the defensible reasons why Sylvia Plath would've been an overjoyed reality television star had she been born fifty years later while the large group huddled up by the front door waiting for me to seat them were making strange noises. Big groups usually reserved tables and I tried asking one of them if they had called ahead. The guy I spoke to didn't say anything. He had good reason not to respond; he hadn't heard a word I said. He and the others were deaf, save the one who promised to translate their hand gestured drink orders. According to finger twitching and palm bending the big guy who looked like he swallowed a pumpkin employed all of them at his Dye Manufacturing Plant in Queens and had dragged them all out for the night because he really loved to drink beer and smoke cigars on his birthday. Obviously hearing is not as important as good eyes when making colored dyes.

By the time I made and delivered drinks for the literary band and the deaf gang there were already five other tables sitting down and a handful at the bar. I didn't recognize anybody. 5:30 PM, I was hustling, the sort of action that gets your adrenaline going. I was very happy to see my bartender finally walk in the door. He jumped right into the mix and it was a good thing because four more small groups walked in the door right behind him. I wondered if there was going to be a full moon or maybe the Stock Market had a stellar day because those two things often explained a packed house by 7:00 PM. Though it had been a gorgeous day and sometimes that's enough to get New Yorkers up-and-at-em in the mood for drinking and smoking.

The waitress finally showed up and that was a lifeline because the bartender and myself were going under. We could have used three waitresses. By 8:00 PM there was still no busboy and I was already running down to the basement to change two kegs of beer and to bring up more booze, especially more gin. By 10:00 PM the backup busboy finally called to say he couldn't make it and I was back downstairs for vodka, rum, more olives and more gin. Gin was turning out to be the evening's drink of choice and that might've been reason enough to call the police or fire department ahead of time. There's something about that white, grain based alcohol deftly fragranced and infused with botanicals because the history of gin's effect is pretty much the opposite of what flowers, berries and whimsical scents are supposed to do for you. Gin is more a cruel medicinal than a liquor and those who routinely drink it usually operate from a different center of gravity than the rest of us. Anyone could order a few and go for a twirl. Be advised, that juniper jive might open a few holes in your head, let some light in, help you see what fun it is to bounce off walls, start a one-man revolution, or experience a frightful collapse in territories unknown.

By midnight things hadn't let up. Making your way through the room was like walking through a mutating and chancy maze made up of backs, chests and curious fingertips. Every time I managed to get into the two bathrooms to empty trashcans, refill soap or toilet paper or hand towels there was evidence of coke snorting everywhere. Three young ladies the bartender had to ask for ID from were dancing on top of the bar. I'd already given up trying to get them down because every time I did and went back to bussing tables or delivering drinks or getting food out of the kitchen the three of them were right back at it and the crowd was only encouraging. The table of deaf dye makers were drinking plenty and somehow making a bigger racket than everyone else in the bar. Their pumpkin gut boss had been lighting up joints for all of them on and off all night, which made the waitress's job of getting drink orders like a slapstick version of The Miracle Worker. I'd already opened a couple of cases of new glasses because customers must've thought there was a contest going on to see who is best at knocking everything off tables and the bar. A serious fight nearly broke out at one of the tables up in the front because the big guy who had been arm wrestling anyone who dared finally lost to a guy half his size and the wrong girl was impressed. A free round of shots squashed that match fast and only added to the fact that everyone in the bar was smashed.

A little while earlier one of the bathrooms was blocked up because gray haired Judith decided she needed to have more than four martinis and the only way that was possible was if she emptied her tiny gut to make room for more; that along with enough paper hand towels to dry an elephants butt was crammed down the toilet making a literary mess of things. I thought of locking the door and leave the customers one bathroom to use so I could deal with it later. But with a crowd like this they might've started pissing in the corners or on the side of the bar if they had to wait too long. I could've been mad at Judith but she was providing first-rate entertainment for everyone in the joint. Somehow she was talking and dancing with the deaf gang and anyone else within her reach, had them spinning and blending in perfectly with the room full of recklessness. It showed how intention goes far beyond verbal communication.

I must've cleaned double the normal rate of ashtrays, sold more cigars and cigarettes than usual, bar sales were skyrocketing and people were still coming in the front door. It didn't take long before the waitress was wiped out and her feet were dragging across the floor. That meant I was backing her up and grabbing drink orders any chance I could. My bartender's lower back was killing him because he was breaking in new shoes so I was jumping behind the stick on and off all night to keep the action flowing. My left palm was burned from a piping hot bowl of spinach dip; my fingers were sponged from loading the dishwasher a hundred-and-one times; and the room dense with smoke had my chest working double-time for air. At 1:00 AM a mid-sized charter bus pulled up in front and I was about to lock the front door because enough is enough. Mercifully it turned out to be transportation for the deaf gang. The joint smoking pumpkin gut boss thoughtfully hired a ride home for all of his employees. He paid for everything and left an incredible 50% tip. They all poured out of the place with enough gleeful and silent goodbyes that had me thinking I'll never crack my knuckles the same way again.

There was some relief after they left. Food orders stopped going into the kitchen and that meant nothing to prepare and no more dishes to clean. The waitress caught a second wind and finally caught up with her tables. By 3:00 AM I had a free minute and needed a drink. There were a couple of empty barstools so I grabbed the one in the corner facing out to the room where I could keep an eye on things. De La Soul's The Magic Number was playing and the place was a mess, still filled with smoke and half filled with unwound revelers, alcoholics, harlequins, lonely hearts, and people without jobs. Feeling queasy and altogether sapped I lit up a cigarette and ordered champagne. "Whatever you have open," I told the bartender. I downed a glass of flat Prosecco and then took a long hard drag on my smoke and looked around realizing I'd forgotten that it was my last night at Circa Tabac, the end of it all. After my ten-hour work surge and with the disastrous shape of the bar some nameless reason had me thinking about the collapse of civilizations, how societies fall apart not because of invasions or plagues or earthquakes but when the people finally give up on their rulers, when the aristocrats have worn out their welcome by taking more and delivering less. I figured my life's work has always been delivering as much as I could and if I could just keep up that momentum I would never have to worry about anything.

It would've been a perfect moment of adornment if I weren't feeling a lot older than I once was and wiped-out because of it. My second glass of champagne went straight to my head with puffed up if-I-could thoughts of things I might like to do with my life after Circa Tabac. Instead of a new career or a new business I could only think of shifting richness and the power to know what's good for your soul from the irresponsible few into the hands of the responsible and worthy many. The guy and the girl sitting next to me were talking about a rode trip someone they knew had taken to the Grand Canyon and how they got lost. "How do you miss something like that?" the girl wanted to know. The guy told her, "They took the wrong map." I figured a lot of people would rather have the wrong map than no map at all and maybe that's one way the value of life gets lost.

By 5:00 AM there was only one table left, they'd paid up but were lingering. The waitress and my bartender had done a great job, tips were in, checks were straight, and they were finished. They wanted to chase out the last table but because it was gray haired Judith I thought I'd let her and her new friend sit a bit. The guy she was talking with had wandered into the bar on his own at around 3:00 AM. He was short, bald, needed a shave, and was wearing a NY Yankees sweatshirt, jeans and dirty sneakers. He was drinking draft beer and smoking a crappy cigar. He was probably my age or younger, obviously harmless and blatantly unmatched with Judith. The dumb grin on his face explained this was the first time in his life he had picked up a woman in a bar and he was unsure how it happened. He was listening intensely to her talk but I'd bet a hundred bucks he didn't understand a word she was saying. They were both in that post drunk state, still not sober, exhausted and awake with easy means of expression or listening, maybe hungry, and far away from making responsible decisions, and far, far from noticing they were the last people in the bar.

Despite running on absolute empty I told the waitress and the bartender they could leave. "I'll close up," I said. Another twenty minutes or so wasn't going to make a difference. I turned the lights up a bit and started to clean because the place was in ruins and I wanted a better last impression of Circa Tabac. While sweeping up cocktail napkins, straws, broken glass, cigarette and cigar butts, unpaired earrings, a lost cell phone, a couple of lighters, a five dollar bill and a clump of unidentifiable matter, I had a sudden, frightening visceral sensation. A quake rolling in my gut and through my chest that converted instantly to a burst in my head. It felt like my heart instantly hardened and cracked and most of me was like a door that somebody fiercely kicked open. My knees were quivering and fast enough I was down on them. A vacuous pain in my gut matched the gorging soreness in my eyes and the fast spreading numbness in my limbs. Judith and her guy were sitting at the table in the back and the room could've been still filled with people but inside of me was so unnaturally open it had me feeling turned inside out, terrified and alone in the face of something mighty. I was hoping it was the first abrupt effects of a hard-hitting flu but with my body beginning to thrum with electricity, spark plugs going haywire, I knew it was more serious. There was big and painful pounding in my chest, it was slowing down, skipping beats and getting ready to stop.

A friggin heart attack, that's what I was thinking, not the way I was supposed to go, thought I was stronger. A sense of detachment, a loss of gravity, security, warmth and dissolution was taking over. In my peripheral small shadows like ghosts of cockroaches, parasitical phantoms, figments and subliminal excuses that I could blame things on scurried in panic. It was the end for me. A crystal clear sendoff reflection came in the face of oblivion: everyone meets the same fate alone and it's awful we don't have the chance to give each other a big hug and pat on the back before we go. I heard an eerie last breath coming out of my chest in unison with that last irresistible fear and then a sudden wooosh. My soul was yanked from me and it was as if what was left of me had been thrown into the sea. The entirety of my life was known in a splash. Everything that had remained hidden or forgotten, the meaningful and the trivial, all of it vividly revealed at once – gigantic and daunting. At long last my true genius was visible and obvious. It was far from incredible. It was common.

On my knees I could still hear Judith and her new friend in the back corner booth talking until my awareness shifted to something unusual between the barstools on the side of the bar. It was beautiful, some kind of an expression more than love, an aura of stained glass floating or a sort of flame changing its colors from the blues to greens and browns and into colors I couldn't recognize until none of them seemed important or distinguished. It was letting me know there were a few things that needed explanation. Cognizant of the choices I could've and should've made in life had me feeling deformed, unwanted and ashamed. Why did I do the things I did with my time? I hurt people and plenty of them I didn't even know about. Easily there were better choices. Mindful choices. Best choices. I begged for forgiveness and mercy. Then I could only think of things I didn't want in my life anymore.

I looked for the flutter on the side of the bar but it was gone and then the loudest thought: I have honest things to do. Instantly it felt like I stepped in front of the #4 train running express and it knocked me into a subway tunnel for a rattling ride nearly bringing me to pieces. Time must've passed but there was no sense of it or a way to calculate it. Rapid transit eventually slowed and when all was calm I was standing on my feet and my eyes were closed and with a little effort I opened them. My back was stiff and my feet were sore and my lungs were filled with cigarette and cigar smoke, there was booze and beer and wine in nearly empty glasses everywhere when a whisper in my ear declared life has just begun. The experience had me reverberating and petering like a struck bronze bell. Soon and sure enough I was back to familiar feelings again. I instinctively went back to sweeping because the only thing that was clear was that life has a purpose. By the time I was at Judith's table with the broom I was feeling exhausted but fine, and they understood it was time to leave. I walked them to the front door because I had to unlock it for them and more so because I had something very important to say to the two of them. I wanted to say goodnight.

They barely noticed me as they walked across the floor in

front of me. I looked at the way she was grabbing onto his hand like maybe she was holding onto a secret, something she'd learned about life, something she'd known about for a long time; like holding his hand was maybe the last hand in the world to hold and if it were truly the bitter end any hand would do because in her heart a hand is a hand. As she stepped outside onto the sidewalk I got a good look at the shape of her, slim, strong and lovely at nearly six in the morning. It had me wondering why a woman like her was retiring when it appeared she was capable of so much more. Maybe she was asked to leave. Maybe our new world has no room for smart ladies or maybe her boss was just making room for more. With her gray hair and her dimmed glow and a man's hand in hers she was great. It had less to do with her appearance and almost everything to do with how smart she was and how much she liked people. There was no mysterious core to her. She was meaningful. Somewhere along the line she identified the deathless design of life and embraced it with arms and legs. I knew that about her the same way I knew in less than a half an hour the sun was going to shine. What I didn't know was how one life can turn out one way yet another life can turn out altogether different. I wondered why Judith was alone at sixty and meeting men in a bar just before sunrise. She looked incredibly happy.

While poking my head out the front door to say goodnight I saw the guy try to kiss her. She turned away but let him plant one on her cheek and also let his hands get a firm hold of her hips. She wasn't mad at him for trying, only put her forehead to his and whispered to him. After that he walked away, headed west. Judith turned to walk east, to the corner of 6th Avenue for a taxi. With my head already out the door I told her, "You were the life of the party, thanks for that." She jerked her head around and gave me a rough and peculiar look for maybe eavesdropping on her or more than likely she thought I was a complete idiot for not knowing that about her from the first moment I set eyes on her. It almost looked like she was ready to tell me something quick and nasty but she let it go and rolled her eyes instead, turned and walked away. I hollered, "Get home safe. Or wherever you're going, arrive alive." She turned back again, like suddenly remembering something, maybe left something in the bar. She took a few steps toward me then stopped and with a depleted but guaranteed smile she told me, "It is a far, far better thing that I do, than I have ever done; it is a far, far better rest that I go to than I have ever known."